TO
Steal, Kill & Destroy
IN THIS
GAME CALLED LOVE

AN URBAN EROTICA TALE

JEN TURNER

This book is dedicated to Mateal (mother), Vince (father), Vickey (sister), Christy (sister), Dayvion (son), and Josselynn (daughter). Thank you for believing in me and loving me unconditionally.

Table of Contents

I want to acknowledge God! Thank you for everything you have done, continue to do, and will do for me. I am nothing without you, Lord.

I want to acknowledge my close family members, best friends, and close friends. There are too many people to name. Just know I love you all dearly. I appreciate the cheers and constant support. You all bring out the best in me!

This novel contains mature content that may be disturbing or triggering for some readers. Please be advised that the following themes are present:

• **Violence**: Depictions of physical violence, including street fights, gang-related activity, and domestic violence.

• **Drugs and Alcohol**: Scenes involving drug use, addiction, and substance abuse.

• **Sexual Content**: Explicit sexual scenes, including references to sexual assault.

• **Abuse**: Emotional, physical, and verbal abuse in relationships and family dynamics.

• **Death and Grief**: Death of characters and the emotional impacts of loss and grief.

• **Criminal Activity**: Theft, illegal business operations, and police encounters.

- **Mental Health Issues**: Depictions of depression, anxiety, PTSD, and other mental health struggles.
- **Strong Language**: Frequent use of profane and derogatory language.
- **Racism and Discrimination**: Exploration of racial tensions, systemic inequality, and discrimination.

Reader discretion is advised. This book is intended for mature audiences and may not be suitable for all readers. If you find any of these topics distressing, please proceed with caution.

Today was moving day for the Coleman family. Patrick Coleman, the man of the house, fought back tears. They were losing their beautiful two-story home located in Pearland, Texas. He watched as his wife Charlene began to pack dishes in the kitchen. He wondered how in the hell their lives could change in the blink of an eye. Patrick has worked at Houston Hobby Airport for the past 18 years as the lead Aviation Engineer Supervisor. He earned a 125k yearly salary. He was proud that his family never wanted for anything.

Patrick was from Alief and was no stranger to street life. He met Charlene in 9th grade at Hastings High School. By the end of 10th grade, she gave birth to their daughter, Trinity. At the age of 18, he opted out of college and earned an aviation technician certification. He landed a job working at Hobby Airport as an aviation technician. Within five years, he worked his way up to being one of their top aviation engineers. Patrick was ecstatic when they offered him the supervisor position.

Fast forward to the present, he was no longer with the company.

Six months ago, the human resource team called him into the office. They informed him that he was being laid off due to budget cuts. The company didn't even give him the option to work in a lower-paying position. They gave him severance pay, but it wasn't enough to sustain the mortgage or bills that kept piling up. Patrick didn't require his wife to work, so they lived off his income. Her only job was to take care of the home. He stood in the hallway to the kitchen and let his mind wander back to the day he was let go.

It was just past 2:30 pm when Patrick received a call from Mr. Nguyen in Human Resources to report to the main boardroom. He was currently going over emergency landing modules on the computer in the training lab. Patrick made his way into the room eager to hear what the meeting was about. Brenda Kensington, the new operations manager, was mesmerized when she laid eyes on him. He was a fine specimen from head to toe. Patrick stood before her at 6'5 feet tall, had smooth, dark black skin, and a strong, muscular stature.

Not one blemish on his face. As he greeted everyone, his perfectly aligned white teeth shined bright. His eyebrows were thick, and his hair was nicely cut into a low-cut fade. His hair was cut low and nicely edged up. Brenda almost wanted to cancel the meeting; he looked so good. At that very moment, she was imagining fucking him. She quickly snapped out of her daze. The three members of the HR management team sat side by side. Mrs. Holland instructed Patrick to sit across from them so that they were all looking directly at him. The long, wooden mahogany table they sat around was well polished and beautiful to look at. Its oval shape almost filled up the entire boardroom.

Two faces in that room he knew very well. Mr. Nguyen was an Asian man in his 60s who was skinny, short, and bald only at the top of his head. He wore a crisp blue suit to the meeting. Mrs. Holland was a dark, brown-skinned Black woman. She was heavyset and in her mid-50s. She had on a red shirt with ruffles on the sleeves and black slacks. Her hair was short and wavy. A gold butterfly chain hung from her neck. Mr. Nguyen and Mrs. Holland worked at this company for many years and always treated Patrick with respect. However, at this very moment, they both seemed uneasy and quiet. There was an unfamiliar face in the room. A skinny middle-aged Caucasian woman, with straight blonde hair, brown glasses, and wearing a tan suit, seemed to command the room.

It was completely quiet for a few minutes as she scanned through some papers in a brown vanilla folder. She looked up at Patrick and informed everyone it was time to start the meeting. Patrick's nervousness began to kick in. He thought to himself, "What the hell could this be about?" The Caucasian woman began to speak.

She said, "Hello Mr. Coleman, my name is Brenda Kensington. I've been with the company for about three months, so I apologize that this is our first time meeting one another. However, I want to get straight to the point."

Patrick thought to himself, *"Bitch, please do,* because you're about to come with some bullshit."

Brenda Kensington continued. "We're making some major changes and want to hire more qualified people to keep up in this industry. We now require your position to have a bachelor's degree." Patrick cut his eyes at Mr. Nguyen and Mrs. Holland as they sat there quietly. He realized they were not about to stand up for him, so he put his focus back on Brenda Kensington.

Looking confused, Patrick said, "Qualified? I have been working here for 18 years, so who is more qualified than me? You think because somebody earned a piece of paper and walked across the stage, it makes them better for the job than I am?" Brenda held up the palm of her hand, instructing Patrick to let her finish talking. Shaking her head, she replied, "Times are different than what they were 18 years ago; education is important, and we want to hire more individuals that went to school for this line of work."

Pat quickly blurted out, "That's some bullshit."

"Excuse me!" yelled Brenda. "Mr. Coleman, I will not tolerate that type of language from you!" She immediately struck a nerve. He was trying to remain calm and professional.

Patrick looked at her angrily and said, "I don't care what you tolerate, woman! I have been working here 18 years, and you're talking about hiring more QUALIFIED people! How the hell did I train the majority of the people in this bitch if I'm not qualified, huh?"

Brenda snatched off her glasses and said, "That's enough, Patrick. This meeting is over. We will email you the details on when to expect your severance pay."

Patrick jumped up from the table and screamed, "LADY, FUCK YOU. I know this was all your idea because I never had any issues working here until your pink and pale face ass got here." Mr. Nguyen held up the church finger and began talking.

"Now hold on, Mr. Coleman…" Patrick quickly waved him off, which interrupted what he was about to say. Mr. Nguyen looked appalled and sat back down quietly. He had never seen Patrick so angry or rude.

Patrick looked at Mr. Nguyen and Ms. Holland and said, "Obviously my loyalty to this company doesn't mean anything to y'all. I thought you two were better than this. I expected this from her stuck-up ass!" pointing to Brenda.

He opened the door to the boardroom and was about to walk out. However, he calmly turned around and said, "You know what? Since you're letting me go, fuck it. I'm going to say what I wanted to all these years." The pettiness in him wouldn't let him leave quietly. "Mr. Nguyen, your old ass is musty as hell. You smell like straight wild hyena piss. Go see a hygienist fast! I guess you want more qualified people but not clean ones, funky ass motherfucka. Mrs. Holland, you faithfully wear that big-ass diamond on your fat finger to show everyone that somebody eventually fell in love with your big, back ass. Well, I'm happy for you because for years you were a pitiful ass woman. But God don't like ugly, and bitch, you are ugly!"

"GET OUT NOW, SECURITY!" screamed Brenda. People out in the hallway began to look concerned. Patrick turned back around and proceeded to leave the building. Mrs. Holland was still sitting down in her chair. She took a deep sigh and said, "Welp, that went well." When Patrick got in his car, he couldn't even start the car up. He just sat in the parking lot and replayed what had just transpired. He wondered how he would break the news to his wife.

He was supposed to be the provider of the family. After a few minutes of just sitting in the car, Patrick spotted Keith, his security buddy, walking up to the car. He rolled down the driver's side window and laughed a little bit. He asked Keith, "They want me to leave, huh?"

Keith chuckled and replied, "Hell yeah, them hoes are scared as fuck that you might do something crazy. They told me you had to leave the property immediately."

Patrick shook his head and said, "Aight, man, be easy. I'm gone." Keith said his last goodbye and told Patrick to keep his head up. Patrick cranked the ignition and headed home to give his wife the bad news.

As Charlene continued to pack up dishes, he stared at her beauty. The light from the kitchen window shined in on her angelic face. Charlene was 5'4 feet tall and drop-dead gorgeous. Her natural hair was platted into two thick pigtails that stopped a little past her shoulders. She had the best grade of soft black hair. She was exotic looking. Her complexion was dark brown, mixed with a reddish undertone. Her eyebrows were perfectly arched, with the right amount of thickness to them. She had small freckles on her face that brought out her beauty even more. She was the definition of slim-thick. She weighed 160 pounds with a small waist, thick thighs, and a round booty that often draws attention.

"Hello, earth to Patrick," Charlene said, snapping her fingers in his face to bring him out of the daze he was in. Patrick leaned against the staircase wall and placed one hand behind his head. He looked at his wife with so much sadness before speaking.

"I was just thinking about the day they laid me off from work. It's been like a domino effect after that. Now we're losing the house."

Charlene walked straight into his chest. She placed both hands around his back for a warm embrace. Holding on to his large frame, she stood on her tippy toes to place a soft kiss on Patrick's lips. Staring into his eyes, she said, "Stop beating yourself up. You did nothing wrong, baby. Shit happens! It's time to make the best of our situation and move on, literally. Plus, trouble doesn't last always, ya hear me. We will bounce back from this."

Instantly, Patrick stopped having a pity party and smiled down at Charlene because she was much shorter than him. He was madly in love with this woman, and it wasn't just because of her undeniable beauty. She had a way of making him think he could conquer the world. His spirits weren't the only thing she managed to lift. Suddenly, Patrick felt his dick rise in his pants. He was rock hard and ready to put Charlene into several different positions. Biting his lip, he stared at Charlene lustfully. She gave Patrick a huge smile and said, "Oooh no, I know what that look means."

She tried to hurry up and walk away. He grabbed her by the waist with both hands and backed her into his pelvis. He slowly started grinding his pelvis on her ass. She felt the hardness of his wood through his jeans.

"Baby, we don't have time for this. We gotta finish moving," she said softly, but horny at the same time.

"Where is Trinity?" Patrick asked his wife while planting kisses on her neck.

"She's upstairs in her room packing," Charlene said. That's all he needed to hear.

Charlene was already wearing a short black sleeveless dress with a slit on the side that exposed a large part of her thigh. With his large hands, Patrick placed both hands on Charlene's thick thighs and began to caress them softly. Both hands started making their way up her thighs and under the dress. He quickly flipped the bottom of her dress over her stomach, exposing her lace black thong. His fingers teased the lining of her underwear until he quickly found the entrance to her warm lady-box.

Charlene spread her legs apart to assist with the pleasure. Picking up speed, he used two fingers to gently massage her pussy.

His touch had her moaning, and she was trying her best not to yell. Her kitty was passionately on fire.

He parted her pussy lips like the Red Sea, and his fingers penetrated her insides. Charlene's eyes began to roll to the back of her head, and her legs began to shake. Patrick quickly dropped to his knees behind Charlene and removed her underwear entirely. With one hand gripping her side and the other still playing in her juices, Patrick started planting kisses all over her booty. After about the fifth kiss, he dove his face into the middle of her butt cheeks.

Charlene felt his long, moist tongue slide between her ass. His wet tongue went crazy going in and out of her asshole. The simultaneous action Patrick gave Charlene made her explode from her gushy spot.

She felt her juices drip down her leg. Patrick quickly pulled down his jeans and exposed his nine-inch chocolate pole. His dick was so beautiful it deserved an award.

"Hurry up, P," whispered Charlene. She didn't want Trinity to catch them having sex. However, she wanted the dick so bad it was a risk she was willing to take. He quickly guided her over to their gray sectional couch. He ordered her to bend over and spread her legs apart. With full access to her bare bottom, he stuck his dick inside her fat pussy. Charlene moaned out in pleasure.

"Fuuuck." That turned him on even more.

With both hands squeezing her waist, he jammed his dick inside of her, giving her one long stroke.

"Shittt," she moaned. Patrick sped up the pace, quickly taking her to pound-town from behind. Charlene covered her mouth to keep from screaming. He loved to watch Charlene's round ass bounce from behind after every stroke. Finally, he pulled out and released his cum on her booty cheeks. Out of breath, they quickly put back on their clothes. Charlene went upstairs to check on Trinity and clean herself up. Patrick walked outside to enjoy the blunt he had stashed in the kitchen drawer. He was happy that he got to fuck in that house one last time. It could be the pussy he just got, but he finally felt okay about moving.

While Patrick was outside smoking, he saw his friend Keith swerve into the driveway with the U-Haul truck blasting Rick Ross music. He hadn't seen Keith since the day the HR managers sent him to tell Patrick he had to exit the parking lot. He hopped out of the truck with it still running, the passenger side door wide open, and talking loud as hell.

"Say, nigga, you ready to load the truck up?" said Keith, giving Patrick a handshake at the same time.

"Yeah, almost everything is in boxes, and the big stuff we can take first," replied Patrick. Mary J. Blige's angelic voice on the "All I Need" track was booming from the truck's speaker system.

"Damn nigga, turn that shit down. The neighbors will come outside bitching."

Making a joke, Keith replied, "You right, dawg, I don't want them to kick you outta here."

Patrick quickly gave Keith the side eye. "Boy, you a hoe-ass nigga," said Patrick, while laughing at the same time.

Putting both hands up to his chest, Keith said smiling, "My bad man, too soon, huh?"

"Ya think?" questioned Patrick as he walked over to lift the back of the moving truck door up. Trinity came outside smiling from ear to ear. She was wearing blue distressed jean shorts, a black spaghetti Guess top, and black and gold Guess sandals to match her shirt. Her thick and wild curls bounced as she headed towards her father.

At 15 years old, she was the spitting image of her mother. She was gorgeous with a blend of African and Native American features that added a richness to her overall appearance.

"What are you so happy about?" Patrick asked Trinity while giving her a hug.

"What, I need a reason to smile?" said Trinity.

"I guess not," Patrick said, smiling back at his daughter.

"Mom told me you were beating yourself up because we had to move. Dad, I'm okay. A house is just a place. A home is what you make it. We will be okay because we have each other." Keith chimed in, "Now that's some good raising you and Leannie did with this girl right here."

Patrick looked at Keith and agreed by shaking his head. Suddenly, Patrick replayed Keith's words back in his head. "Nigga, who the fuck is LEANNIE?"

Keith started laughing hysterically. "Man, you know who LEANNIE is, your wife, Charlene."

Patrick pretended like he was going to punch Keith by jumping at him playfully. "Bruh, don't be giving my wife no cute little nicknames. The fuck wrong with you, nigga?" Trinity starts laughing at her father and his friend joking around. She knew her dad was dead serious, though.

"Y'all play too much," Trinity said while making her way inside the house to grab her boxes. Charlene stepped out on the front porch and informed her husband and Keith it was time to load the big furniture while she and Trinity loaded the boxes in Patrick's black Ford F-150 pickup truck.

Keith responded, "Okay, Leannie," while waving to her.

"Ouch!" yelled Keith. He felt a small punch in his side from Patrick. Charlene shook her head and disappeared inside the house.

Three hours later, the U-Haul was packed up, and the house was completely empty.

Charlene took one more look at the empty place before locking the doors. She fought hard not to get emotional. She also didn't want to make Patrick feel bad again, so she controlled her emotions. Keith drove the U-Haul, while Patrick, Charlene, and Trinity rode in the pickup truck. They put the suburbs behind them as they headed to an area that they worked so hard to get away from. The Coleman family were now Southwest Houston residents.

I sat in the back of the truck trying to get the images of my parents fucking out of my head. I should be used to it by now, because they stay getting caught having sex. The majority of the time, I don't mention it to them. They fuck all over the house thinking they're being discreet. I was in my room packing and ran out of duct tape for my boxes. I remember it was an extra roll of tape in the kitchen drawer. As I'm walking down the stairs, I can hear movement under the staircase.

I thought they were arguing at first, so my nosey ass stopped to listen. Soon I heard a bunch of moaning and felt utterly disgusted. I quickly walked back up the stairs and closed my door. They should be ashamed of themselves. Why not have the decency to go into their bedroom? I mean damn, we were in the middle of moving, and they want to get their freak on. A few minutes later my mom comes into my room asking me if I am finished packing. I responded, "No, are you finished doing what you're doing?"

"Whew, yes. I'm finally done packing up the kitchen. I didn't realize we had so many dishes, pots, and pans!" she said. That's not the type of finish I was talking about, but I let her be great in that moment. It was the middle of summer, and it was scorching hot outside.

This Texas heat is not for the weak. One thing about living in Houston, Texas, is our weather was bipolar as fuck! In the same day, we can get the merciless sun beaming down on us, rain, and an ice storm. Today, the sun was showing its ass! The heat was uncomfortably smothering us, and I fantasized about rain. Now, I was so glad to be in the car with the AC blowing cold. Why did my parents choose one of the hottest days to move on? Loading all our stuff nearly burnt me up.

Now, we're headed to unpack all our stuff at the new place. I hate to sound bougie, but why didn't my parents pay for movers? Well, I guess I know the answer to that. Our funds have been kind of low lately. I heard my mama ask my dad which route he was taking. I quickly rolled my eyes because they loved to argue about directions.

"I'm taking Sam Houston West to I-59 North," answered my father.

"What! Why you just won't take the feeder roads until you get to Braeswood Street. Ride Braeswood all the way down until you hit Fondren Road," said my mother in a demanding tone. My dad gave my mom a sideways look and shook his head.

"Now that's just retarded. All the lights we would hit before getting there. You must want to arrive tomorrow? Look, just sit back and let me drive," my father said with an attitude.

My mother waved him off but didn't say another word. I gazed out the window, enjoying seeing parts of Houston. I watched as the neighborhoods went from better to worse. In about 40 minutes, we pulled into some apartments. The apartments weren't bad to look at, but nothing spectacular to look at either. This was certainly going to be an adjustment for all of us.

As we turned into the driveway of the apartments, a security officer standing outside a white guard shack waved to us. He opened the steel black gates with the remote in his hand and allowed us to pass through to the other side. As we were entering through the gates, I read a huge brown stone with green letters that read Acorn Forest Apartments. The apartments look like small brick cottages with tall green trees planted all around the buildings. I couldn't help but notice the tall brick walls surrounding the property for safety.

What was strange to me was the sharp broken glass they had placed along the top of the walls. I assumed management wanted to keep people from jumping over the walls and onto the property. We came to a two-way intersection and stop sign. We could either turn left, right, or keep straight to the circular driveway out in the middle. My dad continued straight to the circular driveway to find parking.

I heard my dad say, "Oh lord, look at all these lil niggas." I stopped looking out my side of the window and sat up straight to get a good view of the guys. My dad turned around, looking at me crazy.

Laughing, I threw one hand up and said, "What, Dad?" He ignored me and proceeded to drive a little way ahead. Focusing back outside the car, my heart started pounding. Daddy was right! There were quite a few teenage boys and young men standing out front. Suddenly, a little boy on a scooter darted out in front of the truck, which caused my dad to step on the brakes super hard. I used my left hand to grab the back of the passenger side seat and stop my face from flying into it.

My dad rolled down his window and said, "Come here, little man." The boy came up to my dad's side of the truck, still holding on to his scooter. "How old are you?" my dad inquired.

"I'm 8," said the kid.

"Well, that means you're old enough to know that you should look both ways before crossing the street."

The boy obviously was raised pretty good. He responded, "Yes, sir," looking down at his red and black Jordan dunks on his feet. He was a handsome little thang. He had a black, curly, high-top hairstyle. His smooth, light-skinned complexion almost matched his light brown eyes. Next thing you know, a nice-looking woman with a caramel complexion walked up to the truck. You can tell she was naturally beautiful, even with that bonnet on. Her skin was flawless. She was wearing a purple bonnet on her head, a retro DMX t-shirt, black tights, and purple furry slippers.

She looks irritated. "Excuse me, what did you just say to my son?" She asked my dad. My mom, who was comfortable in her seat, quickly leaned up to stare at the woman. "Well, what I told him," … were the only words my dad was able to get out of his mouth before my mom interrupted him.

"WHAT HE SAID WAS THAT YOUR SON IS OLD ENOUGH TO LOOK BOTH WAYS BEFORE RUNNING INTO THE STREET. WE ALMOST HIT HIM!" my mama said aggressively while pointing her trigger finger at the lady.

Both women looked at each other for a couple of seconds without blinking. "Oh, okay, just asking. My name is Jeanette, but people call me Netta. This is my son Malik," she said, rubbing his curly hair. "Welcome to the neighborhood," she politely stated. Thank God her kind words shifted my mother's energy. If she would've had an attitude with my mom, it was going down. My mom would have hopped out of this car and dog-walked that chick. My mom's face softened, and she nicely replied, "Thank you." Something told me that lady could sense the hostility in my mother's voice and knew she wanted all the smoke.

I suddenly thought back to seeing my mama drag this one chick outside my dad's job in broad daylight. I'm shocked he wasn't fired back then. I don't know all the details of that situation, but I know it had something to do with my dad. I was nine years old at the time and watched from the car as my mom put both hands and feet on every part of that woman's body. I wasn't as naïve as my parents thought I was at that age.

I knew my dad got caught doing something he had no business doing with that woman. I remember him apologizing to my mom for months until she finally forgave him. Snapping back into reality, I saw Netta wave to us goodbye. She turned around and walked into one of the apartments off to the left side of the complex. Her son continued to ride his scooter all in the driveway. His little ass didn't learn anything.

My dad chuckled and shook his head at my mom. "Now why did you have to do that lady like that?"

"She was trying to check you, and I had to let her ass know you have a wife that don't play about you. Period," my mom said, rolling her neck around.

"We're already off to a rough start," my dad said worryingly.

"No, we're not. You saw that quiet exchange between me and that woman? Black women have a way of expressing themselves with each other without saying one word. We quickly got an understanding, and everything is good now," my mom assured my father.

One thing about my mom is that she didn't play with people. She can be a motherfucka when you piss her off. People think she is some spoiled housewife. That is true. However, before she met my dad, she lived a rough life in Acres Home. Everyone knows women from that part of town are bat-shit crazy.

The leasing office was closed for the day, so my dad parked in the spot reserved for potential residents. The landscaping was beautiful. They placed four large, marbled rocks out by the leasing office with a beautiful flower garden around each one. Off to the side, there was a long wooden bench for people to sit on. There were three guys sitting on the bench and four guys standing around.

Every one of them had their attention on us. They were no longer laughing and holding conversations with one another. I jumped down from the truck, and I could feel eyes on me. I felt weird and uncomfortable. I haven't had to live in an environment as crowded as this one. Our old neighborhood barely had any kids around. It was mostly retired old folks that lived there. Now I feel like I'm being thrown into the jungle. As I'm walking to the back of the truck to grab boxes, I can hear some of the guys talking amongst each other.

One said, "Sheesh, she bad, and the mama too!" They were horrible at whispering. Picking up a box, I headed in the direction of the guys out front. My dad quickly rerouted my ass and told me I can get to the apartment quicker by walking through the grass and crossing over some small bushes. He pointed to the location of our new place. "We're apartment 1612, baby," he informed me.

As I'm walking through the grass, I felt an energy over me. It was intense. As much as I tried not to look in that direction, I couldn't help it. I turned around, and there was this fine-ass tall boy with tattoos on both arms staring at me. He was wearing a white muscle shirt, red basketball shorts, long white socks, and black and red Nike flip-flops. His hair was cut short in a small fade. His eyebrows were thick and gave him some uniqueness. He had a full set of lips that I immediately thought about kissing.

His skin was smooth, and light brown in color. I couldn't quite guess his age. This boy already had a small goatee beard. He had a grown man physique with a baby face. He didn't even smile at me. He just tossed a football up repeatedly without breaking his stare.

It was like he was looking through my soul or something. There was something about him that I was immediately drawn to. He was mysterious. My dad must've thought I got lost. He came up from behind me and guided me with his hand on my shoulder into the building where our townhome was located. *Isn't he thoughtful?* I thought to myself but was really being sarcastic.

I kind of was mad he was treating me like a damn child! My dad turned to give the boy a stern look, but he didn't cower away. I almost thought I saw a smirk on his face. Now I'm intrigued! He was different, and everything about him screamed, "bad boy."

Who was this boy who was clearly rough around the edges and had a huge growth spurt for his age? I was surely going to find out.

I walked into our townhome, and it was nice on the inside and spacious. I really wasn't expecting it to be that nice because of the area we moved to. I mean it doesn't compete with our last home, but it was decent. The front emerald-green door, gold doorknob, and metal brass door knocker gave the place some charm before stepping in. There is a narrow foyer as soon as you walk in. There is a half bathroom on the right side.

The kitchen was a little past a huge wall and vertically across from the half bathroom. The landlord added stainless steel appliances to the kitchen to give it more of a modern look. After the kitchen was a huge open space that fits our dining room table and living room furniture. Across from the living room was the master bedroom. My parents had their own full bathroom. Past the living room were two sliding doors with huge glass windows that led to a small outside patio. The patio was closed in by dark green wooden gates.

My mom already put up gold and black curtains to keep people from looking inside. Upstairs, there is a laundry closet built into the center wall. After you turn the corner from the stairs, there is a second full bathroom. My room was in the far corner and on the opposite side of the laundry closet. We still had a lot to be thankful for. Honestly, I didn't mind the move. The previous neighborhood was boring, and I had no peers to talk to when I got home from school. I was so anxious to meet new people. I was exhausted. I let my dad, mom, and Keith unload our things for a while without my assistance. I sat in my room on the floor not doing much of anything. After about an hour, I decided to be helpful again. I made my way downstairs and out of the house.

The sun had gone all the way down. As I'm walking towards the U-Haul truck, I see my dad and Keith struggling with our large oakwood entertainment center. Half of it was leaning off the ramp. My dad was trying to pull it up from outside the truck, and Keith was trying to pull it up from the back of the truck. They both were trying their best not to drop it. It was too heavy for either one of them to try to move it on their own.

I heard a car speeding up to us. I turned around, curious to see who was inside the car. The car stopped in the middle of the circular driveway, just a few feet away from the U-Haul truck. A milk chocolate guy jumped out of a black Mercedes Benz and jogged over to my father. I think time slowed down as my heart raced inside my chest. I was mesmerized. I never experienced this type of feeling before; this was different. If it didn't sound ridiculous, I would say it was love at first sight. Well, at least on my end it was. He was beautiful to look at. He had shoulder-length dreads in small 2-strand twist plats all over his head.

The end of the plats was a goldish-brown color. He had the smoothest skin. That man could be an oil painting in a museum. I stood there admiring the man before me. You can tell that he was young but had a grown man on his shit type of vibe. As fine as he was, he still had a street essence to him. I noticed there was a female sitting on the passenger side of his car. She was cute, but not cuter than me. She was light-skinned, and I could tell she was on the thick side.

The low-cut tank top she was wearing exposed her cleavage and arms. She rocked Chinese bangs with long, wavy burgundy hair. My attention went right back to the guy who insisted on helping my father and Keith. He immediately grabbed the bottom of the entertainment center, and they both began to lift the object back onto the truck. His physique was immaculate.

I watched as his arm muscles protruded from under his T-shirt. Together, all three men carefully guided the huge dresser off the truck. They proceeded to carry the large item to our new place. The men disappeared into the doorway. I stood outside waiting for them to return. I couldn't wait to get another look at this guy. Suddenly I remembered the chick sitting in the car. I turned around and she was staring dead at me. She wasn't even trying to be subtle with her mean-ass looks either. It's almost like she was challenging me with her eyes.

Damn, did she notice me lusting after her nigga? I thought to myself. Oh well, I take after my mama. I stared right back at that bitch, letting her know I'm on whatever type of time she's on. The men headed towards us laughing and chattering amongst themselves, breaking our stare contest. She rolled her eyes and pulled the sun visor down to touch up her Chinese bangs.

I overheard my new crush telling my father to get an alarm system in our home because we have some nice furniture. "These apartments turn into Gotham City at night. Protect your valuables, sir," he warned my father.

My dad chuckled and responded back, "I got all the alarm systems I need right there in that house," he said, pointing to our crib. "Anybody that wanna to come into our place uninvited will get a free one-way ticket to the spiritual realm. My two bodyguards, Semi and Automatic, are there all day to keep us safe."

The guy chuckled at my dad's joke. "Damn, that's what I'm talking about."

"What's your name, young man?" My father asked him.

The guy held out his arm to shake my father's hand. "My name is Tyreese, but everyone calls me Reese."

"Nice to meet you, Reese; my name is Pat, and that's a firm handshake you got there," my father acknowledged.

"Thank you, sir," Reese politely stated.

"If you don't mind me asking, how old are you? I hardly see young men with your type of character anymore," my father said with curiosity. Reese answered back, "I just turned 18 two weeks ago."

I stood right in the middle of their conversation, staring at his perfectly aligned teeth. I couldn't even find one blemish on his moisturized milk chocolate skin. He noticed me looking at him because he took his eyes off my father for a second to glance down at me. I almost thought I saw him smirk, but I could be tripping.

"Okay, you did your good deed; now it's time to go. We got places to be!" I heard the chick shout out with an attitude. She was leaning against the car with her arms folded. I didn't even see her get out of the car. Oh, she pressed. He turned around so quickly and gave her a serious look. Chuckling to avoid the awkward moment, Reese shook his head and informed us it was time for him to go. I don't know what came over me, but I suddenly felt like being petty. I replied loud enough for her to hear.

"My name is Trinity, and we appreciate your good deed. How can we show our gratitude?" I said in a flirtatious tone while twirling my bountiful curls with my finger. My dad looked at me and rolled his eyes. Reese turned his attention to me. He gave me a big smile, and my heart skipped a beat. I'm crushing hard on this guy!

He gently patted me on the shoulder and said, "See ya later, kid. It was nice to meet you." The grin on my face quickly turned into a frown. Did he just stick the needle in my balloon and let all the air out? I felt so insulted. He headed for his car. I noticed my father standing there laughing at me. He was getting pleasure out of knowing Reese put me into the friend zone.

Reese ordered the girl to get back in the car. He hopped in his vehicle and sped out of the apartment complex. Walking back to our apartment, I suddenly felt like I was being watched. It was the weirdest feeling. I looked around and didn't see anyone. I just shook the feeling off and called it a night. I was exhausted from moving boxes and furniture all day.

I just saw the most beautiful girl in the world. I felt like my heart was about to jump out of my chest watching her big curls bounce from side to side. Her light brown eyes made me weak in the knees. She had a rich, dark-brown skin tone with light freckles on her cheekbones. She looked mixed with Indian. She had a nice petite shape. Her mother is her twin, so she will grow up to be a true dime-piece.

I couldn't stop staring at her and didn't give a fuck if her daddy was around. I saw him giving me the death stare. He will have to come a lot harder than that, because his daughter is on my radar, and I'm not letting up. I'm going to make it my business to get to know her. I have been dating Kyra for about six months, but I'm done with her ass for good now. She will be mad, but it is what it is. I met my future. I saw the way she was interacting with that nigga Reese too. That angered the fuck outta me.

I watched her be so infatuated with dude. She didn't see me because I was sitting in an upstairs windowpane from a distance. I know we are meant to be together because she felt my presence. Before going into the house for the night, she stopped to look around. Yup, our souls are connected. What is it about that nigga Reese that these hoes are drawn to? Kyra looks at that fool like she's in love with him too. Sometimes I want to slap the shit out of her. Honestly, I care about Kyra, but there is no chemistry.

Kyra was the homie, and we shouldn't have been in a relationship. Kyra was gorgeous. She was a redbone with long, ginger-colored, coarse hair. She had the body type of a track star. She will bounce back with no problem. Dudes lust after her daily. That was no longer my concern. I got to make this new chick mine before she belongs to anyone else.

As I lay in bed staring at the ceiling, I couldn't stop thinking about this new girl. I had been fantasizing about her for the past couple of hours, and I didn't notice the television wasn't on. My thoughts were interrupted by my mama's loud-ass voice. I could tell she was upset about something because she was screaming at the top of her lungs. Rolling my eyes, I jumped out of the bed to see what her problem was. I walked down the hallway and entered the living room to witness my mama pointing her finger at my dad's face. She was hurling insults at him.

"You're such a fucking dumbass, George. I told you to stop and get a 10-piece wing dinner from Timmy Chan's, not no damn Taco Bell," she complained. All this commotion over some fucking chicken.

"Sydney, does it matter? I didn't feel like driving down Bissonnet. Taco Bell was close by the house. Eat it or don't; I'm tired," stated my dad.

"Why can't you ever do shit right?" my mom asked.

"Well, why can't you cook?" my dad shouted. I laughed because my dad had some nuts tonight. He was provoking her, knowing she was violent.

POP!

My mama started slapping him all in his face. He just covered his face to block the blows. I never understood why my dad didn't knock her ass out. No matter how much abuse he took from her throughout the years, he never hit her. I don't care if that was my mother. She stayed attacking the man of the house. He just worked an 8-hour shift fixing people's cars.

It was crazy he still had to buy dinner on his way home. My dad taught me not to be a weak-ass nigga because he was for sure one. My woman will respect me. I wish the bitch would even think about hitting me. I took my last beating from my mom at 14 years old. About three years ago, I was in my room playing Madden on my PlayStation. She kept calling me to take the kitchen trash out, but I didn't hear her.

She burst through the door, accusing me of ignoring her on purpose. After she kept accusing me of ignoring her, I waved her off while she was still talking. That set her off even more, and she slapped the hell out of me in my face. I saw stars immediately. That was the straw that broke the camel's back. Without giving it much thought, I punched her ass dead in the lip. It split immediately as I saw blood leak out the side of her mouth. She ran out of the room crying.

One hour later, I was being taken out of the house in HPD handcuffs. I spent a week in the juvenile detention center. My dad came to my court date and told the judge I was a good boy. He convinced the judge to drop the charges against me. My mother didn't want me back in the house, but my dad informed my mother he would leave her. She was violent but not crazy. He paid all the bills. I don't regret popping her in the mouth either because she never hit me again.

My dad should've taken some notes from me. My mom and dad were an odd-ass couple anyways. She was as ratchet as they come but acted like she lived for the lord. She was a light-skinned woman who smoked cigarettes, drank alcohol all day, and cursed like a sailor. She wore colored wigs and dressed provocatively most of the time, exposing a lot of her breasts and legs. She reminded me of the Black version of Peggy Bundy. She wore the tackiest shit, and her wigs looked cheap.

My dad was a dark-brown-skinned man. He didn't smoke or drink, barely cursed, and often wore suits. He was short and fragile looking. He was bald-headed, thin, and wore reading glasses. There were several moles on his face. I can't lie; my dad looked lame. However, he was a provider, and nothing was lame about that. I guess opposites attract, but I doubt they are in love with one another. They are just comfortable, and one of them settled for the other. My father and I are extremely close. That was the one person that always had my back. Although I love my mother, I always thought my father could do better.

Why be with a loud and obnoxious woman every day? He worked too hard to put up with her bullshit. It made no sense to me. I was used to living in a toxic household. I made my way back to my bedroom under the covers. I heard a knock at the door. My dad opened the door and informed me he was off work tomorrow. "You want to go fishing in Galveston tomorrow?" he asked me. "No, Dad, I have plans tomorrow," I said, feeling sorry for him. He looked so unhappy. Usually, I wouldn't mind going with him, but I had other plans in mind. Tomorrow, I'm going to make my move on the new girl. I thought about her until I drifted off to sleep.

The light shining through my room woke me up. The sun was out bright and early. I tossed and turned all night thinking about what I was going to say to my new crush and Kyra. Thank God Kyra and her brother Jaycee will be at a family reunion all day long. I can handle that situation another time. It was Sunday, and I knew everyone would be at the pool. It was mid-June, and the Texas heat kept us in the pool.

I grabbed my phone to see what the temperature would be today. Damn, it's hot, I thought to myself as the forecast on my home screen read 97.5 degrees. That's crazy because it's only 9:45 am. I walked into the living room and noticed my mom sitting on the couch drinking coffee and watching the news. She was wearing a pink bonnet on her head, a black nightgown, and pink fluffy socks. On Sundays, she doesn't go anywhere, so she stays in her pajamas all day. A Click2Houston news anchor advised everyone to be cautious of the heat before going outside. The news ticker instructed everyone to drink plenty of water. My mom turned to look at me and asked me if I heard the news warnings.

"How can I not hear what they said, Mama? I'm standing right here," I sarcastically replied.

She stared at me with an attitude for a second and said, "Boy, don't be answering me with no damn question. Did you just hear what the fuck they said?" She asked me again in a challenging manner.

I don't have time for her shit today, so I just said, "Yeah."

"Yes, ma'am," she waited for me to correct myself. Walking to the kitchen, I couldn't help but roll my eyes. She really was on one today and looking for a fight. "YES, MA'AM," I said with more bass in my voice. As I'm pouring my cereal, my dad walks past the kitchen and heads toward the front door. He had on his beige fisherman hat with the matching vest, white undershirt, blue jean pants, and water boots. He was carrying his black and silver fishing pole and box.

"Bye, son," I heard him say right before leaving out. I didn't have time to respond back before hearing the door close. It was clear he was trying to get away from this house. He is probably still mad at my mom attacking him last night. I felt bad I wasn't going with him. He didn't say a damn thing to my mother. She continued to watch television until she heard the front door slam.

"I can't believe I married that loser and had a crazy-ass son by him too," she said, looking at me with a great deal of animosity. I ignored her. After fixing my bowl of cereal, I headed straight to my room. I didn't feel like being around her. Man, she was extra all the time. I quickly ate my food and placed the empty bowl on the dresser. I grabbed a pair of aqua blue swim shorts out of the drawer. I decided to be shirtless for the day. I changed into my swimming trunks and slid into my aqua blue and white Nike slides. I examined myself in the bathroom mirror and acknowledged I looked good as hell.

Realizing I missed a dosage yesterday, I reached to open the medicine cabinet. Before I could open it, I saw my reflection in the mirror staring at me with an evil smirk on his face. The man in the mirror sized me up and down.

"Yeah, do like your daddy tells you and take your medicine."

"You can't keep me hidden for long," he assured me.

"No, not now. Go the fuck away!" I shouted at the mirror. My reflection began to laugh at me. I placed both hands over my face, trying to drown out the noise and not panic. Then I quickly opened the medicine cabinet and grabbed the white bottle labeled Fluoxetine.

I took one capsule and placed the bottle back where it was. I have been taking this medicine since I was seven years old. Besides my mom and dad, nobody knows I struggle with a mental illness, and I want to keep it that way. I remembered to grab a large drying towel out of the hallway closet. As soon as I stepped outside, it felt like the sun jumped on my back. As I'm walking down the concrete sidewalk, I could hear loud talking and laughter in the distance. I could already tell people were at the pool.

When I got to the pool gate, I spotted two little kids' dogpaddling in the pool with their floaties on. The little boy was showing his little sister how to swim. Their mom was lying on the lawn chair scrolling through her phone. She wasn't paying attention to them at all. I saw my homeboy Z sitting on the edge of the pool in the corner. Behind him was his bitch-ass brother Reese, Sean, who was exposing his large, flabby stomach, and an older nigga we call Two-Tyma because he can't stay faithful to any woman. They all were standing around drinking and eating on a tall, circular table.

I pulled up the latch on the pool gate to open the door, and Z lit up when he saw me. "What go dine baby?!" He excitedly waved me over. Sean and Two-Tyma gave me the what's up nod, and Reese's hoe ass just looked at me and turned his attention back to the other guys.

Two- Tyma felt his energy because before he took a drink from his beer, he chuckled at our exchange. I popped a squat right next to Z on the edge of the pool and stuck my feet in the warm water. This is Texas, so I was surprised the water wasn't boiling hot. One thing I can say is that the people who owned these apartments tried their best to make our landscape and pool area nice. You almost forget you're living in the hood until you walk outside the gates. Then you're reminded you live in the heart of the Southwest side of town. I always loved coming to the pool.

The maintenance men kept it clean, and it immediately gives off a serene vibe. I loved coming here to smoke my blunt and just think about life in general. There was a small waterfall at the opposite end of the pool. The water stream flowed consistently down the sculpture of natural rocks before falling into the pool. Sean interrupted the peaceful moment I was having.

"Hey, why do you all say, 'What go dine?'" Sean was from Indiana and a classmate of Reese and Jaycee. He has lived in Houston for the past five years and always had questions for us regarding our southern lingo.

Looking at Z with his hands on his hip, Sean asks, "Are you trying to say, 'What's going down?'"

Reese laughs and answers for Z. "Nah, nigga, he said it right. We don't say no 'What's going down? That sounds weak as fuck. H-Town niggas say, "What go dine or What's going dine."

Laughing hysterically, Sean tells us we are too country for him and jumps into the pool. His fat ass splashes me and Z all in the face.

"Damn! Go splash yo big ass somewhere else," Z yells out. Sean proceeds to swim to the other side of the pool. Z digs in his pocket and pulls out a blunt and lighter. After lighting it, he takes a couple puffs and hands it to me. As I'm enjoying the blunt, I see the girl I have been thinking about all night and her parents headed towards us. I quickly held the blunt down to my side before her parents saw me with it. Z looked at me with confusion.

"Why are you hiding the blunt? Your parents know you smoke weed and don't care."

"Man, I'm trying to talk to that girl, and I don't want her parents thinking I'm a bad dude," I told him. We both watched them as they were approaching the pool gates.

"Give me my blunt back then," he demanded, grabbing it from me. He began to puff on it and didn't care who saw him smoking.

"Wait, nigga, what about Kyra?" Z was looking at me with a stone face. Kyra was considered everyone's precious baby, so he wasn't too pleased about her getting hurt.

"I'm ending things with Kyra. What do you care for anyways? Now you can go ask her out," Z thought I really didn't know he was in love with Kyra.

"Huh, what do you mean?" he asked curiously.

"Huh," I mocked him in the same manner. "Dude, don't try to act like you're not in love with Kyra. I have known you had a thing for her since we were little," I admitted.

"Well, why talk to her then with yo hoe ass?" He responded with some bass in his voice.

"Touché, you got me. It doesn't matter because we really didn't get far in the relationship. Hell, I ain't even fuck yet." That seemed to make him feel better because he dropped the subject. He began to puff on the blunt some more.

I watched as her father opened the gate so his family could enter. Sean was swimming his way back to our side of the pool. When he got close to us, he was cheesing from ear to ear.

"Man, is that the mama in the yellow bikini? Aye, she is Michael Jackson bad. The whole family is good-looking, including the dad. No homo."

Z wasn't feeling his comment. "That was some gay ass shit you just said, Sean."

"Man, I'm not gay. Anyone can see that's a nice-looking man." Sean shrugged his shoulders.

"Ahh, you think that man is sexy," Z teased Sean. I had to laugh because Z can be funny as hell sometimes. Sean couldn't help but laugh at Z's comments himself. He quickly waved him off, made his way out of the pool, and grabbed the bag of chips sitting on the table.

I watched as the family got settled on the other side of the pool. They placed their belongings on the lawn chairs next to the waterfall.

"I got my eye on something else," I told Z while staring at my crush. She made eye contact with me but quickly turned away. Not trying to stare at the girl and creep her out, I began to look around. I noticed Reese was mugging me. I twisted up my face at him, because why the hell is he looking at me like he's ready to run the fade? Z started looking at the both of us back and forth.

"Aye, I know why you don't like my brother. You don't like him for the same reason I had an issue with him for a long time. Everyone loves him. You are jealous of him. It's cool. I have been there. Once you get over your jealousy, you can see he is a solid dude," he informed me, patting me on the shoulder. I juked my elbow backwards to knock his hand off my shoulder.

"I've got an issue with yo brother because it's clear he got an issue with me." I aggressively stated.

"Well, whoop that nigga if you think you can," Z suggested while waving me off. "I'm tired of the secret animosity. Either you both fight it out to get it over with, or just stop all the bullshit." I could tell Z was irritated with the both of us. Z has been my friend since the third grade. It's crazy how we are so close, but his brother and I have always been at odds with one another. Honestly, the only reason I haven't fought him is out of respect for Z. I can tell, though, that one day, I'm going to have to knock his ass out.

"Fight what out and kill what bullshit?" Reese asked his brother while walking towards us for clarity. He must've heard what Z said. I just stood there ready for whatever.

"Hello, Reese, good to see you, man," I heard my future girl's dad tell Reese as he was walking towards him. Reese broke his concentration on us and walked to shake the man's hand. They began having a conversation and walked off. I'm almost positive that man stopped up from having an altercation just now.

Reese is already getting in good with her dad. Fuck it, here goes nothing. I got up from sitting on the edge of the pool and made my way over to her. She was standing in the 3ft part of the pool pouring water on her chest. Her mom was sitting off to the side in the water. I got as close as I could to kneel and speak to her from outside the pool.

"Hey, what's your name?" I asked, smiling with the perfect teeth I knew I had. She looked up at me and gave me a smile right back. The water on her moisturized skin glistened.

"Trinity," she answered back while smiling. I could feel her dad and mom eying us from different sides of the pool. Her dad was still standing on the other side with Reese, but he was focused on us now. I didn't care.

"Well, Trinity, my name is Jervonte, but people call me Von. You know you've been on my mind, right?"

"Oh really, don't try to run game on me," she said, smirking at.

"I'm being serious. You're gorgeous to me. Are you mixed with Indian?" I asked her.

"No, I just have good genes. I hate when chicks try to say they're mixed with something other than Black like it's some type of flex.

We are some beautiful people, and I'm proud of my Blackness. I'm Black, period. Nothing else," she said.

Holding my fist in the air, I jokingly replied, "Well alright, Miss Angela Davis."

She burst out in laughter, showing off that beautiful smile again. I was tired of kneeling down, so I sat on the edge of the pool again and placed my feet back in the water. To my surprise, she joined me. She climbed halfway out of the pool and sat next to me. She was rocking an all-black bikini. She had the perfect shape. I couldn't help but notice her small waist and thick thighs. She began to wiggle her pedicured feet in the water. Those painted white toenails were sexy. Curious to know, I asked how old she was.

"I'm 15, but I'll be 16 in August, she spoke proudly. My dad says I can't have a boyfriend until I'm 16," she informed me.

"Who said I wanted to be your boyfriend?" I asked, teasing her.

She just giggled. "Yeah, you're going to be my girl, lil mama. I can wait 2 months," I assured her.

She stared at me, and the sun shining in her face made her light brown eyes sparkle. Her dad left Reese standing in the corner and passed up his wife to make his way over to us. He approached us, but I couldn't stare straight up at him because the sun was bright. He hopped in the pool to face us.

"What are y'all over here talking about?" he asked, floating on his back.

"Nothing really, sir. I'm just trying to get to know your daughter."

"Why?" He quickly interjected and stood straight up in the water.

"Well, sir, I think she is beautiful, and I am curious to know more about her," I stated.

"She's not allowed to date, son." This man calling me son pissed me off. Thinking to myself, *I'm not your damn son, nigga; plus, I have a father.*

"I understand," I said out loud.

"I can't date yet, but in 2 months I can," Trinity said, looking at her father irritated.

"Pat, leave them alone and come chill with me. I've been over here by myself." The man turned to look at his wife and then back to us. He decided to listen to his wife and made his way through the water to get to her. I watched as he walked between her legs while she was sitting on the steps, and he bent down to kiss her. "Girl, your parents are young as hell," I presumed.

"I know; they had me while in high school," she acknowledged.

I started teasing her about her mom's beauty. "Aye, your mama is A-1. She fine as hell," I joked. She looked at me sideways and joked back.

"Well, go holler at my mama then; just watch out for my dad's right hook."

"Nah, I'm good. I know who I want," I said seductively biting my lip. I guess I was too focused on Trinity because I didn't notice Reese walking up until he kneeled to tap Trinity on her shoulder. My entire expression changed to irritation. My blood instantly started boiling, but I had to keep it together. Now is not the time to be spazzing out.

"Hey Trinity, I just wanted to speak to you before leaving for work," he said. She lit up like a Christmas tree. All that was missing was a star on top of her damn head.

"Hey Reese! Aw man, I wish you didn't have to work. Well, enjoy the rest of your day," she said with all 32 teeth showing.

"It's all good. I will catch you later, kid," he ended the conversation. He glanced at me with his mug on mean, and then proceeded to walk out the pool gates.

Trinity noticed the exchange between us because she looked puzzled. "I hate that he calls me kid. He is not that much older than us," she said, rolling her eyes. I could tell she was offended. I remained quiet. I didn't want her to see I'm bothered by their little interaction. It's too early to act a fool, plus I know everyone is being nosey and low-key watching us. The pool gate squeaked open, and we both turned to see who was coming in.

Miss Lisa's extra thick ass was entering into the pool area. She was a heavy-set woman but still had curves. She was a pecan brown-colored woman with thick, black, straight hair that stopped at her shoulders. One thing I can say about her is that she was a confident woman. She wore a bright orange two-piece bathing suit. Her flabby belly shaking when she walks, and her large rump bounced underneath the plain blue towel wrapped around her waist. She passed by us and rolled her eyes at me. Her face was scrunched up like something stank. Her ass ain't liked me ever since she caught me stomping on a cat's head when I was a little boy. She looks at me like I'm the devil.

I can't stand her nosey ass. She is always in somebody's business. "Damn, did she roll her eyes at you?" Trinity asked while being amused.

"I don't know," I said, laughing back with her. "You sure are popular in these apartments," she said jokingly.

"Yeah, you can tell people love me, huh?" I continued to joke with her.

"I want to exercise. You want to do a couple of swim laps with me?" she asked.

I loved to work out, so to do it with her was a plus.

We both jumped in the water and began to do swimming sprints back and forth. I enjoyed spending time with her. After about two hours of swimming and making light conversation, she and her parents left the pool. I was tired myself. I said goodbye to the fellas and headed home to relax. I smiled all the way home because Trinity and I were starting something beautiful together. I know she is the one for me.

I came out of my bedroom and heard a bunch of loud talking and yelling. As I hit the corner to get to the living room, I spotted my big brother Jaycee and his two friends sitting at the dining room table playing cards. I walked over to be nosy and immediately blurted out, "I know you fucking lying." I'm thinking these niggas are yelling over a game of Spades per usual, but to my surprise they were playing UNO. My brother was screaming at Reese.

"Hoe ass nigga, quit cheating. You didn't say UNO when you had your last card, so now you can't call UNO UNO out!" Reese jumped up in my brother's face.

"Bullshit. You didn't call me out on it, so now I won." I started laughing hysterically.

"Y'all must be bored," I assumed. Reese's younger brother, Zion, stood up to give me a hug.

"Hey, Sweet Pea," he said, smiling down at me and not letting me go.

"Hey Z," I said while embracing him back.

"Damn nigga, how long are you going to hug her?" My brother Jaycee jokingly said to Z.

"Forever," he joked back while squeezing me tighter. All three of them loved to joke and play all day. They get on my nerves a lot. Reese and Zion were two good-looking brothers. Zion had a lighter-brown complexion and was bigger in size. He wasn't in shape like Reese, but his weight was solid. He kind of reminded me of Ice Cube in his younger days.

Z was just as handsome as Reese, and his looks made the girls act crazy over him. Reese had shoulder-length dreads, and Z sported a low-cut fade. Z had the most perfect set of waves. Reese was 18 years old and known as the mature brother. Z was 17 years old and known for being wild and goofy. Z finally let me go after that long embrace. Reese stopped arguing with my brother for a second to give me a hug. He didn't squeeze me tight or hold his embrace like Z did.

"Hey, lil sis," he uttered. Man, I hated he called me sis. I have been in love with him forever. I was born in these apartments, so everyone was like family. My nickname was Sweet Pea, but he always referred to me as lil sis. Since knowing him, I think about him every damn day. I dreamed about him every night. I couldn't wait for the day that he saw me as something more.

"Bro, check the rules of the game. You have to call UNO first in order to win," my brother stated, refusing to let go of the argument. Reese continued to shake his head.

"Nah, fuck them rules. You ain't catch it, plus we're playing the Black people version."

Jaycee found Reese's remarks to be hysterical. "Nigga, it's only one version of UNO."

Reese and Z both shouted out, "No, it's not!" There was a knock at the door, which made everyone quiet down. Reese went to answer the door because this was pretty much his house too. We have known them since the sandbox days, so my family and their family are extremely close. I saw Reese answer the door, but he quickly closed it and sat back down at the table. He didn't say anything but started reshuffling the UNO cards. We all were waiting for him to tell us who was at the door.

"Nigga, who was at the door?" my brother asked.

"Oh, nobody," Reese responded nonchalantly. For some reason, I decided to go look outside anyway. Opening the front door, my boyfriend Von was standing outside waiting on me. I immediately knew Reese was being an asshole.

I stepped out further to give him a hug. His demeanor was off and a bit dry. I saw something was wrong in his face but figured it was Reese closing the door on him. I always knew they both didn't like each other, but there was never a clear reason why on both ends.

"Hey, can we talk?" he asked.

"Yeah, let me go grab my shoes, and I'll be back out." Walking to my bedroom, I made it a point to stop and roll my eyes at Reese. "I thought you said nobody was at the door; Von is out there," I said with an attitude.

"Exactly," Reese said. My brother and Z found Reese's remarks to be funny. On that note, I headed to my room to put on my shoes. Headed back out the door, Z stopped me.

"Hey, don't let anything get you down today. I'm here if you need me," Z sincerely spoke. Why was he telling me this? "Okay, I guess," I replied awkwardly.

When Von spotted me, he started walking, and I followed right behind him. We stopped when we made it to the wooden benches located at the center of the apartment complex. We both sat down and stared at each other quietly for a moment. I was anxious to hear what he had to say. He began to speak.

"Pea, I have known you a long time, and I care about you, Mama. I just think we are better off as friends. There is no real spark or passion between us. You've been the homie for the longest, and I just can't get past that type of vibe with you." To be honest, I wasn't even mad. He didn't tell one lie. I never felt like Von was my soulmate.

We've been dating six months, and it's been okay, but I want that feeling that Reese gives me. That feeling where I'm head over heels in love with someone. I don't want to settle, and neither should he.

"Von, I agree with you. You're right. Although I care about you, I'm not in love with you at all," I admitted. "Damn girl, you ain't gone at least shed a tear for me or act heartbroken?"

We both laughed, and I began to focus on the person in the background. I have never seen this girl before. She was absolutely gorgeous and heading our way. She had the most beautiful, thick, curly hair I had ever seen and looked like a real Black Indian. Yes, I say true Indian because a lot of these hoes be lying by claiming they're mixed with something. She walked our way and gently smiled at me.

Her eyes met with Von's, and she softly said, "Hey, Von." My mouth dropped open because it suddenly hit me why he wanted to break up. I cut my eyes at him, and he made sure to not look at me. The way she looked at him told me it was something between them.

I wasn't mad, but he was busted. People tell me I'm crazy and outspoken all the time, so of course, being me, I didn't disappoint. "Wait, come back here," I jokingly said, grabbing her attention. She turned around looking confused.

"You talking to me?" She said, pointing to her chest.

"Yeah, so what's your name?" I asked her.

"Pea, don't," Von said, grabbing my arm.

She folded her arms and answered, "I'm Trinity; what's yours?" "My name is Kyra, but people call me Sweet Pea." Next thing you know, I see nosey-ass Z peeping his head out my front door.

"Oh shit, y'all niggas come peep this," Reese requested. Reese, Jaycee, and Z walked outside and made it a spectacle. I just rolled my eyes and turned my attention back to Trinity.

"So, how do you know Von?" I asked her.

"We met yesterday at the pool. He surely didn't tell me he has a girlfriend," she uttered with an attitude while looking at Von. Von looked like a sick puppy. I have never seen him so bashful.

"Had," I corrected her.

"Huh?" she said with a scrunched-up face.

"He had a girlfriend. He just broke up with me, and now I see why," I spat, looking at her sideways. I really didn't have a problem with her, but I was checking her temperature. I needed to know what type of female she was before I could be cool with her.

She kept staring over to where my brother and his friends were standing, which made me turn around to look at them too. I didn't think more of it. Maybe they made her nervous or something. Focusing back on her, it was clear she was in defense mode. "Well, I don't like to be in drama, so y'all figure this shit out. Bye." She chunked the deuces and was about to walk off.

"Trinity, it's already figured out. We're not together, and I'm okay with that," I let her know with a shrug of my shoulders.

"So, why are you mad at me?" She inquired.

"Who said I was mad at you? I just wanted to know a few things. Now I know. Plus, this apartment is filled with boys and men! It's nice to be around a female for a change. Let's walk to the Valero corner store. I want some Cheeto Puffs."

She tried to see if I was genuine, and I guess her gut feeling told her I was. "Okay," she obliged.

"What just happened?" Von stated with confusion.

"Me and her are cool; that's what happened," I spoke with sarcasm. Leaving him sitting on the bench alone, we started walking out of the apartments.

My brother and his friends started jokingly booing us. Z yelled, "Y'all could've at least pulled each other's hair or something." I turned around and yelled out sarcastically, "I don't pull hair. I beat bitches the fuck up."

She yelled out after me, "Yeah, me too!" I chuckled because that was her way of letting me know she can throw hands. I made up in my mind that I liked this girl, and we're going to be great friends. "Can I ask you a serious question? I want you to be honest too," she looked at me for confirmation.

"Sure, you can always count on me for honesty."

"You really don't care about losing your boyfriend?" she asked, looking puzzled.

"Hey, I've known Von for a long time, and we have only been dating six months. There is no spark between us. I think we both always knew it. He is more of a friend. Now Reese, that's who I have loved since I was a little girl. That nigga gives me butterflies just by looking at him," I informed her.

"Oh, the one with the dreads?" she pointed out.

"Yes, how did you know?" I curiously questioned.

"I met Reese yesterday. He helped my father move a dresser into our place. I mean, I can see why you like him," she said. It was almost as if she shared the same feelings or was crushing on him too. There was a sparkle in her eye the way she agreed with me. "Uh-huh," I said, looking at her with the side eye.

"Well, you just focus on Von," I joked but was dead ass serious. She could have Von, but Reese is off-limits. That was my heart, and nothing or no one was going to get in the way of us being together.

He just needs more time to see I am the woman for him. We crossed over the two-way street as fast as we could because cars were speeding on by. We made our way into the store, and I could hear the legendary Brandy Norwood's classic record "I Wanna Be Down" blasting throughout the store. I danced straight to the chip aisle. I have been craving Cheeto Puffs all day. I looked behind me to see where Trinity was, and she was just standing by the entrance.

I walked over to her and asked why she wasn't getting anything to snack on. She said, "Oh, I didn't have time to go grab any money." I told her not to worry about that and grab some chips and a soda just like me. She politely declined my offer and tried to assure me she was ok. I insisted on her getting some chips and a drink until she finally caved in.

She went to grab some hot fries, and I grabbed some Cheeto Puffs. The drinks were in the freezer at the back of the store. I asked Trinity what soda she wanted, and she informed me to get her a Sprite. I grabbed two 20 oz Sprite bottles and heard the doorbell go off because somebody had entered the store. In this neighborhood, you had to always be alert. You didn't want to spend a lot of time inside the store. I learned years ago to grab my junk food and get the hell out of here. This store has been robbed more times than you can count, and several people died right outside those doors due to gun violence.

Usually, it seemed like I had just missed an incident at the store, or it missed me. Either way, I'm grateful the good Lord has protected me all these years. My arch nemesis, Sabrina Taylor, walks in. This was the girl who currently had the man of my dreams wrapped around her pinky finger. Sabrina and Reese have been together on and off for 4 years. They met each other during freshman year at Sharpstown High School.

She was light-skinned with a big booty, and that's why niggas loved her. She was cute, but that was it. She always had the worst attitude, and for the life of me, I couldn't understand why Reese put up with her. She walked in and gave Trinity a salty look. Trinity quickly put down the chips she was holding and looked Sabrina up and down repeatedly. I walked up front to where Sabrina was standing.

"What the hell is your problem?" I asked, staring at Sabrina. She was about to speak when her phone rang. Answering the call in her fake-ass tone, she said, "Hey baby, what do you want from the store? Oh, your little fake love-struck sister is in here with your little girlfriend from yesterday."

Trinity chuckled and shook her head. I was wondering why she said little girlfriend the way she did. That shit low-key bothered me. Was Trinity not telling me something about her and Reese? Sabrina held the phone, listening to Reese on the other end. He must be getting on her case because she was rolling her eyes all over the place.

"Whatever, I'm not thinking about these little hoes," she yelled into the phone.

"Ha, but you are! You're super pressed, boo," Trinity sarcastically shouts back at her.

"Lil girl, don't play with me," Sabrina warned Trinity while making her way past me. Trinity laughed hysterically.

"Who is playing?" Trinity sarcastically challenged her. Furious, Sabrina bumped me on my shoulder, and one of the Sprites I was holding fell to the ground. I used one hand to shove Sabrina in her back.

"Girl, don't bump into me," I told her. She quickly turned around and shoved me harder. I went flying into one of the shelves. I watched as a bunch of different snacks fell off the shelf. I also dropped my bag of chips and the other Sprite due to being knocked off balance.

"Hey, you all stop that. You break something in here, you will pay for it," said the Black woman behind the counter. She was dark-skinned and rocking a pixie cut hairstyle. I didn't care what she was saying to us. Oh, it was time to set it off in this motherfucka like Lil Boosie from Baton Rouge would say.

I ran straight at her and started throwing hands. I was punching her all in the face. She couldn't stop my punches, so she tried to use her weight on me. She was much bigger than me in size, so she had that advantage over me. She put me in a headlock and tried to tackle me to the ground. I wasn't going down without a fight. Suddenly, I saw an extra pair of feet kneeing Sabrina in the stomach. She quickly let go of me. I could see Trinity had a large grip on Sabrina's hair and was landing punches all over the top of her head.

I immediately jumped in to assist Trinity. I grabbed some more of her hair, and together we beat on her. I popped her real good in the nose. She instantly went down to the ground and curled up in a fetal position. We landed punches and kicks all over her body. *Ding Dong*. In the middle of whooping Sabrina's ass, I heard the bell to the door sound off again. Soon we all were being pulled apart by Reese, Jaycee, and Z.

Jaycee and Z picked up Sabrina while she was kicking the air and kept screaming, "These hoes jumped me." She looked a hot mess. Pieces of her burgundy-colored hair were on the ground, and her lip was busted up pretty bad. They carried her out of the store to calm things down. Reese was furious. I saw it all over his face.

"Kyra, what the hell? So y'all jumped Sabrina? That's not cool, mayne. This isn't you!" He scolded me while turning his attention to Trinity. He obviously was blaming her for the altercation. I began to explain my side of the story.

"Reese I'm sorry. Sabrina…"

"Aht aht!" Trinity interrupted what I was trying to say. "You don't have to apologize to him, Kyra. She came in here on 10, and we gave her exactly what she was looking for." Reese cut his eyes at Trinity.

"You're a little troublemaker. Don't come here starting problems." Trinity was taken aback by his comments. She rolled her finger in his face, and he gently knocked her hand down. That didn't stop her from finishing what she had to say.

"Excuse me, your girlfriend is the one with the problem. She has a stank attitude. Do you know she hit Kyra first? It's not my fault your dumb ass can't see the type of female you have. But that's fine, because we gave her attitude a readjustment today. Next time she will think before she acts. You're welcome!"

The challenge was on as they both stared at each other out of pure annoyance. Reese smirked at Trinity, "Girl, you better watch with the name-calling." Trinity wasn't fazed at all. She stood on her tippy toes because Reese was much taller than her. She moved closer towards him and uttered "whatever" in a nonchalant manner.

She looked at me and asked if I was ready to go. I shook my head yes, and we headed out of the store. I couldn't put my finger on it, but there was something between those two. It was the same feeling I got watching her and Von interact with each other. I had an uneasy feeling in my stomach watching how Reese looked at her. He was mad at Trinity but obviously intrigued by her too. Walking outside, I saw that Jaycee and Z managed to put Sabrina in the passenger side of her car.

When she saw us, she desperately tried to get out of the car. Jaycee and Z made sure to block her from getting out. I heard Trinity say calmly, "Yup, run your stupid ass up again, sis." She was feisty as hell. Reese jogged over to the driver's side of Sabrina's car and hopped in. He cranked the car and sped off. Jaycee and Z joined us as we walked back to the apartments. Of course, Z got to joke around.

"Oh, so you two are the new Mighty Morphin Power Rangers, huh?"

"Shut up, Z," I said while pushing him in the shoulder. Jaycee told Trinity she didn't look like the fighting type. I thought the same thing, honestly.

I lived a very privileged lifestyle. However, my dad taught me how to fight at an early age. He wanted to make sure I could defend myself. My mom used to get mad at him for roughing me up during our sparring sessions, but he assured her it was for my own good, she informed us. Trinity was my type of girl. She had my back, and I would say this was the start of an epic friendship. First day meeting her, and we are already jumping bitches together. I have to low-key laugh at that.

"Let's go to my house to rest a little bit," I suggested to Trinity.

"Cool," she agreed. I needed to unwind after what had just transpired at the store. I was sick to my stomach knowing Reese was mad at me. We were sitting on my couch laughing hysterically at rerun episodes of the Wild 'n Out show. Katt Williams was ripping the Black team to shreds during the rap battle session. There was a knock at the door. We both looked at each other nervously, wondering who that could be. I was praying it wasn't the police. Slightly opening the door, Z held out a white plastic bag up to my face.

"What's this?" I asked while grabbing the bag out of his hand. 'Well, I couldn't let you leave the store empty-handed. I mean, you did just get your ass beat, so it's the least I can do," he teased.

"You're a damn lie! She didn't beat me up," I said, laughing. That was Z. He loved to joke but was a sweetheart. Looking into the bag, I noticed it was a bag of hot Cheeto puffs, a bag of hot fries, and two cans of Sprite in it.

"Hey, how did you know what snacks to bring us?" He smiled, and for a second, I felt myself blushing.

"I asked the clerk, and she told me," He shrugged. "Aw, thanks, Z." I leaned over to hug him.

"Ha! Big face ass," Von jokingly insulted me. I didn't even see him standing off to the side of us.

"Shut up, Von," I rolled my eyes at him. I was about to close the door when Von foot stopped it.

"Aye, where's my girl at?" he asked me while trying to make his way inside. I shoved him backwards. "Damn Kyra, let me in," he chuckled. I closed the door on them and locked it.

"Who was that?" Trinity asked me as soon as I entered the living room. That was Z, Reese's brother. He brought us the snacks we wanted from the store.

"How did he know what to get?" she curiously asked.

"He said he asked the clerk, and she told him."

"Wow, he really cares about you," she said, grinning.

"Z is like that with everyone. He has a big heart," I informed her.

"Mmkaaay," she said sarcastically. I didn't have time for jokes. I ignored her and started watching TV again.

I woke up extremely early on a Saturday morning. I grabbed my phone off the nightstand to find out what time it was. It was only 6:14 am. I tried my best to go back to sleep, but after an hour of tossing and turning in the bed, I was up for good. I jumped out of bed to wash my face, brush my teeth, and throw on some fitness clothes. I got the sudden urge to go for a walk. I always enjoyed the outdoors and nature.

I stared in the mirror, rocking my purple and white Adidas sports bra and tights that hugged my curves. After confirming I was fine as fuck in the mirror, I grabbed my headphones and headed for the front door. The sun was beginning to come up, but it was still quite dark outside. I looked around to be aware of my surroundings this early because who knows what crazy person could be lurking in the bushes?

Watching the ID Discovery channel be making a bitch paranoid, but on her Ps and Qs at the same time. I headed to the basketball court to sit down on one of the metal benches and to listen to some Beyoncé.

My girl B makes us Houstonians very proud. I'm not a crazy beehive fan, though. Her grown-ass fans dress up like it's Halloween at her concerts, wearing bee costumes and aluminum-style jumpsuits.

I just like her music, nothing more. I can already hear a basketball bouncing from a distance, which tells me somebody was on the court. As I'm walking, I spotted Miss Lisa sitting upstairs in an old wooden chair on her porch. She smiled and waved at me. I decided to talk to her for a few minutes.

"Hey, beautiful. What are you doing up this early?" she asked me. Well, I thought I would get a workout in. I have to stay fit if I'm going to get a track scholarship for college.

"That's great! A young girl focusing on her future," she said, nodding her head up and down. I didn't know Miss Lisa well, but she was always so pleasant to me.

"I was unable to carry my babies to full term. I had a lot of miscarriages, so I gave up on having children. I would've loved to have a daughter like you."

"Wow. I'm sorry to hear that, Miss Lisa. Thank you so much for the compliment." She suddenly had a worry on her face.

"Hey, I know it's none of my business, and I'm not your mother to tell you what to do. Please take my advice, baby girl."

"What is it?" I nervously chuckled. The expression on her face turned serious.

"Run away from that boy Jervonte as far as possible. He is not good for you and will eventually be your downfall," she assumed.

"Miss Lisa, why are you always giving Von a hard time? I'm asking because you are never nice to him. Did he do something to you?" Miss Lisa paused for a second and placed one hand on Trinity's shoulder.

She said calmly, "Baby, I have been on this earth a good amount of time. I have an extraordinary gift of reading people. I'm telling you something is not right with that boy! It's evil lurking inside him, you hear me. He tries his best to hide it, but I see right through him."

I chuckled at Miss Lisa's assessment of Von and just shook my head.

"That's not fair. You have to give him a chance," I replied.

"Shitttt. I ain't got to do nothing but stay Black and die. You will see, though; just watch."

"I got to go, Miss Lisa; enjoy the rest of your day." I turned around and headed for the stairs.

"The Devil can only hide for so long without turning red!" Miss Lisa yelled at me while I jogged down the stairs."

Walking up to the basketball court, I could spot Reese's sexy ass shooting the ball around. He must've been here for some time because his face and exposed chest were sweaty. He looked like he had just completed a full workout session. As I entered the gates, I couldn't help but stare at the fine specimen before me. He was shirtless and wearing some light blue shorts that stopped at his knees.

He was sporting the Air Jordan 11 Retro 'Cool Grey' sneakers. I watched as he bent down low while still dribbling the ball with his right hand, quickly moving the ball to his left hand, pivoting his foot like he had an opponent in front of him, and pulling up for the jump shot. That jumper was effortless and precise as I witnessed the ball fly into the net. Not to mention that dick was bouncing in those shorts. I started clapping, which obviously surprised him to see me standing there in front of the goal.

"Okayyy," I said, giving him props on his hooping skills. He started to blush and walk towards me. Damn, those teeth are pearly white and straight. Guys with nice teeth are my weakness. I can't stand a yuck-mouth person. What the fuck type of toothpaste does he use? I thought to myself. His cheekbones were visible, making him even more attractive at that moment.

Damn, without even trying, Reese sure knows how to make my pussy jump.

"Why are you up so early, kid?" he asked, looking at me with a smirk. I smacked my lips and put my hand on my hip.

"I'm not a kid; I'm almost 18 years old. Put some respect on my name," I said in a sassy tone. He put both hands up to surrender.

"Oh shit, my bad. So you're grown now?" Reese sarcastically shot back at me.

"Yes, I am," I said, rolling my eyes and head around at the same time. He laughed at me and just shook his head. I felt offended because why does he always look at me like I'm some little ass girl! He is only three years older than me. He thinks he is so old. Reese walked over to his gym bag that sat on the bench and pulled out a little towel. I just stared at him while he wiped the sweat off his face.

I walked over to Reese with an attitude: "I don't know why you act like you're that much older than me, because you're NOT." He took a seat on the bench and then looked up at me with no emotion. He just stared at me intensely. Damn, this dude is hard to figure out. I can tell he cares about me; I'm just not sure how deep that care goes.

He chuckled and responded in one of the sexiest but calm tones. "Trinity, why are you so mad? I mean, why do you even care what I think?" He waited for an answer.

"I don't," I said quickly. He stood up and walked directly in front of me. Our bodies were so close, it looked like we were about to kiss.

Looking down at me, he said, "Nah, you care. It's all over your face. I want to know WHY you care so much that I see you as a kid. Be honest with yourself." I immediately got butterflies in my stomach. I couldn't speak because I knew the truth would get me in a world of trouble. What the fuck was I doing? I never could help my feelings when it came to Reese. It's always been something about Reese that made me so weak in the knees. It was the grown man demeanor that turned me on. He speaks as if he is guiding you.

Reese saw I was uncomfortable. He spoke out softly, "You don't have to answer that question. I think we both know why you care. For the record, I know you're not some little kid. You're a beautiful young woman, Trinity." I immediately started to blush. Reese turned away from me and walked over to pick up his basketball off the bench.

"Since you're up early, you might as well get a workout in. Let's play 21," he said, dribbling the ball again.

"Okay, cool, you can take this L right quick," I said, walking on to the court. He threw the ball to me as I stood in front of the 3-point line. Facing me, he grabbed his shorts while nodding his head up and down.

"We will see who is going to take the L," he said forcefully. I looked cute, but I was very competitive. I was naturally a tomboy thanks to my father. Faking left, I went to the right side of the goal. As I stopped abruptly a few feet from the goal to make a jump shot, I felt the ball being slapped out of my hand.

"Get that shit out of here!" Reese yelled. I couldn't do anything but laugh. Well damn, I guess he wasn't about to take it easy on me. We played two games back-to-back. Reese won both games, but I didn't go out like no sucker. I made him work for those wins. After the games, I was exhausted. I could barely catch my breath.

"You alright?" Reese asked, handing me his water container. I looked disgusted, refusing to drink his water.

"Boy, I don't know where your mouth has been," I said, rolling my eyes. He walked up to me and put both his hands around my neck. My short ass stared directly into his muscled chest. My heart was pounding fast. I looked up at him cheesing.

Biting his lip, he replied, "You wanna see what this mouth do though?" We both just stared at each other. Within seconds, I heard someone clear their throat. I quickly turned in that direction and saw Von holding a basketball right in front of us. He looked pissed! Reese didn't even break a sweat, nor did he remove his hands from around my shoulders. He just kept his stare on me, smiling. I quickly knocked his arms down.

"Hey Von, we were just playing a game of 21," I informed him nervously.

"I can see that," he said, looking at me with some animosity. Reese started walking over to the bench and began picking up his things.

"I'll catch y'all later; I got to get ready for work," he said, walking past us. Von didn't say anything to Reese or even look at him as he passed by. He kept his focus on me. As soon as Reese disappeared from our view, Von started bouncing the basketball. I followed him onto the court. The bouncing got heavier and heavier as I watched Von slam the ball on the pavement repeatedly.

I said to myself, "Oh, this nigga is big mad." I begin to smooth things over.

"Look, Von, it's not what it looked like." Before I knew it, Von grabbed the ball that he was holding and, with all his might, slung it at me. At an alarming rate, it landed precisely in the center of my face. He had to have thrown it with his strong arm because I felt every bit of that hit. He damn sure can go pitch for the Houston Astros. Stumbling back, my vision became blurred. I was in a daze. It landed directly in the center of my face.

I felt the blood run out my nose, down my lip, and onto the pavement. I looked at the ground being showered by my blood. I touched my nose and stared at my bloody fingers that couldn't stop shaking. I was in complete shock that this fool hit me.

"Oh, it's not what it looked like, huh? Hoe, you think I'm crazy! I should hit you in yo shit again," Von yelled, running up in my face. I just stood there with tears running down my face and my nose all bloody. I could feel my nose starting to swell up. I tried to walk away and felt the ball fly into my back. I hollered out in pain.

"What the fuck, Von!" I cried out.

"Where the fuck do you think you're going? You think you can disrespect me and just leave? Nah, sit your hoe ass down on that bench," he screamed. I couldn't believe he assaulted me again. Thinking about my next move, I froze for a moment. I wanted to go home.

"No! I'm going home," I yelled and tried to run out the gate at the same time. Von chased me right before I was able to make my exit. He forcefully choked me up against the gate with both of his hands around my neck. I couldn't move and could barely breathe. I clawed at his fingers, but that didn't help. His grip around my throat got tighter. I almost passed out. I felt my body go limp, and the next thing I know is that I'm being thrown to the ground. I hit the ground hard from the side. I quickly sat up gasping for air.

He bent down in front of my face with no remorse. "I've been letting you slide with a lot of shit, but today you crossed the line. You literally flirted with that bitch-ass nigga like you don't have a man."

I was livid! I said sarcastically, "Why didn't you call him a bitch-ass nigga when he was standing right here?" Von quickly raised his fist but stopped himself from hitting me.

"Oh lord, that blood on your face must taste like Wendy's strawberry lemonade or something."

"No way you're still trying me!" He said, looking at me sideways. It's no laughing matter, but I almost wanted to chuckle. I didn't respond. I just sat there full of tears. He got up, grabbed his basketball, and left me sitting on the ground. Thank God he was gone. I sat there thinking about what to do next.

After about 15 minutes, I got up and walked home. I entered the door and tried to hurry up to my room. I can immediately smell the food my mom was cooking in the kitchen.

"Hey baby, I didn't even realize you were gone. You hungry? I'm cooking breakfast," she notified me.

"No, I'm fine," I said quickly.

"Trinity," she called softly, stopping me in my tracks. She moved closer to look at me.

"Whoa, what the hell happened to your face?" she inquired. She reached out and touched my bruised nose.

I put on a fake laugh and replied, "I tried to catch a basketball pass with the men on the court, but my face caught it instead."

She shook her head and said, "Girl, you know men don't know their own strength. You're going to learn to stop trying to run with those guys, girl." I made my way upstairs and into my room to clean myself up. I locked my door to prevent anyone from disturbing me. I sat down at my vanity desk and looked at myself in the mirror. My face was red, and my nose swelled up badly. The blood coming from my nose dried up. I touched my nose to feel how swollen it was and hoped it wasn't fractured.

Staring at myself in the mirror, I noticed stains of blood on my sports bra. I looked a hot mess.

"Run away from that boy Jervonte as far as possible. He is not good for you and will eventually be your downfall."

Suddenly, Miss Lisa's words replayed in my mind. Was she on to something? I broke down crying but was careful not to alarm my parents. There would be hell to pay if they knew what really happened to my face. My dad would most likely send Von to the emergency room over at Memorial Hermann Southwest Hospital.

Why was I even trying to protect him anyway? I still love him, that's why. In a way, I feel guilty because he watched another man all over me. It was partly my fault, although I don't think any man should hit a woman. I know Von loves me, but seeing Reese's arms wrapped around me made him snap. If I caught a girl all over him, I would probably lose it too. Damn, I'm thinking just like an abused woman by making excuses for another nigga's actions. I don't care; my situation is different. I'm taking accountability for my part. He never hit me before, and we've been together over two years.

He is not a bad person. I'm in the house for the rest of the day. No way do I want to see Von right now or anyone else. I got up to take out some comfortable panties, shorts, and a T-shirt from the dresser drawer. I needed a relaxing shower, so I made my way to the bathroom out in the hallway. I stayed in the bathroom for over an hour thinking about everything that transpired earlier. I love Von. He is my first real boyfriend, and I'm confident he didn't mean to harm me. Von treats me like a queen. He worships the ground I walk on. I won't hold this incident against him.

Yesterday, I woke up early in the morning to get a good workout in. Trinity loves to go jogging in the neighborhood with me. I knocked on her door, and Mrs. Coleman informed me she was already gone. I decided to look for her because I knew she couldn't have gone too far. Imagine my surprise when I found Reese's hands all over her at the basketball court. I wanted to beat that bitch to a pulp. I had to hurry up and leave before I seriously hurt that girl.

I can't let loose on her ass like that right now. Her parents would have a fit. No nigga ever put fear in my heart, so her insinuating that I'm scared of Reese almost made me spaz the fuck out. At the end of the day, Reese wasn't my girl. She is! What the fuck is wrong with her?

Truth be told, though, I should've two-pieced his ass up for having his arms around Trinity's neck. Then he had the audacity to not even give a fuck that they were caught. He was low-key challenging me. I always knew that hoe-ass nigga wanted her. He wasn't fooling me with calling her that "kid" shit either. All that shit is mind games. I know niggas and the chess moves they be making on women.

That's okay. I got something for his ass real soon. I'm the king of chess moves, baby. He will pay for this shit here. Trinity has been my girl for over 2 years. No way I'm letting anyone take her from me. I nearly died seeing her stare at that nigga with so much admiration. I've never seen her look at me that way. She was really into that nigga, because I was standing there a couple of minutes. I'm happy she didn't drink after that motherfucka too.

She might as well kiss him if she did that shit. I would've really had to kill her. She got some sense. I don't give a damn who it is. Anyone standing in the way of me and her has got to go. He doesn't even know it, but he's on borrowed time now. He done fucked up. I know her feelings are hurt because I hit her ass twice with the basketball. I'll go check on her tomorrow. I don't regret my actions at all. She deserved everything I did to her today, plus more. I see how these niggas look at her, and she just loves the attention.

She plays around with these lame-ass niggas in the hood too much. I don't even say shit. I've been letting it slide because up until this point, it was never anything that serious. Reese is officially a threat to me. I get rid of niggas who I see as a threat. At nineteen years old, I've already caught a few bodies. It was necessary to take over the dope game. My name is just starting to ring bells in these streets.

It was about time Trinity knew who she was fucking with.

She hasn't seen the other side of me. I've been very careful not to unleash that evil motherfucker who lives inside me. That nigga is crazy for real. Any woman of mine will know not to entertain these thirsty niggas. I bet she knows now, though! I felt my head pounding. I scurried to retrieve some Tylenol from the bathroom medicine cabinet. As I shut the cabinet, I saw my evil reflection staring back at me in disgust. He began to talk.

"You a pussy. You let that girl and nigga play in your face."

"Man, don't start. I'm not in the mood," I yelled back. My reflection started laughing uncontrollably.

"She's going to do you exactly how your mom does your weak-ass dad."

"Shut the fuck up!" I ordered him.

Knock... knock... knock.

My talking reflection vanished. The mirror appeared to be normal again. Someone was on the other side of my door.

"Yeah?" I called out.

"You ok in there, son?" my dad inquired. He opened the door slowly and waited for an answer.

"I'm good, Pop." I could tell he didn't believe me. He stared analyzing me for a moment and then asked if I took my medication.

"Pop, I said I'm good."

"Alright then, well, take your meds," he suggested while closing the door. I was hiding a secret from everyone in the outside world. I didn't want people looking at me like I was some crazed freak.

Sunday morning came in no time, and I already knew Mr. and Mrs. Coleman had just left for church. By now, this was their routine every Sunday. They loved to make the 10:00 am service. I threw on some clothes and headed to their place. As I got closer to Trinity's house, I saw Netta dressed in business attire and getting into the car with her son. She gave me a quick wave before starting her vehicle and pulling off. I knocked on Trinity's door.

I stood outside for a couple of minutes before knocking again. I almost thought nobody was home until I heard the chain and locks being messed with from the other side of the door. Trinity opened the door but not wide enough to let me in.

"What, Von?" She said in a low and irritated tone.

"We need to talk. Let me in," I said, looking at her beautiful face. Even with her nose swollen, she was still stunning to look at. She left the door open and headed back upstairs to her room. I followed her up the stairs, watching her nicely shaped ass bounce under her black shorts. She had on a long retro T-shirt with a picture of a Nintendo remote on the front side. Upon entering the room, she had clutter everywhere.

Clothes were piled on top of her vanity desk and chair, different pairs of shoes were spread out on the floor, and hair products crowded her TV stand. The mess annoyed me because a girl this pretty should always be neat. I kicked a tennis shoe out of my way. She climbed into bed and pulled the covers over her face. I could tell she was still very much upset with me. I sat on the edge of the bed on the opposite side of her. It was completely silent in the room for a moment.

"Most niggas who hit females come bearing gifts soon after. Not that I'm going to forgive you, but how do you come empty-handed?" Trinity snarled at me. The nerve of this backstabbing heifer. I almost thought she was joking. The look on her face told me she was dead serious. My head spun around so fast.

"Girl, the gift is I didn't knock your entire head off your body. The fuck," I responded, getting angry all over again. I heard her smack her teeth. She quickly tossed to the other side, turning her back to me.

"Oh, so you're the one mad even though I'm the one that was being disrespected yesterday?" I asked her.

"Von, kiss my ass because you were wrong to hit me like you did. My face still hurts." I heard her voice cracking like she was about to cry. I bent down to take my shoes off. I got under the covers and searched for her body. I wrapped my arm across her waist, pulling her close to me. I begin to express the hurt I felt.

"Nitty, you know we've been together two years, and I never put my hands on you. Seeing dude lust over you made me furious, dawg. It made me even more upset that you seem to like it. Aren't I enough? Why did you wait this long to break bad on me?" I moved in closer to rest my chin on her shoulder and get a better look at her face. Her eyes were bloodshot red, and I saw a tear fall down the side of her face.

"Von, I'm not breaking bad on you. We were just playing basketball. I only want to be with you," she said softly. Her beautiful brown eyes stared into mine. This girl can just crumble a nigga into pieces with one look.

"I believe you, baby. Let's forgive each other and move on from this. Okay?" She shook her head up and down to agree with me. It wouldn't be long before her parents arrived home, so I wanted to make love to her. Turning her over to face me, I placed one hand behind her natural curls and began to kiss her passionately on the lips. We were in a full-blown make-out session. She sat up and removed the T-shirt she had on.

I snatched my shirt off and scooted under her small frame to lay flat on my back. She mounted me cowgirl style. My dick began to rise in my pants the moment I felt her pussy lips straddled on top of my manhood. She still had on her shorts, but it didn't take a lot for Trinity to get me hard. She grinds her hips back and forth slowly to the music. I caressed every inch of her back with my large hands. I began to unbuckle the straps to her bra. Succeeding, her bra dropped below her breast, and she snatched it off. I watched as she tossed her bra on the bedroom floor.

"You didn't want to fold that up, baby?" I asked her. Looking down at me irritated, she ignored my question. That would usually piss me off, but she was looking too damn good with her perfect-size B-cup titties exposed. I sat up and began to plant kisses softly across her bare chest. Taking one of her breasts in my mouth, I twirled my tongue around her nipple. She softly moaned with her body leaning backward. I held her up with one arm while she straddled me. My free hand slowly made its way down her stomach.

I quickly found her panty line barrier and slid my hand inside her shorts. My fingers infiltrated her warm box. My middle and index fingers gently massaged her clit. The pleasure from my fingers was enough for her to spread her legs wider apart. Using the palm of my four fingers, I caressed her pussy lips in a circular motion. Her moans became louder. She slightly lifted her butt, and I assisted with removing her shorts and panties.

I laid her down and removed the rest of my clothing. Naked, I lay on top of her with a full erection. My dick entered her insides with a deep thrust. She caressed my back and moaned with each stroke. Her fingernails dug into my back.

"This my pussy, ain't it?" I asked while my wood explored every inch of her woman cave.

Trinity moaned. "Yes, it's yours." After about a half hour, we were done having sex. I quickly began putting on my clothes.

"Where are you going? You're leaving right after having sex with me?" she murmured. I walked over to her and planted a kiss on her lips.

"Yes, I have an important meeting. I'll see you later."

I left Trinity's place to freshen up at the crib. As soon as I walked outside, Two-Tyma ran past me with the speed of lightning. If I didn't have good reflex skills, he would've knocked me over. He was only wearing boxers and barefoot. What the fuck was going on? Then Netta flew past me, chasing him with a butcher's knife. Her face was red like she had been crying.

Damn, I thought she left earlier. She must've been back home and caught his stupid ass cheating.

"I'm going to kill your trifling ass," she yelled after him.

Damn, I know I saw her leave earlier. Then I saw a young woman in her bra and blue jeans run out to a parked champagne-colored Toyota Camry. She was carrying her shoes and purse in her hand. I watched as she quickly tried to open the car door with her keys. She was trembling, and in a hurry, to leave. She was able to make it inside the vehicle when Netta turned around to harass her. Netta quickly ran up to the driver's side of the window.

"Where are you going, hoe? Get out of the car now!" she screamed. The woman was able to lock the door before Netta could open it. Netta pulled on her car door a few times but was unsuccessful in opening it. The lady quickly reversed her car. Netta ran and beat on her window until the woman drove past her and sped out of the apartments. I just shook my head. It's never a dull moment in these apartments. Obviously, Two-Tyma got caught fucking that woman. Netta was Two-Tyma's baby mama. They had an 8-year-old son together.

That nigga stays cheating on her, and they are always fighting. This ain't nothing new. A week from now, they will be right back together. I continued my walk to my crib, and right before I got to my door, I heard somebody trying to get my attention.

"Psst! Psst!"

"Two-Tyma, what the fuck, boy. What did you do, run behind the building?" I asked him. He was hiding behind the bushes near the neighbor's window.

"Aye, where's Netta's crazy ass at?" he whispered.

"She's somewhere looking to gut yo ass open like a fish," I said, amused at him all sweaty and dirty.

"Man, please let me lay low at your place for a minute," he begged.

"Hell no. I don't feel like hearing my mama's mouth."

"Man, yo mama low-key likes my ass. She won't mind," he blushed.

"Man, fuck you," I said, walking into my apartment. I closed the door on him as he called out to me one last time for help. Walking past the kitchen, I spotted my dad standing over the kitchen sink. He was coughing into a white handkerchief and didn't look well.

"Hey Dad, what's up? You okay?" He quickly tried to hide the handkerchief behind his back.

"Yeah, son. Just coming down with a cold," he informed me. I walked behind him and saw the handkerchief was covered in red spots.

"Is that blood?" I asked him in a panic.

"What the fuck kind of cold do you have that has you coughing up blood, pops?"

"Von, watch your mouth. I'm okay," he said in a weak tone. He walked past me and went into his room. I was still standing in the kitchen worried about what I just saw. My mom came through the front door carrying shopping bags and talking loudly on her cell phone.

"Hahahaha, girl, now you know she loves to steal people's shit," she gossiped with whoever was on the other end of that phone.

"Mama, Dad was coughing up blood," I said, interrupting her conversation. She ignored me, but I know damn well she heard me. She walked into the dining room area and put her bags down on the table. She began to laugh hysterically into the phone.

"Baby, whenever you go around her, wear a fanny pack. If you leave your purse around her, won't shit be in there but lint when you come back?"

"MAMA!" I screamed her name to get her attention. She looked at me like I had lost my mind.

"Did you hear me? Pops is coughing up blood," I informed her once more.

"So, what! Don't you see I'm on the damn phone, you psych patient?" She yelled. I just looked at her trifling ass in disgust. She didn't give a fuck about my dad, and it showed. She continued her conversation, and I just shook my head at her trifling ass. Right before I headed to my room, there was a knock on the door. I opened it, and it was Trinity standing there smiling.

"Girl, what the hell. Didn't I just leave your house?" I asked her.

"So. I'm bored. I want to hang over here with you," she said, hugging me around my shoulders and kissing me on my cheek.

"Trinity, I have a meeting to go to," I said while blocking her from walking inside the house.

"Von, why the hell do you have my door open?" My mama yelled, coming to the door. She pushes me aside and sees Trinity standing at the door. She absolutely hated company, so I knew she was about to fuss.

"Hey Miss Sydney!" Trinity smiled big and wide. The irritation on my mother's face immediately went away. She smiled at Trinity and embraced her.

"Hey girl, let me call you back," my mama said into the phone and immediately ended her call. You got to be fucking kidding me. Just a few minutes ago she acted like that call was so important.

"Why you got her just standing outside? MOVE," my mama screamed and led Trinity into the house. That shit low-key burnt me up. My mama loves the fuck out of Trinity. She has never hugged me in her life! She doesn't speak rudely to Trinity and nurtures her as if she wishes that was her daughter. I closed the door after them, and we all walked into the living room.

"Trinity, what are you up to, girl?" My mama asked her, cheesing.

"Nothing, I wanted to hang with Von, but he has a meeting to get to." She replied.

"What meeting? This nigga doesn't work," she asked with her face all screwed up. "The none of your business meeting," I sarcastically spat back at her. She rolled her eyes at my response.

Focusing back on Trinity, she replied, "Well, you're more than welcome to hang out with me. I can make us something to eat and then find a good Lifetime movie for us to watch."

Trinity's eyes filled with excitement. "Yes, we can do that!" I left them standing there and went to my bedroom. I opened my closet door to find a business casual outfit to put on. Trinity walked in behind me and sat on the bed. She began to take the navy-blue flip-flops she had on off.

"My mama is an evil woman. I wouldn't hang around here today," I suggested. I didn't trust my mom being around Trinity. My mama probably would try to break us up.

"Aw baby, your mama is cool. She is beautiful on the inside and out." That statement pissed me off because what the hell does she know? I have been dealing with that lady for 19 years.

"You think you know my fucking mother better than me?" I yelled, running up in her face. I instantly frightened her. I really had the urge to punch her in the face, but I didn't. It just made me furious that my mother was so damn nice to her but treated me and my father like shit.

"Whatever, Von. I'm leaving." She quickly tried to put her flip-flops on, but I stopped her.

"Hey, I'm sorry. My mom has never been kind to me. I'm lashing out, but you don't deserve it," I apologized. She eased up and stood up to hug me.

"I understand," she empathized, wrapping her arms around my waist. I embraced her back and planted kisses on her cheeks. I had to go so I wouldn't be late.

I asked Z to take me to this meeting at the Saldana's mansion. He said he had to ask his brother to borrow the car. I told him not to mention he was giving me a ride. I know damn well his brother wasn't going to let him take the car if he knew I needed a ride somewhere. Z pulled around to the circular driveway in the apartments.

I hopped in the passenger seat, and as we were leaving, Reese was walking down the sidewalk and saw us passing by. He stopped dead in his tracks. Boy, if looks could kill, me and Z would both be dead. I smirked and pointed my finger at him. Z couldn't do anything but laugh. As he kept driving, he informed me to stop pissing his brother off all the time.

"Man, fuck Reese. I never did anything to him, but he has a problem with me for some reason," I exclaimed. Z ignored me and turned the radio on. I don't care. I only cared about making it to Sugar Land, Texas, on time. It took us about 28 minutes to arrive at the massive iron gates. Once they opened, we both dropped our mouths at how gorgeous this mansion was.

The mansion is a grand, fortress-like estate on several acres. Tall trees and gardens were planted all over the property. We pulled up to the driveway. Multiple men walked the premises carrying AR-15s and semi-automatic weapons.

"You coming in?" I asked Z.

"Hell nah," he responded.

"Scary ass," I mumbled before getting out of the car.

A grand staircase made of large, weathered gray stone steps led up to the front entrance. On each side of the bottom steps were two giant, reeling horse statues made of steel. At the top of the staircase was a stony gray pathway leading to huge double doors made of iron with glass panels that allowed me to see inside. I rang the doorbell and was greeted by an older Black man who I assume was the butler.

"Welcome," he politely spoke, and he bowed simultaneously. He was impeccably dressed in a tailored black tailcoat, a crisp white shirt, a perfectly tied bow tie, and polished black shoes. I was mesmerized by the home immediately.

The grand foyer boasts marble floors, a sweeping staircase, and an enormous crystal chandelier. The living spaces are decorated with dark leather, rich fabrics, and priceless art. Every detail of the mansion, from the heavy drapes to the gleaming mahogany study off to the side, is designed to convey power, wealth, and an underlying sense of danger. The house speaks for itself and gives off vibes that the family living there is notorious.

I had a meeting with the Saldana Mafia Family. I have plans to be on top of the world one day, and by any means necessary, I'm going to get there. The Saldanas were an Afro-Latino family. The father was Dominican, and the mother was Black. They had a reputation in Houston for being the most ruthless family this city has ever seen. I desperately wanted to be in business with them. Donvincio Saldana was the head of the family. He was an older man, married to Karena Saldana.

A lot of people say she is actually the one who calls all the shots and is more brutal than Donvincio if you get on her bad side. My dream is not to be a drug kingpin. However, we often have to take big risks to get to where we want to be in life. My passion is real estate. I want to be one of the youngest and richest niggas in the city to own commercial and residential properties. To do that, I need money and lots of it.

School is a fucking scam to me, so I refuse to take classes and end up with a mediocre career. I don't want to struggle half my life trying to pay on a business loan from the bank either. Nah, I'm going to skip the line and do this shit my way.

"Do you know about me?" he asked me.

"Yes, the entire city of Houston knows who you are, sir."

"Yeah, but do you REALLY know me?" He emphasized the word really and asked me in a more serious tone.

"You want to know the real reason why I haven't let my son into this business? It's because this type of business can be ruthless, even to your own family. Once I let him in, I can't baby him anymore. I won't baby him. This is a big boy's game. I'll treat you like I would any other man if you cross me. I don't care about any fucking excuses, and I don't play about my money. A violation of my rules will have your head detached from your body and sent to your mom in a cardboard box. Once I let you into my organization, you will know too much for me to ever let you out. You better make damn sure you know what that means for you and anyone you love."

We both held our stares with one another for a few seconds. "I understand," I said, nodding my head.

"I'm going to start you off with a trial period. I'll give you one week to get rid of 2 kilos of cocaine and bring me back my money. If you're successful with that, we can talk business. Rafael," the man yelled. A tall man in his mid-40s came walking into the room. He was muscular and had tattoos all over his arms and face.

"Dale al niño dos kilos de cocaína," Mr. Donvincio spoke to him in their native language. The man quickly left the room. It was an awkward silence. I slightly turned to my side, and his son was sitting in the corner mugging me. I can tell that pretty motherfucka was mad his dad was putting me on. Letting out a chuckle, I found amusement that he was so bothered by me. I smirked and winked my left eye at him.

Turning my focus back on Mr. Donvincio, he leaned back in his chair, giving me a smirk of his own. I realize I shouldn't be trying to antagonize his son, but I couldn't help it. He briefly turned to acknowledge his son, but he wasn't fazed at how his son was acting. He ignored him.

"Kid, I can tell you got heart. I like that about you. My son is too damn emotional for this line of work right now." His son smacked his teeth and got up and walked out of the room. Rafael came back and dropped a black duffel bag at my feet. I bent down to open it, and there were two kilos of cocaine on the inside. I stood up to shake his hand. He nodded his head no at me.

"I'll shake your hand when you complete the task. My respect isn't given freely. You earn it."

"Fair enough," I replied, shrugging my shoulders at the same time. We were just about done with the meeting when his wife walked in the room looking all curious.

"Vince, what's wrong with Alejandro? He is upset." Mr. Saldana got upset with her. He pointed at her with his index finger.

"Stop babying that motherfucker all the time. Now get your ass out here. Don't you see I'm in a meeting?" She looked at him like he had lost his mind, but she didn't say shit. She intently looked at the both of us and rolled her eyes. Then she quietly left the room. He stood behind his desk, shaking his head in irritation.

"Listen, if we're going to be working together, I'm going to let you know this up front. My wife is very overprotective of her children. Don't ever disrespect them or hurt them because she would have you killed," he nonchalantly stated.

I thought to myself, "Nah, I'll have her killed first." But of course, I didn't say that. I grabbed the bag off the floor and made my way out of their beautiful mansion. One day, I'll be living just like them, if not better. This was going to be a busy week for me. Z was in the car smoking a blunt.

"How did the meeting go?" he wondered.

"Nigga, it went well. He is starting me off with two kilos. Bro, I need you to be on my team. We can rule the world one day."

"Man Von, that type of lifestyle ain't for me. I like to chill and smoke my weed. I'm not trying to live the fast life, bro. Plus, I can't do prison. I'll drop more names than DMX on the witness stand."

I just laughed because he was hilarious and dead ass serious. Oh well, I was determined to work with the Saldana Mafia Family, so I needed to build me a strong team full of certified goons.

It was a month away from the big fight. Tank versus Valdez was the most anticipated fight of the year. I've finally made it in my career. Valdez was the man to beat, and I was the underdog. I arrived at the press conference. The room was packed with reporters, cameras flashing like lightning, and at the center of it all was my opponent, Emilio Valdez.

The press conference was supposed to be a routine event—a few questions from the media, some promotional banter, and the usual stare down between the fighters. From the moment I walked onto the stage, I could feel the tension in the air.

Valdez had built his career on being loud and obnoxious, using his sharp tongue to get inside his opponents' heads before they even stepped into the ring. He had a talent for trash talk, and today, he was in rare form. I, however, wasn't one for words. I let my fists do the talking, and they spoke volumes.

Valdez and I took our seats at the long table, separated by a handful of officials. The promoters gave their usual spiel about how this was going to be the fight of the century, but I barely listened. My eyes were locked on Valdez, who was grinning like a cat that had just caught a mouse.

When it was time for us to speak, Valdez grabbed the microphone with a smirk. "I've been waiting for this one," he began, his voice dripping with mockery. "Everyone's been talking about how tough Tank is, how he's got fists of stone, but all I see is a big, Black, dumbass who doesn't know when to quit."

The crowd murmured, the reporters scribbling furiously in their notepads. I remained silent, his expression unchanged, though his jaw clenched slightly.

Valdez didn't stop there. "You know, Tank," he continued, leaning forward as if sharing a secret, "I've heard a lot about your past. How you grew up tough, how you fought your way out of the streets. But I gotta ask—what would your mom think about all this? Oh, that's right," he added, his voice dripping with venom. "She's dead, isn't she? Must've been really proud of you, huh? Too bad she's not around to see you get your ass handed to you."

The room went dead silent. The air seemed to freeze, and every eye in the room turned to Tank. He was trying to use my weaknesses against me. I talked about how my mom was my motivation all the time. I slowly stood up, his massive frame casting a shadow over the table.

Valdez's grin faltered for a fraction of a second, but he quickly recovered, leaning back in his chair with a cocky smirk. "What's the matter, Tank? Did I hit a nerve?"

My hands clenched into fists. The microphone in front of me creaked under the pressure as I gripped the edge of the table. I'm making it my mission to destroy that punk in the ring! "You can say whatever you want about me. But you never, ever talk about my mother, you clown," I said in a calm and warning tone.

Valdez laughed, though it sounded forced. "What are you gonna do about it, tough guy?"

"I'm going to show you what happens when you cross the line. I'm going to make you regret every word that came out of your mouth. In that ring, there won't be a referee who can save you. You're going to wish you'd never opened your mouth."

I turned and walked off the stage. There was nothing left to talk about. The press conference was now over. The reporters began scrambling to write their stories about the exchange that had just unfolded.

The weeks leading up to the fight were filled with speculation. Some said I had lost my cool and that Valdez had successfully gotten under my skin. Others believed that I was more focused than ever. I was destined to prove a point. I was no longer fighting for me but for my mother's honor.

Weeks went by, and fight night finally arrived. The arena was electric with anticipation. I could hear the crowd chanting all the way from the locker rooms in the back. I danced around in place, throwing quick jabs to prepare for the fight. One of the event coordinators walked in and announced to my manager, Vinny, and me that it was time for the fight to start.

Since I was the underdog, I walked out first. I had the DJ play the song "Stand Up" by T.I., Lil Wayne, Lil John & Trick Daddy. I chose that song for a reason, because it was time for Valdez to stand on everything, he said to me. I hopped inside the ring, and I could hear cheers and boos from the loud crowd. I spotted my girlfriend Rosalinda seated up close. She looked like a million bucks, rocking her designer dress and heels.

Valdez strutted to the ring, playing up to the audience and cameras. He beat on his chest like he was a wild ape. He threw fake jabs on his way down the walkway. His eyes locked on me as he got closer to the ring. He entered the ring and stared at me with hate in his eyes. He didn't intimidate me at all. I didn't come to play with this boy. I didn't sleep many nights because I was up thinking about physically hurting this man.

The bell rang, and from the first moment, it was clear that I wasn't just there to win. I was there to punish this fool. Every punch I threw was calculated, every move a testament to my skill and strength. Valdez tried to dance around me, to taunt and tease, but I was relentless, cutting off the ring, cornering my prey.

By the third round, Valdez was already looking tired. His flashy footwork had slowed, his jabs weaker, and the cocky smirk he had worn so proudly at the press conference was long gone. I had barely broken a sweat, my focus unbroken.

The moment came in the fourth round. Valdez, desperate and tired, threw a wild punch that I easily dodged. It was the opening that I had been waiting for. I stepped in and unleashed a devastating uppercut that lifted Valdez off his feet. The crowd gasped as his head hit the ground, the referee rushing in to start the count. I don't know what came over me. I pushed the referee out of the way and pounced on Valdez with the speed of lightning. I continued to throw blows to Valdez's face.

Blood leaked from his mouth and nose, but I kept hitting him as quickly and powerfully as I could. A huge knot instantly formed at the top of his head. People from Valdez's team and my team jumped in the ring to stop the fight. I heard the bell sounding off, but I didn't care. Finally, enough people were able to hold me down until they were able to rescue Valdez. I kept my vow to defend my mother's honor. The fight was over, but this was one lesson Valdez would never forget.

The decision came down that I was indeed disqualified. I was full of disappointment and rage. I quickly left the arena and could hear the crowd booing me. The boxing world would forever remember the Valdez's versus Tank fight. I was indeed a champion, but a fallen one. It was no debate that I beat Valdez. However, I still lost the fight because I couldn't control my emotions.

The next day, the media on damn near every news station replayed me losing my control in the ring. They reported that Valdez was rushed to the hospital and is now in a coma. My manager Vinny rushed over and informed me The World Boxing Association (WBA) had a meeting today and will be calling after they make a decision about my boxing career. I assumed they would suspend me for the entire year.

My manager, girlfriend, and I waited patiently in the living room for the answer. My manager's phone rang, and he quickly picked it up. He listened intently and then said, "Okay, thank you for the update," before hanging up.

He lowered his head and got quiet. "Vinny, what they say, man!" I screamed.

"I don't know how to tell you this, but you're suspended indefinitely, Tank. You will never be allowed to box again," he mentioned.

"Whattttt," I screamed louder. I couldn't believe it. Boxing was my life. One mistake has ruined my career. My girlfriend went upstairs to probably cool down.

"Look, kid, if the decision is ever reversed, give me a call." Just like that, he was gone. I sat on the couch in tears. Twenty minutes later, my Rosalinda came downstairs with her luggage. She headed for the door. I jumped up and grabbed the one she was dragging on wheels to prevent her from leaving.

"Where are you going, Ma? You are leaving me just like that?" I asked. Her thick Spanish accent came out.

"Look, Papi, I don't do broke. Sorry, okay?" I watched her walk out of my house forever. I knew that bitch wasn't shit, but she looked good on my arm. I was alone now. I walked to the kitchen cabinet where my alcohol was stored and began to drink my sorrows away.

Three months went by, and my world totally crumbled. Vinny called me a while back and said the WBA decided not to pay me all the money I was guaranteed to make because of my disqualification. My money was dwindling fast. I stayed in a drunken slumber. I often thought about suicide. I sat on the couch naked, getting my dick sucked by a transsexual. I was driving down Bissonnet and thought I was picking up a thick-ass redbone woman. I started to drive off when I realized it was a man.

He said, "I can make you feel really good." Everything in me wanted to leave. I watched as that lady-man licked his lips. That tongue looked juicy. All I wanted was to feel good, even if it was just for a second.

"Hop in," I advised. He began to talk, and I ordered him to shut the fuck up. We rode together in silence the entire ride to the crib.

"Oh, this is a nice house," his gay ass blurted out. We walked inside, and the stench must've hit his nose. I haven't cleaned up in months.

"Eww, it stank in here," he hissed.

"Man, come on," I growled. I led him to the living room and undressed myself. I just sat back on the couch with my eyes closed and my thighs spread apart.

He crawled between my legs and wrapped his thick, juicy tongue around the tip of my dick. I instantly moaned out in pleasure. My God, look how far I've fallen. He spat on the shaft and massaged his saliva with both hands up and down the veins on my pole.

"Damn," I moaned again. It was too late to stop now. He swallowed me whole, and his jaws suctioned my wood like a vacuum. Stroking my dick with his mouth, the warmth from inside his cheeks made my dick rock hard. He sped up the pace. I placed one hand on the top of his head to assist him with eating my dick up. His head swirled around as he continued to suck on me long and hard.

"I'm about to BUST," I whimpered. Lifting my legs off the floor, I forcefully released my cum down his throat. He wiped his mouth and giggled at my uncomfortable pleasure. I pushed him over and got up to use the guest bathroom. When I closed the door, I stared at my reflection in the mirror. Guilt rushed through my body, and I instantly felt ashamed. Tears ran down my face. After getting myself together, I left the restroom to find this bitch taking pictures of my world title belts and medals locked up in a glass display case.

"What the fuck are you doing?" I barked. He jumped back.

"Well excuse me, but I now know who you are! I knew you looked familiar; it's just you look so rough right now. Do you know how much money the blogs would pay me for this type of information? I probably can get at least 40k for an exclusive interview with TMZ."

"You can't be serious?" I asked with fury in my eyes.

"Oh, I'm serious, boo. How much are you willing to pay me to keep quiet?" He teased with his hands on his hips. This motherfucka thinks he can blackmail me in my own house. I literally lost just about everything that meant the world to me. All I had was my dignity. He had just fucked up. I started walking towards him.

"I don't need to pay you to keep quiet. I'll shut you up my damn self," I calmly spoke while grabbing a long iron fireplace poker from the mantle. His eyes got big, and he tried to run to the front door. I was quicker and stronger than him. Just as he got to the door, I powerfully clocked him on the top of his head. The blow instantly punctured a hole in his head, and he dropped to the ground immediately. I continued to strike him with the iron rod across his face and head.

Flashbacks of me punching Valdez to death clouded my brain. Blood splashed all over my floor and walls. I continued to beat this man until his face was unrecognizable. I stood over his lifeless body and decided to wrap him up in an old sheet and duct tape. Then I cleaned as much of the blood up as I could with a sponge, bleach, soap, and water. I waited until it got dark to transport the body to the car. Once the body was in the car, I decided to wash up and threw on some fitness clothes. I drove over an hour to dispose of the body. I decided to dispose of the body in Galveston Bay. I turned down a deserted dirt road and threw the body off a bridge and into the water.

Wanting to blow off some steam, I headed to the gym back in town. I just wanted to get some cardio in and lift some weights. While I'm lifting weights, I see two guys in the mirror discussing me. They were off to the side eyeing me and making jokes. In a blind rage, I dropped the weights and cornered them.

"We have a fucking problem. I'll beat y'all asses," I warned. They were instantly shook.

"No man," one of them blurted out with his hands out to surrender to me. They both quickly exited the gym.

"Don't worry about them fools, Tank," I heard a voice say. A tall, lanky nigga sat up on the bench press. He looked around my age, if not younger.

"You're a warrior, Tank. I noticed it after watching your fight with Valdez. You stand on business, and I need a dude like you on my team," he pointed out.

"Look man, whatever you're selling, I'm not buying," I informed him.

"I'm not trying to sell you anything. I'm working on something big with the Saldana Mafia Family. They gave me 2 kilos of cocaine to get my business started. I'm only telling you this because I can tell that you a real nigga, bro," he reasoned. I sat down on the weight bench next to him to hear more. The gym was empty at this time of night, so nobody was listening to us. He kind of had my attention.

"I'm building my own empire. Boxing was your purpose, and now you've been cast out. I'm offering you a chance to be my muscle, my head guy in charge. I'm giving you a new purpose. With you by my side, we're going after money, power, and respect in the dope game and in the real estate industry. We will own half of Houston one day. People that counted you out will see you on top of the world one day. What do you have to lose?" he asked.

He was right. I literally had nothing to lose. I was down on my luck, and I always heard that the Saldana Mafia Family was super loaded with cash. "Aight, I'm in," I told him.

"My name is Von. Let's put together a team called the 163 Mafia Family. We are both from the Southwest and were raised on Fondren Road. I know a little about you already," he admitted. He got up from the machine and reached to shake my hand.

"Tank, let's take over Houston," he boasted. I shook his hand, and we exchanged numbers. This was the start of a multi-million-dollar enterprise.

Man, fuck Von and his feelings. I saw him the moment he walked on the court, but I pretended not to see him. Trinity had no idea he was there. It might have been wrong to put her in that predicament, but fuck it. It was time I stopped playing around when I'd always known Trinity had my heart. She's too good for that hoe-ass nigga. I never liked Von.

I can't quite put my finger on it, but something about him is not right with him. He walks around feeling entitled to women, like they were his property. He treated Kyra like she was beneath him and always had an attitude like a little bitch. My brother loves that nigga. They have been best friends since elementary school. I see the envious looks he gives me, but I let him slide out of respect for Z. He gets no more passes, though. Trinity will be eighteen soon and heading off to college.

It's time I let her know how I feel. There has always been a huge spark between us. I believe in my heart that Trinity will choose me. I know for a fact her father doesn't approve of Von. Patrick tolerates his ass, but he is not too fond of him either. He would always say it's something about that lil nigga that don't sit right with me. Now he never told me he wanted me to date Trinity, but it was apparent he respected me.

Von has been missing in action this week. He hadn't shown his face in days. Z told me he is trying to be the next drug kingpin, so maybe that's why. I respect my brother for not getting involved in Von's bullshit. I decided to walk over to Trinity's place and have a heart-to-heart talk with her parents. Over the past two years, her father and I have gotten close. I go over there and watch sports with him, and they are always inviting me to stay to eat dinner as a family. My phone started buzzing. I picked it up off the nightstand and answered.

"Reese, what the fuck has been going on with you lately? You've been very quiet these last couple of weeks. I know something is wrong. Just be a man and come out with it!" Sabrina screamed in my ear. I held the phone for a minute, trying to decide what I was going to say. I just decided to tell her the truth.

"Sabrina, you're right. I apologize for being standoffish. I just think we should break up for good this time." Since high school, Sabrina and I have been on and off. The relationship has been draining me.

"Okay, Reese. I'm tired of the back and forth myself. You're confused as fuck, and I know it's somebody else. Don't ever call me again."

Click.

Sabrina hung up the phone in my face. I really thought she was going to put up more of a fight. I was relieved she didn't. I guess she could sense my heart was no longer with her. My heart has been with Trinity since the first time I laid eyes on her. She's such a beautiful, feisty little thang. Seeing her with Von absolutely drives me insane because I know she deserves way better than him.

When I arrived at Trinity's place, her father Patrick was outside talking to Z, Keith, and Two-Tyma.

"What's up, Big Reese?" Patrick greeted me.

"Nothing much, mayne," I chuckled.

"Well, I gotta go, 'cause I got a date with a big booty chocolate chick," Two-Tyma bragged.

"Man, you still ain't learned nothing from cheating? Yo ass going to be on the morning news! Netta going to kill your ass, boy," Z joked but was dead serious. We all burst out in laughter.

"You can learn a thing or two from me, little nigga." Two-Tyma popped his collar like he was big shit.

"I can't learn nothing from you but how to get caught! Not only are you a cheater, but you're bad at it," Z teased.

"Forget you," Two-Tyma waved Z off while walking off.

"Hey, is Trinity in there?" I asked Patrick.

"Yeah, she is in there with that nigga," he spoke in a disapproving tone.

"Oh okay, I'll wait until that fool leaves then. I need to talk to all of you about something," I informed him.

"Mayne, y'all need to quit doing my boy like that," Z shouted. Von walked outside, and I could tell my presence annoyed him.

"Aight, I'll fuck with you later," Von told Z.

"You leaving already?" Z asked him.

"Yeah, I got some business I gotta attend to.

"What business is that? You looking for a job?" Patrick asked him with a stone-cold face.

"Something like that," Von responded.

"Did Trinity tell you I got a new job, and we're moving back to the suburbs? She will be eighteen soon, so it's time she starts focusing on going away to college," Patrick informed him. Von looked caught off guard by Patrick's statements.

"No, she didn't tell me that," he said in a confused tone. He continued to walk away.

Keith pulled out his car keys from his jean pocket. "I think I'm about to head home to get a nap in before my shift tonight." He gave all of us fist bumps before heading out.

"Well, I'm about to go smoke a blunt," Z shrugged his shoulders. Miss Charlene came outside to announce she had just finished cooking. Patrick and I washed our hands at the kitchen sink and then sat down at the dining room table. Trinity came out of the room looking beautiful as ever. Her hair was tied up in a big, fluffy ponytail.

She was wearing a peach-colored spaghetti strap dress. My heart pounded in my chest just by looking at her.

"Hey, Reese," she cheesed big at me.

"Trinity, come help me with these plates," her mother called out. She walked into the kitchen and came out carrying a plate. She placed it down on the mat in front of me. Miss Charlene brought out Patrick's food. Once they both fixed their plate of food, they took their seats at the table.

The food looks delicious. I stared down at a plate with baked macaroni and cheese, turkey wings, collard greens, rice and gravy, and buttered cornbread.

"Reese wanted to talk to us about something," Patrick informed the ladies. Suddenly, I felt nervous. It got really quiet due to the fact I had everyone's attention. Trinity's beautiful brown eyes pierced through my soul. Clearing my throat, I began to speak.

"Trinity means so much to me. Not just as a friend anymore, but as somebody I could see myself being with." Her eyes got big, and I could tell she was caught off guard. I continued my thoughts.

"She's almost 18, and I wanted to be respectful not just to her, but to her parents. I know she is with Von, but he's not her forever person. I am. I'm the one for you, Trinity. I believe deep down you know it's true too. So, if it's okay with Trinity, I would like to take her out on a date," I admitted.

"I think that's an excellent idea! Reese, you have my blessing." Patrick hit the table with his fist, being overly excited.

"Whew, you are so messy," Charlene laughed at Patrick.

"Baby, I don't care. It's up to Trinity," Charlene informed me.

"What do you say, Trinity? Can I take you out tomorrow?" I asked. She blushed and shook her head yes.

"Well, I want to hang out with you most of the day, so our date will start around noon. Is that okay with you?" I asked her.

"Yes, that's fine," she responded. We all finished our food, and I thanked Miss Charlene for a wonderful meal. I wanted to get home to prepare for me and Trinity's date tomorrow.

I woke up early, excitement buzzing in my chest. Today was Saturday, and I couldn't wait to spend the day with Trinity. I wanted to surprise her with a series of fun and romantic activities, creating memories she would cherish forever.

I knocked on the door at exactly noon, and she came out of the apartment smiling. As always, her smile made my heart skip a beat. She was dressed in an off-the-shoulder blue maxi dress that flowed to her ankles. Her shoulder curls bounced as she walked, and I couldn't help but think how lucky I was at that moment. As soon as she slid into the passenger seat, I handed her a small bouquet of roses I picked up at a small flower shop.

"Thank you," she said, blushing.

Our first stop was a cozy little café downtown called Day 6 Coffee Co. It was one of those places with an old-world charm—wooden tables, bookshelves lining the walls, and the smell of freshly brewed coffee in the air. We ordered lattes and shared a plate of buttery croissants while sitting by the window, watching people pass by on the bustling street.

"I don't know what you see in Von's goofy ass," I said with my nose turned up at her. I couldn't take my eyes off Trinity as she laughed at me like I was joking. Her eyes sparkled in the morning sunlight. We sat down there and talked for a few hours.

After the cafe, I had another surprise up my sleeve. I drove to Buffalo Bayou Park. There was a bike shop where we could rent bikes for a couple of hours. The idea of renting bikes and exploring the park's sprawling paths had been on my mind forever, and now I get to share this moment with Trinity. I loved the idea of being outdoors with her, surrounded by nature and the vibrant energy of the city. A friendly attendant helped them choose a pair of sturdy bikes.

The sun was shining, casting a soft golden light over the lush greenery, and the air was filled with the sound of laughter from families and the distant hum of city life.

I adjusted the seat on my bike while Trinity tested the brakes on hers, her excitement evident in the way her eyes sparkled. We set off down the main path, pedaling side by side.

The park was alive with activity. We passed families having picnics on the grass, children chasing after frisbees, and couples walking hand-in-hand. The scent of blooming flowers wafted through the air, mingling with the earthy smell of the trees. Trinity pointed out a group of ducks waddling near a pond, their reflections shimmering on the water's surface. We slowed down to watch for a moment, smiling at the sight of the ducklings trailing behind their mother.

Further along, we came across a group of artists set up along the path, their easels facing the picturesque landscape of the park. Trinity and I stopped to admire a painting of the park's iconic fountain, its water sparkling in the sunlight. The artist, an elderly man with a gentle smile, nodded at us as we complimented his work.

"Isn't this place just perfect?" Trinity said, her voice filled with awe.

"It really is," I agreed, glancing at her with a warm smile. "I'm glad we did this."

As we biked deeper into the park, the city sounds grew fainter, replaced by the rustling of leaves and the chirping of birds. The path took us through a shaded grove where the trees formed a natural canopy overhead. Sunlight filtered through the leaves, casting dappled shadows on the ground. We rode in comfortable silence, simply enjoying the peacefulness of the moment.

Eventually, we emerged from the grove onto a hill that offered a breathtaking view of the park's central lake. We got our bikes and walked to the edge of the hill, where we could take in the view. The lake was a shimmering expanse of blue, surrounded by weeping willows and dotted with white swans gliding across the surface. Trinity leaned her bike against a tree and stood by the edge, taking a deep breath of the fresh air.

I joined her, slipping my arm around her waist. "This place is like a little escape from the city," I said softly.

Trinity nodded, leaning her head on my shoulder. "It's so peaceful here. I could stay all day."

We stood there for a while, just taking in the scenery and the quiet beauty of the park. Trinity turned to face me, a playful smile on her lips. "Race you to the bottom of the hill?" she challenged.

I chuckled. "Okay, cool."

We hopped back on our bikes, and with a burst of energy, sped down the hill, laughter filling the air as we raced each other. When we reached the bottom, Trinity was breathless and glowing with happiness. Of course, I let her win.

After our playful race, we found a quiet spot near the lake where we could sit and rest.

As the sun began to dip lower in the sky, casting a warm, golden hue over the park, we decided it was time to go. "Let's go eat. I've got one more surprise for you," I informed her.

As we walked back to the car, Trinity slipped her hand into mine. "I'm having a wonderful time," she said softly. "It was exactly what I needed."

I squeezed her hand, my heart swelling with affection. "Anytime, Trinity. I loved every minute of it."

Finally, we pulled up to the last spot of the evening, Rooftop Cinema Club. "Omg! I always wanted to come here," Trinity shouted. This movie theater was one of the city's hidden gems in the heart of downtown. The rooftop was adorned with string lights, comfortable lounge chairs, and a large screen that overlooked the stunning Houston skyline. As we stepped out onto the roof, the lights from the tall buildings cast a golden glow over the city.

This wasn't your regular movie theater. They had the best food and only showed classic films. Tonight, the movie premiering was Dirty Dancing. "My mother and I love this movie," she spoke with excitement. We found our assigned chairs and got comfortable. A waiter came over and took our order. I ordered buffalo wings, fries, and a Sprite.

Trinity ordered fajita tacos, a side of Mexican rice, and a Sprite. Together we enjoyed each other's company and the movie. We left the movies, feeling closer than ever. When we pulled up to the circular driveway in the apartments, I told Trinity to sit with me for a minute. Monica's R&B classic song 'Why I Love You So Much,' started playing on the radio. I turned the music down just a little so we could talk.

"Trinity today didn't do anything but reassure me how I feel about you. I love you, girl. I watched you blossom into a beautiful young woman. I think about you constantly. I know you're with Von, but he can't love you like I can. I haven't touched your body yet, but I know I touched your soul. I can't go another day seeing you with Von. I want us to be together," I confessed. We held each other's gaze for a moment.

"Today was amazing. I never felt this way about anyone before. From the beginning, it was always you who I wanted. I knew it then, and I know it now. I never want to break anyone's heart, but I'm going to tell Von I can't be with him anymore," she assured me.

"Do you need me to be there? Hell, I will even tell him for you." I told her with a smirk on my face. "I bet you would. No, I will handle it on my own," she stated. There was an awkward silence, and you could cut the passion between us with a knife. I leaned over for a kiss. A passionate kiss it was.

As our lips met, there was an undeniable connection, a magnetic pull that felt electrifying. The kiss was deep and full of longing, a slow and deliberate dance where every movement conveys desire and affection. Our breaths mingled, hearts pounding in unison, and time felt suspended. It's a kiss that speaks volumes about our love, need, and the unspoken promise of something more together. When we finished kissing, Trinity turned to look out the window.

"Omg Kyra," she mumbled. Holding on to her flowers, she quickly exited the car. I hopped out of the car right behind her. Kyra was standing next to the car crying.

"How could you, Trinity? You're supposed to be my friend. You knew how I felt about him!" Kyra scolded her.

"Kyra, let me explain," Trinity said with her voice trembling.

"Hold up, Sweet Pea, don't be mad at Trinity. I need to talk to you because there is a misunderstanding between us," I interjected.

"Don't ever talk to me again," Kyra spat and started power walking away from us. Trinity took a deep sigh and lowered her head. I raised her head back up with my finger.

"Everything will be okay. Let me walk you to your door," I spoke to her softly. After calling it a night with Trinity, I headed over to Kyra's place to do some damage control.

Jaycee opened the door. "Man, Kyra is mad at you! Don't worry, bro. She will get over it. She just has this puppy love crush on you," he said, chuckling. Z hopped in my face the moment I stepped inside.

"How dare you break my girl Kyra's heart, who ain't even my girl because she always wanted to be your girl, but you went on a date with a girl who's also not your girl, but is Von's girl." Z rambled on.

"Man, shut yo ass up!" I yelled at him and shoved him out of my way.

"Z, you stupiiiiid," Jaycee flopped down on the couch laughing.

I went into Kyra's room, and she was sitting on her large plush beanbag chair watching TV. Her eyes were puffy red. I took a seat on the bed facing her. "What's wrong? Come on, talk to me," I encouraged her to speak her truth. She smacked her lips.

"Go away, Reese," she ordered with her arms folded.

"Nahh, you had a lot of shit to say outside to Trinity. So don't hold back now. Put your big girl panties on and express how you feel."

There was a moment of silence before she began speaking. "I told Trinity the day we met how I felt about you. I let her have Von; now she went after the one person who I always saw myself being with forever. Since we were kids, I dreamed about marrying you," she sobbed. That broke my heart because I never want to see her cry.

"Sweet Pea, Trinity didn't go after me. I went after her, and just so happened she felt the same way.

Listen, I never want to hurt you. I love you and Jaycee; you both are my family. The keyword is family. I have known you since you were a baby. I've never looked at you in that way because I really see you as my sister. You're not losing me. You have me forever. I will literally die for you. Plus, girl, you've been looking at me for so long; you can't see who really does adore you!" Her eyes got big, and I saw her starting to feel better.

"WHOOO?" She jumped up and asked.

"It's not my business to tell. I do want you to make up with Trinity, though. You really hurt her feelings." Kyra rolled her eyes but gave me a smirk.

"Okay, fine, I'll make sure I go talk to her. Leaving out of the room, Z and Jaycee began stumbling over one another in the hallway.

"Y'all niggas nosy," I uttered before leaving out. It was a long day. I was ready to go home, take a shower, and crash.

A week went by, and I decided to go purchase Trinity a bracelet from Katy Mills mall. Her birthday was next weekend, and I thought it would be a nice gift. I was in high spirits as I drove towards the mall.

The streets were busy, but I navigated the traffic with ease, humming along to the R&B music playing softly on the radio. My mind was filled with thoughts of Trinity, imagining her reaction when I presented her with the delicate piece of jewelry. It was a simple plan for a perfect day.

Just a few blocks from the mall, I noticed an unmarked police car pull up behind me with the lights flashing. Confused but not overly concerned, I signaled and pulled over to the side of the road. Two Black detectives stepped out of the car and approached my vehicle on both sides. They had stern looks on their faces.

The first detective, standing outside my window, appears to be in his mid-50s. He has a strong, serious demeanor. He has close-cropped black hair, neatly trimmed. He's dressed in a dark gray suit, tailored to fit his athletic build, with a crisp white shirt and a dark tie.

The second detective, standing by the passenger side window, appears to be in his late 40s. He has a slightly heavier build. His head is bald, and he sports a neatly trimmed goatee. He wears a tan jacket over a dress shirt, which has the top button casually undone, giving him a slightly more relaxed, yet still authoritative, appearance.

"Good afternoon, officers," I greeted them, rolling down my window. "Is there a problem?"

"Step out of the car, please," the older detective said, his tone flat and authoritative.

My heart skipped a beat. "Is something wrong?"

"Out of the car," the detective repeated, more firmly this time.

I complied with his order; my mind was racing. What could this be about? As I stepped out, the younger detective moved around to the driver's side door and began searching the interior of the car without explanation.

"Do you mind telling me what this is about?" I asked, trying to keep his voice steady.

The older detective ignored my question, focusing instead on the search. The younger detective was thorough, checking under the seats, in the glove compartment, and finally, the trunk. That's when he found a black duffel bag, tucked away in the corner of the trunk. "Look at this Fulton," he observed.

"Sir, that's not mine," I said immediately, my pulse quickening. "I don't know where that came from."

Both detectives exchanged glances. The younger one unzipped the bag and pulled out several clear plastic bags filled with white powder drugs.

My stomach dropped. "That's not mine!" I protested, panic rising in my voice. "I swear, I don't know how that got there! Someone must have planted it in my car!"

"Sure, they did," the older detective said, his voice dripping with skepticism. "You're under arrest for possession of narcotics with intent to distribute."

I couldn't believe this was happening. I had no idea where those drugs had come from. I tried to explain, to plead with the detectives, but my words fell on deaf ears. The younger detective roughly cuffed my wrists behind my back, and I felt the cold metal clamp down on my skin.

As they led me to the police car, I could see people staring; their judgmental looks were obvious. I was innocent, but there was no way to prove it. The day that had started with so much promise had turned into a nightmare.

In the back of the police car, my thoughts raced. Who would do this to me? How did that bag end up in the trunk? The weight of my situation settled over me like a dark cloud.

By the time we reached the station, all I could think about was how to prove my innocence and how to clear my name. But for now, I was just another suspect being processed. As they led me into the holding cell, I could only hope that somehow, the truth would come to light.

Today was August 23, 2014. It was a warm Saturday morning in early fall, the perfect day for a birthday celebration. Charlene and I were full of joy and anticipation. Our baby girl, Trinity, had just turned eighteen, and today was all about her. The smell of her favorite pancakes filled the kitchen, and the sunlight streamed through the windows, casting a golden glow over the dining room.

"Happy birthday, sweetheart!" Charlene said, beaming as she placed a stack of pancakes topped with chocolate chips in front of her.

I came from behind, wrapped my arms around her, and gave her a big bear hug. "Eighteen, huh? I swear you were just running around in pigtails yesterday. Now look at you, all grown up," I proudly stated.

Trinity laughed, sitting at the table, feeling the moment's warmth. "Thanks, Dad. Her smile subsided, and she had a sad look on her face.

"What's wrong, beautiful?" I asked.

"I wish Reese were here to celebrate my birthday," she sobbed. That instantly broke my heart.

"Yeah, sweetie, I heard what happened. I don't believe for one minute he was distributing drugs. Everything will be okay." I informed her.

I smiled, ruffling her hair playfully. Charlene sat down across from her, a proud yet bittersweet look in her eyes.

"Let's not talk about any sad stuff. Today is a special day. We've got a big night planned for you. The party's going to be amazing," Charlene assured her.

Trinity's friends were all coming over later that evening. We reserved the apartment's party room, which Charlene and Netta had decorated beautifully. We set up a DJ booth and catered for the party. We couldn't wait to celebrate, but this delicious breakfast felt perfect for now.

We spent the next couple of hours together, reminiscing over old memories. Photos of Trinity as a child were scattered across the living room, reminders of how fast time had flown by. Charlene couldn't stop crying tears of joy. She even made Trinity a new scrapbook filled with pictures from every stage of her life. This moment felt special. She wasn't a baby anymore but will always be our baby girl. We laughed, joked, and enjoyed the peace of the morning.

As the afternoon sun began to set, Charlene and I exchanged secretive glances.

"We've got something special planned for you before the party," I said, standing up. Charlene smiled, her eyes sparkling with excitement.

"We'll be back in a bit, okay? We need to run a quick errand."

Trinity furrowed her brow but grinned. "What are you guys up to?"

"You'll see," Charlene said with a wink, kissing Trinity on the forehead.

Trinity watched as we left, not knowing we had planned the ultimate surprise of buying her first car. She'd been dreaming of getting one for years, and we had saved this money since I lost my job. I texted the number contacted about a week ago regarding a used 2013 champagne-colored Chevrolet Malibu vehicle. The pictures the guy sent me looked great. The car was parked inside a mechanic shop over on Bellaire Boulevard. We pulled up to a shop located on a back street. It was pretty dark out, and it didn't seem like anyone had arrived yet. A few minutes passed, and Charlene began to get anxious.

"Where did you say you found this guy?" Charlene asked out of worry.

"I didn't; he found me. He called and said he heard I was looking for a car for my daughter. He gave me the information about the Malibu," I confessed. Charlene's eyes got big.

"Patrick, you never saw this guy before or checked him out?" she asked.

"No, I just figured if the car wasn't good, we don't have to buy it. Charlene, I know how to inspect cars," I told her.

"It's late, Patrick, and something feels off," Charlene stated.

"Okay, we will wait a few more minutes, and then we'll leave," I said. It was pretty dark on this street. The only lights on were coming from my pickup truck and an alleyway.

Just as I decided we couldn't wait any longer, a dark figure ran out in front of the truck. The man's face was hidden under a ski mask and hood, his movements quick and deliberate. Before we could react, he already had a machine gun pointed towards us. Charlene looked at me with panic in her eyes. In the blink of an eye, bullets flew through the windshield. Glass breaking and live rounds of ammunition sounded like the Fourth of July came early.

I watched as the light in Charlene's eyes faded. He ran to her side of the car and fired more bullets into the vehicle. Her body shook from the impact and slumped over. Blood poured from her chest. It felt like little fireballs hit me in the arm and side. I managed to open my car door and crawl on my stomach. The gunman ran over to me and fired more rounds into my legs and back. At that moment, I briefly thought about Trinity; she will miss us. The last thing I felt was a bullet to the back of my head. I was out instantly.

Back home, Trinity's party had started. She kept asking where her parents were and that they should've been back home by now. She was blissfully unaware of the horror that had unfolded and how her life was about to change. She checked her phone, wondering why her parents were taking so long, but she shrugged it off. They always went out of their way to make things extra special, so she assumed they were putting the final touches on whatever surprise they had planned.

I knew her parents were never coming home. I made sure of it. Her biological father wanted to move her away from me and send her to a college out of state. He never wanted us to be together. I ensured Tank's first role was to get rid of her parents. With the new partnership with the Saldana Family, I was able to get rid of Reese's ass too. Nothing stood in my way now. I have Trinity exactly how I wanted her; to myself.

A couple of days ago, Kyra called me upset. She informed me that Trinity and Reese went out on a date. I knew then that my days with her were numbered if I didn't act quickly. I was already on edge because I stopped taking my medication. Without my meds, I couldn't control my impulses. I planned on taking them again; there's just been a lot going on.

After a few more hours of partying passed, Trinity couldn't shake the feeling that something was off. Her parents still hadn't returned.

Finally, a knock came at the front door. Trinity rushed to open it, thinking they had finally arrived. However, two detectives walked in, their faces grim. "Trinity Coleman?" one of them asked softly.

Her heart sank. "Yes?" The music was cut off, and they had everyone's attention. "My name is Detective Fulton, and this is my partner, Detective Carter. I'm so sorry, but there's been an incident," he informed her.

The words that followed blurred together as Trinity's world shattered around her. Everything she had known, the morning's joy and the warmth of her parents' love, was ripped away in that instant. The birthday celebration, the laughter, and the anticipation for the night were all drowned in the overwhelming weight of grief.

Her parents had been murdered. They would never walk through the door with that surprise, hold her again, or see her grow into the woman they had dreamed she would become. Everyone was comforting Trinity. I assured her I was there for her and that she could stay with my family until she figured things out. I pulled her in for a hug. Embracing Trinity, my eyes met my mother's eyes. Her look pierced my soul and made me feel uncomfortable. She looked at me with so much disgust. If I didn't know any better, I would think she knew I was responsible for all this. She rolled her eyes at me and left the party room. My mom did not know what I did, so I wasn't worried. Trinity left with Kyra to gather her things so she could stay with me. The rest of us stayed behind and cleaned up the party room.

Over the next couple of days, Trinity weighed out her options. She decided to stay with me until she finished her senior year. She was never close with her other family members, so she didn't want to live with any of them. She decided that she would go off to college like her parents wanted. For now, I wasn't going to argue with her about that. Tank and I were busy breaking the drugs down and giving them to the corner boys to sell. I got a call from Ben Taub's hospital that my dad was on life support. That hit me like a ton of bricks! I rushed downtown to figure out what was going on. My mom and I arrived at the same time. An older Indian gentleman wearing a white coat invited us into a vacant room to speak to us.

"Hello, my name is Dr. Ryuji, and I'm the head oncologist at Ben Taub's Medical Center," he stated. I wish I had better news to give you. Unfortunately, George has stage 4 lung cancer, and his condition has taken a turn for the worse," he continued.

"What! He doesn't even smoke; how can he have lung cancer?" I asked.

"You don't have to be a smoker to get lung cancer. There are various reasons why one might be diagnosed. For example, he is a mechanic, so he could have been exposed to certain pollutions and chemicals for years," he informed us.

"You're his wife, correct? We need you to decide to pull the plug," he told my mom.

"Okay, bring me the paperwork, and I'll sign," she said.

"You don't have any questions! You will agree to sign the papers without seeing if there is a treatment to help him!" I stood up and shouted.

"You heard him, Jervonte; nothing can help him now. This has to be done, and I'm doing it."

"What room number is he in?" I asked with tears falling from my eyes.

"Room 424," the doctor said. I had to leave that room before I did something I regretted to my mother. I found his room and walked in. The hospital room was bathed in a sterile, white light. The rhythmic hum of the machines filled the silence, their steady beeping the only sign of life. A ventilator pumped air into my father's lungs, the rise and fall of his chest entirely mechanical. Tubes snaked around the bed, barely keeping him alive.

I held on tightly to the bed guardrails, watching the slow rise and fall of my father's chest, each breath taken not by his own will but by the machines. He lay in the bed unresponsive. I cried, knowing this would be my last time seeing him. He was such a sweet and beautiful soul.

My father was nothing like my mother, and I loved him for that even more. I sat there and watched him for hours. My mother never came inside once. I couldn't help but feel like this was my karma because of what I did to Trinity's parents. I was losing the only person that unconditionally loved me. I wanted to remember the last real moments we shared. I instantly regretted not going fishing with him that day. Life could change in an instant. I couldn't believe this was happening.

The following day came, and the doctor informed me it was time to unplug him from the machines. Not more than an hour later, he was gone forever. My eyes were puffy from crying so hard. I walked into the men's bathroom. I stared at myself in the mirror. My reflection began to talk to me once again. I guess my psych medication was wearing off.

"Stop hiding the real you. I'm the real you! It's time I come out of this mirror and become the version of Von that people need. You're too soft. You know I'm telling you the truth. I want to be free, Von. Let me out of here," my reflection begged.

I had just lost my father. Nothing was stopping me from keeping the other Von hidden anymore. I agree; it's time I stop taking my meds and accept the real me. When I got home, my mother was watching TV on the couch. She looked completely fine for somebody who just lost a husband. I walked up to her and informed her that we needed to start planning my father's funeral service.

"We're not having a funeral. He will be cremated," she spoke without even looking my way.

"No, we're not! We need to celebrate his life and put him away nicely," I demanded.

"What the hell did I just say? I'm not burying his ass!" she said harshly. I snapped. I ran and choked the shit out of her. I squeezed her neck with both hands, and she tried to kick and scratch my face to get me off her. I kept choking her until she almost went unconscious.

Then I let her go. She jumped off the couch, holding onto her neck. "You're crazy!" she said. I cornered her against the wall.

"Bitch, I'll kill you," I spoke softly. Her eyes got big, and she scurried to her room. Trinity walked inside the house and embraced me.

"How are you holding up?" she asked.

"I'm fine, baby. My mom and I just got into it. She is going to cremate my father and deny him a funeral service," I told her.

"I'm sorry; we can always have our memorial service for him. Even if he is cremated," she smiled and tried to make me feel better.

That's why I loved her. She was such a sweetheart. My mom came out of the room with her luggage. "I'm leaving!" she yelled.

"Trinity, if you have the sense God gave you, you will run as far away from him as possible," she advised before leaving out the door. I shook my head.

"What are we going to do for money?" Trinity worried.

"I have some money saved up and more money coming in. I'll take care of both of us from now on," I assured her. This was the start of our lives. Z came over and chilled with us for the rest of the day. All three of us lost critical people to us in different ways. It was mostly my wrongdoings, but that's beside the point. We all had each other to lean on.

I left Z and Trinity in the living room and headed straight to the bathroom. I opened my medicine cabinet and stared at my psych meds. I tried to silence the noise in my head. It began to get louder.

"Be the real you. You don't need those meds," the voice reassured me. I picked up the bottle that read Fluoxetine and tossed it in the trash.

A lot has changed over the past nine years. Von got finer each year. At 29 years old, he had Houston in a chokehold. The women were crazy about him and gave zero fucks about his fiancée. They desperately wanted the life Trinity was living. The men wanted to be part of his team. He was the epitome of a professional thug. He made his fortune as a real estate investor buying up land, commercial properties, houses, and vacation homes all over the world.

He used severe scare tactics to muscle people out of their properties for his own benefit. He had street soldiers ready to do whatever he wanted them to do. Von transformed himself into quite an eligible bachelor. The only problem was that he wasn't supposed to be eligible for anyone but Trinity. Taking care of himself was a top priority.

He brushed his teeth multiple times a day to maintain his beautiful smile, moisturized his skin, which gave him a rich glow, and he stayed in the gym. His 6-pack abs were easy to spot when he was shirtless. Not to mention he had a nice goatee beard and mustache. His hair was cut low and wavy. At 6'4 feet tall, he was GQ quality. Von dabbled in almost everything illegal you could think of. He sold high artillery weapons, ran a drug operation, and stole people's assets. He was ruthless.

Trinity went into residential real estate as well. She was known as one of Houston's most beautiful and successful real estate brokers. She was almost 27 years old, and the definition of a boss chick. She is a strikingly beautiful woman with smooth, rich, dark skin that glows with warmth under the sunlight. Her thick, luscious curls cascade past her shoulders, each strand full of life and bounce, framing her face in an elegant halo.

Her eyes, deep and almond-shaped, exude confidence and mystery, with a gaze that captivates anyone who meets it. Her full lips curve into a mesmerizing smile, and her high cheekbones accentuate the regal structure of her face. Her presence radiates a sense of power and allure, with an effortless urban chicness that turns heads everywhere she goes. Her style is a perfect blend of bold, modern fashion and timeless grace.

She owned a firm called Goldstone Investment Group, but Von was listed as a silent partner. He allowed Trinity to manage a legitimate company without his shady dealings in case the Feds came around snooping into their business.

However, Von owned other companies that he laundered dirty money through. They lived downtown in a luxury penthouse that had a balcony that looped around the entire 28th floor. The suite had expansive glass windows that allowed the ray of sunshine to illuminate the space in the daytime. At night, the city lights were captivating. The balcony view felt magical as tall buildings glowed from a distance and the stars above lit up the sky.

For many years, the 163 Mafia Family ran Houston with an iron fist. They had corrupt cops and politicians on the payroll. The community felt like the gang was unstoppable. They ran their organization on three main elements: fear, respect, and loyalty. Anyone violating these three elements was harmed or murdered. Von was at the head of the table. Standing right next to him was the underboss, Tank. He kept everyone in line and was second in command. He was tall, baldheaded, and buff. Tribal tattoos covered his mocha-brown skin body. He had a thick black beard that stretched down his neck. Tank looked like an absolute beast. He put fear in many people's hearts just by looking at them.

The next head street soldier was Kentrell. He was Black, skinny, and short. He rocked a bald fade haircut and still wore clothes too big for him. It was like he was stuck in the 1990s. He got into a gang fight in prison a couple of years back, and somebody sliced him across his left eye with a shank. The scar healed but is very visible.

These two men were Von's most valuable street soldiers. He could give them any order, and they executed it without problems. They caught many bodies for Von.

Wakumbe, Marquees, and Boogie were making their way up the ranks. There were other low-level gangsters spread out over Southwest Houston, carrying out Von's plans to distribute narcotics and commit other heinous crimes.

Von walked into the empty warehouse that they referred to as The Cozy Corner. It was called The Cozy Corner because when they brought people there, they never left alive. Tank, Kentrell, Wakumbe, and Boogie stood around waiting to see why Von called an emergency meeting. They were the only men Von let come in and out of that location. You could hear dogs moving around on chains, barking in the background.

Von walked in wearing a tailored business suit as usual. "Here's why I called a meeting. Apparently, Larry Anderson didn't take heed to our threats. I just received a call from David McAllister, the manager over at Navy Federal Credit Union. His application for the Vanderbilt property is going through the approval process as we speak! I can't lose this deal. That Vanderbilt property is a huge investment for my operation. Its location is right next to the airport. I can easily get large shipments in and out of the country. Now he will see what it's like to be my enemy. I sent his home address to Tank's cell phone. Bring that fat motherfucka to me. Make sure y'all suit up so your faces are not revealed," he demanded.

Tank, Kentrell, Wakumbe, Marquees, and Boogie walked to the van they normally carry out assignments in. Tank opened the back of the van and grabbed a large black duffel bag that contained all black work boots, black gloves, black long-sleeve shirts, and black ski masks. They got dressed right in the parking lot. They grabbed another large duffel bag that contained pistols, AK-47s, and AR-15s. Each one of them grabbed the gun of their choice. Tank hopped in the driver's seat, and Kentrell sat in the passenger seat. The other men piled into the back of the van. Now they were on a mission.

It was 7:15 pm in the evening. The Anderson family was an upper-class Caucasian family that lived in River Oaks. The Anderson family just sat down at the dining room table to eat dinner. Larry Anderson conversed with his 17-year-old identical twins, a boy and a girl, about school.

"So, did any of you learn anything new today?" he asked them. Both ignored their father and proceeded to text on their phones. Larry's wife, Mary Anderson, instructed the teenagers to put their phones down.

BOOM!

They heard the front door burst open. The 163 Mafia Family barged into the house with guns pointed at the family. The wife began screaming. Boogie ran over to where she was sitting and clocked her in the head with his gun.

"Please don't hurt my family," Larry pleaded. The teenagers were whimpering but scared to make any loud noises.

"GET THE FUCK UP, ALL OF YOU!" Tank screamed. The family quickly moved from the table, and the men rushed them outside and into the back of the van.

"LAY DOWN NOW," Tank ordered the family. Wakumbe, Boogie, and Marquees climbed in the back with the family. They began zip-tying their hands and duct-taping their mouths. They all left in a hurry before the police arrived.

Tank picked up his cell phone and dialed Von's number. "Yeah," Von answered.

"It's done. We're on the way back," Tank stated.

"Bet," Von replied. The line was disconnected. The tank continued to drive to the warehouse.

The gang walked the family into the warehouse in one straight line. Von stood in the middle of the warehouse holding a pistol. The family was seated on the dusty concrete floor. Von walked by each one of them, giving them the death stare. Larry tried to talk, but his words came out muffled because his mouth was duct taped.

"Remove the duct tape from his mouth," Von told Wakumbe.

Wakumbe snatched the tape off Larry's mouth, leaving a red ring around it. Larry licked his lips to try to get the feeling back.

"Larry, you didn't tell your wife how much of a snake you are?" Von asked.

"I can fix it. Please! Let me fix it," Larry cried.

"One thing about you cracka motherfuckas is that you will literally do anything to win. I don't know how you got your paperwork to be at the front of that pile when I have been working on this deal for a long time. I was told I needed to be patient because it was a lot of red tape. Motherfucka, YOU WERE THE RED TAPE!" Von yelled.

"PLEASE, PLEASE LET US GO! I don't want the property anymore," Larry sobbed.

"Nah, it's too late. I gave you a chance to do the right thing. I gotta make an example out of you. Nobody will ever go against me again," Von declared. Von snapped his fingers and instructed the men to kill the family. The family's muffled cries through duct tape got intense. They began squirming on the floor trying to get away. It was too late for them. Von watched as bullets punctured the bodies of Larry's wife and kids. The sound of firepower hitting their flesh was loud. Within seconds their bodies lay lifeless on the cold concrete.

"Noooo, you son of a bitch," Larry cried and tried to rush Von. His attempt was unsuccessful because his hands were still tied, and he was too overweight. Kentrell kicked him in the face, which knocked him on his back. Finally, Larry met the same fate as his family. Kentrell lifted his pistol and shot Larry in the head and three more rounds in his chest.

"Clean this up and make sure y'all burn everything," Von instructed. He turned around to walk away, but Tank stopped him.

"We just killed a prominent Caucasian family, including two white kids. We might've just put a target on our backs," Tank expressed. "

Nothing we haven't been through before. Just make sure y'all clean this place from top to bottom and that nobody is ever able to find their remains," Von stated.

A few hours later, Tank went to the penthouse to inform Von that the warehouse was cleaned, and the bodies were disposed of. "I got one more person to visit. Let's go." Von quickly grabbed a folder sitting on the kitchen counter.

"Who?" Tank asked as they walked out to the hallway and towards the elevators. Von pushes the down arrow button located next to the elevator doors. The elevator opened, and they walked inside.

"I got Phillip Motley's address. He is the CEO of Revolt Investment Properties. He currently owns the Vanderbilt property, and for some reason he and his team allowed Larry Anderson to outbid me. I'm going to make sure that property is mine and that he never ever tries to fuck me over again," Von fumed.

The men pulled up to Phillip's two-story brick home. "How do you want to do this?" Tank murmured.

"He stays alone. His wife left him after he had an affair with his secretary."

"We're just going to go right up there and ring the doorbell," Von stated.

Ding Dong. Ding Dong.

They heard the bell sound off inside the house. Moments later, Phillip opened the door halfway, wearing his reading glasses and thick white robe. "Mr. Westley. It's 4:00 am in the morning. How did you even get my address?" He questioned. Von didn't answer. He just burst through the door, knocking the man backwards into the wall. Von and Tank rushed in and closed the door.

"I'm calling the cops," Phillip said while trying to run off. Tank grabbed him by the back of the neck and walked him over to the living room area. He then slammed him down on the couch. Von flicked on the light switch and took a seat in the recliner, while Tank just stood over Phillip. "What is this about?" he asked.

"Tell me something, Phil. How is it that my bid for the Vanderbilt property has been in since it first went on the market but hasn't been approved yet? I know because I made sure to keep tabs on the facility until it was ready for buyers. How is it that now Larry Anderson's paperwork is going through the approval process? You deliberately stalled my paperwork," Von said calmly.

"Larry Anderson is a pillar in this community, and he was eager to purchase the property just like you!" Phillip screamed at Von.

Von hopped up out of the chair and backhanded Larry in the face. "You're doing some shady shit, and you know it. What, you don't think a Black man should get the property over them white motherfuckas, huh? Bitch, you better make sure I get that property, or they'll be fishing parts of your body at the Braeswood Bayou," Von warned.

"I can't just stop the approval process. Larry could sue us," Phillip said.

"Oh yes you can, and you will. Larry Anderson no longer qualifies to have that property. Dead men can't own shit. Because of you, I wiped his entire family off the map. I'm not worried about you going to the cops either," Von mentioned.

He grabbed the folder and placed pictures across his coffee table. He pointed out each person. "This is your wife and two smaller kids. They moved to Conroe, Texas, about 6 months ago. These two individuals are your parents. They stay about 25 minutes from here, over on Gessner Road. This young lady is your oldest daughter, and she's a sophomore at Rice University. I have eyes and men everywhere. If you don't make sure I get that Vanderbilt property, I'm going after your loved ones first and then save you for last."

Phillip's lips quivered as he tried to keep from sobbing. "Okay, okay. I'll go into the office and make sure the property is yours," Phillip said, shaken up.

"Good. You better not utter a word to anyone about this. I'm not playing with you," Von demanded. He and Tank left the house. As soon as they got in the car, Tank asked a question he was curious about.

"Man, how did you get all these addresses and information on people?"

Von smiled and replied, "I got a contact over at the FBI. This little chick I smash from time to time is an administrator and helps me out," he boasted. Tank was impressed by how Von leveraged his resources.

The next night Von wanted to celebrate getting the Vanderbilt property. He invited the 163 Mafia Family to the exclusive strip club "Sapphire Dreams."

All sorts of foreign cars owned by members of the 163 Mafia Family pulled up to the club's valet service. They walked inside the club like an army. The neon lights flickered above the entrance, casting a purple and gold hue over the scene. Inside, the bass-heavy beats of trap music vibrated through the walls, welcoming the night's special guests.

Von was wearing a designer collared gold shirt with matching corduroy pants. The iced-out earrings, Cuban link necklace, and bracelet enhanced his look. His team was ready to party after a long week of distributing narcotics. These were not your average street hustlers that were crumb chasers. They moved large packages of cocaine, bringing in millions to Von's enterprise.

"Yooo Von, you finally got the Vanderbilt property," said Kentrell, flashing a wide grin as they made their way to their usual sitting area. They were greeted with nods of respect from the bouncers. Inside, the scent of champagne and expensive perfume mingled with the faintest hint of cigar smoke. The air was electric.

Women danced on every stage, and ass was bouncing everywhere. Bodies glittered as they moved in perfect harmony to the music. The attention was now on the infamous gang, and all the dancers wanted to be in their section. D'avyonne, the club's head dancer and building owner, decided which girls made it into the section. Years ago, she started off as a low-level dancer, but Von quickly took a liking to her.

She was a badass, light-skinned chick with curves for days. Ron, the club owner, treated her like trash, so Von eventually bought the building and gifted it to her. Ron was pissed he now had to play nice and treat her like an equal partner.

The crew settled into the VIP section. They bought out the bar, making sure no bottle was left unopened, no glass unfilled. A bartender set up rows of glistening bottles of Hennessy, Ace of Spades, and Patron.

"Tonight, I celebrate you niggas! 163 boys up!" Von toasted with his drink in the air. Sitting down on a plush leather couch, Von's arm draped over the backrest as the finest dancers in the room drifted toward their section.

A woman named Nyeir caught Von's eye. She was stunning, with skin the color of mocha and curves that made every step hypnotic. As she approached, she smiled, her eyes locked on his. She was wearing a sparkly green G-string, and her exposed titties bounced as she walked. She enticed him with her every move. Moving her body like a snake to the music, she reached down to caress her pussy. She grinded her thick hips with such ease.

"You must be the man in charge," she teased, sitting down on his lap.

Von chuckled, sliding a stack of bills onto the table, signaling for her to join him. "I'm just here to enjoy the show."

The rest of the crew was already lost in their own worlds. Tank had two dancers on either side of him, laughing and throwing cash in the air like confetti. Smoke filled the air from the blunts being passed around, the scent blending into the night's haze.

Behind the bar, DJ QKing switched the music up, dropping a heavy beat that sent a ripple through the club. The dance floor lit up as more women flooded the stage, each one more mesmerizing than the last. The energy hit a new level; everyone in the room could feel it. The club had become a playground of rhythm and seduction, where money meant nothing, and the night was endless.

Von leaned back, taking in the scene around him. His crew was in their element, the women were stunning, and the drinks flowed without pause. This was what success looked like. They had what most men wanted, which was money, power, and respect.

Nyeir leaned in close to his ear. "You look like the type of man who knows what he wants."

He smiled, his gaze intense. "And tonight, I want you," he whispered in her ear. With the quickness, Nyeir was snatched off Von's lap by her hair.

"Bitch, get your ass out of here! You know better than to touch my man," D'avyonne yelled. Nyeir rushed out of the VIP section. Von sat there shaking his head at D'avyonne. When she got jealous, it low-key turned him on.

"I'm not your damn man. Don't tell people that shit again," he exclaimed. D'avyonne straddled Von cowgirl style.

"You should be my man. When are you going to leave Trinity?" she asked softly. Now Von was irritated. He reached up and grabbed her around the throat. She gasped for air.

"Hey, we do what we do, and it works. Don't try to buck the system and end up getting your fucking feelings hurt," he informed her. He removed the grip he had around her neck. She decided to let the topic go and enjoy the rest of the night with Von.

"Give me some head," he demanded.

"Okay, let's go to the back," she replied.

"No, right here," he firmly stated while leaning back on the plush couch.

"Out in the open, Von? You can't be serious," she nervously chuckled.

"We're in the corner, and it's dark. Nobody really paying attention anyways," he reasoned with her. She just stared at him.

"Look, give me some top, or I'll call another bitch over here to do it!" he spoke out of frustration. She knew he wasn't playing. D'avyonne got up and kneeled between his legs. She started unhooking his pants. What Von wants, Von gets.

"Damn, Trinity, hurry up. I don't wanna be late!" Von yelled at me from downstairs. "I'm coming!" I yelled back. Tonight, we were attending the city's Annual Prestige Real Estate Gala. This is the most anticipated event of the year, drawing together Houston's elite, a who's who of the local property market. The highlight of the evening is the awards ceremony. The most successful residential and commercial real estate professionals of the year are recognized for their outstanding achievements.

The awards range from "Top Sales Agent" to "Best New Development" and "Lifetime Achievement in Real Estate." Each winner is called to the stage, where they are presented with a custom-designed trophy, symbolizing excellence and their contribution to shaping the city's skyline.

I was sitting in front of the mirror in our spacious bathroom putting on my ombre-colored lipstick. My hair was in a high curly ponytail with a curly bang that flowed down the left side of my face.

My earrings were red, medium-sized diamonds in the shape of a circular flower. I wore a sleeveless, silky, red dress that exposed my entire back. On my feet were some patent leather black high heels with a red bottom sole made by Christian Louboutin. My face was beat for the Gods.

I normally don't wear makeup unless I'm attending an important event. Von loves my natural face, so I usually keep it bare. However, when I do wear makeup, I look even more stunning. Von rushes into the bathroom to see what was taking me so long. I must admit, he was killing it in that suit. He looked so handsome standing there in a burgundy custom-made suit, a black undershirt, and black Versace shoes. There was a crisp burgundy handkerchief tucked in his vest pocket. The edge-up on his haircut was evenly on point.

"Stand up; let me inspect you," he demands. I swear he can make me feel like a kid. Rolling my eyes, I stood up to do as I was told. He repeatedly looked me up and down.

"Now turn around," he demanded. I did a 360 turn, and he stood there trying to decide if I looked okay. "You're lucky we have to go. You might as well be naked. If you wanna be a hoe, just say that," he said. Hearing him say that pissed me off so bad. As violent as he has been to me over the years, I sometimes try to push his buttons.

"I wanna be a hoe," I shouted back to be petty. He snatched me by my face with his right hand and squeezed my chin as hard as he could. It felt like my jaw was going to break from the pressure he was applying. Not letting go of my face, he pulled me towards him until my body was smashed against his.

"I'm gonna let you make it because I have an important ceremony tonight." With one hand, he shoved me against the glass shower door. The back of my head hit the glass.

"Get yourself together and let's go," he snapped. I watched as he adjusted his suit and walked out of the bathroom. I looked in the mirror and quickly fixed my makeup he managed to smudge. I still looked beautiful. I grabbed my red Louis Vuitton clutch purse and left the room.

We pulled into the circular driveway, and the valet escorted us out of the car. You could hear the soft melodies of violins playing from inside. Von walked over to me and grabbed my hand. Before we could walk towards the entrance, we were interrupted by what appeared to be a mad lady. She was dark-skinned like me but wasn't as cute. She reminded me of an off-brand Keke Palmer. She was wearing a black baggy T-shirt, black joggers, and some cheap brown sandals. Her toes weren't even done. She definitely wasn't dressed for tonight's event. She clearly had been crying. Her frizzy box braids flowed past her buttocks.

"Von, so you think you can keep ignoring me and I'll go away? Yeah, I knew I would catch your ass eventually. I'm fucking four months pregnant with your baby!" She hollered. I quickly let go of his hand. He looked at me, looked at my hands by my side, and then back up to me like I did something wrong. I rolled my eyes at him. He turned his attention back to her.

"Shut the fuck up right now and go home," he told her while gritting his teeth.

"No, fuck you! I'm going to hit you where it hurts, nigga. Right in your pockets!" Tank came running up and tried to defuse the situation. He placed one of his hands on her back and tried to turn her away. She jerked away from Tank, but he was still right on her heels. Some guests walking by began to look worried.

"Okay, let's talk tonight. Did you drive up here?" he asked her.

"Yes, I did," she said, calming down.

"Cool. Tank, take her to relax at one of the properties, "The Cozy Corner," and then notify me when it's done."

Tank paused for a second, and he and Von exchanged looks. Von nodded his head at Tank. It was something about that exchange that didn't seem right to me. What the fuck was the 'Cozy Corner,' I wondered. I've never heard of that property before.

"That's right. I deserve to live a life of luxury. Not just her!" she said, looking at me with a stank face. I just looked at her raggedy ass. I didn't have the energy to engage with one of Von's hoes tonight. "You're absolutely right. Tank will drive your car and escort you to the property. I'll be there soon so we can work everything out," he spoke to her softly. I tried to walk off, but he quickly snatched me by my wrist and squeezed it. Tank and the woman walked off together. Von turned to face me and pulled me in for a hug.

He whispered in my ear, "Don't start. This is an important day for me, so lose the attitude. I wouldn't test me," he warned. Von planted a few kisses on the side of my face, and people smiled as they passed us up. We both turned to walk towards the entrance.

As attendees enter the building, they are greeted by a red carpet flanked by photographers capturing the moment. The town's top real estate moguls, agents, developers, and investors mingle over champagne, dressed in their finest evening attire. We were escorted by butlers wearing white suits into a lavishly decorated ballroom. The evening exudes opulence, with crystal chandeliers casting a warm glow over tables adorned with fine linens and floral centerpieces. An older Caucasian lady approached us smiling.

"Good evening, sir and madam. Do you know your table number?" she asked.

"Table number 4," Von answered back.

"Right this way," she guided us with her hand, which suggested the direction we should be going, and then led us to our table. We took our seats, and I recognized a few important faces already sitting down at our table. Mayor Turner, Texas Representative Coral Jackson, Pastor Rasmus, and Rapper Trae Tha Truth were all tied up in conversations about politics, lucrative investment deals, market trends, and upcoming projects. There were two older white men sitting at the table, but I had no idea who they were.

Von left to mingle amongst the crowd. I sat there enjoying the small talk from some of Houston's finest. A female waiter walked past me carrying glasses of water. I stopped her and asked where the restrooms were.

"Down that hallway, make a right, and the restrooms are on the right side of the wall," she guided me by making hand gestures. I headed for the restroom. When I hit the corner on the right, I could see the sign for the women's restroom hanging above the door in the distance. Walking briskly through the crowded hallway, my heels dug into the thick patterned carpet. My foot catches a small object, and I instantly begin to stumble. I didn't notice the tube of lipstick that someone must've dropped. My arms flailing uncontrollably as I try to regain my balance. Just as I feel myself going down, a strong hand reaches out, catching me by the arm.

The person's grip is firm but gentle, and with a quick, effortless motion, I'm pulled back to my feet. I looked back to see who my savior was. I was caught completely off guard. I looked up to see a tall, handsome man in a perfectly fitted, tailored suit, his dark eyes filled with concern. His other hand remained on my waist, steadying my footing. I could feel the warmth of his touch through the fabric of my dress. He smiles, revealing a set of straight, white teeth, his expression reassuring and calm. I felt butterflies in the pit of my stomach.

"Are you alright?" he asks, his voice smooth and deep.

I nod my head yes, still catching my breath. "Thank you. I didn't see it." He glances down at the offending lipstick, now resting harmlessly by the side of my shoe.

"It's a good thing I was close by," he says with a chuckle, releasing my arm gently.

I nervously smile back at him, my heart still racing from the near fall but also from the unexpected and slightly thrilling encounter.

"Yes, it certainly is," I replied, feeling a wave of gratitude—and maybe something more—toward the man who saved me from what could have been a very embarrassing moment. I scurried to the restroom, leaving the man watching my backside. After I was done using the bathroom and fixing some out-of-place hairs, I returned to my seat. Von had his arm resting at the top of my chair. As soon as I sat down, he removed his arm from behind me and began caressing the back of my neck and shoulders. He smiled at me, and anyone looking at him would've believed he truly valued me.

"Okay everyone. Now it's time to honor our city builders."

A beautiful, brown-skinned woman with shoulder-length bohemian braids and flawless makeup spoke boldly at the podium. She wore a tight-fitting nude brown dress that had an opening on each side, revealing some of her flat stomach. She leaned into the microphone to announce the next category.

"The winner for best architect of the year goes to Jatavion Mathews. The crowd started clapping. That's when I saw the guy who stopped me from falling stand up and begin to make his way to the front. The applause continued. I nearly bit my lip looking at him. I heard a couple of women holler as if they were in heat. I instantly noticed the discomfort on Von's face. I focused my attention back on the stage. Jatavion walked on stage, and a gentleman handed him a glass trophy. He held the trophy in the air to salute the audience before making his speech.

Wow! I am truly honored to stand before you today as this year's recipient of the Architect of the Year award. This moment is one that I will cherish for a lifetime, and it serves as a profound reminder of the power of collaboration, creativity, and vision in shaping the world around us. Architecture is more than just creating structures; it is about crafting spaces that inspire, that bring people together, and that stand as lasting symbols of our shared dreams and ambitions. This award is a testament not only to my work but also to the countless individuals who have contributed to these projects—my dedicated team, our clients, and everyone who believed in the vision we set out to achieve. This honor is as much yours as it is mine, and I am deeply grateful for your support, your trust, and your partnership. Looking forward, I am excited by the possibilities that lie ahead in our field. We live in a time where the challenges are great, but so too are the opportunities to innovate and to leave a meaningful impact on our communities and the world. I am humbled, and I am inspired to continue pushing the boundaries of what we can achieve together. Thank you.

I was completely mesmerized by this man. He spoke with so much poise and class. Von watched me as I watched Jatavion. I didn't even care; that was until I turned around, and he had that crazy look in his eye. He knew to be on his best behavior in front of all these folks, though.

After Jatavion left the stage, more awards and speeches were given for about another hour and thirty minutes. When the formalities were over, the event transitioned into a glamorous after-party with live music, dancing, and networking. The music was turned up louder, and people flocked to the dance floor. The two white guys sitting at the table made small talk with Von.

"Who is this beautiful lady?" One of them asked while smiling at me.

"Baby, this is Mr. Cushier. He is one of Houston's most successful real estate brokers. The guy sitting next to him is Mr. Baugher, and he is a real estate attorney."

"Hello," I politely spoke and waved my hands at them. Startling me, Jatavion approached us from the side. He came and stood directly in front of me. Von's entire demeanor changed. He looked at the man as if he was confused why he was standing there. The dude's eyes were locked dead on me. He paid Von no mind. I wish I could curl up and die at that moment.

"Hey Miss Lady, just checking on you to see how your foot is feeling?" he asked me.

"Oh, thank you. It's doing fine." I quickly looked away, trying not to make eye contact.

"Wait, y'all met?" Von asked, looking at the both of us.

"Indeed, we did," he answered. He continued to explain how we met.

"She almost fell in the hallway. I'm glad I was right behind her to catch her. That could've been a nasty fall," he stated while finally staring at Von. What the hell is up with these two, I thought to myself. I know Von wasn't a fan of his, and now it seems like he was perfectly trying to antagonize Von. Von nodded his head and chuckled.

"Well, aren't you kind?" Von asked him, but this time he wasn't smiling.

"I am," he quickly responded but wasn't smiling either. They stared at each other as if they were in a who-can-blink-first contest. The entire table was quiet and nosy as hell. It was almost as if they were entertained by this foolishness.

"Mr. Westley, the men and I have some lucrative business propositions we wanted to speak to you about regarding the Vanderbilt property. I hear you will soon be the new owner! Let Mr. Mathews take this young lady on the dance floor while we speak. You're not insecure, are you?" Miss Coral Jackson asked him with her eyebrow raised.

"Oh no, I'm fine," I tried to quickly interject.

"Nonsense, dear. A dance won't kill you while we talk business," she waved me off. Von nodded his head yes to agree to the dance. Jatavion quickly stepped to me with his hand reached out. I grabbed it, and he led me away to the dance floor.

My heart felt like it was about to pop out of my chest. I knew in my heart Von was steaming inside. There was no way he was okay with another man touching me in any way. As soon as we stepped on the dance floor, the song "Sittin On Top Of The World" by Burna Boy went off.

My favorite 90s R&B track, "Slow Jam" by Usher and Monica, blasted through the speakers. The mood instantly changed to a more intimate setting. The mid-tempo melody relaxed everyone on the dance floor, and people found partners to slow dance with. Jatavion wrapped his arms around my lower waist, and I moved his arms up until he rested them in the center of my back. Our bodies began to sway from side to side to match the beat. My breasts were pressed up against his chiseled body.

"What's your name, beautiful?" he inquired.

"Trinity," I answered. "Your name is Jatavion, right?" I asked him.

"Oh, somebody has been paying attention to me," he teased. I rolled my eyes.

"Don't get ahead of yourself. I'm just good with names," I informed him. He chuckled and smiled those pretty teeth at me.

"Just messing with you. Yeah, ma, my name is Jatavion, but I go by the name Ja." Usher's smooth and sensational voice continued to serenade the room.

"Why are you with such a horrible person? You don't strike me as the type of woman who would be with a man like that." That pissed me off.

"First off, you don't know me well enough to know my type. Also, I don't appreciate the stunt you pulled earlier. If you know Von is a horrible person, why antagonize him? Because of you, I'll pay for your actions later," I told him, trying not to tear up.

I didn't realize I was poking him in the chest with my finger until he looked down at it. For a moment we stopped dancing. His facial expression showed he was concerned for me. He pulled me back into his embrace, and our feet began to move again.

"What do you mean by you will have to pay for my actions later?" he asked.

"Nothing," I quickly avoided his question. His eyes search for my soul, or so it felt like it. He dropped the subject and dug his face deep into my neck while caressing the center of my exposed back. This might sound crazy, but at this very moment, I felt loved. Only one other person in my life made me feel like this. The slow song was over, and I was happy. The DJ started playing some new and old hip-hop tracks. We danced for another 30 minutes.

I was enjoying myself so much, I almost forgot about Von. Von didn't forget about me, though. He walked by us, and it felt like a dark cloud floated over us on the dance floor. I could feel Von's energy. He just kept walking, and the lady that was at the podium earlier pulled him to the side for a conversation.

"I'm ready to sit down," I informed my dance partner.

"Okay, no problem. Thanks for entertaining me tonight. I wasn't going to come, but now it was worth it," he said.

"You're welcome," I smiled and quickly walked away. I almost made it to my seat when I decided to turn around to get another look at Ja. He was still standing on the dance floor watching me. My heart skipped a beat. I sat down at the table alone with my thoughts. Everyone at our table left to mingle or network with other guests. I patiently waited for Von to return.

After a few minutes passed, Von came walking up and took his seat next to me. I grabbed his hand that was resting on his lap and gave a half smile. He turned towards me with the coldest look, and chills ran down my body. His eyes cut low, and his brows had a wicked frown. I could almost see the fires of hell in his eyes. His lip was pressed together tightly. He quickly released my hand from his and leaned towards me as he placed one hand on the back of my neck, pulling me closer in.

He whispered in my ear, "You think you know pain; wait until we get home."

A handsome older gentleman with a gray afro and beard walked over to us. The man's excitement snapped Von out of the rage he was in.

"My man V, I hear you're going to close on that 50 million commercial property deal! I don't know how you do it, but you tend to close deals that other companies can't seem to close. Teach me the ropes!" The man politely begged with his hands in a praying position. Von let out a friendly laugh.

He got up from the table and began walking off with the man. I watched as they smiled at each other and exchanged fist bumps. You know you're evil when you can switch personalities in a second. I thought to myself, *What a crazy-ass nigga.* I can't lie and say I wasn't happy the attention was taken off me. I just sat in my chair frozen, unable to move. I realized I had been staring at the floor, and as I picked my head up. My previous dance partner, who just got me in trouble with Von, was staring at me with a sincere look on his face.

I can tell he felt sorry for me. It's crazy because although I knew I was about to get the shit beat out of me later on tonight, I couldn't help but think, God, this nigga Ja is finer than a motherfucka. I gave Ja a friendly grin and let my eyes quickly search for Von.

Yup, I found him across the room by the bar, staring directly at me. The man who pulled him away just a few minutes ago was still talking to him, but it didn't seem like Von was paying attention as he was dead set on focusing on me. I know he just saw the little exchange between me and Ja.

Damn! I was considering making a run for it, but he always catches me. I can't even prepare for the ass whooping I'm about to get because he is unpredictable with it at times. I just hope I don't die.

"It's time to go. I need to use the bathroom and say bye to some people first. You can head to the front. I'll be there shortly."

I waited patiently by the front entrance for Von to say his goodbyes to all his colleagues and business partners. Ja walked past me, but he didn't stop to make conversation. He winked at me and kept going out the door. I believe he could sense there was trouble in paradise and didn't want to make matters worse for me. I was blushing on the inside. I tried to search for Von, but he was nowhere in sight. 15 minutes went by, and I was still standing at the door by myself.

I walked back to the party area and still didn't see him. I continued my search down one of the hallways. As I was passing up the restrooms, I spotted him with the woman presenting the awards. They were tucked off in a corner. He was leaning against the wall with his hands in his pants pocket. She was all in his face, giggling and carrying on a conversation. She made sure to have her thick thigh completely exposed in her split dress. I stopped dead in my tracks.

"You ready to go?" I asked him annoyed. The woman looked pissed that I interrupted them. I returned the same look right back at her.

"Yeah," he answered and gently pushed her away with one hand in her midsection. He grabbed my hand as we were leaving the building. He is so fake and full of shit. He loves to keep up with impressions or make people think he is good to me. The moment we got outside, he let go of my hand. A guy working as a valet brought the car around. Von tipped him twenty dollars. We both got in, and before pulling out of the parking lot, Von began texting someone. I watched as both of his fingers moved swiftly across his phone keypad.

On the drive home, Von was quiet. That was scary to me because usually he would be screaming from the top of his lungs by now. He would have at least slapped me or something.

With a stern look, he just clutched the steering wheel with one hand and drove in silence. I just knew he was steaming on the inside but trying to control his anger. This type of reaction was new to me.

"Von, I didn't want to dance with that man," I explained. His facial expressions tensed up even more. He opened and closed the same fist he was driving with. At that moment, I knew to be quiet. There was nothing else I could do but wait to see what my fate was. We pulled into the garage, and Nate the bellboy, was standing by the elevators leading up to the floor of our penthouse. He waved at us and used his keycard to open the elevators.

Von reversed into our reserved parking spot. He hopped out of the car and walked over to my side to open the door. I stepped out and tried to bend down for my purse. He stopped me by pulling on my arm, and I went flying forward. He slammed the door behind me, and we made our way to the elevators. Passing Nate, he softly smiled at me.

He was used to Von's behavior towards me. I could tell he felt sorry for me. Nate was 20 years old and a college student at Texas Southern University. He was a skinny, dark-skinned guy with thick eyebrows and a small afro. He wore a black tailored suit that had a gold nameplate attached to his pocket that read *Nate C. Douglas*. Nate was always so polite to me. I believe his future was going to be bright. Von and I had so many altercations in this garage; he has seen me at my worst.

"Enjoy the rest of your night," he said before sending us up on the elevator. As the doors were closing, he made eye contact with me, and I could see the pity across his face. I hated that so many people low-key felt sorry for me. I watched the screen above the elevator door change, blinking red numbers when we passed up a floor level.

Ding.

The elevator announced we were on floor 26, and the doors opened for us to get out. I was nervous and didn't know what to expect. We entered the condo, and I went straight to the bedroom. It was dark throughout our place beside the hall light. I cut on our bedroom light, and it immediately went dark again. I turned around, and Von had cut the light back off.

I backed myself all the way against the wall. I was trying to prepare myself for a brutal beating. "Don't move," he ordered me.

Von's phone rings. "Yeah. Okay," he says, holding the phone against his face. He leaves the room. Scared to move, I remained standing in place. Maybe he got a business call and must leave. I only hoped. I could hear him leave out the front door. For a moment, I felt peace. I was glad he was gone. However, that feeling was short-lived. About 5 minutes passed, and I heard the front door open. He walks into the room and begins to undo his tie. He stares at me with malice.

"So, you want to dance with niggas and have them rub all over your body, huh?" he sarcastically asked me.

"Von, it wasn't like that. Why did you agree to let me dance with him?" I shouted. I entered his personal space to get an answer and soften his heart towards me. He looked at me like I did something wrong. Biting his lip, he snatched me by both of my shoulders and guided me to the bed.

"Get yo ass in that bed and don't move," he said while shoving me down on the mattress. He scurried out of the room again. I'm left there, wondering what he was up to. Next thing you know, my eyes got big from utter shock. I couldn't believe the sight before my eyes. Von walks back in holding the hand of some bitch. She barely had any clothes on. She was wearing a black trench coat and champagne-colored heels.

Her hair was curly and in a half-up, half-down hairstyle. Her bundles flowed all the way down her back. I can't lie; she was a beautiful woman. Although the room was dark, I could tell her makeup was flawless. The light from the hallway still gave me enough visual to see inside the room.

He proceeded to take his clothes off. His masculine physique stood in the middle of the dimly lit bedroom, and his massive dick hung between his thighs. I stared at him with so much hatred. Was he about to make me watch them have sex? This was a new low. Standing there in all his nakedness, he began to massage his third leg. Come suck this dick, he nodded his head for her to approach him. She slowly unbuttoned her coat and unhooked the belt that was wrapped around her waist.

The coat fell off her shoulders and onto the floor. She was completely naked. I continued to watch as she smiled and sashayed over to him. Rubbing the middle of his bare chest, she slightly turned to acknowledge me.

"I sure will, Daddy," she said lustfully and dropped to her knees. I was disgusted. I turned my head away from them.

"You better look at us, or I'll make you suffer, Trinity," he warned. Afraid of what he might do, I turned back around to watch this freak nasty ass shit. She happily took Von's curved rod into her cheeks. She placed both her hands on his legs and slobbered on the shaft of his 9-inch stick.

Von rested his left hand on the top of her head and leaned his head back in pleasure. His eyes were completely closed. She challenged herself to go deeper. Her head bobbed back and forth with a steady motion. Her plump ass cheeks bounced as she slurped and sucked on him loudly.

"Shitttt," I heard him moan out loud. He moved his hips around her mouth. He moaned out in pleasure. Opening his eyes, he focused on me.

"You see this? She is a woman who knows how to respect and please her man." I rolled my eyes and swatted him away with my hand. That must have pissed him off because he started fucking her mouth hard. He pumped in and out while grabbing her ponytail for support. Her head rocked back and forth fast. She began choking, but he didn't care. He kept going, forcing every inch of her mouth down his manhood. She screamed loudly with each stroke. He never took his eyes off me. I could tell he was about to cum. He abruptly stopped her before nutting in her mouth. His facial expression eased up.

"Stand up." He quickly ordered her off her knees. She stood up and began to tongue kiss him. I watched as they both locked lips with each other with so much passion. She was trying to swallow his face with her mouth, and he allowed it. This motherfucka is insane, I thought to myself. He flipped her around and palmed both her breasts in his hand all while watching me. She was now facing me and loving every minute of this. She smirked at me as he rubbed on her titties and kissed her passionately on the side of her neck. She moved her body like a snake, grinding her bare ass across his manhood.

They both stared at me seductively, and that sent chills down my spine. They were disgusting. He walked her over to the foot of the bed and bent her over. She positioned both hands on the bed and arched her back. Her long weave fell between their bodies. Grabbing his thick pole, he entered her from the back. She let out a pleasurable moan. Tears fell from my eyes, knowing that this man didn't respect me.

Placing one hand on her shoulder, he continued to fuck her from the back like I wasn't even there. He slowly rolled his hips inside her. She tilted her head in my direction to taunt me. She wanted me to see her getting pleasured by my man. He was obviously making her feel good because he had her eyes rolling to the back of her head. Speeding up his strokes, he slammed every inch of his stiff dick inside her. She screamed out in blissful pain. I couldn't stop crying.

This can't be happening, I thought to myself. Tears flooded my face watching those two have sex.

"I'm about to cum," he announced, looking at me with his sadistic ass. After a couple more pumps, he pulled out his manhood and exploded his cum all over her ass cheeks. Thank God it was over, I thought. Now this bitch can go home, and I can get some rest. She got up and went to pick up her coat.

"Wait, D'avyonne, I want you to eat my girl's pussy," he said, smirking at me, with his hands clenched together across his sweaty chest. She was taken aback for a second but dropped her coat on the floor. This bitch will literally do anything he say.

"What? Hell no!" I shouted and tried to get off the bed. With one finger pointed towards the ground, he jumped at me. "Bitch, don't you dare get up or I'll break every bone in your fucking body," he assured me. I quickly sat back against the headboard.

"Goddamn you, Von, don't you do this!" I pleaded with him not to let this happen. He walked over to me, and I grabbed the palm of his hand.

"Von, please," I begged again. He yanked his hand away from me and began to hike my dress up. He forcefully removed the yellow thong underwear I had on. He waved his fingers for her to come over to me. She bent down to kiss me on the lips, and I tried to move my head away. Catching me off guard, I wasn't fast enough to dodge the peck she gave me on my lips. She laughed. She was really enjoying this. This bitch was sick in the head just like him.

He reached over to rub my head. I guess that was his way of trying to keep me calm.

"You're going to do this," he demanded, yanking my hair backwards. He gave me a look that told me he would hurt me if I didn't comply. She walked back to the foot of the bed and bear-crawled between my legs. My heart sank into my stomach. There was nothing I could do. She massaged both of my inner thighs in a circular motion. She lay face down and started planting kisses on my inner thighs. Von left my side and walked over to our black and gold marble dresser.

He grabbed something and walked back over to us. Holding whatever it was in his hand, he put it in his mouth and lit it with a lighter. Now I see; he went to get his blunt. This chick was trying to torture me and tease me at the same time. My adrenaline was rushing throughout my body like a raging river. I took deep breaths to control my emotions. With each kiss, she moved her tongue closer towards my pussy.

I felt a tingling sensation when she arrived at her destination. She slurped on the inside of my lady box. My legs jumped at the feeling of her tongue inside me. Her mouth felt cold and soft on my lady parts. My mind didn't want this, but my body was reacting to it in a different way. Von inhaled on his blunt and blew smoke in the air. He watched as she spread my legs farther apart and nose-dived deeper into my wet goodies.

Her head twirled with the motion of her tongue. She went crazy giving me head. I clenched the covers with both hands. She sucked profusely on my clit, and her tongue slipped down my ass. I couldn't believe this girl was eating my ass, but it felt good. Her tongue worked its way back up to my g-spot, and she flicked on it fast. My legs began to shake uncontrollably. The muscles in my pussy tightened up and started convulsing. I couldn't stop it, and within seconds, I exploded in her mouth.

This was wrong, and I cried softly due to feeling guilty. Von was still puffing on his blunt. I turned away from him, not wanting to look at the man standing before me. I felt sick to my stomach. The lady got up and began putting on her jacket. Just like that, she was gone after violating me.

Von didn't even say bye to her. It was like she knew what time it was. I curled up in the bed wishing I was anywhere but here. I hated him so much. I could feel him standing over me. Suddenly I felt small kisses on the top of my forehead. I could smell the weed on him.

"You did good," he said while placing his hand on my thigh. I quickly knocked his hand off me. I wanted to say, "Bitch, don't touch me," so bad. I wasn't stupid, though. He quickly replaced his hand back on my knee to let me know he was in control.

"Nitty, let's get in the shower and clean off." I used to love that nickname. Now, I cringe every time he calls me Nitty. I wanted to say so badly, "Boy, fuck you and your slavery pet name."

I knew better, though. He gently helped me out of the bed. We both walked into the restroom. I couldn't help but look at my reflection in the mirror. My eyes were puffy from crying so much. Von slid the shower glass back and turned on the faucet. After being satisfied with its temperature, he instructed me to get in. He followed right behind me after grabbing two small towels. Our shower was huge and had multiple shower heads we could stand under. I made my way under the farthest shower head against the opposite wall.

"Here," he said, handing me a towel and squeezing some Dove soap in the middle of it for me. I quickly began scrubbing my body, trying to erase that bitch's saliva and scent off me. Von soaked up his body and began to wash off the sins he had just committed. He didn't touch me, and I thank God for that. I don't want him touching me ever again. We both went to our side of the bed and buried ourselves under the cover. Von scooted over to my side and wrapped his arm around my waist. I wanted to remove his arm from around me so badly but didn't have the energy to get into a fight with him.

"You did good tonight," the dummy thought he complimented me. I couldn't help but be sarcastic.

"Yeah, I don't even think I need a man. She ate pussy better than you," I boasted against my better judgment. Von burst out into laughter.

"Oh word? I'll make sure to make this a reoccurring thing then," he happily stated. I got quiet.

"Hello, cat got your tongue? I thought so. Girl, stop playing with me," he warned. He turned back over to his side of the bed, and soon I heard him snoring. I just lay in bed, completely lost in my thoughts. I couldn't help but replay this night's events over in my mind. When I thought about the man I danced with, it soothed me. I saw visions of his handsome face in my dreams all night long.

The morning came, and I was still upset. I was so tired of Von disrespecting me. I just couldn't bear the sight of him anymore. Forcing me to watch him have sex with his side piece was the final straw. Then he made her nasty ass perform oral sex on me. I couldn't sleep all night after what took place.

I decided to leave Von without notice. He already left the penthouse to get his day started. I just needed to get away from him as quickly as possible. I left all my belongings at the condo besides the clothes on my back, driver's license, social security card, credit cards, and my keys. I just know he has a tracking device in my car or on my phone.

He always seems to know my exact location. Fuck it, I'll buy new clothes, a purse, a phone, and a car. I couldn't wait to leave the office so that I could stop by the bank and head to my hotel. I would stay there for about a week until I come up with a solid plan to leave town. I know I should've had the plan put together before trying to leave Von, but I couldn't stay another night with him. As I'm walking out of the office, my assistant Zoya stopped me. She was from India, 28 years old, and absolutely gorgeous. Zoya looked just like Jasmine from Aladdin in real time.

"Oh, you're not even going to say goodbye?"

Her accent had a bit of an attitude, and I thought it was cute. I smiled at her and gave her a hug. She hugged me longer than I expected. I knew that was her way of telling me she was going to miss me. I saw the sadness in her face once she let go of our embrace. She has been my personal assistant for the past 6 years, and we have grown close. I really saw her as a friend. While Kyra has been away at medical school, she helped fill a void in my heart. Nobody can ever replace Kyra as my best friend, though.

"When will you be back?" She asked in a concerned tone.

"I'm not sure, Zoya. I need to figure some things out. I know that you are more than capable of running things here until I return. The staff has direct orders to report to you for right now," I informed her. I turned to walk away, and she gently grabbed my hand.

"Trinity. You have been my dear friend for a long time now. You can't hide too many things from me. All I'm going to say is please be safe, and I pray you really get away this time. I'm here if you need me. It don't matter the time or day. If you call, I'm coming."

Tears filled her eyes, and I embraced her one last time before exiting the building. The truth is, I would never call her if I was ever in trouble. I care about her too much to involve her in my problems or to see her get hurt behind me. I jumped into my Bentley Bentayga SUV and headed towards the bank.

I walked into Navy Federal Credit Union and was greeted by one of the staff members.

"Hello, ma'am, would you like to go up front and speak to a teller or see a personal banker today?" she said with a big smile. "I would like to speak to a personal banker," I informed her.

She quickly walked off to the side where there were a bunch of cubicles. I saw her stop at one of the cubicles located near the back wall. She began speaking to someone. I couldn't see who the lady was talking to because the cubicle was blocking my view. She happily waved me over. Approaching them, I finally saw who the lady was speaking to. It was a middle-aged Caucasian man wearing a beige suit. His brown hair was slicked backwards and stopped at his shoulders.

He guided me to the chair across from him with his hand. He said, "Have a seat right here. My name is Paul, and I would like to assist you with your financial needs today. Can I please see your ID and bank card for the account? I also need you to verify your PIN code to the account." I dug into my pocket and pulled out my driver's license and bank card.

"Here you go, sir, and my PIN code to the account is 4479." I politely provided him with the requested information. He began to enter some data into the computer.

"Okay, your account is verified. What can I do for you today?"

"I would like to withdraw $500,000 from the account," I stated.

"Wow, such a large withdrawal. I'm sure I can do this for you. Anything over 20k requires my boss to approve the withdrawal. Stay right here, and I'll be back." He got up and disappeared into an office located off to the side. I sat there patiently waiting for about 5 minutes, and he came back accompanied by a heavy-set Caucasian man wearing a brown pinstripe suit and reading glasses.

The man had hair around the side of his head, but none at the top. His face had bad acne scars. "Hello there. My name is David McCallister, and I'm the branch manager. Paul tells me you would like to withdraw 500k. Is that correct?" He asked me for confirmation.

"Yes, that is correct," I said.

"Okay, I need to ask you some questions due to federal regulations. "Are you or any loved ones being held for ransom?"

"No, sir," I answered. "Are you withdrawing this money out of your own will?"

"Yes sir, I am," I answered.

"Okay, last question. Do you plan on participating in any money laundering activities?" That question took me by surprise. I ain't never heard of banks asking this shit.

"No, I do not and will not participate in money laundering activities," I responded with a bit of agitation in my voice.

"Thanks for answering these questions; it's just protocol," he tried to convince me. He turned his attention to the personal banker.

"Paul, do you have the account up? I would like to take a look real fast," he told the gentleman.

"Yes, boss," Paul said as he moved over so Paul could sit at his computer. I watched as the branch manager stared into the computer. Suddenly his eyes focused on me and quickly back to the computer. After a few minutes, he got up from the chair.

"We're almost done, Miss Coleman. I just must check something on my end."

He grabbed my ID and scurried back into his office. I saw Paul give an awkward look to the manager, but he tried to play it off. He smiled at me and stood there quietly. I got this uneasy feeling in the pit of my stomach. Something was off, but I figured it was just nerves because I was leaving Von. After about 15 minutes, David came out of his office smiling while carrying a blue Navy Federal Credit Union handbag.

"Sorry for the hold-up. We rarely have a withdrawal this big, so I had to verify your documentation one more time. I'll put your funds in this bag." I was ready to get out of there, so I didn't question anything he said or did. I was happy he was giving me the money with no issues. You know banks always think Black people are trying to commit fraud and don't have that type of money. It wasn't that long ago that I read a story about a young Black female doctor being denied service at a Chase bank in Sugarland, Texas, when she went in to cash a 16k check. I heard that she sued that branch for discrimination. Good for her! Here I am withdrawing 500K with no problems.

Thank you, God. I know Von will be mad, but it's my money too. I've made millions of dollars from being a real estate broker. It wasn't fair I had to share an account with him. That was just another chess move he made to control me. I know for damn sure he had other accounts without my name attached to them. He can only be mad that I took the money without letting him know, but I wasn't stealing anything. After Paul and David counted the money for me and placed it in the bag, I was headed to The Four Seasons downtown. I was tired. All I wanted to do was shower and go to sleep.

I loved the view I had from my office building on the 19th floor. I was sitting at my desk looking at the cars pass on Hwy 59. It was a beautiful and sunny day in Houston. I was reminiscing about the events that had taken place last night. I know Trinity was pissed off at me. I decided to take her to Steak 48 when I leave the office this evening. That would be my way of apologizing to her. I was lost in my thoughts when my phone started vibrating on the desk.

The name David Mc Callister flashed across my phone screen. I couldn't help but roll my eyes. Leaning back in my leather Rockefeller recliner, I answered the phone. Before he began talking, I beat him to the punch.

"Dave, man, you should've received the funds for the Vanderbilt property last week."

"Yes, the Vanderbilt property is now yours, Mr. Westley. That's not why I'm calling," he assured me.

"Okay, so what's up?" I asked, confused about what the call could be about.

"I'm calling because your girlfriend is here pulling out $500,000 from one of your joint accounts. I never met her before, but this withdrawal seems legit. Her ID and passwords match up to what we have. You've been so good to us. I just wanted to give you a call to make sure you know about this," he said.

I quickly sat up in my chair. "Wait a minute, are you sure my girl is there withdrawing 500K from my account?" I asked loosening my business tie from around my collared shirt.

"Well, technically it's her account too, but yes, she is. Her name is Trinity Coleman, and she has big, curly hair. Very beautiful young lady," he acknowledged.

"Hold on, David. Let me check something real fast, and I'll be back on the phone," I assured him.

"Sure thing! I'll wait," he responded. I removed the cellphone from my ear and went directly to the Now You See Me app on my phone.

As soon as I opened it, I saw Trinity was indeed at the Navy Federal Credit Union Bank in River Oaks. I closed my eyes and tried to keep my breathing at a steady pace. After a few seconds thinking about my next move, I got back on the phone.

"Hey David, you still there?"

"Yeah buddy, I'm here," he happily replied. I hate when this fool calls me buddy because we're not friends.

"Listen, give her the money, but please do not tell her you talked to me. Got it?"

"Alrighty, got it. Talk to you soon." I hung up the phone and grabbed my car keys to head home. It was obvious this bitch was trying to leave me. I told David to give Trinity the money because she won't be able to spend a dime of it anyway once I get my hands on her. I wanted her to leave the bank thinking everything worked out. I was about to pull the rug right from up under her. I wondered what items she may have taken from the house. My nerves were bad thinking she probably robbed the penthouse of all my luxury items. I drove over 100 MPH on the freeway. I'm happy I didn't get pulled over by the police. When I got to the penthouse, I started searching for any missing items. I entered our walk-in closet, and all her clothes were still hung up. Her accessories were still hanging up on the jewelry racks. I opened her dresser drawers, and each one was filled to capacity. Nothing seemed to be out of the ordinary. I sat on the bed and pulled out my phone to call her.

I heard her phone ringing in the distance. What the fuck? I got up to follow the sound. I spotted her phone sitting on the kitchen counter. Right next to her phone was the big diamond engagement ring I proposed to her with, and her purse. If she left me, why are all her things still here? Then it dawned on me. She thinks she is so smart. I had to laugh a little because this shit is comical. When will she realize she's not smarter than me? I bet she knows I have a tracking device on her, so she decided to leave everything here. Well, almost everything; she failed to locate where it's at.

She must think I only planted one in her clothes, shoes, phone, or car. Nope, I knew that would be the place she would suspect first. She hasn't figured out yet that there is literally a tracking device on her keychain. It's small and hidden on the inside of her mini-Louis Vuitton key pouch. I couldn't believe she was this bold to steal our money. We are a team and share that account, so it's stealing. On everything, I was going to fuck her up. The tracking device was leading me to the Four Seasons Hotel located downtown. I decided to take Tank along with me.

The heavy oak doors of the Four Seasons Hotel creaked open, allowing the warm evening air to mix with the coolness of the lobby. Tank and I stepped inside and began our walk to the receptionist desk. My black Timberland boots echoed on the marble floor. I'm instantly hit with the subtle scent of fresh flowers, arranged in elaborate displays throughout the lobby. Comfortable, high-backed chairs and low, elegant sofas are strategically placed, inviting guests to sit and relax. The fabrics are rich and tactile, a blend of silk and velvet that feels luxurious to the touch.

The security guard stood against the wall and nodded his head at us as we moved through the lobby. The receptionist behind the front desk was texting on her phone and laughing hysterically at her messages. She was every bit of ratchetness with that stiff-ass blue wig on her head and long, colorful nails she was rocking. She didn't bother to look up until my shadow fell over her.

Her eyes finally locked in on me, and she gave me a lustful smile.

"How can I help your fine ass?" she teased. I wasn't in the mood for small talk.

My jaw tightened. "I'm looking for someone by the name of Trinity Coleman. She checked in earlier. Give me her room number and keycard," I ordered.

The receptionist raised an eyebrow. "Now sir, you know I can't give you that information. I might help you out. What are you willing to do for me?" She asked, twirling her hair around with her finger. I turned to look at Tank. He chuckled because he knew this girl was annoying me.

"Don't play games with me." My voice was a low growl, the kind that sent shivers down the spine of anyone with a shred of common sense. She rolled her eyes at me.

"LIKE I SAID…" she began to get sarcastic. I quickly reached across the counter and choked her with my left hand. I yanked her ass as hard as I could towards me. She clawed at my hand with her long nails, but that just made me squeeze tighter. She struggled to breathe and quickly felt for the mouse on her computer. Once she grabbed it, I shoved her backwards.

"Hurry up," I barked as she looked up the room number.

"She's in room 412 on the 4th floor. She opened one of the drawers. Here is the keycard," she whispered while rubbing her neck. As we walked away, I heard her yell at the security guard.

"Wayne! You useless piece of shit. Why you ain't help me?" She screamed.

"Aye, those are the 163 Mafia niggas. You clearly didn't know who you were fucking with," he stated.

Tank and I got on the elevator, and I couldn't wait to get my hands on Trinity. Once we arrived at the door, I slid the card across the electronic card reader, and the light flashed green. Just like that, we were inside the hotel.

"Hey, I'll be out here in the living room area," Tank informed me.

I walked to the bedroom, and there she was, sleeping peacefully in the dark. Her hair was pinned up into a ponytail, and the cover lay across half her body, exposing her lace black bra. I loved when she slept in her undies. Damn, she was gorgeous.

I stood in the doorway and watched her sleep for a minute. Remembering she ran away and stole money, I finally shut the door to the room and locked it so she wouldn't be able to leave. Deciding to watch her a little while longer, I sat in the olive-green accent chair next to the bed. The room was filled with a heavy silence, broken only by the soft hum of the air conditioner.

Trinity slept peacefully under the thick comforter, her breathing steady, unaware of my presence in the room. For hours, my eyes never left her, following every rise and fall of her chest as she slept in the pitch dark. Trinity began to stir in her sleep as if she was having a nightmare. She abruptly opened her eyes and sat up in the bed. Squinting in the darkness, she began to search the room. Finally, her eyes fell upon my shadowy figure in the darkness.

"Hhhhh," she took a deep sigh. I sat there motionless and in rage. She knew she was in danger, and I needed my presence to be feared.

I was sleeping well, until I felt an extreme sense of darkness come over me. I tossed and turned for a while and couldn't shake the feeling. Something just didn't feel right. My hotel room no longer felt safe. I sat up and scanned the room. It was hard to see because the room was dark but illuminated only by the faint light filtering through the sheer curtains.

One thing I noticed is that my door was closed. I know I didn't close that door. Trying to remain calm, I kept looking around. The quiet of the room felt oppressive, and an inexplicable chill ran down my spine. Then I saw a manly figure sitting in the chair by the bed staring at me.

"Hhhhh," I let out a loud sigh. I tried to improve my vision but couldn't make out who it was. He remained sitting there quietly. He moved his head around as if he was analyzing me. For a second, I wondered if the boogeyman was real, because this felt like a scene straight out of a horror film. Fear took over my body. My heart pounded in my chest, and I couldn't catch my breath. Suddenly, I remembered there was a lamp on the nightstand next to me. I fumbled with the switch, finally casting a dim glow around the room.

The light revealed Von's presence. His eyes gleaming with a mixture of disappointment and anger. My pulse raced as the realization dawned upon me. This was no stranger, but the man I desperately wanted to get away from.

"Von?" My voice trembled with fear and disbelief.

He shook his head in a disapproving manner. "When will you fucking learn, Nitty?" He got up from his chair, and his tall frame was already overpowering me, just by standing there.

"Your problem is that you think you're smarter than me. I will always find you. There is no place you can hide from me. Then, you stole money out of our account. So now you're a fucking thief!" he scolded me.

"Come on, Von. You know that's not true. I'm no thief. I earned millions of dollars, and I only took 500k. That's nothing compared to what's in that account. Honestly, we're not married! We shouldn't even be sharing accounts!" I exclaimed. My words instantly pissed him off. He flew over to my side of the bed.

Yelling in my face, he replied, "We move as one unit. You don't do shit without me. Ever! It's stealing because you went behind my back." He slapped me, and my head jerked back.

He turned away from me for a second, and I decided to make a run for it. I jumped out of bed half naked and ran to the door, quickly unlocking and opening it. I ran out of the room as fast as I could. Von moved slowly. Now, I know why. Tank was blocking the front entrance, so I kept going until I got to the sitting area. I had nowhere to go. Von walked towards me.

I stood there shaking in my bra and panties, bracing myself for the impact. He backhanded me, and my vision instantly went black. I stumbled backwards, and he pounced on me like a lion that saw his prey. As soon as we hit the ground, he kneeled over me and pinned my arms between his thighs. He sat his big body down on my chest, and I couldn't move. I tried to free my arms from his grip, but the squeeze he had on me was unbreakable.

"Bitch…I…fucking…told…you…to…stop…playing…with…me!" he yelled. Each word was in unison with forceful slaps on both sides of my face. I wanted to shield my face, but my arms could not escape his strong grip. My face burned, and I was helpless. I screamed and cried out for him to stop, but he didn't let up. He continued to slap the hell out of me, and I felt myself losing consciousness. These definitely weren't no love taps.

POW. POW. POW.

The slaps turned into punches. My face weakened with every blow to it. My eyes rolled to the back of my head, and I began to drift off to sleep.

"Stop, stop, stop, bro! You gone kill that girl," I heard Tank say.

"Yeah, you're right. I am gone kill this motherfucka," I heard Von respond.

POW. POW.

He hit me two more times before getting up off me. I felt myself being dragged back to the room by my hair. All I could do was try to hold on to my hair, so he doesn't rip it off my head. When we got to the room, he yanked me up on my feet by my arm.

"Go back to sleep," he ordered before shoving me down on the bed. I quickly buried myself under the covers until I drifted off to sleep. I wanted to dream about a beautiful place far away from him. I dreamed I was sitting by a beautiful river surrounded by mountains. I was watching a waterfall and felt one with nature. I must have dreamed all night and later part of the next day. I didn't want to wake up and face reality.

When I did wake up, it felt like a ton of bricks hit my face. I suddenly had to pee. Cutting on the light in the bathroom, I was completely startled. Seeing my face saddened me. It was bruised and swollen like a pumpkin. I stood there crying my eyes out. I heard the bathroom door open, and I already knew who that could be.

Von walked in shirtless and wearing some all-black gym shorts. He stood behind me and softly planted kisses on my neck and shoulders. I wanted so bad to slap the fuck out of him. Of course, I did nothing. We just stared intently at one another through the mirror. I hated this man so much. He wrapped one of his arms around my bare stomach and dropped a beautiful jewelry box on the bathroom counter.

Tears streamed down my cheeks as I cut my eyes low at the box. I was not in the mood for gifts. The jewelry box looked like a stunning piece of art. It is crafted from rich, dark mahogany wood, polished to a mirror-like finish that gleams softly under the light. The box is small with smoothly rounded edges that give it a timeless, classic feel.

"I thought about what you said earlier. You said that we're not married, so we shouldn't even be sharing bank accounts. You're right. It's about time you become my wife." He reached past me and flipped the jewelry box open. I wanted to die right there. The box exposes a huge, beautiful, oval-shaped diamond ring sitting on a velvet blue plush pillow. The diamonds on the ring sparkled beautifully.

Any woman would be happy to sport this ring, but I wasn't because of the monster behind it.

"We're getting married," he said, smiling. He grabbed my left hand and placed the ring on my fourth finger.

"Are you asking me or telling me?" I turned around to ask him.

He paused for a few seconds, and then the bastard retorted, "Both." I just remained quiet as much as I wanted to fight this. I don't think I could afford to be hit by him today. He embraced me and began caressing my back. I just leaned against him, my hands down at my side. No way in hell was I about to hug him back.

Grabbing my waist, he picked me up and sat me on the counter. He eyed my bra and panty set. I saw the lust in his eyes. Having sex with me after hitting on me was a norm for him. I think it turned him on. He reached behind me and unhooked my bra. My voluptuous breast popped out, and he began caressing one with his hand while kissing the other one.

Damn, this felt good.

"Was I sick in the head like him too?" His kisses trailed down to my underwear. He kissed on my lace panties, and I felt the warmth of his saliva between my legs. I was completely aroused. Von's two fingers slipped inside my panties and began massaging my pussy. His fingers stirred my honey pot until it made its very own juice.

I held on to his head for support. He kept a steady pace as he rubbed my pussy lips around until I creamed on his fingers. He removed my undies all the way off and threw them to the side. Von quickly undressed, and his dick stood at attention. He leaned me back some more and held my thighs, while inserting every last inch of his rod inside me. The long thrust caused me to exhale. I had no choice but to hold on to his shoulders. Every time he took deep strokes, I clenched my pussy muscles on his dick.

I know he loved that and would be done sooner. He moaned from my wet box hugging on to his meat like a long-lost-friend. After a few more strokes, he came inside me. His cum dripped down my legs. I went directly to use the toilet. I needed to try to pee out all his sperm, or as much of it as I could. Von hopped in the shower while I sat there ashamed of my life. This can't be the rest of my life, I silently pleaded to God.

I was sitting at my work cubicle when Desmond came from behind me and whispered in my ear. "Will I see you tonight, beautiful?" The sound of his deep voice almost made my coochie purr like a hungry kitty. I hurried up and slid over to the side in my rolling chair.

"Des, you can't be doing that type of stuff out in the open. People will start to suspect something between us," I whispered in an agitated tone. He rolled his eyes and rested his hand on his gun belt. I couldn't help but stare at the gorgeous man in uniform.

I mean, he was wearing the fuck out of that uniform too. His shirt fit tightly across his broad chest, and his muscular arms were nicely oiled down. A silver nameplate right above his left pocket on his shirt read the name D. Biles. His pants fit perfectly on his toned waist. His chocolate skin glistened. His hairline edge-up was neatly cut and enhanced his low-top fade. I glanced down at his feet, and his black penny loafers were shiny. Desmond was sharp from head to toe. Damn, I almost creamed in my panties watching him.

"Hello Jean, are you there? he said, waving his hand in front of my face. Get dressed up tonight. I'm taking you to dinner, and then we will spend the rest of the night making love at my house." I looked around to see if anyone was watching us. Of course, Miss Rhonda's nosey ass was staring hard at us from across the room. Miss Rhonda was older than the majority of the police officers in the precinct. She was very wise because she had been on the police force for 28 years, but man, was she super nosy.

She stayed in everyone's business and didn't mind telling it too. I think the only reason she hasn't retired is because everyone's business is her entertainment. I love her, though. She gets on my nerves, but she is the most giving and thoughtful person I've ever met. Why is she staring so hard over here? I thought to myself. I turned my nose up at her, and she couldn't help but giggle. I quickly turned around to block her view from hearing what I was about to say to Des.

"Yes, that sounds good," I responded back to him and watched as his beautiful smile formed across his face. Damn, I thought to myself, admiring him once again. He stared back at me with so much passion. I can't believe me, and this man, have been in a secret relationship for two years. Our gaze with one another was quickly interrupted by Captain Dan Marley.

"Whitfield!" he screamed while hurrying towards me.

"The Texas Parole Department is asking us for surveillance videos our officers confiscated on August 23, 2014. The Deontae Wiley case is coming up in about two weeks, and they want to reassess any evidence they can about the night in question."

"Deontae Wiley?" I asked him, confused.

"Wait, that case sounds familiar." I scanned my brain for the answers, and it was like a light bulb went off in my head.

"Oh my God, I remember him. He was the 18-year-old kid that committed arson. He burned a local Chinese restaurant down to the ground, and the owner was still inside!" I informed Captain Marley.

"Yes, that's him. Great memory. He was only charged with manslaughter because the prosecution was able to prove he didn't know the man would still be in the building. Anyways, I need you to find that camera footage of that night. Log into our online portal and search the database until you find any video of that incident. Notify me when you do."

"Aww, come on, Cap. Who has time for that? Right now, I'm trying to work on bringing down the 163 Mafia Family. I got numerous reports they're running drugs through our neighborhoods and intimidating multiple residents out of their properties."

"Whitfield, did I ask you to do that? Leave that work to the FBI and our detectives," he ordered me.

"What you got time for is what I just asked you to do. Your application for detective is still in review. You're not one yet. We base promotions on one's ability to follow instructions. Now if you don't want to stay past work hours, I suggest you get started now," Captain Marley barked.

He then turned his attention to Desmond. Giving him a stern look, he said, "Don't you have some work to do? You stay over here." He glanced at me. Desmond held up his hands to surrender to Captain Marley. Desmond, fine ass, never takes anything seriously. He just laughed and backed away from my desk.

"I'm gone, Captain," he assured him.

"I'm serious, Whitfield. Get started on that, and I want an update by the end of the day", he said while walking away. I logged into the Texas Criminal Justice database, and I clicked on the evidence tab. Then I scrolled down the video footage tab and clicked it.

The system asked me to input a date. I entered the month, day, and year in the search field and hit the go button. The system advised me to wait a few seconds, and hundreds of videos popped up. How in the hell was I going to find the video I needed? I started scrolling, and there were so many videos to look at. The system must have given me all the footage from that day in the entire State of Texas.

"Hey!" A voice and body abruptly appeared behind me. I jumped from being frightened. I soon noticed it was Desmond again.

"What the hell, Desmond. Get from over there now," I snapped at him.

"Girl, calm down. I'm trying to help you narrow your search down because I can see from across the room that you're confused as hell," he stated. I felt him move closer behind me. He bent down over me and grabbed the mouse my hand was on. His face was pressed tightly against mine while he helped me. For some reason I wanted to glance at Rhonda's ass. Yup, she was watching and had an amused look on her face. I ignored her and returned my focus to my computer.

"Okay, this is how you narrow your search down. At the top right-hand corner of this screen is an option to select the city. Once you select Houston, scroll down to select one of the city's regions. What region did this happen in?" he asked me.

"Southwest Houston," I responded without looking back at him. Okay, so select South Houston and then select the zone that is Southwest. You see how the system now divides up the videos based on streets and intersections?

"You should be able to work through these videos a lot quicker now," he said.

I turned my body around to thank him. He didn't move back to give me space. Our faces were damn near in a kissing position. "Thank you, Des. This helped me out a lot. I would've been searching forever," I smiled bashfully at him.

"No problem, happy to help," he said, backing up off me and leaving me once again. I turned back to my computer to begin my search. I'm hoping this shit won't take long at all. Four hours later I'm still on the computer searching through videos. I'm tired and need a lunch break. I got up from my desk and headed to the break room. Desmond was already in there leaning against the wall talking to two of the precinct's best male detectives.

Detective Carter and Detective Fulton were both chatting it up with Desmond but got quiet when I entered the breakroom. "Hey, Miss Whitfield," they both said simultaneously.

"Hello, guys," I replied. I looked at Desmond but didn't initially speak to him. I went straight to the refrigerator and pulled my lunch bag out from the far back. I set my bag on the counter and walked towards Desmond. He continued to stand in front of me and was unknowingly blocking me from using the sink.

"What's up?" he asked me in a confused manner.

"Nothing, I just need to wash my hands," I said sarcastically.

"Oh shoot, I'm blocking the sink," Desmond noticed. Detective Fulton pointed at us and looked at Detective Carter for answers.

"What's up with these two?" he curiously asked. Detective Carter rubbed his chin and smiled.

"Man, they're acting all awkward because they're fucking and think nobody knows," he said. Detective Fulton's mouth dropped wide open, and they both began laughing hysterically. I was completely flustered and speechless.

How the hell did he know about me and Desmond, I wondered.

"What? Why would you say that?" I asked him nervously.

"Because it's true," he said, shrugging his shoulders. I turned to look at Desmond with an ice-cold stare.

He threw his hands up and replied, "Hey, don't look at me. I ain't say shit."

"Uh huh! So, it's true?" Detective Fulton shouted.

"Man, be quiet," Desmond told him. Stop embarrassing her, nigga," he said, irritated.

"Man, almost everyone up here knows y'all are messing around. Y'all really ain't that slick. Desmond, you STAY at her cubicle, dude. You both make googly eyes at each other all day, and anytime you leave for lunch, you're together!" Carter enlightened us. Well, I guess we haven't been doing a great job hiding it, I thought to myself. I was nervous now because I didn't want to get reprimanded by Captain Marley for this.

"Well damn, I guess I'm slow then, huh?" Fulton asked while looking at all three of us. Carter shook his head yes to indeed signal to Fulton he was slow. I proceeded to wash my hands in the sink and went and sat at one of the empty tables in the room. Desmond followed me and sat down next to me.

"Really, Des? Co-workers already know we're messing around, and here you come sitting next to me."

"So. Who cares?" he nonchalantly asked.

"I do. I care about my job. Captain Marley will fire our ass so quick," I reminded him. He chuckled and shook his head.

"You don't take nothing seriously, do you?" I asked, frustrated as fuck at him.

"Jean, I have known Captain Marley since the day I was born. He ain't firing us," he tried to assure me. I still wasn't convinced.

"So, you might've known of him, but that still doesn't mean anything." Desmond looked at me with a side eye.

"I didn't say anything about knowing of him. I know him really well! Captain is my family," he informed me.

"I meeean, we're all family up here; that doesn't mean he won't throw our Black asses out on the street," I said.

"No, Jean, he is literally my family. Captain Dan Marley is my uncle." I smacked my teeth so hard at him.

"Stop it, that white-ass man is not your uncle." Desmond laughed again. I watched as his shoulders bounced up and down in amusement.

"Captain Marley has been married to Charissa, my oldest auntie, for almost 40 years," he said, staring at me more seriously.

"Oh damn, I didn't know that," I stated.

"Nobody does," he responded.

"Now that I think about it, this makes perfect sense. You do whatever the fuck you want to up in here and don't get in trouble for it. Plus, you're never working," I teased him.

"Oh really? It's like that?" He rolled his eyes due to my current statements.

I knew he wasn't really mad at me. He is a legitimate goofball and sweetheart. After that, I ate my food while enjoying Des's company. He never brings a lunch to work. He just helped himself to my food without my permission. I didn't care. He can eat my food anytime because of the way he eats my pussy and ass. I was still going to be discreet with him at work. I don't want to draw any unwanted attention to myself. I don't need anything jeopardizing my chances of becoming a detective.

Des and I managed for two years to keep our relationship a secret, and that's how I would prefer it. I love him dearly. We were friends for three years before even being romantically involved. I never like to mix business with pleasure. However, he eventually wore me down being all charming. After an hour passed, I returned to my desk to finish the task I was given. Another hour passed, and I was becoming anxious. I still haven't found what I was looking for. I continued to scroll, and then I saw three videos packaged together. The caption on the videos read Bellaire Medical Center District. That sounded about right to me.

I clicked on the first video and almost jumped for joy. The first video was approximately 4 minutes long, and the time started at 10:04 pm. The camera was located across the street on a lamp post at the Wells Fargo Bank parking lot. It pointed down at the front entrance of the Chinese restaurant. After about 54 seconds into the video, Deontae appeared on the camera carrying a huge red gas jug. He began looking in the windows with both hands. After about another minute of staring into the building, he looked around to see if anyone was watching him. He pulled an object from his pocket and walked up to the door.

He quickly shattered the glass attached to the door. It was hard to tell what he had in his hand because the footage was kind of dark, since it was captured during the night. He stuck his hand between the shattered glass to unlock the door. He quickly began pouring gasoline all over the front entrance. He disappeared inside the building with the red gas jug. At 10:07 pm, he ran outside. He must've left the red gas jug inside the restaurant. He stood there for another minute, staring inside the restaurant. The flames engulfed the inside, lighting up the entire building.

At 10:08 pm, the video ends. I click on the second video. The quality of the video was better than the last since the alley had lights from the street poles. However, the footage was still dark because it was late into the night. The video catches Deontae sprinting down the side alley. At the same time, a tall male figure wearing a ski mask and hoodie was running in his direction. The guy pulls a gun from his waist and points it at Deontae's face. Deontae quickly throws his hands up and says something to him. They exchanged a couple more words.

The guy puts his gun back into the band of his shorts and runs off. One thing Jean notices about this mysterious man is he had a tattoo on his calf muscle. She couldn't determine what it was. Deontae stood there a few more seconds watching the man. He then continues to run away until he disappears from the camera's view. The video ends at 10:10 pm. Now that was interesting. The third video was 1 hour and 28 minutes long.

I was exhausted and decided to watch it another time. I have these two videos, which should be good enough for Captain Marley at this time. I emailed the two videos to him. I emailed the last video to myself and called it a day. All I was thinking about was going home to relax and later on meeting Des for dinner.

Later that evening….

Desmond had planned this night for months. He stood in front of the mirror, adjusting his black suit. His crisp white undershirt, subtly patterned tie, and polished leather shoes completed his sophisticated look. His hair is neatly cut, and a touch of cologne adds to his magnetic charm.

He stared at his reflection, feeling both excited and nervous. The anticipation of what he was about to do made his heart race. His reflection mirrored a confident, handsome Black man ready to take a significant step in his life. He decided to wait for Jean in the living room.

After a few minutes waiting, Jean's presence almost took his breath away. She looked stunning in a silk turquoise dress that accentuated her bodacious figure. The dress had a high split on the side that exposed her thick, moisturized thighs. Her diamond turquoise heels enhanced her look. Jean's warm caramel complexion glowed softly under natural light. Her shoulder-length curly hair cascades in voluminous, well-defined spirals that frame her face beautifully.

Her makeup is elegantly understated, with a hint of shimmer accentuating her features. Delicate jewelry and a pair of elegant heels add the final touches to her glamorous ensemble. Making eye contact with Des, she instantly showed him that radiant smile of hers. Tonight, they were going to the city's most prestigious restaurant, Le Chateau Vineyard.

As they entered the restaurant, the soft glow of chandeliers and the gentle hum of classical music set a romantic ambiance. Des led Jean to a private table in a quiet corner with a breathtaking view of the downtown skyline.

The evening unfolded with delicious courses and delightful conversation. Des found it hard to concentrate on the food, his mind racing ahead to the moment he had been envisioning. Finally, as the waiter brought dessert, he knew it was time.

"Jean," Des began, his voice steady despite the butterflies in his stomach. "These past few years with you have been the happiest I have ever been. You make every day brighter and every challenge easier to face. I can't imagine my life without you by my side."

Jean's eyes widened in surprise and then softened with love. Des stood up, reached into his jacket pocket, and pulled out a small red velvet box. He knelt on one knee, looking up at her with a gaze full of hope and adoration.

"Jean, I knew you were the one for me since the first time I saw you at the police academy. You walked past me wearing a black jogger's suit, carrying a red duffel bag across your shoulders, and your wavy hair was blowing in the wind. You took my breath away then, and you take my breath away now. You're beautiful from the inside out. I don't wanna change a thing about you, except your last name. Baby, will you marry me?" he asked, opening the box to reveal a sparkly, oval-shaped diamond ring.

Tears welled up in Jean's eyes as she saw Des, the man she loved wholeheartedly. She only dreamed of him asking her to spend the rest of their lives together. Now, her dreams were coming true. She could hardly speak but managed to whisper, "Yes, I will marry you."

The restaurant erupted in applause as Des slipped the ring onto Jean's finger and stood to embrace her. They kissed passionately, sealing their promise to each other. It was a magical moment they would cherish forever, a beautiful beginning to their new chapter together.

They finished dinner and headed home. Jean was on cloud nine. She couldn't believe she was one step closer to being Des's wife. Both Jean and Desmond didn't utter a word to each other in the ride home. They just passionately glanced at one another every few seconds. What was understood needs no understanding.

They both were ready to make love to one another, fuck, and anything in between. Jean's pussy was throbbing as she tightly clenched her thighs together. Des's dick was stiff inside his dress pants. Jean's eyes lit up when she saw the bulge in his pants. His dick was so hard his pants looked crooked. She just knew she was about to get that work.

They pulled up to the beautiful one-story home that was gifted to Des by his parents. Des hopped out of the car and jogged over to

Jean's side of the car. He opened her door and grabbed her hand to assist her getting out of the car. Before she could head towards the front door, he gently shoved her against the car. He passionately kissed her on the lips and twirled his tongue inside her mouth. She left markings of her lipstick all over his mouth. He didn't care. Both of their lips were in sync, twirling and sucking on each other's tongues like it was their last supper. Jean placed her arms around his neck, and her lips never skipped a beat as she continued to tongue wrestle with Des.

He quickly got down on his knees and stuck his head under her dress. He pulled her maroon bikini panties down to her ankles. "Des, people are going to see us; stopppp," she began to moan in pleasure. Her eyes began to roll to the back of her head. He stuck his moist tongue at the top of her wet pussy and began flicking it on her sweet-tasting pearl. His head danced around her dress.

"Ouuuu Shitttt," she moaned some more.

"Des, the neighbors are going to catch us," she looked around nervously. Her legs started to bend a little from all the pleasure she was receiving.

"You like that?" Des asked while fast stroking the inside of her pussy with his tongue.

"You sure you want me to stop?" he asked her while slurping and licking on her wet goods simultaneously. He had that pussy leaking.

"No, don't stop," she whispered. He opened her legs wider and took small bites on the outside of her thighs. He rubbed two of his fingers across her swollen twat. After massaging the outer entrance of her neatly shaved box, he gently slid his fingers inside of her.

"Fuckkkkkk," she moaned some more.

She quickly soaked his fingers with her juices. He began to finger fuck her while placing small kisses on the outside of her pussy. She felt every thrust of his fingers sliding in and out of her at a steady pace. Her legs began to shake. He didn't want her to cum just yet. He removed the panties from her legs and quickly got up off his knees. Des picked Jean up and carried her across his shoulders into the house. He headed straight for the bedroom.

Arriving at their final lovemaking spot, he put her down on the bed. She quickly removed her dress, exposing her voluptuous body. Her titties bounced as she slid closer to the headboard. Des was removing every piece of his clothing as quickly as possible. Finally, he stood before her naked with a curved dick on hard. The veins on that thick monster he was blessed with looked like he could be mixed with part horse.

As he crawled into the bed, Jean invited him between her legs. She opened them as wide as they could go, but Des had another position in mind. He flipped her over on her stomach and arched her caramel-colored ass in the air. He quickly inserted his thick shaft into her pussy. Jean's face was smashed into the mattress. Des began to grip her perfectly shaped cheeks with his strong hands and slow-grinned his manhood inside her.

"Damn, this pussy is mine forever," he said while slapping her on the ass with a little force. Jean gripped the sheets tighter. Des began to speed up his strokes.

"I said this pussy is mine forever, right?" He slapped her on the ass again.

"Yes, baby, this is your pussy forever," Jean acknowledged in a pleasurable tone. That turned him completely on. He now wanted to punish her body, but in a good way.

Her ass cheeks clapped as he quickly pumped in and out of her. Jean buried her face deeper into the mattress. Her muffled screams continued to arouse him. He gave her pussy quick and forceful pounds. "MRS. BILES, take daddy's dick," he shouted. Jeans's entire body was jerking forward from the intense fucking Des was doing.

"Oh shit, baby. I'm about to come, "he hollered. Jean's body started trembling. Within seconds, Des exploded his cum inside her, and Jean's juices dripped down her thighs. They both climaxed at the same time. It felt magical. Together they lay in bed with their bodies intertwined until they drifted off to sleep.

After a couple of hours of sleeping, Jean's eyes popped open in the dark. She remembered the video footage she emailed herself earlier. Jean was curious to know what was in this last video. She felt around the nightstand for her phone. Her fingers tapped the screen, and her phone lit up, allowing her to see a little better in the dark. Her phone showed the time of 3:25 am. Jean got out of the bed and headed for Des's home office to use his desktop computer. Walking down the hallway, she realized she was still moist between her legs, and her thighs were sticky.

"I need to get my ass in the damn shower," she spoke to herself. She rerouted to the bathroom. She absolutely loved Des's bathroom.

It was like stepping into a serene, spa-like bathroom filled with natural light. The centerpiece is a large, freestanding garden tub with sleek, curved edges. It sits under an expansive window that offers a view of a lush, private garden in the backyard, bringing a sense of calm and nature into the space. The white marble tiles extended across the floor, adding a touch of luxury.

To the side, a frameless glass shower stands in a corner, with floor-to-ceiling glass panels that make the space feel open and airy.

Inside, the shower is lined with mosaic tiles in earthy tones, echoing the natural feel of the garden. A rainfall showerhead hangs from the ceiling, while a built-in bench and toiletry niches add comfort and practicality.

Des parents remodeled the home before gifting it to him after they retired and moved to Phoenix, Arizona. Jean couldn't wait to share this home with Des once they got married. She stepped her naked body inside the glass shower and turned on the shower head. The warm water ran down off her glistening body. Turning around to let water hit her backside, she was startled to see Des in all his glory standing before her on the other side of the glass.

"What the hell," she blurted out. His thick man-pole was standing at attention. She glared back at him with those intense bedroom eyes. At that moment, he was the hunter, and she was his prey. He was ready to pounce and gobble her up. He opened the glass door and stepped inside the shower. Des wrapped his left arm around Jean's waist to press her up against his body. He bent down to suck on her round breasts. Her nipples became hard from the lip action Des was giving her. His lips felt soft on her wet skin. Jean arched her back, and the water soaked her hair, giving it the wet and wavy look.

"Des, I got to get started on some unfinished work," she informed him. He smirked and guided her down to her knees. She looked up at him, and he gently grabbed her chin. Leaning against the shower wall, he spoke to her softly.

"I got some work for you. Suck this dick, bae", he ordered. Water continued to pour down on the couple. Jean took her wet hands and grabbed Des's thick pole. She began to give it a two-twist twirl in a repetitious motion.

Jean started with the tip by giving it soft kisses. She slowly swirled her tongue around the shaft of his dick. She made sure to flick her tongue across his urethra hole.

"Yeah, that's it, baby, keep going," Des motivated her. She removed her hands from his piece and forced as much of it as she could down her throat. Making sure to not use any of her teeth, she continued to suck backwards and forwards on his manhood. Des grabbed the back of her head to assist her.

He slowly moved his hips around to face-fuck her. Jean sucked faster and harder. His eyes rolled to the back of his head. Des picked up speed and began to fuck her mouth harder. With both hands on the side of her head, he pumped his dick in and out of her mouth.

"OH SHIT, I'M ABOUT TO BUST," he called out while gripping her head tighter. With a few more pumps, he exploded his nut all over her chest. Jean quickly got up off her knees. They both soaked their bodies up with soap and rinsed off. Des went to lie back down in the bed. Jean grabbed her robe on the back of the door and headed for the office room.

She sat at the computer and typed in the numbers 1234 to unlock the computer screen. All she could do was shake her head because Des chose the easiest password ever. Anyone would be able to hack into his computer. Jean logged into her email and downloaded the video she sent to herself at work. The video started playing, and the camera is facing the backstreet of the restaurant.

The backstreet is narrow and dimly lit, with only a few flickering streetlights. The atmosphere appears to be quiet. The alleyway entrance on the side of the building casts some light onto the backstreet pavement. Jean was tired, so she didn't feel like watching this video for an hour and a half. However, she was determined to see what was on it. For over an hour, Jean was watching literally nothing. She was bored out of her mind sitting there. Suddenly, at 9:55 pm, a dark- colored pickup truck pulls up and parks on the side of the street.

The driver leaves the headlights on. There was literally no activity until about 10:06 pm. Suddenly, Jean spots the same masked individual wearing a hoodie from the second video she watched earlier. He ran out into the front of the truck with his gun pointed at the truck. He instantly let off shots that flew into the windshield.

He walked around to the passenger side and fired a couple of rounds inside. The driver-side door opened, and somebody slid out of the truck. They appeared to be crawling on their stomach. The gunman ran to that side of the vehicle and fired rounds into that person's flesh. The body stopped moving. The gunman took off running and turned down the alleyway.

"What the fuck. Two crimes were committed around the same time," Jean spoke to herself. That's how he ran into Deontae, she thought to herself. She wondered how come she hadn't heard about this story.

"Who the fuck was in that truck?" she whispered out loud. She was definitely going to get to the bottom of this. She forwarded the video to Captain Marley before heading off to bed.

The next morning, Jean couldn't wait to get to work. Her and Des pulled up to the police station separately as if they hadn't just left each other's side. Jean marched into Captain Marley's office while he and Detective Carter were having a private meeting.

"Excuse me," Captain Marley said, agitated.

"Don't you see two men in here handling business?" Detective Carter joked.

"Sorry, Cap, this can't wait!" Jean walked behind Captain Marley's desk. I sent you a video to your email. Click on it for me.

He looked at Detective Carter in a confused manner. Detective Carter shrugged his shoulders.

"You're kind of bossy this morning, aren't you?" he sarcastically blurted out. Jean looked at him and placed her hands on her hips.

"Come on, Captain, this is serious," she informed him. He pulled up the video. It appeared to be nothing.

"Okay, what are we looking at here?" he asked. "Fast forward the video until the time reads 10:06 pm. After doing what he was told, he finally saw what Jean was so intense about this early.

"WOAH," he yelled. Captain Marley quickly grabbed his glasses out of the center drawer. This now had Detective Carter's attention. Carter scurried behind the desk, and all three of them watched the homicide of what appeared to be at least two people.

"Where did you get this video from?" he curiously asked.

"Sir, it was part of the evidence used against Deontae Wiley years ago. You asked me to pull the videos from that incident, and this was one of them. Don't you see, Cap? It was multiple murders that occurred that night, around the same place, and around the same time!" she stated.

"I don't fucking believe it," Detective Carter had a shocking expression on his face. Jean and Captain Marley both turned their attention to Detective Carter.

"I don't recall ever seeing this video. All evidence has to come through me. What homicide case is this? Refresh my memory," Captain Marley asked. Detective Carter held up his index finger while jogging off. A few minutes later he came jogging back into the office carrying some manila folders with Detective Fulton.

"Jean, replay the video from the time the truck pulled up," Detective Carter politely asked. All four of them watched the video.

As the video was playing, Des walked by looking curious. He was wondering what was going on. He was so nosy. Jean saw him standing at the door from the corner of her eye but continued to ignore his presence. After the video was done, detective Fulton shouted, "I recognize that scene from anywhere. That is definitely the Coleman couple!"

"WHAT!" Shouted Captain Marley. Captain Marley continued, "How did you two drop the ball on this case is the better question?"

"What do you mean, Cap?" Detective Fulton asked.

"I mean, this video could have potentially helped solve the murders of two people. How did y'all miss this?" he scolded them.

"I don't know, Captain, maybe we thought nothing was on the video," Detective Fulton said.

"It's clear you both didn't thoroughly look at all the video evidence that was confiscated from that night," Captain Marley said, annoyed.

"Who are the Coleman couple?" Desmond asked while walking in.

"We were assigned to the case, but it went cold a few years ago when we failed to find any leads. Their teenage daughter was cute as a button. I will never forget the sadness in her eyes when we told her that her parents were murdered on her birthday." Detective Carter spoke.

"There's more! There is a second video that is a couple of minutes long. It shows the gunman running down the alley, and Deontae Wiley is coming from the other way. The gunman must've thought Deontae was a threat to him at first because he held him at gunpoint. They exchange words before the gunman takes off and leaves Deontae standing there.

"This shit is crazy!" Detective Fulton yells.

"I say talk to Deontae. Maybe it's something he can remember about the dude that we can't see from the cameras," Jean suggested.

"That's a great idea. Detective Fulton and I will schedule some time to go see him," Detective Carter announced. "I want to go with y'all," Jean stated excitedly.

"No. Leave this to the big boys," he spat. Her smile turned into a frown, and Desmond could see her feelings were hurt.

"Well, it seems like the "big boys" dropped the ball on this one. If it weren't for Jean, you wouldn't be one step closer to solving this old-ass case. So, the least you can do is take her." Desmond wasn't playing with Detective Carter. He was deadass serious and gave Detective Carter a stern look. Captain Marley was amused watching Desmond stand up for Jean.

"I have to agree with you, Officer Desmond," Captain Marley spoke up. "Take Jean with y'all to the jail when you go visit Deontae Wiley."

"No problem, Captain," Detective Fulton obliged. Everyone was leaving the office when Captain Marley stopped Jean at the door.

"Officer Whitfield," he commanded her attention. She turned around to face him.

"Good work today. That's great DETECTIVE work," he winked and complimented her. Jean smiled big before exiting his office.

I was sitting in my car outside the station steaming mad. My mind was racing as I thought back to the night of the double homicide. It had been a messy job. The crime scene was horrific, and it spooked the community that someone could be evil enough to harm people like the Colemans. I texted Detective Carter to come outside so we can talk where no one would be listening to our conversation.

I couldn't believe what I just watched on Captain Marley's computer. The surveillance footage sent chills down my spine. It had been years since that awful night, and I thought the evidence had long since been forgotten and destroyed. But now, it had resurfaced, and it won't take long for somebody to go snooping and possibly find the culprit responsible for those murders.

Officer Whitfield had found the video while trying to find footage regarding the Deontae Wiley case. The footage from the Coleman murders must've been accidentally picked up and misfiled with Deontae's case. I saw Carter exiting the building and heading my way. He hopped in the car, and I didn't wait to go off on him.

"You DUMB motherfucka. I specifically told you to destroy all the footage gathered by the team that night. How is it that the video ended up in our database system?" He sighed and threw his hands up like he didn't know what happened.

"Look, mayne. It's not my fault! When Marcus from the tech team came to grab all the tapes, I insisted he destroy that one and told him nothing was on it. He is the one to blame, not me," he stated. I slammed my fist on the steering wheel, cursing Carter out immediately. I trusted him to handle it, and now everything was at risk. If that tape got out, it wouldn't just be the killer going down—it would be both of us too.

"No, it's your fucking fault, dumbass! Marcus wasn't paid ten bands to destroy the evidence. YOU WERE NIGGA!" I yelled.

I knew the city of Houston was disappointed that the killer was never found. Everyone wanted answers, including our state politicians. "Carter, do you know this new evidence could blow up in our faces once people like Officer Whitfield start digging around? This type of corruption could bring the police force down to their knees if anyone knew we had anything to do with preventing the case from being solved. Our lives would be over," I explained.

Detective Carter rubbed his hands over his face, looking extremely troubled as Detective Fulton felt. A few years ago, a young man named Jervonte Westley reached out to us with a referral from Mr. Donvincio Saldana. He said he had some propositions for us and would pay both of us 10k. We heard him out and agreed to work with him without a second thought. Money from the dope game is always lucrative. These police salaries don't pay us enough for the bullshit we deal with daily.

I made it clear to Detective Carter to destroy any evidence we found that night, including surveillance footage. The kid was an upcoming boss in the dope game and didn't want any heat coming down on him and his squad, who are now known as the infamous 163 Mafia Family. Carter and I were both opportunists and had taken the money without a second thought. We were homicide detectives, so destroying evidence was supposed to be an easy task. We are usually pretty good at making sure there are no loose ends.

Thanks to Detective Carter, we now have some. "We must see what Deontae Wiley remembers from that night. Let's head over to the prison now before Officer Whitfield gets a chance to see him. You call Von Westley to explain the situation and that you fucked up," I ordered. I cranked up the car and sped out of the parking lot.

Carter's face hardened. "Don't pin this all on me, Fulton. We've both done things we're not proud of. This isn't just on my shoulders," he hissed. I could tell he was scared to call Von and was deflecting.

"Just call him!" I yelled. Carter nodded, his expression grim. "Fine, I'll call him after we see Deontae Wiley. What about officer Whitfield? She's going to be mad when she finds out we went to see Deontae without her."

I smirked at that question. "We're just gonna tell her we were already by the prison, so we stopped to see him. We will tell her that he doesn't know shit. For her sake, she will leave this alone."

"She is young and full of determination. Not to mention, she is trying to be a detective. She is not leaving this shit alone," he warned. What Carter was saying was true. As much as I hoped she would, Jean ass wasn't going to let this go. We both rode in silence for the remainder of the ride. We pulled up to Beauford H. Jester prison in Richmond, Texas.

We stepped out of the blistering Texas heat and into the cool, sterile corridors of the state penitentiary. The heavy steel door clanged shut, sealing us off from the outside world.

"Hey Penelope. We're here to see inmate #8974, Deontae Wiley. I spoke to the guard at the desk. She nodded, checking the roster before buzzing us through another door leading further into the building. A male guard I didn't recognize walked us down the narrow, dimly lit hallway.

The room we entered was stark, with a single metal table bolted to the floor and chairs on either side. We took our seats and waited for Deontae to arrive. Shortly, one of the guards walked Deontae into the room, and he sat on the other side of us. He certainly has grown up these past few years. He was medium built, had a small goatee beard, and a thin mustache. His hair was parted into plats. His eyes were light brown, and they matched his skin complexion. He gave us both blank stares, which told us he was ready for us to explain our reason for seeing him today.

"Mr. Wiley," Carter began with his interrogation. "We appreciate your time. You're not in any trouble. We need to ask you a few questions about the night on August 23, 2014." Deontae shifted in his seat.

"I already told y'all everything about that night. I'm serving my time, so what more do you want from me?" he asked.

"We're not here to accuse you of anything," I spoke up. "We think you might have information that could help us solve another case. That same night there was a double homicide. You had to have run right past the vehicle with the dead bodies in it. You were seen on camera running into a gentleman fleeing the scene of the crime. Can you tell me what you remember about that man?"

Deontae's eyes flicked to me and then Carter and back down to his hands. "I really don't know anything. The man thought I was a threat. When he realized I wasn't, he let me go. Once he was gone, I ran and didn't stop to pay attention to any crime scene," he explained, his voice low and guarded. I analyzed his demeanor to detect any form of deception.

"You briefly spoke to that man. Tell us anything you can about him. We want to know how he sounds, his height, and any scars." Carter pressed.

"Whatever you tell us can help us out a lot." Deontae shook his head.

"I'm telling you there is nothing! Dude had a hoodie and face mask on. It was dark that night, and the only thing I cared about was getting away from that restaurant. I have no idea who that man was or what he looks like. That's the truth," he ranted. The room fell into a tense silence. Carter and I shared looks, knowing we wouldn't get more out of him today.

I gazed sharply at him and leaned forward with my finger pointed downward on the table. "Okay, we believe you. Just make sure you stick to that story. For your sake, you better stick to that story and don't EVER deviate from it. Deontae glared at me with his head tilted sideways. He could sense the threat in my voice. He signaled for the outside guard to come get him. He stood up, and before he walked away, I encouraged him again to keep his mouth shut.

"You don't know nothing Deontae; keep it that way." He didn't utter a word; he left the room quietly. "See, he doesn't know anything," Carter sounded relieved.

"That motherfucka lying. If he keeps his mouth closed, I don't give a fuck," I nonchalantly replied.

As we were signing out at the receptionist desk, Sergeant Marley with the Internal Affairs Bureau came from the back. I absolutely loathed her. It was like she had it out for cops when she was supposed to be one of us. She had the biggest log up her ass; I won't even say stick because that's putting it nicely. "Well, if it isn't HPD's finest detectives. I didn't know you guys were here. What inmate are you here to see?" she spoke in a curious tone.

"We were visiting Deontae Wiley. Why are you here?" I asked in a condescending tone.

"Well, you know, I'm here taking inmate complaints regarding their cases as usual," she answered.

"Well, you do know most of them are lying to get out of prison, right?" I questioned her. She gave me a casual smile.

"Maybe, maybe not. It's my job to determine who is lying and who is not. I ALWAYS get to the truth," she stated in a stern tone.

The way she said that made me feel uncomfortable. It was almost as if she was implying something. "Anyways, how is my husband treating y'all over there at precinct 49?"

"Captain treats us well. We can't complain," Carter blurted out.

"Good." She patted him on the shoulder and exited the building. We left right out, right behind her. As soon as we got in the car, I instructed Carter to call Von. He took a deep sigh and dialed the number.

"Put it on speaker, man," I whispered. The phone rang twice before Von picked it up on the other end.

Von: Hey, what's up?

Carter: Von, I called to notify you of a little situation.

Von: What little situation?

Carter: Well, one of our police officers found surveillance footage of one of your guys fleeing the scene from the Coleman murders.

Von: WHAT! I paid you two fucking idiots to get rid of any evidence. How in the hell did y'all let this happen?

Carter: Calm down. You can't see the dude's face in the video. His entire face was covered. However, the video shows him running into a guy who is now serving time for another crime on the same night. They exchanged a few words before your guy took off.

Von: Don't tell me to calm down! This shit should've been handled years ago. Now I have to clean this shit up. Who was the other guy in the video, and what prison is he serving time in?

Carter: His name is Deontae Wiley, but we already interrogated him. He doesn't know anything.

Von: Man, you two got me fucked up if you think I'm going to rely on your information. That nigga gotta go, and so does that cop! I'll clean this shit up myself. Send me their information NOW!

Click. Von hung up the phone in Carter's face. "Man, just send him the information. It's out of our hands now," I told him. I started the car engine and headed back to the precinct. We got back to work, and I saw Whitfield sitting at her desk.

"Hey Jean," I called out while approaching her.

"Listen, we were already in the area, so we went ahead and saw Deontae Wiley. Her facial expression quickly turned to disappointment. "Look, you would've just wasted your time. He is adamant he doesn't know anything regarding the suspect from the Coleman murders," I informed her.

She got up from her seat and walked around her desk to speak with me. "Detective Fulton, maybe I can speak to him and help him remember the smallest detail. I need to talk to him. Why didn't y'all wait for me?" She continued to blab.

"Jean! Let it go. I'm telling you to let this one go," I pleaded with her. Our eyes challenged one another.

"I promise, I'll take you with us on the next case," I tried to reason with her. If only she knew they were a target now. I hated that because she was innocent in all this. Von would do whatever it took to protect himself and his men. Even if it meant destroying anyone who stood in his way, including police officers. She waved me off and went back to her seat. I left to finish my workday.

"Jean! Let it go. I'm telling you to let this one go," Detective Fulton's words played over and over in my head. I abruptly woke up in the middle of the night and sat up in bed. Des rolled over and placed his hand on my thigh.

"You aright, baby?" he asked me.

"Fulton," I mumbled.

"Fulton? What the fuck you dream about him for?" Des asked me.

"Shut up, Des. Something is not right with Fulton. I can't quite put my finger on it."

"Why do you say that?" he inquired.

"It's the way he looked at me when he told me to let seeing Deontae Wiley go. It was almost as if he was warning me versus telling me. Fulton, for some reason, does not want me to speak to Deontae. I don't know why, though. That's what I can't figure out, but I'm going to get to the bottom of it."

It's been a week since Detective Fulton and Carter went to see Deontae Wiley without me. I made it up in my mind that I was going to speak to Deontae Wiley myself. I can't ignore this gut feeling I have. Maybe I was grasping at straws, but I didn't care. If Deontae was going to trust me, I had to try an unorthodox approach. I went back to sleep for a few more hours before heading into work.

When I got there, I immediately looked up Deontae Wiley's personal information. His mother's address was listed. I decided to pay her a visit regarding her son. I saw that his mama stayed in Southpark off Martin Luther King Blvd. I passed up Burger Park and immediately got hungry. Their food is so damn good, but I'm on a mission right now. Pulling up to the house, I saw it was a young woman sitting on the porch. She was watching a young girl ride her bike in the yard.

"Excuse me. Is Miss Glenda here?" I asked, walking up on the porch. She looked at me with a mix of wariness and curiosity.

"No, she went grocery shopping at Fiesta. Can I ask what you want with her?" she replied. The girl ran over and asked her mom if something bad happened.

"My name is Officer Whitfield," I began, pointing to my badge hooked to the belt of my pants.

"I need to speak to her about her son, Deontae Wiley."

The woman's face tightened, her hand instinctively reaching to rest on the girl's shoulder. "Well, I'm his baby mama, and this is his daughter. What about him?" The little girl had to be around 9 years old.

"What's your name, ma'am?" I asked.

"I'm Joystina, and my daughter's name is Velvet Roots."

"Say what now?" I blurted out.

"Yes, Beyoncé's daughter is named Blue Ivy, but it doesn't compare to my baby. I love velvet everything, and roots are the strongest foundation in the ground. So, we named her Velvet Roots," she bragged.

POW.

I popped her in the face for naming that girl a stupid-ass name like that. I'm just kidding. For a second, I envisioned I backhanded her, but I quickly snapped out of my trance.

"Oh okay, that's beautiful," I lied.

I softened my tone. "I wanted to come by to see if his family could accompany me to the prison to speak with him about helping us solve another crime. He is not in trouble, but I believe he might have some information that could help us. He's been in prison for some years now, and he has a parole hearing coming up. If he helps us solve this crime, maybe he can get an early release." Joystina's eyes lit up with hope.

"You really believe this could help him come home early?" she asked me.

"I don't want to make any false promises, but I would do my best to help him in any way that I can," he informed her. Two of our detectives visited Deontae, but he told them he doesn't know anything. I believe if he is reminded that he has a family to get home to, he might be willing to talk. Thinking about what I said, she glanced down at her daughter.

"Sometimes, the only thing that can reach someone is the voice of the people they care about most," I continued.

"Why should we believe you? Everyone knows the Houston Police Department can't be trusted," she spat.

"That's not true. We are all not bad police officers. Look, I give you my word that I will try everything possible to make sure he comes home early."

There was a minute of silence. Joystina was trying to decide if she wanted to cooperate with me. She sighed, a tear slipping down her cheek. "I'll do anything to help Deontae come home early. This could be the new start he needs and finally be able to put that awful night behind him. Maybe he would feel better after telling what he knows. He could find some peace. When do you want us to go?" she asked.

"NOW," I emphasized. Joystina nodded slowly, as if coming to terms with the decision. She turned to face her daughter and began brushing her misplaced hairs back into a ponytail. "You want to go see your dad?" she politely asked her. The girl nodded her head yes. Joystina rushed

into the house to grab her purse. After she locked up the house, we all got into my patrol car and left.

We entered the prison, and I signed us all in at the receptionist desk. Joystina and Velvet Roots sat in one of the empty chairs. I notified the receptionist we were there to see Deontae Wiley. "Officer Jean Whitfield?" an unfamiliar voice called out to me. I turned around and saw a beautiful older lady with a gray afro smiling at me. She was wearing an internal affairs jacket and holding a bunch of files in her hand.

"Yes," I answered her, confused.

"My name is Sergeant Charissa Marley. I'm Captain Marley's wife and Desmond's aunt," she introduced herself. My mouth dropped, and I walked closer to shake her hand. She looked at my hand like it had mud on it. Then she quickly pulled me in for a hug.

"It's so nice to finally meet you," she said. I smiled and returned the compliment.

"It's so nice to meet you as well. How did you know who I was?"

Every time I come to the station, my nephew points you out. He absolutely loves you! He begs for me not to bother you, because you want the relationship to remain a secret. I chuckled at that because this boy can't hold water. "I can't believe I never saw you before," I said.

"Oh child, I be in and out of that station fast. I worked there for so many years in the past and refuse to stay longer than I should. What brings you here?" she asked.

"I'm here to see Deontae Wiley. I'm hoping bringing his family to see him will help me solve a cold case back in 2014," I answered.

"Detective Fulton and Carter were here last week, seeing the same young man," she spoke.

"Yeah, I know. Captain Marley told them to bring me along when they talk to him, but they purposely left me out."

"Is that right?" she inquired in a curious tone.

I continued giving her information. Do you remember the double homicide of Patrick Coleman and Charlene Coleman? Their pickup truck was shot up over on Bellaire Blvd," I explained.

"Yes, how can I forget? Detective Fulton and Detective Carter were over that case," she acknowledged.

"Right. Well, I found surveillance footage that shows Deontae Wiley running into the killer that night. The killer was about to shoot him but ran off instead after they exchanged a few words. Then Devontae took off towards the direction of the murdered victims. If he can help us solve this old case, I want to help him get released on parole. His hearing is coming up soon.

"If he helps solve that case, you have my word. I'll help him get paroled."

My mouth dropped. "Just like that," I asked her all excited.

"Just like that," she winked.

"Come on. I will walk with you all to the back. Deontae Wiley might be in the room already, since we were talking." She signaled for the receptionist to buzz us through the other side of door. We were guided to one of the rooms for special law enforcement and lawyer visits. Deontae was already sitting in the chair. He looked mad until he saw Joystina and his daughter. He quickly stood up and embraced them with hugs. Sergeant Marley signaled for me to follow her, and we stood outside the room.

"Whatever you learn here today, do not tell Fulton or Carter. I can't tell you everything now, but it's important you protect any information you have. Okay?" She asked for my cooperation.

"Okay," I replied. She walked away, and I went back into the room. Deontae, Joystina, and Velvet Roots were all smiling. And enjoying each other's company. I believe seeing his family is the motivation he needs. I prayed he had some viable information for me.

I stood in the prison yard, my muscles straining as I pushed through another set of push-ups. The sun beat down on my back, but I welcomed the burn. It was better to focus on the pain than the stress I was feeling regarding my upcoming parole hearing.

As I stood to catch my breath, I noticed something out of the corner of my eye. Two men, large and intimidating, making their way toward me. They walked with a purpose, their eyes locked on me, and there was no mistaking their intentions. The yard was crowded, but the noise faded as my senses sharpened. My heart pounded in my chest, and the adrenaline was kicking in.

I kept my breathing steady, assessing the situation. I've seen these two hardened, dangerous men who thrived on fear, affiliated with the 163 Mafia Family. I'm from the hood and have been in enough fights to know when trouble was coming, and this was trouble.

They were only a few steps away now. I tensed up, readying myself for what's about to come. I would have no choice but to try to defend myself. I quickly scanned the yard, calculating my options, knowing that in a matter of seconds, I would be fighting for my life.

Just as they closed the distance, one reached into his waistband and pulled out a sharp object resembling a knife. Suddenly, a loud voice cut through the tension.

"Wiley!" A guard called out from behind the fence, his voice firm and commanding. The two men hesitated, glancing at the guard, then back at me. The guard motioned for me to come over.

"You've got visitors. Let's go."

I didn't waste a second. Not giving away the relief I was feeling, I kept my face neutral. Walking towards the guard, I could feel the two men's eyes boring into my back, but they made no move to attack me. The guard's presence had disrupted whatever plans they had.

As I approached the gate, the guard opened it just enough to let me through, shutting it behind him with a loud clang. I quickly let out the deep breath I was holding in. The guard, a stocky man with a gruff exterior, gave me a nod.

"Are you alright, Wiley?" he asked, his tone low enough that only I could hear.

I nodded. "Yeah, I'm good. Thanks."

"Better watch your back," the guard warned me before leading me toward the visitor's area.

I walked silently, my mind racing on who could be visiting me. These weren't normal visiting hours. Regardless, I'm happy because they had just saved me from a dangerous situation. As I followed the guard down the corridor, I pondered why those two men wanted to hurt me. I can only think of one reason. It was a miracle that the guard's timing saved me. Next time, I might not be so lucky.

In this place, you always had to be ready for the next move, the next threat. But today, for the moment, I was safe. I got to the room, and the guard informed me the visitors were headed this way. I was mad as hell sitting there thinking about how I almost died today. A beautiful lady cop walked in, and that made me more irritated. I was not in the mood to deal with cops. My mood quickly turned to happiness when I saw Joystina and little Velvet tagging behind her.

I immediately stood up and embraced them. I was familiar with Sergeant Charissa. She frequented the jail a lot and spoke to inmates regarding their cases. I heard that numerous inmates have been able to go home because she found inconsistencies in their cases. She spoke to the lady cop outside the room for a couple of minutes. The cop returned, and we all sat down. Velvet and I sat on one side, while Joystina and the cop sat on the other.

The lady cop began to speak. "Deontae, my name is Officer Whitfield. I wanted to talk to you about a double homicide that occurred on the night of August 23, 2014. I know you had nothing to do with it, but I believe you might have some information that can lead me to the killer," she explained. I rolled my eyes.

"Look, I told the other cops that I didn't know anything. Just leave me alone about this shit!" I exclaimed. Before officer Whitfield could say anything else, Joystina chimed in.

"Deontae, tell her what you might know! Your parole hearing is coming up, and helping them might help you come home early. Look at your daughter! I was pregnant when you went to jail. She is growing up before your eyes!" Joystina cried. I took one look at my daughter and lowered my head.

"Deontae," the sexy-ass cop called my name.

"What man?" I spoke, irritated.

"You see that lady that was here earlier? Her name is Sergeant Marley, and she has agreed to help you come home early if you can give us any type of helpful information. This is your second chance and for you to finally start a life with your family," she stated.

If I tell you what I know, I'm as good as dead. The 163 Mafia Family just tried to kill me right before y'all got here. The guard was just in time; otherwise, I would've been stabbed to death. Joystina panicked and looked to Officer Whitfield for answers.

Okay, it looks like they might be trying to kill you before you talk. You might as well go ahead and tell me what you know, and I'll make sure you're safe. I stared at her and decided to tell her what I know. Fuck it, these niggas are already trying to dead me anyways.

"Okay, well, I really don't know much. After I set the restaurant on fire, I ran down this alley. A dude was running towards me and pointed a gun at my head. I held my hands up and told him I just set the restaurant on fire. I informed him I wasn't worried about him and that I was trying to get the fuck away before the cops came. He had a hoodie covering his head and a ski mask hiding his face, so I didn't really know how he looked. He told me that he was with the 163 Mafia and that he can easily end my life. Then he ran off. However, I noticed the dope-ass tattoo on his left calf muscle. It was a tattoo of two snakes.

"Deontae, a lot of men have snake tattoos. That's not enough evidence," she griped.

"I don't think you understand. See, I know tattoos because my oldest brother is an artist. You must have a special skill to do these types of tattoos, and it's only a handful of artists in Houston that can do them. They are referred to as optical illusion tattoo artists. The tattoo looks very real, like it's about to jump out of the skin.

The guy's tattoo was a two-snake striking design, featuring two serpents intricately intertwined with one another in a serpentine dance. One snake is inky black, with its scales glistening with tiny sparkles, giving it an almost ominous presence. The other snake is a vibrant, fiery red, its scales reflecting a deep crimson hue that contrasts sharply with the black snake.

Their heads are positioned opposite of each other. The scales of the snakes are meticulously detailed, each one distinct and giving the illusion of movement, as though the snakes could come to life at any moment.

You find that artist, and you find the killer. Trust me, an optical illusion artist knows his or her work! They pride themselves on having rare artistic talent. That tattoo was so dope; I'm almost positive the artist probably recorded or has pictures of that session.

Officer Whitfield looked at me for a moment as if she was thinking about what I just said. "Okay, that's good information. I'll check this out, and if what you're telling me is true, then we will recommend to the parole board an early release. In the meantime, I must keep you safe."

She quickly left the room. I sat there talking to Joystina and my daughter for about 15 minutes before we were interrupted by Officer Whitfield, Sergeant Marley, and the warden. Come with me, the warden demanded. I'm putting you in solitary confinement until you can be released. I got up to leave and gave my loved ones one more look. They both smiled and waved bye to me. I hoped my days in prison were coming to an end.

CHAPTER 20

JA

It was early in the morning, and I was clapping cheeks. Jenelle was a sexy red-bone stallion. Her body was banging from head to toe. Her big ass cheeks sat up better than two bunk beds. She arched her back while I kneeled behind her, pounding that pussy from the back. She gripped the sheets, moaning out in pleasure. I was punishing that pussy. I dipped my hips lower to ensure every inch of my dick stroked her walls. I instructed her to lie down flat on the bed and to remain on her stomach. I lay flat on top of her.

I slowly gave her deep strokes. Her body moved in sync with mine. Her ass bounced as I filled her insides up with my thick, chocolate third leg. Each thrust she felt in her stomach. She placed both hands on the headboard for support. That pussy was soaking wet, and my dick was riding the wave. She tried to scoot up every time the end of my dick hit the g-spot. I wrapped my arms around her tighter without skipping a beat.

"Uh, uhh, don't run from me. Take this dick," I whispered in her ear. I stroked her kitty long and hard, and that thang was purring. Her juices dripped down my legs, and that turned me on. I pumped her insides harder.

"Mmm, ahhh," she let out a soft moan. I felt my body pulsating from the pleasure. I quickly pulled out and released my nut on her ass. I went into the restroom to wash off. After I cleaned myself up, I brought her a warm towel to clean off with.

"Hey, I got some errands to run," I informed her.

"That's cool. I'll be here when you get back," she replied. She tried it. I looked at her like she lost her motherfucking mind. She rolled her eyes and climbed out of bed.

She stood in front of me naked with her hands on her hips. "Ja, how long have we been messing around? It's crazy you don't want to get close to me or be in a relationship with me!" She screamed. Women were some emotional creatures.

"Come on, Jenelle. I told you from the jump I'm not a relationship type of guy. I'm here for a good time, not a long time," I nonchalantly stated.

"Asshole," she screamed and shoved me in the chest. Jenelle quickly gathered her clothes and left. I was happy because I was starving.

I had a taste for some delicious southern breakfast. There was one place that came to mind, The Breakfast Klub. I know it's fucked up that I didn't invite Jenelle to breakfast after beating her back in. She would've thought we were on a date, and I can't have that. I keep it simple, so it doesn't become complicated. Every time a female tries to cross that line and catch feelings, I remind them what it is.

We enjoy our moment, and then we go our separate ways. The line was around the corner, but I never had to wait. I was a regular there, and they appreciated the Black soldiers who served this county and fought for their people. This restaurant was my favorite. It's known for its vibrant energy and soul food-inspired breakfast dishes. Nestled in the heart of Midtown, it stands out with its colorful, welcoming facade featuring bold murals and signage that reflect the lively spirit of the place.

The menu is the star of the show, featuring signature dishes like "Katfish & Grits" and "Wings & Waffles," which draw long lines of loyal customers daily. The food is hearty, rich in flavor, and rooted in Southern comfort traditions, served in generous portions. Patrons often rave about the crispy fried chicken, the perfectly seasoned catfish, and the fluffy waffles topped with syrup.

The seating is cozy, with wooden tables and booths arranged in a way that encourages friendly chatter between customers. I took a seat at one of the wooden tables, and that's when I spotted her, the woman I met at the gala a few weeks back. She was sitting by the window reading a book. My heart stopped. My God, she was naturally gorgeous. Her hair was in a tight ponytail, and her curls flowed past her shoulder. She wore a flowery yellow headband that gave her a sultry look. The headband enhanced the plain yellow sleeveless dress that sculpted her body. She looked like a beautiful ray of sunshine.

It felt like my heart was about to beat out of my chest. What the hell was this feeling? I'm never nervous to speak to anyone. I got up and walked over. I sat on the empty seat at her table. She looked up, and I was smiling at her, but I didn't utter a word yet. For a few seconds we just took each other's presence in. Then finally she leaned back in her chair.

"Sure, you can join me," she said sarcastically. I couldn't help but laugh.

"Don't mind if I do," I replied, smirking at her. I leaned over and grabbed her book.

"What are you reading?" I asked.

"Well, since you snatched my book, I'll let you answer your own question." She rolled her eyes at me.

Man, this girl is so fine and feisty. I saw that she was reading "How Women Can Dominate in Commercial Real Estate" by Myra V.

"Oh, you like those self-help books, huh?" I asked her. She hesitated.

"Not really, but this woman, Myra, epitomizes Black excellence. I'm in the real estate industry myself, and it's a male-dominated industry. This lady is young, Black, and successful. She motivates women to not see limitations and become a powerhouse," she enlightened me. I gave her the book back.

"Okay, that sounds good," I responded.

"What are you doing here anyway?" she asked. Now it was my turn to be a smart ass.

"I definitely didn't come here to read. I'm hungry as hell." I looked around for the waitress.

"Do you remember my name?" She quizzed me.

"It's Trisha," I blurted out. She immediately frowned.

"Yes, I remember your name, Trinity," I admitted. She smiled, and that sent chills down my body, and not in a bad way. My dick instantly got hard.

"Now what's my name?" I asked.

"Ummmm," she teased.

"Your name is Ja. It's short for Jatavion."

"Oh, you've been looking me up!" I said, tickled by my very own humor. She giggled.

"No, I haven't. They said your name that night before you got your award." I twisted my lip up at her to suggest she was lying. Suddenly, three men crowded around our table. Trinity's eyes were almost bugged out of her head. These men were obviously here to cause trouble. Their hard demeanor told me they were on some bullshit. All three men mean-mugged me and surrounded the table, like wolves circling their prey.

"Oh, don't let us interrupt your little date," the short man with the cut across his left eye said to us.

"Shut up, Kentrell, it's not a date," Trinity spoke. The other two men stood with their arms folded. They were much bigger in size and thought they were intimidating me.

"Ja, these men are dangerous. I don't want to be responsible for you getting hurt. Please leave," she pleaded with me. I leaned back in my chair.

"I don't know Trinity. I kind of like a little danger," I said, smirking. I wanted them to know I wasn't scared at all. The small man's grin fades, replaced by a scowl.

"You better listen to her, boy. You got one minute to get your ass outta here before the hospital has to hook yo ass up to a ventilator." People sitting near us got up and moved out of the way. Trinity was panicking, and I could tell she was scared. It was time she knew that these niggas could be stopped.

"Aight. It's time for yo ass to go," the big, brown-skinned dude grabbed my shoulder. I moved to strike him like lightning.

I bring my hands up, locking onto his wrist. I quickly pull down on his hand and twist outward at the same time. The grip he had on me is broken with a sharp flick of his wrist. This sudden reversal leaves him momentarily off-balance. I'm on my feet now. Before he could react, I put intense pressure on his wrist. He is unable to find his balance, as I grip him tightly with both hands and step inward. With one fluid movement, I rotate my hips while sharply twisting his arm at the elbow joint. Hyperextending his joints past normal range, I heard his arm snap. He cries out in pain. I release the hold I had on him but send one damaging blow to his rib cage. He collapses on the floor weeping.

"He broke my arm! He broke my arm!" He cried.

The huge African nigga, with a nappy beard, tried to rush me. I landed a precise punch to his nostrils. He stumbled, and I gave him no time to recuperate. I gifted him with a sweeping kick to his abdomen. And he flies between the empty tables, knocking them over. The small guy didn't expect his men to go down so quickly. He probably would've moved faster. He reached into his waist to grab his gun. He didn't have enough time to aim it. I had a steady grip on his wrist and controlled the direction it was pointed in. I made sure to hold his hand upward, so nobody is struck with a bullet. With my free arm, I gave him a swift chop to the neck.

He immediately gasped for air. I kneed him in the stomach, and he voluntarily let go of the pistol. I pushed the magazine release button on the pistol to eject the clip. I dropped both the empty gun and the full clip on the table. I lifted dude off the ground by his neck and slammed him on his head. All three men were down for the count. I turned my attention to Trinity, and she was stunned at what just took place.

"My goodness. What kind of architect are you?" she inquired. I shrugged, not knowing how to answer that question.

The restaurant was silent as the three would-be aggressors lay groaning on the floor. Their arrogance thoroughly beaten out of them.

"I'll see you around, beautiful. I'm going to take my food to go. Order you some food too. I'll make sure to cover your bill at the cashier."

"Okay," she obliged and smiled. I went home and thought about her the rest of the day. I got to make sure I see her again.

The guys stormed into the penthouse looking all messed up and injured. Man, what the fuck happened? I asked Kentrell. He covered his face with one hand and shook his head in defeat.

"Man, when we walked in the restaurant, we saw some nigga sitting down at a booth smiling all in Trinity's face." I turned to look at Trinity, but she made sure not to make eye contact with me by staring at our marble floors. The guilt was all over her face.

"Who was he?" I asked with a tight lip. She let out a soft sigh.

"It was Ja, the architect," she confessed.

"We tried to press dude, but it didn't go as planned," he continued. "We walked up to him, and we demanded he get up and leave. He wasn't fazed by us at all. He wasn't your ordinary nigga. He had special fighting skills or some top-secret training mayne. Marquees grabbed him by the shoulder. Without breaking a sweat, he grabbed Marquees's hand, twisted his entire arm around, and bent it downwards until we heard it snap. Wakumbe tried to attack him next, but he karate-kicked him across the restaurant. He took both niggas out in a matter of seconds." I glanced over at them niggas, and they were standing against the wall, all bruised up. Marquees was holding his arm as if it was broken, and Wakumbe held his stomach like he was in agony. All I could do was shake my head.

"Wakumbe, your African ass, just big for no damn reason," I smacked my teeth and insulted him. Kentrell continued telling his story. "He saw me going for my gun, snatched me up by my neck, and slammed me on my head. I saw stars and those cartoon birds flying around my head instantly." Marquees, still nursing his arm, started laughing. I gave him a stern look, and he immediately shut the fuck up.

"Now is not the time to make jokes or think this shit is remotely funny. You niggas are useless!" I screamed. It was utter silence.

"Man Von, I'm still trying to figure out how that nigga moves so quick." Kentrell said.

"So, you mean to tell me this ONE nigga whooped all three of you niggas? Man, I knew I should've had Tank tag along with y'all," I said.

"Eh," Kentrell. blurted out, shrugging his shoulders.

"What the fuck does that mean?" I asked, stepping into his face.

"I'm just saying, Von, I'm not even sure Tank can fuck with this dude! Know what I'm talmbout?" He responded in Houston, Texas, vernacular.

"No, I don't know what you, *TALMBOUT*! I sarcastically spat.

"Tank is a nationally ranked professional boxer. The fuck you mean you don't think Tank can fuck with this nigga?" I asked out of aggravation.

"I'm just saying, bro. Okay, picture Mike Tyson and Jet Li as one super nigga. That's what we're dealing with. Tank maybe got the hands for dude, but that martial arts shit is going to put Tank on his ass," Kentrell assured me.

"Is that right?" Tank asked, walking into the kitchen. Kentrell shook his head for yes. One thing about this little nigga is that he will stand on whatever he said.

"Get up," Tank ordered Boogie, one of my young street soldiers sitting at the counter. Boogie was a new member of the 163 Mafia Boys.

He was about 5'9 feet tall and had a baby face. It could be because he had no facial hair and kept his hair cut low. He was quiet the majority of the time, but he had a demon side to him that I liked. I watched him shoot a man in the head for lying to me about stealing my money. As much as the man begged for his life, Boogie ain't give a fuck. He pulled that trigger with ease, and that's the type of niggas I need riding for me. Boogie got up from his seat.

"I'm not for your shit today, Tank. The fuck you bout to do?" he asked.

Tank laughed while grabbing a Coke can out of the fridge. Walking up to Boogie, he placed the Coke can on his head. Boogie smacked his teeth. "Stay still, and don't move," he told Boogie while taking a few steps backwards. It got really quiet in the room as everyone was wondering what the fuck Tank was doing. Next thing you know, he does a 360 roundhouse kick in the air. He kicks the can with his right leg, and it goes flying off Boogie's head.

"Oh shit," Kentrell shouted out. I stood there clapping my hands because I was impressed with what I just saw.

"I'm skilled in martial arts too. I just never had any competition with you pussy-ass niggas, so I never had to use those skills. It's a lot of shit about me you don't know," he said to Kentrell.

"I can't wait to run into this nigga Ja, though. I love a good squabble," he said, shrugging his shoulders and walking out of the kitchen.

"Yeah, that was a great kick, nigga, but you gonna have to do more than just squabble!" Kentrell yelled out.

"This nigga Ja is a thorn in my mf side. I'm so damn sick of him," I blurted out while rubbing my temples.

"Hmmm, could it be that you finally met your match?" Trinity sarcastically spoke with her head cocked to the side. She had an amused grin on her face. This bitch can't be serious. She was loving every bit of this. Nah, I'm about to wipe that smirk clean off this hoe's face. I chuckled while slowly walking towards her. She was no longer smirking at me.

Instead, she glared at me like I disgust her. As soon as I approached her, I lifted her off the ground by her armpits. She was thick in all the right places but still fragile. I dangled her in the air by her underarms as if she were the character Baby and I were Patrick Swayze from the movie Dirty Dancing. She looked down at me, confused and worried. I started humming the lyrics to the last song at the end of the movie.

"*Now I've had the time of my life. No, I never felt like this before…*"

"HA! This nigga insane!" Kentrell blurted out. I could hear some of the other men chuckling. My look towards her turned cold. I threw her backwards in the air clear across the kitchen. She went flying to the other side.

BOOM!

Her head and back slammed against the counter attached to the stainless-steel kitchen sink. Her body slid down from the counter. She fell to the ground hard. She cried out in pain. I leaned over the counter to get a better view of her. She was curled up on the floor crying. It was obvious she was in pain from being thrown up in the air like a rag doll. That ought to teach her ass, though. It was me that now had a smirk on my face.

I didn't feel sorry for her. She deliberately tries to push my buttons, knowing I'm going to fuck her up. "Did I give you what you were looking for?" I asked her. She lay there sobbing with her big curls covering her face. Tank ran into the kitchen.

"What the fuck was that loud bang?" he asked me. I didn't answer him. Instead, I continued to look at Trinity, who was now in a world of pain. Tank walked up and stood right beside me. He quietly watched Trinity laid out on the floor. I could tell he felt bad for her because he had a pitiful look on his face. He turned to leave the kitchen again.

"Kentrell, I want to hear more about this Ja dude. Let's take the side stairs to our condo." They both left the penthouse.

"Boss, why do I not have a condo here like Tank and Kentrell ay?" Wakumbe asked me in his strong African accent. I looked at that nigga like he was insane.

"Nigga, what? You're standing here with an ice pack on your fucking head after getting your ass kicked, but you got the nerve to ask me about a luxury apartment?" The rest of the men remained quiet. Wakumbe stood there looking dumb.

"First off, y'all ain't put in enough work yet to get those types of benefits." I was speaking to all them niggas in case they were wondering the same thing.

"Aye, I need you, Marquees, and Boogie to get the fuck up outta here. I need some peace right now," I demanded. They all left the penthouse. I heard Trinity weeping.

"Baby, I think I sprained my wrist. I can't move it," she softly cried out to me. I took one more look at her before heading upstairs to bed.

I left her lying there to think about her actions. Right before entering the hallway, I tapped the light switch on the wall to cut the lights in the kitchen off. I woke up out of my sleep a few hours later. I reached over to rub Trinity's shoulder. My hand hit the empty side of the bed where Trinity was supposed to be sleeping.

Where the fuck was Trinity? If she ran away, I was going to beat her ass once I found her. I turned over to look at the clock sitting on the nightstand. It was 4:23 a.m., so she should've been in bed by now.

Pulling the covers back, I got out of the bed wearing my gray Lululemon boxers. The condo was freezing as my half-naked body walked the hallway that led to the kitchen.

Damn, what was the temperature on the thermostat, I wondered. I opened the office door, and she was not in there. Next, I opened the door to the guest bathroom, and she wasn't in there. Entering the kitchen, the floor was cold under my feet. It was dark, so I cut on the light switch. I proceeded to the area I left her at earlier. There she was, lying in the same place.

She was sleeping behind the counter with her bushy hair covering her face. I didn't notice it before, but her body was in an uncomfortable position. One arm was stretched out while the other arm was bent behind her back. I walked over to her and kneeled beside her.

"Trinity," I called out to her. I tapped her on the shoulder to wake her up, but she didn't move or say anything. I removed the hair out of her face and noticed the dry blood at the top of her head and down the side of her face.

Her body felt ice cold. I began to worry. "Trinity," I called her name again and shook her shoulder. She barely opened her eyes, but I was happy to see some kind of movement.

"Von, my shoulder and back hurt. I can't move my left hand," she whispered. With that being said, I began to scoop her up in my arms. She moaned in pain. I carried her upstairs to the bedroom and placed her on the bed.

"Von, my hand. I can't move it," she cried softly. I leaned over her to grab her hand. I tried bending it a little.

"Ouuu ouch," she cried out some more.

"Damn, it might be broken," I suggested with my eyes closed. The guilt was starting to slowly eat me up on the inside. I grabbed my phone off the nightstand and searched through the contacts. I found Dr. Taylor's number and hit the green phone icon button. The phone rang three times before I heard her voice on the other end.

"Good morning, Mr. Westley. What got you calling me at this time of the morning?" she curiously asked. I knew she was being sarcastic because this wasn't my first time calling her this early, nor was it my second or third time.

"It's Trinity. She is in a lot of pain," I informed her.

"What did you do?" she yelled in my ear.

"Excuse you!" I blurted out. There was an awkward silence on the phone.

"I'm sorry, Mr. Westley. What I mean to say is, what happened to her?" she politely asked while correcting her tone.

"She fell. Can you get over here now?" Dr. Taylor loved Trinity and would drop everything to cater to her. I think she looked at Trinity as a younger sister. Over the years, she has cared for her, and they have become extremely close. I don't think she likes me that much or even at all. She knew how to respect me, though, and that's all that mattered to me.

"I'm on my way," she assured me. I ended the call. I walked out of the bedroom and went to our high-tech intercom placed on the wall near the front door. I hit the black, oval-shaped button that read elevator lobby.

"Nate, Dr. Taylor is on her way over. Please let her up when she comes."

"No problem, Mr. Westley. Is everything okay?" he asked. That little nigga was nosey. He was just concerned about Trinity, not me at all. I see the looks he gives her.

"Yeah, just do what I asked of you," I responded with irritation in my voice.

"Sure thing," he responded back to me. I ended the connection between us by pushing the elevator lobby button again. Now, I'll wait for Dr. Taylor. I pray Trinity's hand isn't broken or any other part of her body. Damn, why did she have to test me? It's like she low-key loves getting a rise out of me.

"Yeah, just do what I asked of you," Mr. Westley's attitude came blasting through the intercom.

"Sure thing," I replied to him. He hung up the receiver.

"Bitch-ass nigga," I mumbled and knew he was no longer on the call. Man, I couldn't stand his ass. I hated working around a bunch of rich snobs, but they paid me well. Von was a horrible person. He treated Trinity like shit, and all the staff members working here knew it. I have been working at this building for a year. I've witnessed countless black eyes and bruises on her body. It baffled me how a man can abuse a beautiful woman like Trinity.

He had some deep-rooted issues. I felt so sorry for her. Every time she looked at me, I saw the embarrassment in her eyes. She was such a sweet person. She knew I was a college kid, so she tried to tip me any chance she got. I never saw her mistreat any of the staff here. However, Von probably called every staff member in this building stupid and yelled at us for the smallest things. If I wasn't present to answer the intercom, he would be pissed. Even if I told him that I had to use the restroom. That didn't matter to him.

He told me I should have made sure a staff member could cover my spot while I'm gone. It's not that easy. At night, management only has me working the lobby doors and just one more staff member to work the receptionist desk. He knows all of this but still doesn't care. I told the managers of the building numerous times to let Mr. Westley know that I'm the only one working the elevators at night, and I might have to go to the restroom at times.

Their scary asses still ain't said shit to him. Well, I couldn't wait for him to get his karma. I know you shouldn't pray on someone else's downfall, but I did! That dog will have his day, I just know it. When I look at him, I see pure evilness. I see a man who doesn't love anyone or anything. I don't even think he loves himself. It wasn't unusual anymore for Dr. Taylor to come at this time of night. I was used to it by now.

Every time she came over here, Trinity had new injuries or bruises. I wondered what the fuck he did to her now. After about 35 minutes, I spotted Dr. Taylor's white Mercedes Benz truck pull up to the garage gate. I electronically opened the gate by pressing a button on the intercom. She parked in a reserved spot that belongs to a tenant that is never here. I gave her permission to park there a long time ago. I know her car wouldn't be towed because I'm the one who is responsible for towing unauthorized vehicles.

Dr. Taylor adjusted her sleek, tailored coat as she stepped out of her white Mercedes SUV and onto the pathways leading up to the side elevators from the garage. It was still dark outside, and she was dressed like she was walking the runway of a fashion show. Her designer handbag and polished heels clicked rhythmically against the sidewalk as she approached me.

"Doc, it's too early for you to be this bougie," I teased. She giggled at my commentary.

My humor subsided when I saw her face turn to sadness. Thanks to Von's inability to control his temper, we have become quite acquainted. Dr. Taylor has been here too many times for the same reasons. "How are you doing, Dr. Taylor? I imagine you're here to treat Trinity again?" I asked.

"Well, I can't say anything without violating HIPAA, but yeah, I'm sure that's why I'm here," I stated.

Dr. Taylor sighed, shaking her head as she entered the hallway leading to the elevators. "Between you and me, Von called me to come look at Trinity." Her tone was clipped, and the frustration was clear in her voice. I frowned at this information, but it was nothing I didn't already suspect.

"That guy's no good. I always see him coming in here with a bad attitude, acting like he owns the place," I informed her.

"Every time you come here, it's the same story. He can't keep his hands to himself," I whispered.

"I know," she agreed.

"Doc, every time I think she's going to leave him, she doesn't." I folded my arms, leaning against the doorway.

"She deserves better. I don't know why she puts up with him," I questioned.

Dr. Taylor ran a hand through her silky dark hair, letting out a frustrated breath. "I don't either. I've told her a hundred times, but she's scared. He has a way of getting into her head, making her think she can't do better." I shook my head in disbelief.

"I don't get it. You'd think after the first time."

"You'd think," Dr. Taylor interrupted me softly, her tone knowing what I was about to say.

"But these situations aren't that simple. Trinity is strong, but she's in a relationship with a monster, a rich one. ... those types of men make women feel powerless." I nodded solemnly.

"Well, at least she's got you looking out for her."

"Well, I try to be," she muttered, straightening up and pushing her emotions aside.

"I'm going to check on her now. Thanks, Nate."

I smiled and replied, "Anytime, Doc."

I scanned my elevator key and motioned for Dr. Taylor to step inside. In return, Trinity gave me a small smile, but the heaviness lingered as she entered the elevator, riding it up to the penthouse floor. She wasn't just a doctor; she had been Trinity's lifeline at times when she needed care. It made me feel good that the doctor was here to make sure she was okay.

When the elevator doors slid open, my heels clicked against the marble floor as I approached Trinity's door. I knocked softly, already bracing myself for the condition she was in.

A moment later, the door opened, and Von stood on the other side. "She's in the upstairs bedroom," he said. I walked right by him without uttering a word to him. As I entered the bedroom, I saw Trinity sleeping. I walked over and pulled the covers back to examine parts of her body. The cold breeze woke her up immediately.

"Dr. Taylor," Trinity said, her voice thin but relieved.

"Thank you for coming."

"What's going on, Trinity? Where are you hurt?" I asked.

"I think my left hand is broken. I can barely move it," she said, trying to bend it.

"My back and shoulder are also in pain." She squirmed from all the pain she was experiencing.

"Okay, I'm about to examine you to determine if it's broken.
It might hurt a little." I began to feel her wrists and hands.

"Ouch," she murmured.

"It doesn't appear to be broken. It's swollen, so that's why it hurts so bad. You have a severe sprain. I pulled a compression bandage from my bag and began wrapping her up. I will also prescribe you some Oxycodone tablets to help deal with pain.

"What happened to you, Trinity? What did he do?" I interrogated.

"I slipped and fell," she said with tears falling down her cheeks.

"Don't do that, Trinity. Don't lie to me," I calmly said.

"I'm sorry, Dr. Taylor," she sobbed.

"You know you don't have to apologize to me. But Trinity, this can't keep happening." Trinity looked at me, her eyes welling up with tears.

"I know. I just... I don't know how to leave him."

I heard this a million times from my clients. This was indeed a sad situation. "You deserve so much better than this," I said.

"If I could leave him and be safe, I would," she stated.

"I can help you," I said softly.

"Whenever you're ready." Trinity nodded, but I knew that readiness was still far off. For now, all I could do was patch up the wounds and hope that one day, she would be free from this man. I just so happened to glance at the picture on her nightstand. It was a picture of her and Kyra, one of my residency students at the hospital. "Hey, you know Kyra?" I asked.

"That's my childhood best friend," she whispered.

Von came out of the shadows. "Are you done here?" he frowned. I grabbed my bag and was about to walk past him. He snatched me by the arm.

"Is there something you would like to say to me?" he challenged. I just looked at him with hatred.

"Nope," I replied and removed his hand from me. He didn't challenge me any further. I left the penthouse. When I reached the garage floor, Nate was waiting for me.

"What happened? Is she okay? He hit her, right?" He anxiously hurled questions at me.

"Nate, she's okay. Her body was a little sore. That's all," I informed him.

"Okay, well, I'm glad you came. Enjoy the rest of your day," Nate replied.

I had a few more hours before I had to be at the hospital. I was testing the students all day on live surgical procedures. I rushed her to enjoy a couple more hours of sleep. Four hours later, I was at the hospital watching Kyra struggle with the task before her.

She stood frozen in front of the operating table, the bright surgical lights beaming down at the simulation dummy stretched out on the table. We were waiting for her to make the first incision, but her hands trembled, gripping the scalpel so tightly her knuckles turned white. I watched her breathing speed up.

"Kyra, we don't have all day!" My tone was impatient, bordering on annoyed. My students knew I didn't sugarcoat things.

"You need to cut. Now," I advised. Her hands shook even more, the scalpel wobbling in her grip. Every second that passed felt like a failure, a sign that she wasn't cut out for this. The pressure of knowing that real life would soon be in her hands only made the panic swell.

"Kyra!" I barked, stepping closer. "If this were a real patient, they'd be dead by now. You have to push through it."

Her chest tightened, and she fought back the tears threatening to spill over. The room seemed to close in around her, the sterile smell of the OR amplifying her panic. Her hands, still trembling, lowered as she swallowed hard, her voice barely a whisper.

"I can't… I don't know why I can't do it."

"Put the scalpel down," I ordered, my voice firm. Reluctantly, she set the scalpel on the tray beside her, her head hanging low in shame. She had dreamed of being a surgeon for years and worked hard to get here, but this panic had taken control of her every time she stood before a dummy or a patient.

I sighed, stepping in front of her. "Kyra, I know it's hard. I've seen plenty of residents' struggle at this stage. But you've got to get a handle on it. Panic doesn't belong in the OR."

"I know," she whispered, her voice cracking with frustration.

"But every time I pick up the scalpel, I freeze. What if I mess up? What if I hurt someone?"

"Messing up is part of learning. And right now, you're hurting yourself by letting this get to you." I crossed my arms, studying her closely.

"Surgery requires precision, yes, but it also requires confidence. You've got the skills. I wouldn't be riding you this hard if I didn't think you could do it." She looked up at me, startled by the rare compliment buried beneath my words.

"You think I can?"

"I know you can. But you've got to stop getting in your own way." I gestured toward the dummy on the table.

"It's not about being perfect every time. It's about staying calm, even when things go wrong. That's why we practice on these dummies. You can mess up here, not out there."

Kyra blinked, wiping the corner of her eyes. She had always viewed me as unrelentingly harsh, but now she realized my sharp words came from a place of experience and concern. I wasn't trying to break her down but was trying to build her up.

"Take a breath," I said, nodding toward the dummy.

"Pick up the scalpel again. Slow and steady. Just make the incision."

Kyra nodded. Her breath was still shaky, but steadier than before. She picked up the scalpel, feeling its weight in her hand. Her hands trembled less. She focused on her breathing and on the feel of the instrument between her fingers. With one final look at me, she lowered the scalpel to the dummy's chest. Her hand moved with slow precision, and this time, instead of shaking uncontrollably, it stayed steady enough to make a clean cut.

I watched closely with my arms still crossed. "Better," I said, my voice low but approving.

"You're getting there. Now, keep going." Kyra took another deep breath and continued cutting. It was far from perfect, but it was progress.

As she finished the incision, I looked down at her work. "Not bad," I said, with a rare hint of a smile.

"Now, let's do it again."

Kyra nodded, her hands still shaky, but her resolve was more robust than before. She knew she had a long road ahead but wouldn't let fear stop her.

I was never easy on her, but she finally understood why. I saw something in her, and if she was going to become a surgeon, she dreamed of being, she had to believe in herself, too.

"Okay, Kyra, meet me in my office," I instructed.

Kyra walked into my office, looking nervous. "Dr. Taylor, I swear, I will work on my panic attacks," she began. I shook my head.

"No, that's not why I called you in here. She looked confused. "What I'm about to tell you is a violation of HIPAA law. I'm not supposed to discuss anyone's private healthcare with another party," I informed her.

"Okay," she said curiously.

"Earlier this morning, Von called me to the penthouse to take care of Trinity's injuries." Kyra's face hardened.

"What did that bastard do?" she asked.

"Well, I don't know all the details, but she had a sprained wrist, and her back and shoulder were in some pain, too." She became curious.

"Dr. Taylor, how did you know she was my friend?" she asked.

"Well, I saw a picture of the both of you on her nightstand.

"Oh okay, yes, that's my best friend. She will be okay, though?"

"Yes, she just has some bruising and swelling, but nothing major…this time. I'm afraid that one day he is going to hurt her badly or kill her." Kyra sighed at my remarks.

"I know. I'm afraid of that too," she stated.

"Okay, I just wanted you to know what happened. Go ahead and finish out your workday," I told her. Kyra got up and left my office. I remained at my desk, already feeling exhausted. I had to go right back to class and test more students. This is going to be a long day.

I fixed myself a cup of coffee and sat on the couch to watch television. It was on the local news channel, so I decided to leave it there. My heart sank into my chest when the station posted a missing woman's photo. I recognized her immediately. It was the same young lady that confronted Von outside the real estate gala and informed him she was four months pregnant. I wondered where Tank really took her to that night. The news anchor's voice spoke with urgency.

"This evening, we're reporting on the disappearance of 24-year-old Destiny Daniels. She is described as 5 feet 6 inches tall, with brown eyes and a hairstyle in long black braids. Destiny was last seen wearing a large black T-shirt, black joggers, and brown sandals. She drives a 2018 red Toyota Camry, license plate number VRT 6941. Her family is pleading for any information that could help bring her home."

The news report shifted to a video of Destiny's distraught mother speaking through tears, pleading for help.

The screen cut back to the anchor. "If you have any information regarding Destiny Daniels, please contact the local authorities. Her family is waiting and hoping for her safe return."

Von walked past the couch, and I couldn't help myself. "Isn't that your baby mama?" I asked. Von stopped in his tracks and warned me to never say that shit again.

"What property is "The Cozy Corner" located at? I heard you mention it to Tank the night of the gala." Our stare with one another was broken by a knock on the door.

Von and I looked confused because who in the hell got past the concierge booth and made their way to the penthouse suite? I moved to open the door. Von got up from the couch because he was curious who this visitor could be. He opened the door to find Kyra smiling from ear to ear.

"Hey bestie, I'm so happy to see you," she said, giving me a big hug. Von smacked his lips.

"Kyra, have you ever heard of calling before you come? Also, remind me to have the staff downstairs fired. What good are they if they just let anyone up here?" he said with his arms folded.

"Now Von, you know they couldn't stop me if they wanted to," Kyra quickly teased. Von ignored her and headed towards the back of the condo. All I know is I'm glad my friend is here, and we can spend some quality time together.

CHAPTER 25

KYRA

As soon as Trinity saw it was me, she hopped up from the couch with the speed of lightning and embraced me. I could tell she really missed me.

"Pour us some wine, Trinity, before I tell you about the day I had yesterday," I asked. She went to the kitchen and grabbed two Champagne glasses from out the cabinet. I watched as she poured our drinks. She handed me a glass of red wine and walked to the other end of the couch to sit down. Taking a seat on my girl's luxury sectional black couch, I began to tell her about this guy I recently met.

"Girl, I got to tell you about the awful date I had last night with this dude named King. I knew this nigga was too good to be true. So, we had a romantic date on the Kema boardwalk. He reserved a table on the patio of this really nice seafood restaurant. He had a huge bouquet of red roses on the table. The table was decorated with beautiful, sparkly gold dishes and silverware. There was a guy in the back corner dressed in a black tuxedo playing the violin. The violinist wasn't playing that boring elevator music either. He was playing 90s classic R&B hits."

"Being confused by my story," Trinity interrupted me.

"This doesn't sound like an awful date."

"Bitch, wait. I'm getting there," I assured her.

"I'm loving every moment of the date and really enjoying his conversation. He was so damn fine girl. All I could think about was fucking the shit out of him."

Von was walking by to get to the kitchen and heard me. He just shook his head, and I ordered him to mind his business. He grabbed a Fiji water out of the fridge and headed to the back once again. Finishing my story, I jumped to the part that mattered.

"To make a long story short, we both had sex on our minds. He was too tired to drive back into town, so he paid for a hotel. We were all over each other as soon as we got to our room door. We kissed passionately and took each other's clothes off. I threw him on the couch and hopped on the dick. I'm bouncing up and down on that thang so good I can see his eyes rolling to the back of his head. After a few minutes, he flipped me around, and now I was on my back. He spread my legs apart and started eating me for breakfast, lunch, and dinner, bitch! My eyes were closed shut while he was licking all over my pussy. I had one of the best orgasms off his tongue. His tongue slid down to my ass, and he began devouring my shit. When he was done, he got off his knees and whispered, 'My turn to get pleasured,' in my ear. I got up to give him my best head game. As I'm about to get on my knees, he lies on his back and holds his legs straight up in the air. He bends them back as far as they can go."

Trinity holds up one hand to pause the conversation.

She asks, "Why did he do that?"

I could tell she already knew what I was about to say because she was trying not to laugh. I said to him, "What are you doing?" Peeking through his legs, this nigga gone say, "It's time for you to eat my ass." He looked like a giant ass turtle that flipped over on its shell. His entire ass was tooted up in the air." Trinity hollered so loud and faked passing out on the couch.

Quickly sitting back up, she said, "I know you fucking lying. Well, did you eat his ass?" She must be crazy to ask me that.

"Hell nah, I didn't!"

Trinity was so tickled. She was still laughing.

"I told that nigga he got me fucked up. I don't eat ass. Plus, you know I'm a nurse, and I see firsthand how these niggas don't clean their ass properly. He was mad at me and said I was being selfish because he ate my ass. I was like, so what; you're a nigga. I asked him why he would want anything or anyone near his ass. That fool had the nerve to tell me to grow up, and that's what grown women do. Bullshit! I ordered him to take me home after that. Do you know he sent me back to Houston in an Uber? I know that Uber ride cost him a pretty penny too. Anyways, I changed his name to Donatello in my phone."

"Wait, like the ninja turtle?" She asked with tears streaming down her face from laughing so hard.

"Yup," I said as we gave each other a high-five and screamed out in laughter.

"Kyra, I needed this laugh. I love it when you're around," she said with a bit of sadness in her eyes.

"Trinity, what's wrong?" I asked. She just looked down at the couch and put her left hand over her face.

"You can tell me what happened," I inquired some more. She looked up at me, and her eyes were bloodshot red.

"I'm just emotionally, spiritually, and physically drained. Hell, I'm tired of being tired, ya know? I just want to be free from Von. That's all."

"I know. I told you plenty of times you can stay with me. You know I'm not scared of him."

"Kyra, you have known Von longer than me, but the thing is he respects you. You haven't met the monster that lives inside of him like I have," she informed me.

"Trinity, I need to tell you something. I have been hiding it all these years," I admitted to her. She gave me the side eye and waited to hear what I had to say.

"The night you went out with Reese, I was hurt and jealous. I called Von and told him about the date. I kind of suspected he was a little off because he went ballistic over the phone. He started screaming in my ear that he was going to kill the both of you. I never heard him talk like that. I instantly regretted it. People over the years have speculated that he beats you, but there was never really any solid proof. I'm sorry I left for medical school, and you had to suffer alone. I'm happy to have moved back to Houston to finish my residency program. I'll always have your back and will do my best to protect you from now on."

"The rumors you hear in the streets are true. He is not only a woman beater, but he is a cold-blooded killer. If he believes you're trying to come between us, he will not spare you."

I was about to respond, but Von walked in all dressed up. He completely changed clothes. He had on a gray polo shirt, blue jeans pants, and blue and gray Nike tennis shoes. The diamond studs in his ear could be seen a mile away.

"Aw, you look so nice on your way out to cheat," I said to him. Trinity almost spit out her wine from choking so hard. He leaned down behind me and placed his head on my shoulder.

"You wish I was cheating with you, huh?" he asked me.

"Eww," I blurted out and moved from under him. He winked at me and then turned his attention to Trinity. She rolled her eyes at him. He chuckled and walked over to the kitchen counter to grab his keys.

"I'll be home later," he notified her. She didn't say anything back to him. Trinity and I both stayed quiet until he left the condo.

"He is so damn disrespectful and cocky," I acknowledged.

"I know, sis," she agreed with her head down. She looked stressed.

"Von is cold a lot of the time. It's like he doesn't feel anything. And other times, it's like he's wearing a mask. He says all the right things, but it feels fake. He stays trying to control and manipulate me. I feel like I'm going crazy. Something evil lurks inside that man. He is a damn psychopath or sociopath. Hell, what's the difference?" Trinity asked.

I felt so bad for my friend. Working in the hospital, I was too familiar with everything she said. I deal with mental illnesses all day long.

"Alright, let's break it down," I said gently.

"First off, you're not crazy. You're the main one who has experienced just how crazy Von is. Now, I can explain the difference between a psychopath and a sociopath, but remember, this isn't a diagnosis. It's just to help you understand what you might be dealing with. Trinity nodded, gripping her coffee cup tightly.

"Both psychopaths and sociopaths fall under the umbrella of antisocial personality disorder, which means they both have a disregard for others and tend to violate social norms. But there are key differences.”

She paused, gathering her thoughts. I continued… “Psychopaths are typically more calculated. They’re often charming, smart, and good at hiding their true selves. They don’t feel emotions like guilt or empathy but know how to mimic them. They’re incredibly manipulative and will lie without a second thought if it gets them what they want. Think of them as predators, always calculating how to get ahead but appearing completely normal, even successful, on the surface.”

Trinity’s eyes widened. “That sounds like Von. He can be so charming when he wants to be. However, I see this coldness behind his eyes, like he is a demon in the flesh.”

I nodded. “That could be a sign. But then, we have sociopaths who are a little different. They can also be manipulative but tend to be more impulsive and erratic. While psychopaths are good at hiding their true nature, sociopaths often struggle with relationships and controlling their emotions. They’re more likely to have outbursts or engage in reckless behavior. Their emotions, like anger or rage, are closer to the surface, and they’re less calculated than psychopaths.”

Trinity bit her lip, thinking about what I said. “Damn, I guess the bastard is a psychopath and sociopath.” We both burst out in laughter.

“To me, he sounds more of a psychopath because he can turn his triggers on and off,” I said carefully.

“But again, I can’t diagnose him. What’s important is how you feel. You must get away from him for good if you're feeling manipulated or unsafe. Even if he doesn’t fit into one neat category, it’s still worth paying attention to your instincts.”

Trinity sighed deeply, her eyes welling up. "I just don't know what to do. I have tried to leave him often, but he always finds me. I scooted closer to her side of the couch to hug her.

"You deserve to be with someone who makes you feel loved and safe. Trinity smiled, her grip on the cup loosening slightly as the weight of the conversation settled in.

"Thanks, Kyra," she whispered.

"No problem, girl. I will always be here to uplift you. Plus, you're all I have since Jaycee moved away and is busy caring for his family."

"OMG, I forgot to tell you this! We went to this Real Estate Awards Ceremony. Before we even entered the building, some chick confronted Von about getting her pregnant…"

"I know you lying," I interrupted.

"Wait, that's not all. Right before you got here, the news posted her as a missing person. I remember Tank, Von's right-hand man, leaving with her that night. Now you tell me what could've happened to her," she implied. There was more to this story.

"Wow, that's deep. Are you going to tell the police?" I questioned.

"Hell no! Von has cops on his payroll."

"There is this guy named Ja, who I keep thinking about. I believe he is the only man that is not afraid of Von. He does something to me. My heart skips a beat just by thinking of him," she informed me.

"Well, now, it seems you have a little crush on someone," I teased. I grabbed her hand to comfort her. Trouble doesn't always last, Trinity. Von's day is coming. I'm always here for you," I assured her.

The weather was warm, and it was a lovely day to cruise the streets of Houston. I just stopped at Sweet Haven Wings to pick up some buffalo wings with Cajun fries. Before I could get out of the car, my father called.

"Hey, what's up, Pop?" I greeted him.

"Alex, don't forget to be home by 7:00 pm so we can meet with the other bosses. I'm getting older, and it's time for me to retire. Today is the official meeting where I let our allies know you are now taking over the family business, although it should be expected anyway," he announced. That was like music to my ears.

I always felt like my dad didn't acknowledge the hard work I was putting in. Now I see he was molding me into a man. I know a lot of niggas are not going to like answering to me. It is what it is.

"I got you. I'll make sure I'm home by 7." After the call, I went to order my food. Walking back to my car, I heard the loud noise of screeching tires. A vehicle came flying towards me. A young man leaned out of the car with his arm extended. He was holding a pistol.

I quickly tried to make a run for it. He began to fire shots at me. A bullet struck my left side and right shoulder before I was able to dive on the other side of my car. I was glad they kept driving. I couldn't stay at this location in case they returned.

I managed to get up on my feet. I clutched my side where the bullet had torn through my flesh. My vision blurred as I staggered, desperate to find refuge. I blinked hard, forcing my legs to move. Blood dripped from my fingers as I pressed harder on the wound, each breath sharp and shallow. I saw this woman about to get into her vehicle. Good lord, she was thick and fine. If I was going to die, at least I got to see all that ass sitting up in those blue jeans she was rocking. She froze when she saw me, bleeding and staggering toward her.

"Help..." I croaked, barely able to speak. My knees buckled, and I collapsed at her feet. I was going in and out of consciousness.

"Can you stand?" she asked, glancing around nervously. The other customers had begun pulling out their phones, no doubt recording the scene. Time was running out. She helped me off the ground and opened her back door. I held her around the neck, and I'm sure blood got in her big orange hair. I found some strength to slide into her back seat. She quickly closed the door and sped out of the parking lot.

"Don't fall asleep," she yelled.

"You're going to be okay. Think happy thoughts," she encouraged me. Although there was panic in her voice, the sound of it calmed me.

"Who did this to you?" she asked. I winced in pain as the car went over bumps and dents in the road.

"Doesn't matter. You shouldn't get involved," I replied.

"I'm already involved," she retorted.

She sped through the city. I could hear the engine being pushed to its highest potential.

"We're almost at the hospital. Stay awake!" she yelled. She glanced back at me, not sure if I'd make it. My breathing grew more labored.

"We're almost there," she whispered.

"Stay with me," she sobbed. Hearing her voice weep like that pulled at my heartstrings. She pulled into the emergency entrance and leaped out, running around the car to help me out of the backseat. She waved down a few staff members, who rushed to help as soon as they saw my state."

"Debbie, get him into a room!" she shouted. I groaned, eyes fluttering. She stayed by my side for hours, ensuring I got the care I needed. She had to work there because she knew everyone's names and was also allowed to be in the operating room. At some point, I was put to sleep. I don't even remember closing my eyes. Finally, I just woke up but was tired. I could tell I had been moved to a private room. My eyes were low but landed on a familiar face. There the ginger-haired lady was. She was right next to my bed, checking my vital signs.

"You... stayed," I said. My voice was hoarse but filled with gratitude. She nodded, sitting down beside my bed.

"You asked for help, and I couldn't just leave you." I smiled weakly.

"You saved my life. I owe you."

"I just did what anyone else would've done," she replied. I chuckled softly, wincing from the pain.

"Not everyone would help the son of a kingpin." Her eyes widened slightly, but she stayed calm.

"You're safe now." For the first time in a long while, I felt like I may have found the woman of my dreams. I didn't know what came next, but for now, I was alive. I owe it all to the woman who had risked everything to save me. She was going to be my woman. I'm going to make sure of it.

For the past two weeks, Trinity began to feel extremely nauseous. During dinner, she threw up a bowl of spaghetti. That was her sign to verify her pregnancy. While Von was out, she ran to CVS Pharmacy and picked up a test. Half an hour later, the test read positive. She sat on the toilet distraught and concerned about being trapped with Von forever. There was no way she was going to have Von's baby.

Texas now banned abortion, so women had to travel to get one. Trinity sat quietly in the cab's backseat as it weaved through Atlanta's afternoon traffic. Her hands trembled slightly as she clutched her phone, watching the city roll by. She had flown in alone from Houston that morning, slipping away without a word to Von, her fiancé. He thought she was at work as usual. Trinity was here for something she couldn't bring herself to discuss with him, a decision she had made alone. Von always made it clear he wanted kids with her.

The clinic came into view, a small, unassuming building in a quiet part of the city. Trinity took a deep breath and stepped out of the cab. Her legs felt shaky as she walked inside, and her mind raced. She checked in at the front desk, trying to keep her head down and avoid eye contact with the nurse who asked for her name.

Unbeknownst to Trinity, the nurse, Rainee, recognized her instantly. She had seen Trinity's face many times on social media, always smiling, usually next to the hottest man in Houston. Trinity's social media was massive. She was a charismatic entrepreneur with a lifestyle that seemed plucked from magazine pages. Also, Rainey's cousin D'avyonne was sleeping with Von. D'avyonne recently called her crying about their engagement and sent her photos of Trinity and Von. Rainee knew exactly who Trinity was. Seeing Trinity sitting in the clinic, her heart raced with shock and concern.

As Trinity sat in the waiting room, Rainee slipped into the break room and pulled out her phone. She scrolled through her contacts until she found a familiar name. She pressed the dial button under D'avyonne's name.

"Bitch, what are you doing?" Rainee whispered into the phone.

"You're not going to believe who I just saw... Von's fiancé, Trinity. She's at the clinic up here in Atlanta about to get an abortion."

"Are you serious? Trinity's there?" She asked.

"What?" Von's voice could be heard in the background. It just so happened that Von was over D'avyonne's place at that very moment.

"I'm dead serious. Is that Von, I hear? It would be best if you told Von now," Rainee whispered into the phone.

"That's none of my business," D'avyonne quickly tried to deflect.

"Who is that, and what about Trinity?" Von said in a stern tone.

D'avyonne hesitated momentarily because she didn't want Trinity to have his baby. However, she knew better than to play with Von. D'avyonne rolled her eyes.

"That's my cousin in Atlanta. She says Trinity is at her clinic about to get an abortion." Von quickly jumped out of bed.

"Give me that phone," he demanded with his hand out. D'avyonne handed him her cell phone.

"Hello, you sure it's Trinity?" he asked Rainee.

"I'm positive!" she yelled into the phone. His mind spun, disbelief giving way to anger, then fear he was losing a child.

"Rainee, I don't give a fuck what you have to do. Stall that motherfucking procedure. I'll pay you for looking out," he informed Rainee.

"Cool," she replied and hung up the phone. Rainee returned to the front and removed Trinity's name to the bottom of the list.

Von immediately left D'avyonne's place and called his assistant to charter a private jet to Atlanta. He didn't care how much it cost— those were the perks of being rich. The ride would only take an hour and thirty-five minutes. He made sure to have a rental car waiting at the airport when he got there.

Two hours passed, and Trinity walked up to the receptionist's desk.

"Hello, I had an appointment this morning and wondered why my name wasn't called?" Tasha, one of the other nurses, heard Trinity's concerns.

"I did see you early this morning. What time was your appointment time?" She asked.

"It was for 8:30 am," Trinity answered.

"There must be a mix-up. Let me go speak to the doctor." She tried to smooth things over with Trinity. Trinity nodded and went to sit back down. Rainee was sitting off to the side, looking nervous.

Just as the nurse Tasha was about to call Trinity to the back, the front door burst open.

"Trinity!" Von's voice was unmistakable. Trinity's heart sank as she heard the voice that made her stomach drop.

Von spots her sitting in the corner. Everyone in the clinic stopped talking and stared at Von due to his loud outburst. Trinity was startled, and her face showed nothing but fear. It was as if time stood still for a second. Von mumbles something under his breath while shaking his head disapprovingly. Trinity couldn't determine what he was saying, but she knew it wasn't good. She is frozen in her seat and sits there panicking.

"COME ON! What the fuck are you just sitting there for"? Von says forcefully.

She quickly grabbed her purse, which was sitting on the empty chair beside her, and headed for the door. Everyone was still staring at them. Von continued to hold the door open until Trinity quickly walked past him. Right before he closed the door, an older woman with short gray hair made a comment.

"Young man," she called out to Von.

"It's her body and her right to choose." Von looked at her sideways.

"Man, if you don't mind your motherfucking business and shut the fuck up talking to me! Ain't you a little too old to be getting knocked up anyway?" The lady gasped and seemed shocked at his words.

"Excuse me! You are so disrespectful. I'm here supporting someone else, thank you!"

"Yeah, sure you are," Von replied, quickly closing the door on the lady before she could say anything else. He and Trinity walked to the elevators in complete silence. Once they reached the elevators, Von pressed the down arrow button on the wall. They got on the elevators, and Von pressed the number 1 button to get to the first floor. As soon as the door closed, Von turned to look at Trinity all pissed off.

"Bruh," he murmured while slamming his right fist into his left hand.

"You like getting yo ass beat, don't you?" He let out a sarcastic laugh.

"Yeah, you must like getting yo ass beat, girl. I be trying to let you make it too!"

Trinity just stayed silent. The elevator doors opened, and they both walked out of the building.

CHIRP, CHIRP.

Von clicked the button on the car keys as they walked across the parking lot. He got in on the driver's side, and Trinity got in on the passenger's side. He didn't start the car engine up.

He calmly spoke, "Trinity, I will ask you two questions. Both answers will piss me the fuck off, but one may land you in the dirt, and I'm not even playing right now." Trinity was nervous as hell. She couldn't even look at him, so she stared straight ahead, watching more cars drive past them in the garage.

Von's anger escalated, but he tried his best to stay calm. Pointing his fingers in the shape of a gun near Trinity's face, he began with his questioning.

"Okay, check it. I caught you at an abortion clinic. So that means you are either getting rid of MY baby, or you are getting rid of ANOTHER nigga's baby and didn't want me to find out. I swear you better not lie either. Which is it?"

How in the hell did this nigga know I was at the clinic in Atlanta? I swear he literally got eyes everywhere. I'm sitting in the car, and Von just asked me if I was getting rid of his baby or another nigga's baby. He knows damn well I haven't been with another man but him.

I wanted to say so badly, "Bitch, I was getting rid of your baby, and I would've got away with it if it wasn't for the meddling kids."

Now is not the time to be funny, though. He was in a terrible mood and would probably break my jaw or kill me. I'm not stupid.

"Trinity, did you hear what the fuck I just asked you?" Von took his hand and slapped the shit out of the side of my face. Tears rolled down my face, and I calmly said, "Come on, Von. I haven't been with anyone else but you."

"So, you were getting rid of MY baby, right?" I paused at the question and just shook my head up and down to give him the answer he had been waiting on. He continued to stare at me and then replied,

"Ok." He cranked up the car and drove out into the streets, leaving the building where I was almost free from carrying his seed. If I was able to get the abortion, the ass whooping would be worth it. Real talk. That's how much I don't want to have this man's kid.

This is just another reason for him to try to control me, and now I'll never be able to leave his ass. He was speeding so fast, and my heart felt like it was beating out of my chest. He wanted to get to the airport so badly that he was running red lights. All I could do was say a silent prayer. I asked God to let me make it through the night with the littlest pain as possible. Von was determined to hurt me in the worst way possible. I worried about how he would hurt me and the amount of time the beating would last. Before I knew it, tears were rushing down my face. I made sure not to cry out loud to avoid annoying him more than I already have.

We arrived home a couple of hours later. Von grabbed me by the arm and rushed me upstairs to the bedroom.

"Get completely naked," he ordered.

"Huh?" I questioned him as if I didn't hear him the first time.

"Huh, my ass, you heard me, Trinity! Take off your clothes, NOW!" he barked.

Starting with my blouse, I begin to remove my clothing. As I undressed, Von disappeared into our huge walk-in closet. I couldn't see what he's doing. He was taking a long time in there. I'm nervous as hell. I'm standing in the room completely naked, looking at my clothes on the floor.

Suddenly, Von walks out of the closet holding handcuffs. He charges straight at me, grabbing for my right hand. He yanked me forcefully closer to him. I watched as he put one cuff on my right wrist and tightened it. He left the other hand free. He walked behind me and guided me with both hands towards the closet he had just left out of.

I ask him in a whimpering tone, "Von, what are you doing?"

He replied, "Teaching your ass a lesson you will never forget."

As we entered the closet, the words "What the fuck?" quickly came out of my mouth. He put a metal stripper pole in the middle of the closet floor. It was bolted down from the ceiling and had a floor base to hold it in place. I don't even know when he had time to do this. I'm thinking, *"I know this fool don't want me to dance."* I'm not in the mood to entertain his punk ass. He walks me over to the pole. He places both my hands around the pole and grabs the middle chain to cuff the free wrist. I'm officially bound to this pole.

It's like he had this shit planned out. I watched him slowly walk over to his belts that were hanging up and organized by the colors. He grabbed a long black leather belt and turned to face me. His look was cold, and not an ounce of sympathy for me could be seen. My eyes got big as hell as I began begging him not to use that on me. I started pleading with him like my life depended on it.

"Baby, please don't, please don't!" I reminded him that I was pregnant.

He calmly said, "I know you're pregnant; hell, that's how you got in this mess. I will be careful not to hit your stomach."

I yelled once more. "VON!" But that's the only word I could get out before he raised the belt and struck me hard as hell on my upper thigh. I wept in pain. I had nowhere to run. I was shackled to the pole and stuck to deal with the blows coming my way.

He screamed, "Bitch, you're an attempted murderer! You almost killed my baby. I have been praying for a child, and you tried to get rid of it!"

WAP!

The belt came down hard on my other thigh. I slid to the bottom of the pole immediately. My thighs felt like they were on fire. He made sure I felt those hits, which were quick and precise.

"STAND UP," he demanded.

I cried out, "I can't." He informed me that if I didn't stand up, the beating would take longer. I found the strength to get back up.

My knees were buckling, but I didn't fall. He walked to the back of me. I couldn't see him anymore. Too scared to turn around, I braced myself for another hit. *WAP, WAP, WAP!* Three consecutive hits came down on my buttocks. I squeezed the metal rail to hold my balance. My breathing picked up as I struggled to adjust to the pain. My buttocks were stinging.

I couldn't help it anymore. I begin to cry uncontrollably. My tears poured down my face and onto my chest. I don't know how I mustered up the courage at that moment, but I looked at him with so much animosity and screamed, "You're a monster! I hate your fucking guts. Your dad would be disappointed to see the man you've become."

Why did I say that? Big mistake. Von looked at me like I had lost my mind. He bit his lip in anger and raised the belt in the air. With every ounce of force in his body, he came down with the belt straight across my back. I instantly made the snake sound *sssssss* because that shit hurt like hell! I wanted to touch my back to soothe myself but couldn't move my shackled hands. He screamed out, "I'm a monster, huh? And you're the one at abortion clinics. Bitch, please!"

Next thing I know, he went crazy with the belt. He pretty much forgot I was pregnant. He swung the belt all kinds of ways across my body. I slid down the pole to ball my body up as much as possible. I took hit after hit across my head, back, arms, thighs, and legs. Every hit stung worse than the last. The pain was so unbearable that I couldn't even pass out. I lay there taking the brutal beating for what seemed like forever. Finally, he uncuffed me and helped me stand to my feet. Trying to walk was painful. He helped me to sit on the edge of the bed. I grabbed the blankets to cover my body.

He was headed out of the room but paused in his steps. "Hey, our engagement party is scheduled for the weekend before Thanksgiving. Make sure you purchase a lovely gown." I couldn't believe my ears. Not wanting to upset him, I nodded in agreement. This was happening too fast for me. It was best he planned everything without me anyway. This would not be a joyous occasion, at least not on my end.

Later that night, my body felt unsettled. I tossed and turned in my sleep. I awoke in the middle of the night, my body drenched in sweat. There was a deep ache that rippled from my abdomen. It felt sharp, unbearable, and wrong. For a moment, I told myself it was just another nightmare. The ones that had haunted me since the beatings started. The pain dragged on, bringing me fully into consciousness.

My heart pounded as I threw the covers back, gasping as my eyes took in the sight beneath me. My legs and thighs were smeared with blood. My throbbing vagina drenched the white sheets. I blinked as if trying to wipe away the image, but it stayed. This was real. I swallowed hard, my throat dry, feeling the hot sting of tears welling up. This wasn't supposed to happen. Not like this.

"Von!" I screamed, my voice a mix of fear and desperation. He was lying next to me, his chest rising and falling rhythmically as if nothing had happened, as if just hours ago he hadn't beaten me senseless during one of his uncontrollable rages.

"Von!" I cried louder, my voice breaking as I shook him awake. He stirred, confused, his eyes blinking open.

"What? What's going on?" His voice was sluggish, but his gaze quickly focused on the blood soaking the bed.

"I—I'm bleeding. Please, help me!" My words came out in a strangled sob, and my hands were shaking uncontrollably. Von's expression hardened for a split second, but then he pulled himself out of bed and grabbed his phone to call an ambulance. By the time we arrived at the hospital, I felt disconnected from everything. The nurses rushed me into a room. The sterile lights of the emergency room made me feel even more exposed, raw.

Hours passed like minutes, my mind clouded, until a doctor finally came in. His facial expression was serious.

"Miss Coleman," he began gently, "I'm so sorry, but you suffered a miscarriage." My chest tightened as I heard the words. Tears welled up in my eyes, but I blinked them away. Von stood near the door, arms crossed, watching me intently. I could feel his gaze pressing me to lie. His look reminded me of the consequences if I implicated him.

The doctor sighed, his expression softening. "Trinity, I need to ask—have you experienced any trauma or abuse? Any incidents or falls that could have led to this? Your body has small lacerations, severe bruises, and swelling. We can protect you. All you have to do is tell us the truth." The doctor moved closer towards me and blocked my view of Von.

I hesitated, my throat tightening as I struggled to get another glimpse of Von. I swallowed hard, my voice barely above a whisper.

"No, nothing like that. I—I think it just happened." The doctor paused, studying me carefully. I could feel his concern, his disbelief, but he didn't push the issue.

"Okay," he said quietly. "I'm sorry for your loss. We'll do what we can to help you recover."

The doctor left the room. Von's eyes remained cold and focused on me. I could have easily said he was the cause of the bruises on my skin, but I feared what he would do to me if I said the wrong thing. The silence between us was deafening. Von finally spoke, his voice low and edged with a dark calm.

"You killed my baby. This is all your fault. I bet you're smiling on the inside."

I closed my eyes, tears slipping down my cheeks as I silently mourned the life I could've had without him. He was right. Part of me was glad I wasn't carrying his baby anymore. I hate that he had to beat it out of me. Von didn't want me to get an abortion, yet he beat me to the point I had a miscarriage. How does that even make sense to him? I guess it doesn't. He thinks this is entirely my fault. I thought about the conversation I had with Kyra. It's becoming harder for him to hide his true self. Maybe he is a sociopath.

The mall buzzed with energy as me and Rainee made our way to the lavish dress shop called "Devine Fabrics." Rainee was my favorite cousin, and I was excited she flew in from Atlanta to be my plus one at the engagement party. We made our way into the store and began searching the racks of vibrant dresses. I gently brushed my fingers across the silky fabrics. Rainee, always full of life, searched beside me with a bounce in her step, pulling one dress down after another.

"This one is fire!" she exclaimed, holding up a fitted gold gown.

"You'll have every guy at that party staring."

I immediately felt a dull ache gnawing in my chest. There was only one guy I wanted, and he was about to get married to another woman. Rainee saw the sadness in my eyes.

"Every guy except Von," I muttered. Her smile dropped.

"Cousin, are you okay?" she asked. I looked up from the racks to assure her I was okay. That's when she walked into the store and right by us. I stared at the woman I envied the most. She was in this elegant boutique, looking for a dress for her engagement party. I wished this party wasn't even happening, but here we are.

Rainee sighed, putting the dress back and turning to face D'avyonne. "Look, I know this is hard. I mean, you've loved him for quite some time now. But you can't go to his engagement looking like you're attending a funeral. You've gotta show him what he's missing." She was right, but my attention was on Trinity at the moment.

D'avyonne scoffed, but before she could reply, her gaze caught something—or someone—across the store. Trinity was standing in front of a mirror, holding up a long ivory gown to her small frame. I scoffed at the vision before. Reality was setting in that I was about to lose Von forever. This woman has the life I only dreamed of. Rainee followed my gaze, her eyes widening.

"Wait, isn't that… Trinity?"

"Yup," I stated as we both stared at her. It was almost sickening how perfect she looked, like everything in her world was flawless. She must've felt the attention because she turned around and spotted me.

"Oh, hell no," Trinity exclaimed, her eyes narrowing as her hands clenched into fists.

"What the fuck are you doing here, you freaky-ass bitch?" Then her eyes zoomed in on my cousin.

"Wait a minute. Weren't you the woman at the abortion clinic in Atlanta?" It must have dawned on her.

"Omg, that's how he knew I was there," Trinity said. My cousin smirked and waved at her.

"Oh, you won't think it's funny when I get your ass fired!" Trinity spat. Rainee quickly dropped her smirk.

Rainee folded her arms and began tapping her foot on the tile floor.

"I don't know what you're talking about. That just happened to be a coincidence."

Trinity rolled her eyes. "Yeah, sure it was," she sassed my cousin.

My heart pounded, a mix of anger and jealousy swirling in my chest. I know Von would be mad at me for starting trouble with his fiancée, but I didn't care.

With Rainee by my side, I made my way toward Trinity. She stood her ground.

"I wish you would come closer. I have been waiting to rock yo shit since you ate my pussy without my permission." Two females were walking past us. One of the ladies elbowed the other after they heard what Trinity said. I forced a tight-lipped smile.

"Yeah, I did that, but only because Von wanted me to!" I snapped. Trinity shook her head.

"He got you out here looking goofy! Do you always do everything he wants you to do? It's pathetic. I bet you're in here shopping for a gown to attend our engagement party."

She chuckled. "You're just mad because he always wants me around," I teased.

"No! I'm mad your pussy is not good enough to make him only want to be with you," Trinity's words cut deep.

"Ooowee," I heard one of the nosy ass females say. They act like they were shopping but were hard up listening to us.

"I feel sorry for you. You want what I DON'T want so bad. If only you knew, honey," she fussed. I could tell Rainee was agreeing with Trinity; that's why she was so quiet.

"I have every right to be upset. Von spends a lot of time with me. He is handsome, rich, and he takes care of business. I would give anything to be the one marrying him," I stated. Trinity shook her head in disbelief.

"Girl, everything that glitters ain't gold. Be careful what you ask for. He's manipulative, abusive, and pure evil," she stated.

"Well, that's your experience. It won't be mine," I informed her. Rainee rolled her eyes at me and walked off.

"I'll tell you what. Make him choose me or you. If he chooses you, I'll be gone immediately!" She assured me.

"Okay, I will," I said, trying to sound convincing that I had no problem giving him an ultimatum, but deep down I feared the outcome of that.

Trinity turned around and left me standing there alone. She went back to searching for dresses. I stormed out of the dress shop to find Rainee. She was sitting on a bench outside the store. I tried to pick a fight with Trinity but ended up getting embarrassed. I sat next to Rainee. She grabbed my hand with tears in her eyes.

"D'avyonne, I know this might be hard to hear, but that woman is telling you the truth. Being with Von is not all it's cracked up to be. Do you want to be a side piece forever? You're better than that! You got a club out that nigga; now go find a real man. Think about this. Why wouldn't Trinity want to have that man's baby?"

She waited for me to answer. "I don't know; it could be for many reasons. Maybe she is selfish," I said. Rainee rolled her eyes.

"A woman like that is not selfish. There's a good reason she doesn't want a kid by him. Let me ask you something. Has Von ever put his hands on you?" She inquired.

"No, he hasn't," I lied. One thing about my cousin is she knows when I'm being dishonest. I looked away from her, and we remained quiet for a few minutes. We sat and reflected on what had just happened. I'm going to that engagement party and will make a final plea with him to be with me.

He either chooses me or Trinity.

The penthouse atop the gleaming skyscraper stood as a beacon of luxury against the backdrop of Houston's skyline. Tonight, it hosted the most illustrious event of the season, an engagement party thrown by the esteemed couple, Jervonte Westley and Trinity Coleman.

As guests ascended the grand staircase, they were captivated by the sight of the lavish penthouse. Soothing R&B music flowed through the air. Glasses clinked, and laughter filled the room as the city's finest mingled and danced beneath the dazzling chandeliers.

Von, looking dapper in a tailored suit that exuded power and elegance, moved through the crowd with the grace of a seasoned host. His charming smile lit up the room as he greeted each guest with genuine warmth and hospitality. At the top of the staircase, Trinity radiated beauty and grace. She looked down at Von as he worked the crowd in the living room area, laughing and making small talk with the guests.

Trinity's stomach was in knots. She wasn't in the mood to party or pretend like she was happy. Von noticed Trinity still hanging on to the rail at the top of the stairs. He waved for her to make her way down to him. She slowly made her way down the steps, and you can hear the taps on the marble tile floor from the stiletto heels she elegantly sported. People gazed up at her in awe. Her striking beauty almost silenced the room, and she commanded everyone's attention by simply walking.

Houston's elite residents showed up in their best fashions. Among the guests were politicians, philanthropists, entertainers, athletes, and entrepreneurs—all drawn together by the couple's hospitality and the promise of an unforgettable evening. Every detail spoke to the couple's impeccable taste and unwavering commitment to excellence, from the polished marble floors to the exquisite art adorning the walls. The wedding planner that Von hired pulled Trinity to the side while she and Kyra were enjoying some wine in the kitchen. The lady wanted to discuss options for her wedding. Trinity wanted to decline but didn't want Von to cause a scene.

Trinity sat at the edge of the large table, staring blankly at the array of appetizers meticulously placed before her. Her fingers absently brushed against the rim of her champagne glass, though she had no intention of taking a sip. The engagement party was supposed to be a celebration, but it felt like a funeral for her. The air was thick with the scent of expensive perfumes, floral arrangements, and false smiles. Her fiancé, Von, stood across the room, laughing boisterously with his corporate friends. His controlling, dark eyes darted in her direction, a silent warning that she better be smiling and grateful.

The wedding planner Von hired sat beside her, trying to engage her in another round of discussions about floral choices and cake flavors.

"Trinity, we really need to finalize the colors for the reception. Do you think we could go with the lavender or the blush pink?"

Trinity barely looked up. "I don't care," she muttered. She couldn't muster the energy to fake enthusiasm. The planner, clearly flustered, tried her best to maintain her chipper demeanor.

"I'm sorry, I just—" Trinity cut herself off. It was pointless. No amount of blush pink or lavender was going to make her feel like this was a good idea. As the night went on, the penthouse buzzed with excitement. From the rooftop terrace, guests admired the breathtaking view of the city below. The sounds of laughter and chatter from inside can be heard from outside. The place was jam-packed from the entrance to the outside balcony.

For Von, tonight was more than just an engagement party—it was a celebration of their success, and a testament to the journey he and Trinity had over the years. Trinity would finally be his wife and promised to him forever. At least that's what he was thinking. For Trinity, she was living a nightmare, and the thought of Von becoming her husband made her nauseous.

As they stood side by side outside on the beautiful patio, surrounded by friends and loved ones, they both didn't share the same interests anymore. A waiter came over and handed Von and Trinity a glass of champagne. Von raised his glass in the air and told the crowd how excited he was for Trinity to be Mrs. Westley. He looked her passionately in her eyes and told her how much he loved her.

His kind words moved the audience before them. "Aww," some of them blurted out.

"To my future wife," Von held the glass of champagne up in the air to toast to their engagement. The guests followed his lead. They all raised glasses in the air. Trinity reluctantly held her glass in the air.

The guests cheered and clinked each other's glasses together while some people applauded. The guests seemed so happy but didn't know about Von's cruel words and the small ways he manipulated her life until it felt like she had no control. They certainly didn't know about the bruise on her arm, still tender from where he had grabbed her during a fight two nights before. He was drinking and thought about the baby she had miscarried. He took his frustration out on her arm, by punching into her flesh like it was nothing. Trinity tried her best to keep a smile on her face.

Suddenly, she felt dizzy, nauseous, and overwhelmed by intense fear and anxiety. As her heart raced and breathing became shallow, she collapsed to the ground. Some of the guests gasped for air in disbelief and crowded around her as she lay there unconscious. Ja watched what occurred from a distance. Von was embarrassed and trying to hide the fact that he was fuming mad at her for fainting at such an important moment.

He instructed Tank to lay her down in the guest bedroom. When she opened her eyes, she was no longer at the table. She was lying on a velvet couch in the downstairs guest room. The murmurs of concerned guests filtered in from the other side of the door. Slowly, she sat up, trying to steady herself. Her head still felt light, but her heart raced less frantically now. "Trinity," a voice called softly from the doorway.

She looked up, and her heart skipped a beat. It was Ja, the mysterious architect she had been crushing on. Someone whose presence soothed her nerves, though she rarely saw him. He stepped inside, closing the door behind him. His gaze was filled with concern.

"Are you alright?" he asked gently, sitting down beside her on the couch.

"I… I don't know," Trinity admitted, her voice trembling.

"It's all too much. I can't breathe. How did you get inside the party?" Ja frowned; his brow furrowed in worry.

"I have my ways. I know you're in real danger with this man. Do you want to be with him? It's obvious you're not happy."

His words hit her like a wave. She hadn't looked happy because she wasn't. She was about to marry a man who controlled her every move, who made her feel small and insignificant. The engagement party wasn't about love; it was about appearances.

"I don't have a choice," she whispered, more to herself than to him. Ja leaned closer, his voice steady.

"There's always a choice."

Tears welled up in her eyes, and for the first time in months, she allowed herself to feel the weight of it all—the fear, the sadness, the hopelessness. She felt trapped in a life she didn't want, with a man who had slowly worn her down until she didn't recognize herself anymore. But sitting here, with Ja beside her, she felt a flicker of something she hadn't felt in a long time: hope.

Before she could stop herself, she whispered, "I don't love him. I can't leave. Von or his men will kill me." Ja's gaze softened, and he reached out to gently take her hand.

"You deserve better than this, Trinity. You deserve to be happy. I'm going to see what I can do to help you." Trinity closed her eyes, taking a deep breath. The anxiety that had overwhelmed her earlier was still there.

"Von is a very dangerous man. I've tried to leave him, but he always finds me. He won't hesitate to kill you too.

"Don't get caught up in my mess," she warned him. When she opened her eyes, she met Ja's gaze, and it melted her heart. The anxiety she was feeling suddenly subsided. He gently rubbed her hand.

"Get up right now and walk out of here with me. I'll put you somewhere safe."

"I can't do that," she whispered, more firmly this time.

"You can't, or you won't," Ja asked, concerned. "Both. This man has shown me he is unstoppable," Trinity answered.

They could hear men walking and talking down the hallway. They were headed towards them. Ja quickly hid behind the large door. Von stuck his head inside the room.

"Are you feeling better?" he asked Trinity. She nodded her head yes.

"Come on, we still have guests to entertain." Trinity got up off the couch and headed for the door. Before making her exit, she gave Ja one last glance. Right then and there, Ja vowed to set Trinity free from her invisible cage.

D'avyonne and Rainee entered the party. D'avyonne quickly adjusted the strap of her shimmering gown as she entered the penthouse. The engagement party was in full swing, with lights twinkling overhead and guests in expensive attire clinking glasses and exchanging hollow compliments. But none of that mattered to her. Her heart pounded in her chest, and her palms were slick with nervous sweat. She was here for one reason only: to stop Von from making the biggest mistake of his life.

Her eyes scanned the room until they landed on her lover and his fiancée. They walked hand in hand across the beautiful living room. D'avyonne's stomach tightened at the sight. Trinity was beautiful, wealthy, the perfect socialite who had everything she could possibly dream of. D'avyonne didn't, including the man she was in love with. She took a deep breath, and they began weaving their way through the crowd, their heels clicking sharply on the marble floor. D'avyonne had to talk to him. Tonight. Before it was too late.

As she approached, Von caught sight of them, his eyes narrowing slightly in recognition. He excused himself from the crowd, leaving Trinity behind, and stepped toward D'avyonne. His smile was smooth but lacked warmth. Rainee walked away to grab a drink and give them some time to talk.

"D'avyonne. You look… stunning," he said, his voice low. She forced a smile, but there was no joy in it.

"We need to talk, Von. Now." He nodded. "Let's go somewhere more private."

They went into the empty guest room. Ja was no longer in there. He was able to slip out of the party without ever being seen. D'avyonne's chest tightened with every step. This was her last chance. She couldn't hold back anymore. When they reached a quiet corner, Von leaned casually against the wall, hands in his pockets.

"So, what's this about?"

D'avyonne's heart raced, but she steadied herself. "I can't do this anymore. I can't watch you marry her." His expression didn't change.

"D'avyonne—"

"No," she interrupted, her voice firm. "I love you. I've been in love with you for years. You know that. And I know you care about me too, no matter what you try to act like. But I won't be a part of this anymore unless you're ready to choose." Von raised an eyebrow, the amusement in his eyes fading.

"Choose?"

"Between me and Trinity," D'avyonne said, her voice trembling despite her best efforts to sound strong.

"I can't keep pretending like this is okay. Like, I'm okay. I love you, Von. I deserve better than this… than being your secret. You need to make a decision." There was a long pause, his face unreadable. For a fleeting moment, D'avyonne thought maybe—just maybe—he would choose her. That he would realize how much he meant to her, how much better they could be together. But then Von straightened, his smile turning cold, and something dark flashed in his eyes.

"You really thought I'd choose you?" he said, his voice dripping with condescension.

"D'avyonne, don't be ridiculous." Her stomach dropped, and the air in the room seemed to grow heavy.

"What?" she whispered. The disbelief clear in her voice.

"Listen," he continued, his tone harsh. "You're fun. We have good times, sure. But that's all it is. Fun. You're the side chick, D'avyonne. That's your role. And I need you to accept that." The words hit her like a punch to the gut, knocking the breath from her lungs. She stared at him, stunned into silence.

Von shrugged. "Trinity. She's the one I'm marrying. She's the one who had my heart since we were teenagers. You? You're just the girl I call when I want something different. That's how it's always been, and that's how it'll stay."

D'avyonne's hands balled into fists, her heart shattering with every word. She had known this wasn't perfect—had known deep down that Von was a selfish man—but she hadn't realized just how little he thought of her.

"I'm not your side chick," she said, her voice low, trembling with barely contained anger. He smirked, leaning in slightly.

"Oh, but you are. And if I were you, I'd play my part real carefully."

D'avyonne stepped back, her skin crawling.

"What is that supposed to mean?" Von's smile widened, but there was no humor in it.

"That building you think I gifted you. The one you're so proud of? It's not really in your name. You don't own it. I do. I can take it back whenever I want. So, I'd watch how you play your cards, D'avyonne. Don't forget who's in control here."

Her breath hitched. She felt as if the ground had been pulled out from under her. The building. The one thing she had believed was hers, the one symbol of her independence, of what she could build for herself. And now he was telling her it had all been a lie, another way to control her.

"How could you—" she started, but the words wouldn't come. She felt sick. Her eyes burned with tears, but she refused to cry in front of him.

Von leaned back, his face smug. "Go back to the party, D'avyonne. Smile, drink some champagne. Play your part. Or you'll find out just how much worse things can get if you try to cross me."

She stood there for a moment, numb, staring at the man she once thought she loved. The man she had risked everything for. And in that moment, she realized how deeply she had misjudged him—how blind she had been to his cruelty.

Without another word, D'avyonne turned and walked away. She didn't stop to look back. She didn't need to. She had heard all she needed to know. As she made her way back into the ballroom, her head held high despite the pain ripping through her chest, one thought echoed in her mind: This wasn't over. Not by a long shot.

I got the contact information of the daughter whose parents were murdered from our database system. I dialed the number.

"Hello, Miss Coleman speaking," she spoke like a true professional.

"Hi, Trinity Coleman, right?" I asked.

"Yes, this is she," she said.

"Trinity, my name is Officer Whitfield, and I would like to speak to you about your parent's case that went cold.

"Are you opening the case back up? Did you find the murderer?" she anxiously asked. I heard a deep voice in the background inquiring about the phone call.

"Who is that? Who's reopening the case?" the man said.

"I don't know. It's a cop on the phone." I interrupted their conversation before they started making assumptions.

"Miss Coleman, can you come down to precinct 49? We're located off Dairy Ashford Road," I informed her.

"Yes, I can come now. And my fiancée wants to come too," she said, pausing for a second. About forty-five minutes later, Trinity and her fiancé showed up. I walked them into one of our conference rooms. Before I was about to shut the door, Detective Fulton and Detective Carter tried to enter the room. I blocked them from coming in. This is a closed meeting. I suggest taking your grievances up with Captain Marley. I closed the door and locked it.

"Hello, Trinity. It's very nice to meet you. First, I want to say I'm sorry about what happened to your parents."

"Man, fuck all that, and get to the point," her boyfriend rudely demanded.

"Really, Von?" Trinity was annoyed by his demeanor.

"I'll get right to the point," I said while rolling my eyes at him. There has been some new evidence in regard to your parent's murder. We believe it will lead us directly to who's responsible.

"Wow, really. What evidence is that?" she asked. There has been a video to surface that matches the location and time of your parent's murder. In the video, a man can be seen fleeing the scene. He was covered up pretty good, but like always, they leave room for error.

"What error is that?" the guy asked me.

"Well, this is still an ongoing investigation, so I can't say much. I want you to know, Trinity, that your parent's case is officially reopened. I won't stop until I find that monster," I assured her. She smiled big.

"I have been waiting to hear these words for a long time. I knew God wouldn't let the killer get away with this," she boasted.

"The two detectives they had on this case didn't do anything to help me, right babe?" She spoke to her lover.

"Yup, they ain't worth shit," he added.

"You will be the first to know when we have the perpetrator in custody," I informed her. Both of them got up. Before she left the room, she turned to me, and thanked me one last time for reopening the case. I smiled and gave her a wink. What a sweet young lady.

However, her man is awful. More weeks passed, and I was working my way down the list of tattoo artists that could possibly be responsible for that tattoo. I had our tech department zoom in on the tattoo to print it out. It looked okay but wasn't great. I was hoping the artist would still spot his work. I really wanted to come through for Trinity. That poor girl suffered enough.

I sat in my car, watching the tattoo shop from across the street. The purple neon sign buzzed with the words "3D Tattoos Here." I had been tracking leads for weeks. I was down to the last three shops that specialize in 3D illusion tattoos. I hoped I was one step closer to identifying the man with the double snake tattoo on his calf muscle. He was a wanted man for a double murder, and the snake coiling on his leg was the key.

I'd shown photos of the tattoo to every illusion artist I could find. Nothing was a hit yet. Venomous Ink was the third shop from last. It was a small, hidden studio that catered to exclusive clients, the kind who didn't want to be found. I heard rumors about a mysterious artist, known as King Hiss. He only specialized in unique designs, including the intricate snakes that haunted my mind. I got out of the car and crossed the street.

My footsteps were drowned by the bustling noise of Downtown Houston. I didn't trust this part of the city. A lot of crazy folks roamed this part of town. My hand hovered over my gun. I couldn't afford to let my guard down, not when I felt unsafe. I had this feeling for days now, and it was getting stronger.

Inside the shop, the air was thick with the scent of ink and antiseptic. The man behind the counter glanced up, his eyes narrowing at me as I flashed my police badge.

"I'm looking for someone. The artist who did this tattoo," I said, showing him a photo of the snake tattoo. The man's face paled ever so slightly, and his hand froze mid-reach for a cigarette. "Never seen it."

I could tell he was lying, but before I could press him further, a flicker of movement outside the window caught my eye. Two men stood by my car, watching me intently. They looked like gang members rocking red bandanas on their heads. It dawned on me that I was followed. I didn't have time to hesitate. I turned my attention back to the man behind the counter.

"You're going to want to cooperate, or your shop's going to be part of a murder investigation," I assured him.

"Now, who did the tattoo?"

The man hesitated, his eyes darting toward the back room, but he never got the chance to answer. The front door burst open, and the two gang members stormed in, weapons drawn. I dove behind the counter as bullets shattered the glass display case. Glass flew everywhere, and I pulled my gun out.

"Officer, you should've minded your fucking business," one of them sneered as they advanced.

"Time to take a long nap."

My heart pounded in my chest. I refuse to let them corner me in the shop. I darted toward the back exit, firing a shot that grazed one of the men's arms. He howled in pain, and his partner returned fire, the bullets narrowly missing me as I kicked open the back door. The alley outside was dark and narrow, the kind of place where sound didn't travel well. Perfect for an ambush. But I wasn't the kind of woman to be caught off guard. I have been in worse situations before and had no intention of losing this battle.

The first man barreled through the door after me, but I was ready. I crouched down behind the door and swept his legs out from under him, sending him crashing to the ground. He groaned in pain as I disarmed him, pressing the barrel of my gun to his temple.

"Who sent you?" I demanded. He smirked through the pain.

"You're already dead, lady. You just don't know it yet."

Before I could react, the second man lunged at me from behind. I twisted his arm and drove my elbow into his ribs. He stumbled back, and I landed a swift kick to his knee, dropping him.

Both men were down. I cuffed them quickly, then stepped back, adrenaline still coursing through my veins. Thank God I practice self-defense techniques with Des all the time. He keeps me on my toes.

"What gang are you two with?" I yelled.

"The 163 Mafia Family," the one I shot, confessed.

"Man, don't tell her shit," the other dude demanded. As sirens echoed in the distance, I realized that this case had just gotten more dangerous. Someone didn't want me finding the man with the snake tattoo. But that only made me more determined.

I turned back toward the tattoo shop, where the man behind the counter stood wide-eyed at the chaos that had unfolded in his shop.

"I'm not asking again," I said, my voice colder.

"Who did the tattoo?" The man swallowed hard, fear creeping into his eyes.

"Dawn," he whispered.

"He is off today but will return tomorrow."

"I'm not waiting another day. Call him up here now."

He nodded and picked up his cellphone to call Dawn.

"Hey man, you need to come to the shop now. I'll explain later; just come," he spoke into the phone.

"He will be here in 20 minutes," he said. Almost a half-hour later, Dawn came through the door looking like a vampire in real form. He looked confused and worried.

"Dawn, I need some information about a tattoo you did. Don't try to lie, or I'll have this shop closed due to a pending murder investigation." He looked at the man behind the counter to see what he should do. The man nodded, so Dawn took the picture of the tattoo out of my hand.

"Yes, I did this tattoo. Sick work, right!" He bragged. I ignored him, and my annoyed look wiped that smile clean off his face.

"All I know is the man goes by the name Tank and runs with the 163 Mafia Family. That's all I know," he shrugged.

"You better not be lying, or I'm coming back with more cops," I informed him. I left happy that I got what I came for. I sat back in my car thinking about how I barely escaped death. Desmond will be mad that I played detective alone in a bad part of town. Okay, time to find out who this Tank person is.

"We got you now, motherfucka," I whispered out loud.

* * *

The next morning, I went to work and headed straight to Captain Marley's office. I entered the room and noticed his wife, Charissa, and Desmond were sitting down having a conversation with him.

"Oh, I'm sorry. I can come back if you all are in a meeting."

"Hey, you've been gone lately. Where you been?" he asked. I closed the door, and Desmond offered me his seat. Sitting down, I began to tell them everything.

"Wait a minute. You've been doing detective work on your own Jean? You could've gotten hurt or even worse, killed," he scolded me.

"I know, captain, but we're now closer than ever to solving this double homicide after all these years. I just didn't trust Detective Fulton or Detective Carter to tag along with me." Captain frowned at my statement.

294

"Those are two highly decorated police detectives. I don't understand," he replied.

"Dan, that's why I'm here and called this meeting," Sergeant Charissa spoke up.

"You're not about to like what I'm about to say. Your precinct is under investigation for corruption. I have a long list of complaints from inmates and members in our community that says Detective Fulton and Detective Carter took bribes, planted evidence, padded charges to convict people, and used intimidation methods to keep people from coming forward. This goes back at least 15 years. We have substantial evidence that proves they're guilty. I was giving you the heads up first before the cavalry storms in here. They are about to be arrested as soon as I give them the signal."

Captain removed his reading glasses and rubbed his face.

"How long have you known about this, Rissa?" he asked. She took a minute to respond. It got very awkward.

"For quite some time. We were building a solid case against them," she confessed.

"Wow. You're just now having the decency to tell me," Captain stated in a disappointing tone.

"Come on now, Dan. You ought to understand I can't compromise my job like that." Captain was speechless.

"And you, missy…we're gonna talk about how you think you're Veronica Mars!" Des pointed his finger at me. I couldn't do anything but roll my eyes at this crazy fool.

"Make the call, Charissa," Dan said sadly.

"Detectives and officers from precinct 32 will make the arrests. This might be too hard for the officers stationed here," she informed. She made a call on her phone.

"Send them in," she advised.

"Okay, let's go watch this unfold," she said. We all walked out and headed towards both of their desks, which were right next to one another. Ten officers stormed the building along with members from the internal affairs office and prosecutors' office. It looked like a mob was headed their way. Almost everyone stopped what they were doing to watch.

A tall, heavyset, bald man wearing a gray suit approached the men. Officers circled around them with their guns drawn.

"Detective Fulton and Detective Carter, put your hands up and don't make any sudden moves," he ordered. The men did as they were told.

"What's this about!" Detective Carter hollered.

"We will tell you; just hold still." The man in the gray suit quickly placed Detective Fulton's hands behind his back and cuffed him. One of the officers followed suit and handcuffed Detective Carter.

They removed both their guns and badges from their bodies.

"Fulton…Carter, you are being charged with the following crimes: bribery, extortion, perjury, obstruction of justice, drug trafficking, assault and excessive use of force, embezzlement, conspiracy, racketeering, civil rights violations, misuse of power, misuse of police resources, tampering with evidence, and fraud. The Miranda Rights are typically recited by law enforcement when someone is taken into custody. The standard wording is as follows: You have the right to remain silent. Anything you say can and will be used against you in a court of law. You have the right to an attorney. If you cannot afford an attorney, one will be provided for you. Do you understand these rights as they have been read to you?"

They acknowledged they understood their rights.

"Don't say shit, Carter. We will get a lawyer!" Detective Fulton yelled.

They both involuntarily participated in the walk of shame by being walked out of the building. Cops shook their heads as they watched two of their coworkers' downfalls.

"Let this be a lesson to everybody in here!" Charissa boldly spoke while pointing towards the former detectives.

"You enforce the law. You're NOT above the law. You will be found out. You will be prosecuted to the fullest extent. Good day, ladies and gentlemen." She left the building.

Desmond walked up to me and placed his loving hands on my shoulders.

"Jean, you're so close to solving the Coleman murders. Finding the tattoo artist is nothing but circumstantial evidence. You need to connect the dots. Find the motive between the suspect and the victims." I nodded in agreement. We couldn't go after this Tank guy with just my information alone. He would walk free. We needed to build a solid case against him that would stick.

"Just be careful because it's obviously somebody trying to harm you. I'm not letting you go alone anymore, okay? It's too dangerous." He gently kissed me on the forehead.

"Can we go to Gringos? I need a good drink and some tacos," I asked him. He smiled.

"Come on. Let's go," he obliged.

I lay on the hard cot in my prison cell, staring up at the ceiling. The gray walls seemed to close in around me, but I've grown used to that over the years. I've been stuck in this prison, and at times I felt like giving up. Years stolen from me because of two crooked police officers who had pulled me over and miraculously found bags of cocaine in my trunk. I was framed, and no one listened to me back then. I still wonder who could've planted those drugs in my vehicle. There was only one name that kept ringing in my ear. I just couldn't prove it. I was young and Black; the courts didn't believe I was being set up. To this day, I maintain my innocence. They wanted me to take a plea deal, but I refused. This is how the system railroaded so many Black people.

I closed my eyes, trying to drown out the constant hum of the prison, the distant clanging of metal doors, and the low murmurs of other inmates. I thought of the life I could've had with Trinity. She tried to visit me a couple of times back then, but I refused to see her.

I didn't want her last memory of me to be behind bars. Finding out her parents were murdered devastated me. I wanted to be there for her so bad. The world had moved on without me, and all I had left was hope and memories. A faint knock on the bars pulled me out of my thoughts.

"Reese, you have a visitor," came the familiar voice of one of the prison guards named Hill.

"A visitor? It's not even visiting hours," I noticed.

"Your lawyer, Yasmine Brown, is here to see you."

She was the lawyer my family found to represent me. She actually did a good job trying to show my true character to the judge. No matter how hard she tried, the detectives testified against me, sealing my fate. Who are the courts more likely to believe, me or two well-known detectives? There must be a good reason for her visiting me after all this time. The guard unlocked the cell and walked me to a room scheduled for special visits. Yasmine was sitting down looking through a folder full of paperwork. When she saw me, she smiled really big.

"Whoa, you've packed on some muscles! How are you, Reese? It's been a long time," she stated.

"What's going on?" I asked.

Yasmine took a deep breath and instructed me to sit down. "Reese, I've got some good news. The two detectives who pulled you over that day have been arrested on multiple corruption charges. This means their entire record is under investigation after evidence showed they falsely accused people of crimes they didn't commit."

I paused, rubbing the top of my dreads, trying to process what she just said. Am I dreaming? I felt a jolt of something—hope, disbelief, anger at the years I lost in this hellhole. But I held it in, trying to stay grounded. I prayed for good news like this for a long time.

"So... what does that mean for me?" I asked cautiously.

Yasmine smiled. "It means the state is looking to overturn your case. They're going through all the convictions tied to those officers, and you're on that list. If everything goes smoothly, you could be released. It might take some time, but there's a very real chance you'll be out of here this year."

I took a deep breath. "This year?"

She nodded. "Yeah, but listen, Reese. I need you to stay out of trouble, okay? No fights, no issues. The state's going to be reviewing everything about you—your behavior in here, your record, everything. If you keep your head down and stay patient, we could be looking at your freedom."

I promised her I would stay out of trouble. I couldn't wait to call Z and my mother to give them the good news! Freedom was something I missed and deserved to have. The world outside seemed like a distant memory, but now there was a real chance I could walk out of here and rebuild my life. "How long do you think it'll take?" I asked.

She sighed. "It's hard to say. Bureaucracy can move slowly, and there are a lot of cases like yours to go through. I'll be on top of it every step of the way. Just hang in there a little longer. Patience is key right now."

I already survived almost ten years. What were a few more months if it meant I'd get my life back?

"I can do that. I've waited this long. I can wait a little longer," I assured her.

"Good. I'll keep you updated as soon as I hear anything. But Reese, I need you to believe this—you're almost there. Just keep it together." I stood and shook her hand.

"Thank you, Yasmine. For everything."

"It's my pleasure. Maybe when you get out of here, you can take me on a date," she teased. I just smiled and made my exit. I didn't want to hurt her feelings because I was not interested. Hill was posted by the door; we walked back to my cell in silence.

When he locked the cell door behind me, I sat down on my cot. I closed my eyes, but this time, instead of the bleak gray walls of this cell, I imagined the outside world. It was almost as if I could feel the sun on my face and a fresh breeze. Freedom was close; I could feel it.

"Thank God for not throwing me away," I whispered.

I'm about to come home!

It was two hours past the time I was supposed to get off work. Von's name lit up on my phone.

"Why are you not home yet?" he asked.

"I'm on the way now. I was just finishing up some paperwork for this deal I closed today."

"Aight," he hung up the phone in my face. He didn't even say congratulations. Zoya came knocking on my glass door.

"You need anything before I head out?" she said.

"No, I'm good. I'm leaving soon."

"Okay girl, see you tomorrow."

I was the last one to leave the office. I locked up and walked to my car. You could hear the sound of my heels tapping the concrete. The parking lot was nearly empty, except for a few cars belonging to the cleaning crew. I clutched my keys and flung my small wallet purse across my body.

Suddenly, a van sped toward me, tires screeching against the asphalt. I fumbled with my keys to open my car door. Panic surged in my chest. The van cornered me, and the door slid open. A man covered in all black jumped out. His face was hidden behind a ski mask.

"Help!" I screamed. I tried to swing at him, but he caught my hand and wrestled me to the ground. He forcefully placed a towel over my face, and it instantly knocked the wind out of me. I could smell some type of strong chemicals. I fell into a deep slumber. Blinking through the haze of disorientation, I woke up on a black leather sectional couch in a modern cabin house.

The smell of wet earth and pine mixed with the faint aroma of coffee in the air."

What the hell," I whispered. I notice I wasn't tied up. I bolted for the door, only to be met with a torrential downpour. The rain was relentless, drumming against the roof in a symphony of chaos. I tried to run through it, but the ground was slick with mud. My foot slipped, and I fell. The rain drenched my clothes as I lay sprawled on the ground. A figure stood over me while water clouded my eyes. He picked me up and carried me. Once we were back in the cabin, he grabbed a towel and started wiping my face. I jerked away from him. That's when our eyes met.

"Ja?" I said, confused. I snarled at him.

"So, you're a lunatic too? Are you going to kill me? Oh lord, don't tell me you're a Black Ted Bundy!" I blabbed. He chuckled.

"Girl, stop being dramatic. I told you I was going to protect you. You're safe. Nobody knows where you're at," I informed her. I was still nervous.

"Ja, you have to take me back. He will kill us both. He always finds me," she cried.

"Trinity, he always finds you because there was a tracking device on your keychain. I took those keys and tossed them out the window."

"Ja, I'm scared. Just take me back!" He left the room and came back with a big towel. I was soaking wet. He placed the towel around my shoulders. Then he brought me a cup of coffee.

"I know you're scared, but this cabin is not even in my name. He won't find you. Take this time to relax and heal. Heal from him, and let your body heal from all those bruises. Regardless, I'll protect you."

I was thinking about his words. My mind was telling me to return to Von. My heart was telling me to trust this man.

"Fine," I reluctantly said.

"Let me show you your room." I followed him into the master bedroom, with a huge bathroom connected to it.

"I'm sleeping in here? Where will you sleep?" I asked.

"I'm right across the hall," he said, pointing. Water ran down my leg, and dirt clung to my elbows and other body parts.

"I just slipped in the mud. Can I take a shower?" I asked.

"Yeah, you don't have to ask. Make yourself comfortable," he stated. When I got out of the shower, he gave me a throw blanket to get comfortable on the couch with. He warmed up some leftover pizza for us and sat on the opposite side of the couch. I watched as this beautiful man searched through the cable channels.

"I love this movie. You want to watch Boomerang?" he asked, showing off his perfect smile.

I was mesmerized. "Y-yeah," I stumbled over my words.

"I love this movie," I stated. This might be the first case in history where a female fucks her kidnapper willingly on the first night. The rain continued to pour down on the house. It was relaxing to listen to. The movie wasn't over yet, and we both were sprawled out on our side of the couch, knocked completely out. A few hours later, I felt soft hands shaking my arms. I opened my eyes, and Ja stood over me.

"Trinity, you're tired. Go get in the bed," he spoke softly. He helped me off the couch, and I went to my new room. I closed the door behind me. For some reason, I felt safe and at peace. Two things I haven't felt in a very long time.

* * *

The following day, the aroma of good cooking hit my nose. I walked out and heard soulful music playing towards the front. I was shocked to see Ja in the kitchen area over a hot stove.

"Girl, you know I…I…I love you. No matter what you do," he sang while flipping the pancakes over. I stood there giggling. He finally noticed me standing there.

"Oh, I'm just messing around. Go ahead, sit," he directed me towards a round cherry oak table. I sat in one of the wooden chairs. Ja came over and placed a plate in front of me that had two pancakes, a small pile of cheese grits, 3 pieces of bacon, and one jalapeño sausage on it.

"Thank you," I said. The food looked yummy. I wasn't used to nothing like this. Von never cooked me a boiled egg. Next, he placed a glass of lemonade on the side of my plate. After he fixed his plate, he joined me at the table.

"Did you sleep good?" he asked. I smiled and nodded my head.

"I slept really good." I just remembered I needed to call Zoya and tell her to hold things down for me at the office.

"Hey Ja, where's my phone? I have to call my assistant and let her know I'm safe and give her some tasks to do. I also need to call my best friend," I informed him.

"Trinity, do you trust me?" he asked. I gave him the side-eye.

"I barely even know you," I said. He holds his hand up to surrender to my previous statement.

"I get that, but hear me out. You got to completely disappear for a while."

I hopped up from the table. "What! You're trying to isolate me. This feels familiar," I angrily screamed.

"I promise it's not like that. Von is a dangerous man. He is smart. He will check to see who has heard from you, and he will harm anyone who doesn't give him the information he wants. If he has connections, he could easily trace the signal to where you're calling from. I know it's not easy, but give yourself a fighting chance. For right now, you have to completely disappear. This won't be forever," he reasoned. Now that he mentions it, he is completely right.

I can't risk Von finding me, not right now anyway.

"Okay, we will try this your way," I agreed. After we finished breakfast, Ja opened the door.

"I love being out here. When it's dry, I'll show you how beautiful it is here," he said, smiling. His large frame leaned against the wooden door. I walked past him until I was outside. I noticed the beautiful dark wood porch swing in the corner. I took my seat and admired Mother Nature. This cabin house was gorgeous.

I should've known he would put his touches on it as an architect. The cabin house exudes rustic charm and timeless beauty. Weathered logs and large stone accents that give it a sturdy, inviting feel. It's surrounded by tall, majestic pine and oak trees, their leaves rustling gently from the breeze. The porch is wide and spacious, made of rich wood that has taken on a soft, warm patina from years of exposure to the sun.

Bright bursts of bluebonnets, Indian paintbrushes, and yellow daisies bloom in clusters around the house, their colors standing out against the deep greens of the surrounding woods. The fragrance of wildflowers and fresh pine fills the air, adding to the cabin's tranquil atmosphere.

"Oh wait, I got a surprise for you!" He sounded excited. He scurried into the house and came back holding a large stack of books.

My mouth dropped wide open. I love to read. I started grabbing the books, and I became overwhelmed with joy. He bought me the latest bestsellers by Black women. Some of the books included Jennifer Lewis's autobiography, "The Mother of Black Hollywood," and "Black Girls Must Die Exhausted" by Jane Allen. "Wow. Thank you. Nobody has ever gifted me books before besides my parents," I confessed. This was the start of a beautiful friendship and maybe something more.

Four weeks flew by quickly. There were times when I woke up in bed crying because I thought I was back with Von. Ja would hear me weeping, enter my room, and just hold me tightly until I fell back asleep. I never knew how much trauma Von caused me until I found tranquility. Ja respected me and treated me like a queen. He never pushed me to be intimate with him. I was starting to think he didn't find me attractive. Maybe he saw me as a wounded animal that just needed help. I often thought about my friends like Kyra, Zoya, and Doctor Taylor. I know they are worried about me or think something happened to me. I pray they find peace in thinking I finally got away from Von.

Later on that night, the cool breeze blew in. Ja prepared a nice setup under the large stone fireplace. The crackle of the fireplace filled the cozy cabin, casting a warm, golden glow over the room. We lay together on a soft blanket spread across the wooden floor, the flickering flames reflecting in our wine glasses. I enjoyed the scent of burning wood mixed with the sweet fragrance of fresh strawberries and grapes, resting in a bowl between us.

"God, you are so beautiful. I will never understand how a man would want to hurt you. I take that back. That fool Von ain't no man; he's a boy. I promise that I will be the man you always needed," he vowed.

"I can't thank you enough for rescuing me. Being here with you has brought me so much peace, happiness, and reassurance that I'm worthy of true love."

I almost wanted to cry tears of joy. In that moment, it was like time froze. We both stared at each other passionately before moving in for our first kiss. Our lips met in a slow, lingering kiss. The kind that made time stop. The fire crackled softly in front of us, and the warmth of the flames seemed to melt into the warmth of our embrace. When we finally pulled away, I flipped over on my back and just stared at the ceiling. My heart felt full.

Trinity was more than three hours late getting home, and I was becoming agitated. The agreement we had was to not let her work life overshadow her home life. I was going to beat her ass. Another two hours passed, and I was in my car headed towards her job. I pulled out my phone to track her location.

It led me to the front of the street where she works. I found her keys in the grass. Damn, somebody knew that tracking device was on those keys. I made my way to her office building. Nobody was there, and the doors were locked. I quickly began scanning the parking lot. I know where she usually parks, so I headed that direction.

Getting closer, I spotted her purse and phone on the ground. My heart dropped. All sorts of things were going through my mind. I needed to think. I wondered if she called herself running away again. I wondered if one of my enemies harmed her. I stood there crying like a bitch, thinking about what could've happened to her. I got in the car and started beating the steering wheel. I picked up my phone and called Tank.

"Hey, gather the team and meet me at the warehouse," I ordered. After about twenty minutes, the team started rolling in. Once everyone was crowded around me, I began to let them know what was going on.

"Listen up, everyone, I got a task for you. My fiancée is missing. I need her found ASAP. I need you to press anyone who might know where she is. Anyone that finds her will get a hefty payday." All the men nodded, and they began their search. The next day I get a call from Kyra. The moment I picked up the phone, she started yelling at me.

"What did you do, Von? What did you do to Trinity? I know you did something to her," she fussed.

"Girl, you better calm your ass down. Maybe you know where she is and playing games. I promise, Kyra, you better not be fucking playing games," I warned.

"Nigga fuck you! Trinity better be okay."

Click.

She hung up in my face. I had to stare at my phone like it owed me money because I can't believe Kyra had the audacity to talk to me like that. I called Z next.

"What's up, man? Have you talked to Trinity lately?" I asked.

"Naw, man. I haven't heard from her in months. Everything okay? What did you do?" he asked. I smacked my teeth.

"Yo, why the fuck is everyone asking me that?" I spat.

"You know why," he said in a dry tone.

"Whatever Z. I'm tired of y'all coming at me like that," I said, irritated.

"Oh yeah, my brother is coming home soon. Those bitch-ass cops that pulled him over got indicted for corruption. They are overturning his sentence." I just hung up the phone on him because I felt my blood pressure rising. Z knows me and Reese never got along, so why would I be happy about him coming home?

Two days passed, and I had no choice but to put out a missing person's report.

"Do you know anyone that would want to harm her or any reason why she would leave without saying anything, sir?" Officer Desmond asked me.

"No, I do not," I half-lied.

"Okay, well we will put out an ABP on her." I left the police station and went home. For Trinity's sake, I hope one of my enemies did snatch her. If she called herself leaving me, I was going to strangle her ass. Weeks passed, and not one lead came up.

Dr. Taylor called and discussed organizing a search party for her. The community really came together to help search for my baby. Even D'avyonne joined the search party. I don't know if she is being fake, but it was cool she was helping. We were still sleeping together. I used her for comfort, but I really wanted Trinity home. D'avyonne was not Trinity, and she could never replace her. I might be mean to Trinity, but I love her and couldn't see myself being with anyone else. I would rather kill her before I let her be with somebody else.

I watched as Kyra's hand trembled as she held the missing person's flyer. She cried, and Z rubbed her back for comfort. The word "missing" was printed in bold red letters above a picture of Trinity. Her beautiful smile froze in time. She had vanished almost two months ago, leaving behind only questions, confusion, and the simmering anger that now gnawed at me daily. People were eager to help. Keith, Mr. Coleman's friend, passed by me with a sour expression on his face.

"Is there something you would like to say to me, Mr. Security Guard?" I asked.

"Nope, just hope we find Trinity," he said. People scoured the city, plastering flyers on every telephone pole, knocking on doors, asking if anyone had seen her. They combed through nearby woods, checked hospitals, and even reached out to shelters, but nothing turned up. There wasn't one clue where she could be. I heard the rumors. Tank told me a lot of people think that I killed her and that I am trying to cover up her murder. They better not say that to my face; that's all I know.

Tank and I jumped in my black Cadillac Suburban after the search party went home for the night. "Man, it's crazy how that girl vanished into thin air," I groaned. We sat there in silence for a minute.

"Hey, what about that architect dude she was having lunch with at the Breakfast Klub a while back?" I looked at him like he lost his mind. "Ja? She barely knows him," I said, shaking my head.

"From what I gathered, he seems like the protector type. What if they planned all this out together?" he stated. I thought he was grasping at straws now.

"I think you crazy, but look into it if you want," I informed him.

"Yup, I definitely will," he assured me. Maybe Trinity's friends didn't know where she was. I wasn't going to take any chances. I called Kershira for a favor again. Hey, I'm going to send you a list of names. I want you to track their whereabouts from here on out. I know the FBI uses a global tracking system to locate people.

"You need a federal warrant for that. It's going to cost you extra for me to hack into their phone lines illegally."

"Duh Kershira. You know I'm going to pay you," I said. Tank's words reluctantly replayed in my head. I decided to throw in Jatavion Mathews name as well. She agreed to get right on that for me, and I ended the call.

My phone buzzed, and I saw it was my mom. She hasn't called me in years. "Hello, Mama, how are you?" I asked.

"Hello Von. Do you have time to meet me for lunch tomorrow?" she asked. I was shocked she wanted to see me.

"Yes, I have time. We can meet at Pappadeaux Seafood Kitchen off Katy Freeway. How does noon sound?" I asked her.

"That's fine." She hung up the phone before I could ask her how she was doing.

The next day, I walked into Pappadeaux and spotted my mom sitting at one of the large booths in the back. She was looking at a food menu.

"Hey mama." She looked up from the menu and didn't even crack a smile. Nor did she get up to hug me.

"Son, sit down, please," she spoke. I sat on the opposite side so that I could face her.

"I see there are large groups of people looking for Trinity. Did things go too far with you two this time? Did you hurt her or kill her?" I couldn't believe she had the audacity to ask me that.

"You have some nerve asking me that. I barely hear from you. I figured you wanted to rebuild a bond with me," I said. She paused. Her facial expression showed she was uninterested in having any bond with me.

"What bond is that? We never had a bond. You're mentally ill just like your father, but he hid it well from you. You need some serious help. You need to give your life over to God and ask for forgiveness for the things I KNOW you have done!" Her words carried a hint of assumptions and accusations.

"Ma, what do you KNOW, hmm?" I asked.

"I'm your mother. I know every time you're being deceitful or lying. Just like when Miss Lisa told me she caught you killing that cat when you were younger. You've always been a menace!"

I rolled my eyes.

"I don't understand you. I never did. Since I was a baby, you always treated me like a disgrace. You never loved me. You treated Dad like shit! I got some news for your ass. I'm more like you than him! You might need God more than me. I don't think I could ever be so low as to turn my back on my own child," I expressed.

Tears filled her eyes. She frowned a sinister look at me. She gathered her purse and left me sitting at the table alone. I decided to order myself some seafood pasta because I was hungry. I decided right there to write my mother off for good.

Fuck her.

It's been six months at the cabin with Trinity. She never went without anything, and I covered all our expenses. I would leave and get things she needed from a local store in Lufkin, Texas. We celebrated Thanksgiving, Christmas, and the New Year together. Time spent with her has been amazing. I have never felt a love like this before. Spring began, and I couldn't wait to take her camping in the woods.

Trinity sat on the porch swing, reading. "I have a surprise for you. Go put on some tennis shoes." She smiled from ear to ear.

"What is the surprise?" she asked, jumping into my arms. She smelled of cocoa butter and cinnamon. I held on to her waist, rocking her from side to side.

"It's a surprise. Now go put on your shoes," I snickered and tapped her on the ass. I grabbed everything we would need for the night and placed it in a wheeled wagon.

The Texas woods offered the perfect blend of serenity and romance. I wanted to show her a side of nature that would bring us closer together, a quiet haven where we could focus on each other. Trinity had a lot of trauma that she had to work through. She needed a clear mind and a new start. I decided not to have sex with her in her most vulnerable state.

I know she wanted me to make the first move. My dick was hard plenty of nights, and I went to bed horny. We shared many kisses, but I haven't made love to her yet. I don't think I could resist her any longer.

We walked down a long dirt path, past open fields and wide skies, until we reached the other side of the woods. The tall, green trees loomed ahead, creating a canopy that seemed to welcome us into another world. I continued to roll the wagon behind me and smiled at Trinity. She looked stunning in the glow of the afternoon sun, her dark curls cascading over her shoulders, eyes wide with curiosity.

"You ready?" I asked, a playful glint in my eyes. Trinity laughed, nodding as she adjusted her backpack.

"Lead the way, adventurer." We walked through the forest, surrounded by the rustling of leaves and the distant calls of birds. The smell of pine and earth filled the air, calming and refreshing. After about twenty minutes, we reached the spot I longed for her to see. It was a secluded area next to a peaceful creek, its water gently bubbling over rocks. A gazebo stood nearby, its wooden frame offering a bit of shade and charm to the scene. I could see Trinity's eyes light up as she took in the surroundings.

"This is beautiful," she whispered, her voice soft with wonder. I set down the blankets and tent, carefully arranging everything to make our campsite cozy. I spread out a thick, plush blanket near the creek's edge, making sure we would have a clear view of the water and the open sky above them when the stars came out.

As we sat down, Trinity leaned against me, resting her head on my shoulder. The sound of the creek mixed with the gentle rustle of the trees, creating a melody that seemed meant just for us. The air was warm, but not too warm. The mood was perfect for cuddling on top of blankets. I carefully thought out this day. I reached into my bag and pulled out a small speaker. Soulful music filled the air, blending with the sounds of nature. Trinity smiled, her fingers intertwining with mine as we watched the sunlight filter through the leaves.

"This is perfect," she said, looking up at me with eyes full of affection.

"You deserve perfect," I replied, brushing a strand of hair from her face. I kissed her forehead, feeling the warmth of her skin against my lips. As the day turned to evening, we decided to take a walk along the creek. The sky was a gradient of orange and pink, the colors reflecting on the water.

I couldn't stop glancing at Trinity. Her beauty, her grace, the way she seemed to fit perfectly in this moment with me felt surreal. When we returned to the campsite, I lit a small fire. We removed our shoes and sat on the blankets, watching the flames dance as the night fully settled in. The stars began to dot the sky, each one brighter than the last. Trinity leaned into me, her head resting on my chest as we gazed up at the universe above.

"I love this," she whispered. "Being here with you… it's like everything else just fades away." I tightened my arm around her, pulling her closer.

"That's the whole point. It's just us. No distractions, no noise. Just you and me."

She tilted her head up, and our lips met in a slow, tender kiss next to the burning fire. I gently positioned her on her back, not breaking our passionate kiss. Our tongues swirled around each other's mouths intensely, leaving us both breathless. I began to plant kisses down her stomach line. She assisted me by quickly removing her T-shirt. I yanked at her shorts. She slightly lifted her ass in the air, and I pulled off her panties and shorts, tossing them to the side. I've been dreaming about eating her pussy for the longest.

I decided I wanted her in a different position.

"Sit on my face." I whispered in her ear. I flipped her around and lifted her upward with both my hands around her thighs. She understood the assignment and moved her bottom up until her pussy covered my mouth. My lips gently clamped down on her pearl. She let out a soft moan. I repeatedly twirled my long, wet tongue across her most precious jewel. My head dove deeper into her box, and I marinated in her juices.

Damn, she tastes like a mixture of pure water and honey-lavender. The scent of her body wash was still strong. She placed her soft hands on my head. That turned me on even more. I swirled my nose around her goods to help with the stimulation. My tongue glided from the bottom of her pussy and back to the top, sucking on her clit repeatedly. I felt her pussy muscles contracting. Trinity began to ride my face cowgirl style. Her ass rotated back and forth on my face. Holding her thighs for support, I sped up the pace. Keeping a constant motion, I sucked long and hard on her clit. She continued to gyrate on top of me like a champion bull rider.

"Don't stop, baby. I'm about to cum," she panted. Her body began to shake, and within seconds she creamed down my mouth. I sat up and removed her bra off her shoulders. Flipping her over on her back, I planted multiple kisses on her neck. It was now time for me to remove my clothing. She helped me slide my shirt off. I tossed it to the side. Then I removed my blue jeans and black boxers from my waist. Trinity stared at me seductively as she eyed me from head to toe. She spread her legs apart, inviting me into her pretty shaved juice box. I couldn't wait any longer. I dove between her thighs, and my rock-hard dick penetrated her walls.

"Mmmm, you feel so good," she moaned. I didn't want to be too rough with her, but I want to fill her up as much as possible.

Her pussy fit my dick like a custom-made glove. I was doing donuts in that pussy, deep stroking every inch of my thick wood inside her. She kissed me passionately while throwing both her legs over my shoulders. She was a glutton for punishment. I accepted the challenge. I got on my knees and held her legs in the air. I pumped in and out of her with as much force as she could take.

She screamed out in pleasure.

"Ouuu Jaaaaa!" My waist slammed against her perfectly round ass, making clapping sounds.

"This my sweet pussy, right?" I asked while pounding her insides.

Her pussy got power. Her walls latched on to my dick, and a white, creamy substance was all over it.

"That's right, cum all on this dick," I said while fucking her senseless. Her legs began to shake. I felt my nut rising up at the same time. Together we climaxed. I realized I didn't even pull out. I never forget to pull out with any woman. Yeah, she's different. As we lay there naked, I gave her news to see how she would respond.

"Hey, when I went to the store the other day, I used the phone there to call my family. They said my cousin wanted to stay out here in the third bedroom for some time to get his life together, and they want to throw him a small party this weekend. The cabin belonged to my grandfather, and it was passed down to his grandchildren. I don't want you to be uncomfortable, so how do you feel about that?" I asked. She looked at me and smiled.

"I'm okay with it. It might be good to see some other people for a change," she said. I kissed her forehead.

"I'm starving," she said. I was just thinking the same thing. I got up and pulled out a fruit tray, waters, and sealed-up sandwiches from the cooler sitting on the wagon. I also grabbed the big bag of Doritos. We sat there naked, enjoying our meal.

Afterwards, Trinity felt tired, so I set the blankets in the tent, and we got comfortable inside. We chatted until she finally fell asleep. I couldn't help but smile. This was everything I had hoped for: a night of peace, beauty, and the woman I know I've fallen in love with by my side. I stayed awake a little while longer thinking about how excited I was that my cousin was finally coming home from prison.

The weekend was here before we knew it. It was Sunday morning, and all I wanted Trinity to do was relax. She was nervous about meeting my family and was up trying to clean the entire cabin. My mother and my cousin's mom were bringing the food. All I did was pick up a vanilla cake at the local bakery. I had them put the words welcome home on the cake. About an hour later I heard cars pulling into the front of the yard. "You want me to remove the top covering the cake," Trinity yelled from the kitchen.

"Yeah, baby, that's fine," I replied. My mom and my aunt Sylvia rushed to embrace me.

"You look good as always, nephew!" my aunt Sylvia, the loudmouth, yelled. She always hyped me up. I saw my two cousins walking out; it melted my heart to see my cousin after all these years of being locked up for a crime he didn't commit. We all stood in the doorway, loving on one another.

"Hey baby, show your cousin this ca…." she said, but unable to finish her statement. The cake slipped out of her hand and splashed on the floor. She never even looked down at the cake. She stared at my cousin Reese. I watched as his smile turned upside down. He was staring right back at Trinity.

"OH SHIT," my aunt Sylvia and Z blurted out at the exact same time. My mom and I were looking confused as hell. Trinity snapped out of her trance.

"I'm so sorry," she said, bending down to try to pick up the cake. Reese moved with the quickness.

"Don't worry about this Trinity. I got it," he informed her. He bent down next to Trinity to pick up the cake, and I caught the glances they gave each other.

"Oh man, this shit is about to get nasty," Z said, gently holding his face.

"So, I take it you two know each other," I asked both of them. They both stood up. Trinity sighed.

"Yes. We've known each other for a couple of years, cuz. She was the girl I was telling you about back then. I got locked up, and that was the end," Reese informed me.

"You made it the end when you refused any visit from me," she told him.

"Girl, I was not about to let you waste your life away. I didn't know how much time I was going to do. That wasn't your cross to bear," he passionately expressed his feelings. It got quiet and awkward.

"I'll go throw the cake in the trash," Reese said.

"Well, hello. My name is Gloria. So, you're the special lady that has been living here with my son," my mom spoke. Trinity smiled and embraced her with a hug.

"Nice to meet you, Gloria." She then turned to my aunt. They embraced each other for a long time.

"I'm happy you're okay. I thought Von killed you," she said almost crying. Reese came out of the kitchen, drying his hands with a paper towel.

"You need your ass whooped! You got everyone thinking yo ass is dead!" Z screamed. Everyone laughed, but he was dead serious. Z embraced her with a hug.

"I'm glad you're okay too," he admitted.

"I'm okay, everyone. Ja has been taking really good care of me the past couple of months."

"I bet he has," Z blurted out. Aunt Sylvia rammed the side of her arm into his stomach.

"Ouch, mama!" he exclaimed. She bit her lip and ordered him to get the food out of the car.

"I'll go freshen up since I got cake on my clothes and feet," Trinity informed everyone.

I followed behind her, closing the door to the room. She faced me with a half-smile. "Trinity, are you okay? You know you can talk to me." She lifted her body up to kiss me on the lips.

"I'm okay. All this just caught me by surprise," she said.

"I understand that." I kissed her on the forehead and left her to clean herself up. I walked out to the dining area where Reese and Z were chatting it up.

"Aye cousin, you love her?" Reese asked me.

"Yeah, I do," I confessed. Reese nodded his head.

"Okay, just asking because we all know you don't settle down," he replied.

"I know, but this is different. What about you?" I asked.

"Me what?" he questioned.

"Do you love her?" I asked. He started looking away.

"Man, that was a long time ago," he said.

"You didn't answer the question, though." I gave him a side eye. He was about to answer me when Trinity came out wearing a purple Tupac shirt and black leggings. No matter what she put on, she was fine as hell. Reese stared at her like he wanted to add her on his dinner plate. I wanted to slap fire from his ass.

The women stayed inside the house after we all ate and reminisced about old times. Reese, Z, and I went outside on the front porch. Of course, Z pulled out a swisher sweet and started smoking. Both of them pulled out their phones and began having private conversations. I sat on the steps for a few minutes just appreciating both my cousin's presence. Then something dawned on me. If they're old friends of Trinity's, their phone signals could be traced here. I jumped on my feet.

"HANG UP! HANG UP!" I yelled at them. They both looked confused but hung up the phones.

"Power your phones off now!" I demanded. "Man, the hell wrong with you? You not on steroids, are you?" Z asked. They both powered their phones off.

"I just realized that crazy nigga Von is probably watching everyone's movements. We can't take a chance with Trinity's life," I informed them. They nodded and agreed.

"Von definitely can't find out that I know where Trinity is. Over the years, he has become more psychotic." Z stated, shaking his head. It was getting late, so Reese went to get settled in the third bedroom. Everyone else headed out.

"I'll come back next week to hang with the triangle. Oops, I mean to hang with the three of y'all," he snickered. Trinity didn't sleep with me tonight. She went back to the room she was usually in. That lowkey bothered me, but I was going to let the issue rest for now. A week later Z showed up, but with another woman.

"Bro, what the fuck. I told you nobody is to come here," I scolded him.

"Man, I had to bring Trinity's best friend. We won't be here long. That girl has been running herself crazy worrying about Trinity," he tried to reason with me. I had a bad feeling about this.

"My name is Kyra. I grew up with your cousins since we were practically babies. How come I've never seen you before?" She asked with her arms folded.

"I really don't know. They mostly came to our house, and I often did my own thing," I stated. Trinity walked outside and spotted her friend. She screamed with excitement. They ran and hugged each other tightly. Both women started crying.

"I'm just glad you're okay and were finally able to get rid of that fool," Kyra told Trinity. Reese joined us outside, and he hugged Kyra. She stood there looking back and forth at everyone.

"This feels like a well-written movie. This whole situation is crazy!" she giggled. I barbecued a bunch of meat and cooked baked beans and potato salad for the sides.

"Ja, you cooked, so Kyra and I will bring out the sides," Trinity said. We all sat at the large picnic table out front.

"Where is the bathroom?" Kyra asked.

"Walk inside, and it's in the first hallway to your left," Trinity explained. Kyra left the table.

"You still a pussy. I guess Kyra will never know you are in love with her." Reese put him on blast. We all laughed.

Suddenly, I heard a noise rumbling through my bushes a few feet away. Pulling my 9mm pistol from the back of my pants, I walked slowly toward the bushes. The moment I stepped behind the bush, a nerdy-looking Caucasian man with a camping backpack on was standing there looking at a map. He noticed me with the gun and put both his ass up to show he is not a threat.

"This is private property," I informed him.

"Sorry sir, I'm looking for the Eagle Crest camping site." He pushed his prescription glasses up with his finger.

"That camping site is on the other side of the road. You made the wrong turn." I suspiciously analyzed him from head to toe.

"Okay, thank you, sir."

He headed back towards the woods. I watched as he walked away. Something seemed off, but maybe I was paranoid. The military taught me things aren't always as they seem and to never underestimate people. I went back to the table, and we all enjoyed each other's company for the rest of the night. Trinity would glance at me from across the table, and I'd give a friendly smirk. I could tell she was struggling with her new feelings for me and old feelings for Reese. As much as I loved her, I didn't mind letting her go. I only wanted to see her happy.

My heart stopped when Tank informed me that Ja's office said he recently took time off work. He's been gone for the same amount of time Trinity has been gone. My team and I have been trying to find them for months. I was convinced that Ja and Trinity ran off together. That sneaky little bitch! I cringe thinking about how she has been laying up with that nigga. I thought about all the ways I wanted to torture her. I knew she hated dogs, so I would let my pit bulls at the warehouse teach her a valuable lesson. A week ago, Kershira texted me some news I had been waiting on.

Hey Von, I got the information you asked about on Jatavion Mathews. That's not all the information I found. Until recently, I had nothing substantial regarding the names you gave me. However, Zion and Reese Pryer's cell phones pinged off a tower in Lufkin, Texas, this past weekend. The location is a rural and secluded area. Both men must've realized they shouldn't be on their phones

I clicked the email app on my phone and selected the document to download. I asked her to research Ja's background, so we knew what we were dealing with.

I saw that Ja did multiple tours in Afghanistan. He returned to Houston as a decorated war hero. He'd seen the worst of humanity and earned a reputation for being unbreakable. He ran with an elite special ops team called the "Iron Hawks" and always brought his men back alive. Ja was awarded the Silver Star for his bravery. Some of his skills are operating under highly stressful situations, camouflaging and moving through environments without being seen, and combat weapon proficiency. I see I'm going to have to send more men after him.

I didn't want any of the 163 Mafia boys fucking this up. I hired a Caucasian man who came highly recommended by Kershira. He was a professional spy that I used to scope out the scene and confirm if Ja and Trinity were indeed hiding out in Lufkin, Texas. That man did not disappoint. In a matter of days, he located the missing.

The picture he sent me fucked me up! It was a picture of Trinity, Ja, Z, and Reese enjoying a meal outside on a picnic table. They all looked like one big happy family. I was confused and hurt at the same time. Z knew where Trinity was and wasn't going to say shit. I wondered how in the hell Ja and Reese knew each other. Maybe Reese hired Ja to kidnap Trinity until he came home from prison. I couldn't wrap my head around this mess. I quickly found out all three men were indeed family. I called Z's phone.

"Aye, I'm fucked up right now. What you up to?" I asked sadly.

"Nothing much, just been working. You aight?" he asked. I tried my best to keep my composure together so he wouldn't suspect anything.

"Hey, come to Sapphire Dreams. I think Kyra knows where Trinity is and is just not saying shit. Man, I'm about to hurt that girl. Come talk me off the edge," I fake cried. I knew he would do anything to protect Kyra and would bring his stupid ass down to that club. I ordered Tank and Kentrell to snatch his ass the moment he arrived and bring him to *The Cozy Corner* warehouse.

Z entered the building with a nervous look on his face. As they walked, Tank shoved him in the back to speed up his pace. I could tell he wanted to know what was going on. He stopped a few feet away from me. Tank and Kentrell stood behind him. He felt uneasy, so he turned around to see what type of energy they were on. They mugged him and held on to their weapons, ready to use them at any moment.

"Why was I brought here, bro?" he curiously asked. Hearing him refer to me as his brother when he betrayed me irritated me.

"Nah, I'm not your bro. That's Reese. What's up with your family? You, your cousin Ja, and your punk-ass brother always want to go after my women. Y'all niggas want to be me so bad! You were like my brother, but I can't trust you anymore. I should've known you would always have Reese's back. Then you betray me for Ja. They're your blood; I get it. You knew he had Trinity this whole time and watched me go crazy without her." I finished my rant.

Z chimed in with an attitude, "Nigga I didn't know where Trinity was at first. Once I learned my cousin had her hidden in his crib, I decided to stay out of that shit, mayne. I never chose sides! You were always at odds with my brother. You and me remained cool, and I stayed out of y'all's beef. Let me ask you this, though," he said, pointing to me.

"My brother seems to think you're the one that planted the drugs in his car. Is that true?" He asked, looking at me sideways. He paused, ready to hear my answer.

"Yeah, I set his ass up," I proudly stated.

"He was coming for Trinity, and I couldn't let that happen," I shrugged, not giving a fuck.

"You bitch-made ass nigga!" he shouted and tried to run towards me. Tank was quicker than him. Z was no match for him. Tank clocked Z in the head with the back of the AR-15 rifle he was carrying. The blunt force to the head immediately knocked Z to the ground. Tank then yanked him up on his knees and held him up by the back of his t-shirt. Z appeared to be dazed but conscious.

"So, what now? You about to have them beat me up?" he asked, short-winded.

"Beat up? We're way past that. You've shown me your loyalty lies with your flesh and blood."

My emotions started to get the best of me because I felt my eyes tearing up. I felt a tear slide down my face, and that pissed me off even more. I hate he put me in this position. Memories of us in middle school banging our pencils on the lunchroom tables because we were freestyling rap lyrics flashed through my mind. I loved this nigga, but things will never be the same between us.

"I hate a disloyal ass nigga," I said with a whimpering voice.

"I'll see you next lifetime." Pulling my black and chrome 9-millimeter pistol out of my waist, I aimed it at Z's head. It was now or never. He managed to hold his head up and look me in my eyes. He knew his time on earth had come to an end. I could see his chest rising as his breathing sped up. I quickly pulled the trigger, and a bullet flew through his dome. Blood splashed out of his head, and his lifeless body dropped to the ground. I stood in place staring at his body. I've killed several people before, but this felt different. This one hurt, but I needed to send a message to anyone that crossed me. Tank gently hit me on the shoulder.

"Don't beat yourself up about this. He wasn't loyal. That man was cool with too many of your ops. Fuck a 25-year-old friendship when there is no loyalty," Tank said.

"Boss, what do you want us to do with the body? Kentrell asked.

"Wrap his body up. It's time to send Ja and Reese a package. They need to know I'm on a warpath. We're going to have a fight on our hands, though, so be ready. I showed Tank and Kentrell the email.

"I told you that wasn't a regular dude," Kentrell's scary ass murmured.

CHAPTER 37

I opened the front door to admire the wilderness. I also wanted to get a feel for what type of weather we would get today. I lived in the country for a while, and the beautiful scenery of nature out here never gets old to me. Dark gray clouds covered the sky. I could tell we were about to get hit with a lot of rain. Stepping out on the wooden porch, I couldn't help but notice the large object rolled up in plastic, leaning on the side of the house.

"What the fuck?" I whispered to myself. A knot instantly formed in my stomach.

Whatever was inside was wrapped up pretty good, and I couldn't make out what it was. Slowly walking towards it, my vision got better. I could see what appeared to be the top of someone's head due to it not being wrapped all the way up. The object was turned face down, so I quickly flipped it over.

"Oh shit," I tripped backwards and landed on my ass. What I saw horrified me. I quickly got on my feet and examined Z's zombie-like body lying in front of me. I could see the kill-shot wound in the middle of his head. Tears filled my eyes thinking about how my little cousin died.

This nigga Von is unhinged. He really just murdered his best friend. Now, I had to go inside the house and be the bearer of bad news. Then a thought hit me. How did they know where I lived? I started looking around from the porch to see if I could see anyone out in the woods. We need to leave this place fast. I quickly walked back into the house and made sure to lock the door behind me. Walking through the foyer to get back to the kitchen, I dreaded being the one to tell Reese his brother is dead and left outside on the porch.

Reese was leaning against the kitchen counter laughing it up with Trinity. As I walked towards them, I couldn't hold back the tears in my eyes. I knew there was nothing Reese loved more in this world than his little, loud-mouth, crazy brother. Reese and Trinity could sense the pain all over my face. Their smiles quickly turned to frowns. I headed straight for Reese. I grabbed him on the side of his arm, hoping he would remain calm.

"Reese, I need you to sit down for a second," I said with tears leaking from my eyes. He could sense I had the worst news for him. Breaking from my grip, he pleaded to know what was going on.

"Get off me, Ja. What is it?" He stood in front of me waiting to hear what I had to say. The words just couldn't come out. I just shook my head and let out a deep sigh.

"Bruh, what is it?!" Reese was irritated that I hadn't spit out the news. Looking at him, I just shook my head in disbelief.

"It's Zion. Z's body is out on the front porch, man," I informed him.

"No," Trinity gasped as she covered her mouth with both hands and nodded her head in disbelief. Reese immediately started to have a panic attack.

"Body? The fuck is you saying!" he cried out. He sprinted to the front door. I tried to stop him, but he was too fast. As soon as he opened the door, he screamed out in agony.

"Ahh, what the fuck, bro," Tears flooded his eyes and ran down his face. I stood in the doorway with my head down, feeling helpless. I could hear Trinity still crying in the kitchen.

Reese dropped to his knees and gently rubbed his brother's head.

"Noooo, not my brother, mayne. Noooo. Why he do this to you, bro?" He asked Z's lifeless body. His cries sounded excruciating. My heart broke for him, and I felt useless at the current moment. What can you say to someone who is literally looking at their dead brother wrapped in plastic and discarded on the porch like trash? I suddenly noticed there was a note sticking to Z's chest from inside the plastic.

I went back inside to check on Trinity. "I need to call Kyra," Trinity said with a trembling voice. She pulled out her phone to dial the number, but her hands were shaking like crazy.

"It's okay, baby. I'll call Kyra," I said, trying to calm her nerves.

"The password to unlock the phone is 442810," she said. I dialed the number, but there was no answer.

"She didn't answer? What if he did something to Kyra too?" Trinity cried.

"What's her address? I'll check on her for you. You and Reese gather your things and leave the cabin immediately," I advised.

I knocked on Kyra's door, but there was no answer. I knocked again. This time harder. Still nothing.

"Kyra?" I called out as I pushed the door open. The place was a mess. It looked like a tornado had ripped through the apartment. The couch cushions were overturned, drawers had been pulled out, and clothes were scattered everywhere. But that wasn't the worst of it. As I stepped inside, I noticed the walls. Spray-painted in big black letters across the living room wall were the words

"Where's Trinity?"

My heart pounded as I scanned the room. My eyes landed on Kyra, sitting in the middle of the floor, knees pulled to her chest. Her thick, orange, coarse hair blocked her face. She finally looked up at me. Her eyes were red and swollen from crying.

"Kyra!" I rushed to her side, kneeling in front of her. "Ja..." she whispered, her voice cracked and hoarse.

"What happened? Are you okay?"

I looked around the room again, my eyes drawn back to the menacing message on the wall. Kyra shook her head, trying to speak but failing as sobs choked her words. I gently placed my hands on her shoulders, trying to comfort her.

"It's okay. You're safe now." She took a shaky breath and wiped her face, but the tears kept coming.

"They broke in. I wasn't here when it happened. I came home from work, and it was like this. Everything's destroyed."

I glanced around again, noticing for the first time how thoroughly the place had been trashed. Nothing was left untouched. I know Von did this. He wanted to send a message.

"Pack your things. You're not staying here," I said. She looked up at me, eyes wide with fear.

"But... my apartment..."

"It's not safe, Kyra. These people can come back." She hesitated for a moment, glancing around the wrecked room before nodding slowly.

"Okay… I'll grab a few things." I helped her to her feet, keeping an eye on the door and windows as she hurriedly gathered what she could into a small bag. When Kyra was ready, we walked out together, my arm protectively around her shoulders.

I picked up the phone to dial Reese's line.

"Hello," he barely spoke into the phone. I could tell he still was hurt behind Z's death.

"I'm sending you an address. You and Trinity meet us there. You can't go to any loved one's house. You will put them in danger," I informed him.

"Okay," he agreed before ending the call. We headed to my military buddy's home in the city. I have a lot of weapons stashed there. That was the place I needed to be. When we arrived at the house, my friend Sharpee welcomed me and Kyra with open arms.

Sharpee was her military name because she was the best sharpshooter the military had at that time. Her aim was magnificent. She was a hardcore Samoan and beautiful. We served in Afghanistan together, and she was very protective over me. Reese and Trinity arrived at the house with their belongings.

"This is where we will be until we solve the problem," I informed them. Sharpee told everyone to make themselves comfortable.

"Any friend of Ja's is a friend of mine," she said. I noticed Trinity's facial expressions. She seemed bothered by my friend. I decided not to press the issue. I called Reese over to the side.

"What did that note on Zion's body say?" I asked. Reese took a deep breath. It said:

One, two, we're coming for you.

Three, four, better lock your door.

Five, six, grab your crucifix.

Seven, eight, gonna stay up late.

Nine, ten, never sleep again.

"This dude is so lame. Anyways, where did y'all take Z's body?"

"I called Reverend Hines, and he called in some favors. Rest Haven Mortuary took his body in," he replied.

"Okay, you all get some sleep. You're going to need your rest," I said. I decided to stay up a little while longer and kick it with Sharpee. It wasn't every day that I got to spend time with my military buddies.

"So which one of those ladies belongs to you, the sexy ginger-headed girl or the gorgeous Black Indian?" she asked. I just laughed because her crazy self had a way with words. I'm in love with the dark one. It gets complicated, though. She dated my cousin as a teenager, and she might still have feelings for him.

"Ouch," she blurted out after taking a sip of her beer. We started reminiscing about our tour in Afghanistan.

"Aye, do you remember the time when you thought the Taliban was attacking us and you ran yelling for everyone to return fire? We all rushed outside with our guns drawn, and it was only a herd of goats passing by. Baaaaa," she teased, making a goat sound. We both laughed hysterically at that. I guess we were too loud because Trinity came out of the room. She was standing with her arms folded. Then she turned around with an attitude and went back to the room.

"Go see if she's okay," Sharpee said. I followed Trinity and closed the room door.

"What's wrong with you?" I asked.

"You're flirting with that woman! Who is she?"

"She's just an old military buddy," I answered. She waved her finger at me.

"No, something's going on with y'all. You like this woman. I'm not crazy!" She yelled.

"Don't do that. I told you the truth. You know what? Stop trying to pick a damn fight with me. If you're torn between me and Reese, just say that!" I barked. Her facial expression softened, and she sat on the bed.

"Why would you say that? That's not what I'm doing."

"You could've fooled me. Why haven't you been sleeping with me since Reese got home?" She remained quiet, looking down at the floor.

"I thought so. I'm going back out there to talk to my FRIEND," I emphasized. She made sure she didn't come out of the room until the next morning.

After a week of planning Z's funeral, today was the day we would finally lay him to rest. Z's homegoing service was being held at Beyond The Sky Baptist Church. The black Mercedes Benz Sprinter we rented for transportation pulled into the parking lot. I took a deep breath to calm my nerves. I knew this was going to be a tough service to get through. I haven't been to church in a long time. My entire family grew up at this church. It's been around for many generations, and the staff has managed to take good care of the property.

The huge white church can easily be spotted off the Southwest Freeway and Beechnut Road intersection. A circular driveway gracefully leads visitors to the church entrance, encircling a serene water fountain adorned with intricate carvings and surrounded by vibrant landscaping. The soothing sound of flowing water welcomes worshippers, creating a tranquil atmosphere for reflection and connection.

Two women ushers wearing black tuxedos and white gloves were standing outside the entrance and welcoming people inside the church. As soon as you walk in, you immediately notice the red carpet and matching rows of red pews. The large windows with stained glass designs depicting Black people in biblical scenes are vibrant, giving the church a colorful light.

You could see the pianist sitting on stage playing a slow southern ballad while people are finding their seats. I could already spot a lot of our relatives sitting towards the front left side of the church, and friends were sitting on the right side. I got chills thinking about Z's body being in that casket. I can't believe we are here to say our final goodbyes to one of my favorite people in the entire world.

Growing up, all three of us were extremely close, and I knew Z looked up to me. The family did a great job coming together and preparing a beautiful service for him in this amount of time. His body lay in a gold metallic casket in the front center of the church. My aunt Sylvia decided to have a closed casket ceremony because she didn't want people looking at the hole in his head from being shot. There were two huge bouquets of beautiful yellow, white, and red roses sitting on each side of the casket.

A beautiful portrait of him smiling with white angel wings extending from his back and clouds in the background was enlarged and placed on a stand near the flowers on the left side of the casket. The picture had a cursive text towards the bottom that read Zion LeMarcus Pryer, with his birth year and death year in bold white letters. I looked around and saw people were already crying. Sadness and grief filled the atmosphere. We were almost to the front when I saw my aunt get up from her seat and gently place her hand on Z's casket.

She was wearing a tight-fitting black dress that hugged her knees. She had black stiletto heels that had straps that wrapped around her ankles. She wore a blonde, middle-part, curly wig. Her nails and toes were painted red. She was considered the "young auntie" in the family because she was always fly from head to toe.

"I will miss you, my baby. Why you had to leave me?" she wept. Reese scurried on up and placed his left arm around her neck. He stood there with her, looking at the closed casket. Reese had on shades, so you couldn't really see his facial expressions, but his demeanor told us he was devastated. Happy to see him, Aunt Sylvia wrapped her right arm around his waist. He planted a kiss on the side of her face. She turned around and saw me, Trinity, and Kyra standing there. She smiled at us and held out her arms for us to give her a hug.

Trinity was the first to give her a warm embrace. She kissed Trinity's cheek and told her this wasn't her fault. Trinity sobbed and moved to the side for Kyra to greet her next. I didn't notice how torn up Kyra was until just now. Her entire face was red from crying, and her eyes were filled with tears. When my aunt hugged her, she broke down crying even more. They held each other tight, and my aunt held Kyra's face in her hand.

"I know, baby. You will be okay. Z loved you so much," she told Kyra. Kyra just shook her head in agreement and moved to the side. When she laid eyes on me, she placed her hands on her hips in a playful manner and smiled up at me. She was such a short, petite woman. I moved in to hug her.

"Z absolutely adored you. Thanks for being his favorite big cousin," she said in the midst of our embrace. There was a long line behind us, so we all went to grab our seats in the front row. Trinity and Kyra headed to the right side of the church to take a seat.

"Where are y'all going?" My aunt stopped them.

"We're going to take our seats, Miss Sylvia," said Trinity.

"Y'all are my family; you sit up here with me," she demanded and guided them to the front row.

Her seat was right up front, right by the aisle. Reese's seat was next to hers. It's like she knew exactly where she wanted us to sit. She had Trinity sit in the seat next to Reese, and for Kyra to sit on the side of Trinity and my seat was after Kyra's. That was strange but no big deal. My mom's seat was on the other side of mine. The rest of the seats on our row were filled with close relatives.

"Take your seats, please. There will be time to offer your condolences to the family towards the end of the service. We're about to begin," Reverend Hines informed everyone.

He stood on stage in a large black robe and stole around the neck. The stole was long with gold patches in the shape of a cross stitched on both sides of the stole. He was a heavy-set man with a kinky gray afro and a fluffy gray beard that hung to his neckline. He pretty much favored a Black Santa Claus. He wore clear reading glasses and held a small black towel in his hand to help with the sweating on his forehead.

He was more than a pastor to me but a mentor and father figure as well. In fact, the reverend used to whoop me, Reese, and Z behind when we used to act up in church back in the day. Nowadays, preachers can't touch other people's kids. This generation has gone soft. The church was filled to capacity. The ushers seated everyone, and people stopped conversing so the funeral service could begin. Reverend Hines stood behind the wooden podium looking out at the church members and guests.

"Brothers and Sisters, I want to start off with the good book of Proverbs. The Book of Proverbs, Chapter 3, verses 5-6, says, Trust in the Lord with all your heart and lean not on your own understanding; in all your ways submit to him, and he will make your paths straight." He wiped his forehead with the towel. The pianist continued to play a slow gospel tune on his keyboard.

"See, we may not understand the plans God has for us, but we have to trust in the Lord. We all have an expiration date. See, we don't know the day nor the hour that we will be called home. That's why it's important you get your affairs in order now. I don't think y'all hear me. Let me put it into terms so you youngsters will understand. Stay ready, so you don't have to get ready!"

"Amen," shouted Miss Earlene as she cooled herself down with the church fan. The pastor continued preaching.

"God never promised us tomorrow. However, if we serve him, then we shall inherit the kingdom of God. I don't know about you all, but I find peace knowing Heaven will be my forever home. Too many devils roam this land. I'm not ready to die right now, but when I do, please don't weep for me. God has a heavenly crown to bestow upon my head. I want all of you to lift your heads up. Zion's memories on earth and the amount of joy he brought to us will never be forgotten. He knew how to live life! He was always joking around and smiling because he wanted to spread love and laughter wherever he went. I thank him for that, and today we celebrate his legacy. I would like Sister Tilly to come up here and sing to us about Zion's transition to our Heavenly Home. Can you do that for us, Miss Tilly?"

Tilly was an older, beautiful, and heavyset, brown-skinned woman. She had small red freckles on her cheekbones. Her natural hair was all gray, and she kept it braided into cornrows leading up into a ball ponytail. She kind of reminded me of the character Cora from the Tyler Perry plays. She was a true woman of God, and her strong southern voice could bring anyone to tears. She had on a purple blouse, a matching purple skirt, and some black flats to ensure her feet were comfortable.

We all watched as she got up from the choir section and joined Reverend Hines on stage. He handed her a microphone, and the pianist began to play a melody that filled the room with the presence of the holy spirit. His fingers glided across the keyboard, creating a melody to uplift anyone feeling defeated and brokenhearted. Tilly lifted her microphone and softly started her song off with some soul-stirring humming.

Mmm, mmhmm, heaven... is where I'm destined to be,
Mmm, heaven is where I'm destined to be,
This earth I'm on is not my home.
Just a place for me to roam,
Ohhh heaven,
One day we all will make it there if we walk the straight and narrow way.
Heaven is where I'm destined to be,
It's heaven for me,
I'll see my savior's face, and I want to praise him all day.
We'll sit and sing,
No crying allowed,
No more sorrow or paying my bills,
Heaven is where I'm destined to be,
Mmmm... Heaven is where I'm destined to be,
I'll meet my sista, my brotha, my father, my mother there.
Don't crown my head until I get to heaven.
My heavenly home.

While Sister Tilly was bringing the house down with her sultry gospel voice, the sound of the door opening caught everyone's attention. I couldn't believe my eyes. Rage was trying to take over my body, but I thought about the safety of the innocent church members in the building. This nigga was bold. The nerve of him to show his face up in here since he was the reason we were having a service today.

As Von and four of his men walked in uninvited, some mourners began to whisper and gossip amongst each other. Others remained shocked but stayed quiet. Von walked down the middle aisle as if he was auditioning for a role on America's Top Model. He wore black Versace shades, a dark blue three-piece pantsuit, and a crisp black dress shirt underneath his vest. A black velvet handkerchief was tucked neatly in his jacket pocket. He wore black suede loafers on his feet. I was disgusted looking at that murderer strut in here like he was the shit.

"Damn. That man is fine, fine, fine", I heard my teenage cousin Latoya say.

She was sitting behind us in the next row. She was 17 years old and had always been what the old folks considered a fast-tail girl. I turned around to give her the death stare.

"Be quiet, Toya," Victoria demanded of her. She was 19, and the mature sister.

"What? I'm just saying," she said, patting her weave. Apparently, my aunt Sylvia heard them. She turned around to scold Toya.

"Girl, act like you got some damn sense and shut yo little ass up. Stop being thirsty all the damn time. You got me cursing in the church. Don't make me snatch you up, you hear me?" she said, pointing at her. Toya straightened up immediately and didn't utter another word. She knew Aunt Sylvia wasn't the one to mess with. People shared disapproving glances at Von while he was walking up, but none of them dared to challenge him.

The choir and Sister Tilly stopped singing. The pianist stops playing his tune. Ignoring the tension, Von approached Z's casket. There was a moment of awkward silence. All the family stood up and gathered around each other. Reese tried to rush Von, but his mother jumped in front of him, screaming for him to stop.

Trinity and Kyra both forcefully pulled on his arms to hold him back. This gave me enough time to overpower him and place him in a bear hug position. One of the men Von was with stuck his hand in his coat pocket. Von smirked but stopped the man from pulling out whatever he had under his jacket.

"Tank, that's the guy who choked and body-slammed me." The guy looked directly at me with revenge in his eyes.

"Yup, and I'll do it again," I informed him.

The guy Tank chuckled at my comment and used his fingers to imitate a gun aimed at me. Tank was a big, swole, bald-headed ass nigga. Reese tried his best to break loose from my grip, but he failed miserably. Our family gathered around him like a force field, making sure all hell didn't break loose in this church.

"Calm down, Reese. It's not the time. Think about all these people in the church," I reasoned with him. Reese looked around the church and noticed their scared faces. I felt his body ease up, and he stopped trying to break free from my arms. I still decided not to let him go just yet.

"I just came to pay my respects. I mean, that is my best friend in that coffin," he said, shrugging his shoulders. He began to rub on Z's coffin, and that set my aunt off. She walked up to him and knocked his hand off Z's coffin.

"Get yo goddamn hands off my baby coffin. You have lost your motherfucking mind, boy!" she yelled in his face. I didn't want to let Reese go, but I knew I had to protect my auntie.

His goons moved in closer to her like they were about to do something. He gently took his shades off and angrily stared down at my auntie. She was a short and feisty little thang. He was about to say something to her, but Pastor Hines intervened. I was thankful the pastor came to calm things down because letting go of Reese would have been a mistake.

"Okay, young man, it's time for you to go so we can finish up in here."

He held out his hand to position them all to leave. Von looked at the pastor up and down and ignored his orders for them to leave.

"All you are sitting up here turning your noses up at me, but I bet you never told anyone how you came to me for help," he pointed to various people spread throughout the church.

"Sean, we grew up together, and just last year you came to me needing five thousand dollars for a business investment. Yo fat ass still owe me some money from that loan, and you still don't own one business. I bet you ain't tell your boys that, though."

Sean sat next to his chubby girlfriend in silence. Von turned his attention to a young woman sitting in the middle section of the church. She had a dark skin complexion and wore a long, wavy weave down her back. She wore a black formal dress with black crystals stitched to the fabric.

"Jazzie, everyone knows you came into some insurance money because the husband that was beating your ass mysteriously died. You over there looking like a million bucks. Do you care to tell the church who you came to for help?" he asked. She scratched the back of her head and quickly looked away.

"Yeah, I didn't think so," he said with sarcasm.

I couldn't do anything but shake my head but low-key wanted to know who else has been using this man for help.

"OH, REVEREND HINES," he yelled with his church finger pointed up. My head jumped back out of pure shock. I heard other people gasp at the pastor's name being mentioned.

"Now son, that's enough," he tried to stop Von from calling him out. Von continued his thought.

"Tell the church how three years ago you were swimming in so much debt that the government wanted to seize this church. You came to me begging me to bail you out. I agreed to do it but informed you the church would be signed over to me until you have paid me back every cent you borrowed. That's right, church! Guess who is the real owner of Beyond The Sky Baptist Church? You motherfuckers that are judging me are sitting in my damn church."

Von and his company began to laugh hysterically. The church became noisy due to everyone gossiping amongst each other. "Pastor, how could you?" my mom stood up asking him.

"Ok, quiet down, church. I've paid Mr. Westley all the money back as of last week. The church will be in my possession again, and we had a legit contract put in place. The church was going to be taken away, and I couldn't let that happen. I apologize to you all, but how many of you believe God will take what somebody bad and make it good?"

"He is right. I'm turning the church back over to him," Von stated. He turned to look at Trinity, who Reese was comforting like it was his sworn duty. Reese was rubbing her shoulders, and I almost felt some type of way. I know she is terrified of her ex, so I understand Reese wanting to be there for her.

"I'll be seeing you, Trinity, very soon," he winked at her.

"I said let's go," Pastor said with more bass in his voice, trying to guide them towards the door.

"Man, if you touch me, you won't have to worry about catching the holy spirit; you'll meet him personally," Von challenged the pastor. Pastor threw up both hands to surrender because he knew Von meant business.

Von rolled his eyes at the pastor but proceeded to leave the building anyway. His goons followed behind him, mugging the pastor as they left the church. As soon as the door closed behind the last man leaving, the pastor began to share his thoughts.

"Church, I need you to find comfort in knowing that man will have his day of judgment soon. His demise is already written. God is working it out; mark my words. You must sit back and be patient. I've been on this earth a long time, and I don't worry about anything because I know God can fix people far better than we can."

I just didn't agree whole-heartedly with what he said. I believe God also uses some people as a vessel to help others and combat evil. This man has destroyed so many lives. I'm about to bring the wrath of God down on his head. Thinking to myself that I'm his fucking karma. I had so much rage built up inside of me.

The pastor went back to the stage to finish the funeral service. As he was turning the pages of his Bible, one of the ushers that greeted us abruptly called out for him.

"Pastor, there is a lot of smoke on the outside," she screamed while looking out the stained-glass window next to the doors. She was a beautiful Creole-looking lady with brown freckles across her cheeks and nose.

She has a reddish skin tone and short, curly hair. Her accent let me know she was from New Orleans. Everyone turned their attention to her as she tried to push on the huge wooden double doors. It was clear she was having a hard time opening the doors. A dude sitting near the entrance tried to assist her. He gritted his teeth as he pushed on the doors with all his might.

"The doors are locked," he informed us all. People began to stand up and crowd the aisles. Something or someone had us trapped inside. The panic started setting in on people's faces. Reverend Hines quickly made his way to the doors.

"What the hell," he blurted out. That was all I needed to hear. I quickly got out of my seat, and so did Reese. We both made our way to the front doors. I tried my luck with opening it but failed.

"It's something on the other side of these doors locking us in," I stated. Suddenly the sound of loud crackling can be heard on the other side of the door. The scent of burnt wood got stronger, and smoke began to slip through the doors. Everything outside went dark and foggy. We could see the roof about to cave in. This was an old church, so it wouldn't take much for it all to fall apart.

"Everyone get back; the building is on fire!" I yelled. People in the church began to run the opposite way. Some children were scared and crying. I headed towards the pulpit to see what I could use to open the door. As I walked and looked around, I didn't see anything of use.

I ran on stage, and that's when I figured a way out for us. I grabbed the pastor's podium and lifted it above my head. It was heavy, but I was able to make my way down the small steps with it. I stopped in front of the first window and threw the podium at it with all my might. The podium flew through the glass, creating a huge hole in the center of the window. I began to kick the rest of the glass out with no problem.

With most of the window gone, everyone began to climb out of it. Reese and I waited until everyone was out safely to make our exit. As soon as we reached the front of the church, we noticed the steel chain and padlock connected through both door handles. The entire front of the building was up in flames. This was the work of Von and his goons. They literally tried to burn us alive.

Reverend Hines stood off to the side, watching his church being destroyed by the fire. "I just paid all that money to Von to get my church back. I can't afford to fix this place up," he said in sorrow.

"Have faith, pastor," Miss Tilly advised him while placing one of her hands on his shoulder to keep him encouraged. My aunt walked over to him and told him he should wait on the fire department while we go to bury Z's body.

"Miss Tilly, can you wait for the fire department? I made a promise to this family, and I plan on keeping it. Z was like family, and I'm going to make sure he gets laid to rest properly."

"I sure can, pastor," she assured him with a smile. The family left the church to put Z in the ground for good. After about an hour, we all said our final goodbyes. Von doesn't even know he unlocked the beast in me.

We had been at Sharpee's house for a couple of days. Ja wanted everyone to lay low until he could get a handle on things. I saw Ja was dressed in a black army fatigue unit. He walked outside and unlocked the door to an underground basement. I was curious about what he was doing, so I continued to follow him. I walked down the narrow staircase into the dimly lit basement. The air was thick with the smell of old wood and damp concrete.

As he reached the bottom, Ja flicked on a light, illuminating the cold, cavernous space. To my surprise, the basement was meticulously organized. At first glance, it seemed normal enough. There were shelves with tools, storage boxes, and old furniture. But then Ja walked toward the farthest wall. Without a word, he reached up and pulled a hidden latch. The wall slid back, revealing a concealed compartment. My breath caught in my throat. Inside the hidden space were weapons, such as guns, rifles, tactical gear, and ammunition that were neatly stacked. The sight of so much artillery sent a shiver down my spine. I felt a deep sense of uneasiness. Ja's face had been unreadable, eyes darker than I had ever seen them. He looked like he was about to go on a killing spree.

He moved swiftly, grabbing weapons and ammo, his movements sharp and rehearsed. He was no longer the man she knew—the one who held her close in the quiet moments and made her laugh with his ridiculous jokes. He was focused, his eyes cold, dressed in black army fatigues that she had never seen before. He looked like a soldier ready for battle.

"What is this, Ja?" I finally asked, my voice barely a whisper. I wasn't sure I wanted to hear the answer, but the silence between them had grown too heavy to ignore. He didn't stop moving. He stuffed weapons into a large duffel bag.

"I've got business to handle," he said, zipping the bag up with one swift motion.

"Business?" I repeated, my heart pounding now. My hand gestured toward the cache of weapons. Ja paused then, finally turning to face me. His expression was hard, eyes like steel.

"The kind you don't need to be involved in," he said, his voice low but firm.

"I told you before, Trinity. Some things are better left unknown. Just know, I'm protecting you," he said. My mind raced as I processed his words. There were parts of Ja's life that he didn't share with me. I always knew he was more than an architect. I thought back to the restaurant incident, where he took down three men effortlessly.

"I gotta go, Trinity," he said, and slung the duffel bag over his shoulder. "

Please, be careful," I advised. He cupped my face gently with one hand.

"I love you," he said quietly.

"That's why I can't let you be part of this." We shared a tender kiss.

"Hey, cousin. I need to roll with you. You don't need to try to handle this stuff on your own," Reese said. I didn't even hear him come in. Reese gave me a look that revealed his hurt.

"Nah, Reese, I need you to stay here and watch over Trinity. Plus, you just got out of prison. You need to keep your head down," Ja said.

As Ja approached the stairs, he looked back at us. "Stay here. Don't leave this house," he commanded. The sound of his boots going up the stairs echoed through the empty basement, leaving me and Reese by ourselves. Reese looked at me as if I broke his heart.

"You really love my cousin, huh?" he asked. My heart started pounding.

"I do," I replied softly.

"That's understandable. I mean, he does have my blood running through him," he joked. His smile almost lit up the basement. After all these years, he is still handsome. He's just bigger in size, and his dreads are longer.

"You might be right about that," I joked back. We both stood there smiling.

"I'm glad you're out, Reese. You didn't deserve prison at all," I said.

"You know who put me there, right?" he asked. I looked confused.

"Yes, the police, right?" I asked for more clarity.

"Von is responsible for all of this, Trinity. I thought about this for a long time. I had no enemies. We went on that date, and the next thing you knew, I'm locked up. I'm telling you; it was him," he assured me. I was processing his words. Honestly, it made sense, because I've seen him do worse to people over the years. Plus, he is very territorial when it comes to me.

"Come on, let's get out of this basement," he said.

Hours passed, and I couldn't help but think how I haven't had access to the world for the past couple of months. I was getting antsy and needed to know if my parent's killer had been found. Sharpee and Reese were chatting it up in the backyard. I knew they would disapprove of me leaving the house, so I decided to sneak out. Ja told me to stay in the house, but he wasn't the boss of me either. I was tired of people telling me what to do. I grabbed Sharpee's car keys off the rack in the kitchen and made sure the coast was clear.

I jumped in her orange candy-painted Dodge Challenger out front and sped off down the road. Fifty-three minutes later, I arrived at the police station. I asked the cop sitting at the front desk to page Officer Jean Whitfield to the front.

"You mean Detective Jean Whitfield," he corrected me. I refused to give him my name, but he called her anyway. I saw her walking up, and when she spotted me, she froze. She no longer wore a uniform. She had on a black suit and heels. Her badge was displayed on her waist area. She quickly looked around to see who might be watching and scurried me into her office.

"Trinity, I have been trying to reach you. Where you been?" she asked.

"I've been safe and hiding out. My ex-fiancé is a dangerous man," I said.

"Oh, I know," she agreed. She reached into her drawer and pulled out a vanilla folder. She showed me a picture of Von and a bunch of other men I saw frequently around the house. They were all posing inside a strip club.

"You see that man there?" she asked, pointing to Tank. "Yes, that's Tank," I informed her. She paused, gathering her thoughts.

"Trinity, I'm almost 100 percent sure this is the man that murdered your parents." My anxiety was about to flare up. I tried to slow my breathing down.

"Our criminal profile database shows he has the tattoo we've been looking for. Also, we had two witnesses who were going to testify that Von Westley paid them to falsely arrest Reese Pryer and to cover up your parent's murder. Von Westley paid Jordan Booker, also known as Tank, to kill your parents," she notified me. That news hit me like a ton of bricks. I cried uncontrollably. She came to my side to console me.

"Wait. You said there were witnesses. Did they change their minds about testifying against Von?" I asked with tears streaming down my face.

Jean sighed. "The officers who were arrested decided to testify for a lighter sentence. However, both men were mysteriously murdered behind bars. So now we need to take a different approach. We don't want to arrest him without any solid proof, and he walks away scot-free. We want to take down the entire 163 Mafia Family," she informed me.

"I'm going to give you one of our extra phones. I will be back," she said. While she was gone, several cops walked by. I had a feeling I needed to get back to Sharpee's house. Jean returned and handed me a cell phone.

"I programmed my number in the phone in case you're ever in danger or need my help. I promise you will get justice soon," she stated. I left the police station and headed back to Sharpee's.

Driving down the highway, I was listening to some good old Otis Redding. Suddenly, a black Cadillac Suburban swerved on the side of me and rammed my side of the vehicle. The windows were tinted, so I couldn't see who was driving the car. I panicked and tried to speed up. The truck crashed into the side of me again, and I lost control of the car. I went flying through a tall grass field. Stomping on the brakes, the car came to a halt. I was completely shaken up. Looking into the rearview mirror, I saw the truck parked directly behind me. Both doors of the truck opened. Tank exited the driver's side, and Von hopped out the passenger side.

Von slowly approached my side of the car while Tank stood back. I just knew I was dead. I was in a full-blown panic attack. As I cried and struggled to breathe, Von locked eyes with me. He had a menacing look on his face. It didn't take long for him to try to open my door. I had nowhere to go, so I reached down to unlock the door.

Once he got my door open, he quickly yanked me out by the front of my shirt. I clawed at his fingers, trying to get him to remove the grip he had on me. He flung me to the ground. I quickly got up. He walked towards me, as I walked backwards. The grass rubbing against my legs itched. Before I knew it, Von cocked back as hard as he could and punched me in the face. All I remember was everything going black.

I woke up, and the blow I took to my face still hurt. I noticed I was in an abandoned warehouse. Panicking, I looked around to see if I could get a clue where I was at. I didn't know what was about to happen to me. The air was thick with dust, and the scent of aged concrete filled the space. Puddles of water dot the floor, remnants of rain leaking through the roof. The concrete walls are bare, with steel pipes clinging to them like industrial vines, adding a touch of mechanical complexity to the desolate atmosphere. It was dim and quiet.

There were small lights around the corner of the walls, which gave me some vision. There weren't many windows on the ground floor. Suddenly, I heard a door open from a distance, and all the lights come on. I heard footsteps approaching me and dogs barking, but I still couldn't see anything yet. The barking gets closer and louder. My heart feels like it is about to jump out of my chest. I absolutely hated dogs. What's so terrifying is that I hear more than one dog. I closed my eyes tightly and began to pray.

"Lord, please save me; get me out of here." I repeatedly begged God for assistance. I'm curled up on the cold floor with my back against the wall. I'm on pins and needles. I finally spotted Von, Tank, and Kentrell coming down the large hallway with two large pit bulls on leashes. One pit bull was dark brown, and the other was white with brown spots all over its body. Both dogs had large gold Cuban link necklaces that were attached to a thick gold chain.

Von was shirtless, and as he walked, his chest muscles and abs bounced. He wore black Nike joggers and Air Jordan Space Jam 11 sneakers. He apparently wanted to match the dogs because he was rocking a diamond-gold Cuban link chain around his neck, too. He held on to the white pit bull tightly while heading towards me. If looks could kill, I would already be dead.

The dogs noticed me in the far back and began barking ferociously. I immediately curled my body up tighter and tried to bury my face under my crossed arms. I knew that they couldn't even protect me, but I couldn't do anything else but wait for what was to come. Von stopped a few feet away from me and extended the dog chain just enough for the dog to bark near my face but not bite me. Tank extended his dog's leash and followed behind Von. *Grrrr,* the dogs growled.

Woof, woof, woof, woof!

Both dogs viciously barked and growled at me. They were ready to eat me alive. The dog's menacing teeth were sharp, and saliva dripped from their mouths.

Making eye contact with Von, he snarled at me. I could see the hate in his eyes. *Woof, woof, woof!* The sounds of their barking echoed throughout the building. I quickly buried my face under my arms and hopelessly wished my knees would be a protective shield. I was too scared to look at those dogs. I cried and screamed for them to stop torturing me.

Von knew I hated dogs. He made sure to treat me like this on purpose. I felt a slight kick to my backside, and I fell over on my side. Both dogs were still barking and trying to lunge at me. Von pulls his dog back and hands it over to Kentrell. Tank pulls the dog he's holding back and stands off to the side with Kentrell. I'm completely shaken up now. Von bent down and grabbed me up by the back of my hair. He positioned me on my knees.

"You disloyal, ungrateful, bitch of a woman," he spat. My neck was in so much pain from him yanking my head back too far. I tried to loosen his grip on my hair with my fingers, but his grip was too tight. I gave up and started pleading with him to let me go.

"Von, you're hurting me," I cried out.

"So, bitch, you hurt me!" He screamed in my face.

"After all we've been through, after all these years, you choose them niggas over me. You ain't shit, just like Z. You saw what happened to him, right?"

"Von, I know you're responsible for my parents' deaths! How could you kill your best friend? What's wrong with you? You're so evil!" I yelled at him.

"What's wrong with me?" He repeated, pointing to his chest.

"Bitch," he uttered and gave me a swift punch to my right rib cage. I winced in pain as I hunched over trying to catch my breath.

"What's wrong with y'all! Everyone I love betrays me!"

"Your father wouldn't want you to do this, Von. Mr. Westley would want you to be better than this!" I encouraged him. I see I wasn't making it any better for myself. I knew his dad was a touchy subject. At the mention of his father, his eyes got big.

Whack!

He slapped me across the face, and I hit the ground. I couldn't do anything but hold my face to ease the pain. Tank and Kentrell stood there holding the dogs.

"You don't deserve to speak on my father. Keep his name out of your fucking mouth," he demanded.

He walked up to me and stared me down for a second. I heard him whistle, and his hand patted his legs, signaling for the dogs to run over to him.

"Bruno. Bricks. Come here." The guys let go of the chain, and the dogs ran right to Von. I thought to myself, this is it for me. These dogs are about to devour me. I covered my face with my hands and could feel the dogs hovering over me.

I cried softly, scared to make any loud noises. Both dogs began to growl at me once again.

"Easy, boys. Sit!" Von commanded the dogs. Immediately the growling stopped. Von kneeled down to remove one of my hands from my face so I could look at him.

"I'm about to go take care of your little boyfriends. I want you to think about your actions, so I'm going to leave you here with my two friends, Bruno and Bricks. They will watch you until I get back to deal with you," he said, smirking.

"No, Von. Take me with you," I softly pleaded.

"Mmm, nope," he rejected my plea. He stood up and grabbed the dog's chains. I watched as he walked both dogs over to the wall off to the side. He attached their chain to large metal clamps bolted on the wall. The dogs still had much room to roam around, but the chains didn't quite reach where I was. It then occurred to me that this was the building he probably did most of his killing in. After chaining the dogs up, Von walked back over to me.

He kneeled to me once again to look me in my eyes.

"Sit up for me," he asked. I did as I was told. I quickly sat up against the wall and hugged my knees. I looked at him with defeat in my eyes. There was a silent, awkward moment between us. He stared into my brown eyes and shook his head as if he was disappointed in me. He always said staring into my eyes made him weak in the knees.

"I wouldn't try to escape from here if I were you. Those clamps on the wall probably can't hold these big-ass dogs, so don't make them chase you," he said while gently rubbing my cheek and moving a piece of my hair behind my ear. He stood up, and all three men began to walk out of the room. Suddenly, the lights went back to being dim. They cut the main lights off, and I was stuck in the room with two vicious pit bulls.

"God, please save me." I started praying again.

CHAPTER 39
THE LAST TESTAMENT

Ja had been out of the military for a few years, but he hadn't lost his edge. The precision, the discipline, and the ability to see things others missed were all there. And now, he had a mission. The entire 163 Mafia Family needed to be stopped. It was time to pay for the crimes they committed throughout the years. Von was the devil, and his street soldiers were demons. It was time to send them all to hell. It didn't take Ja long to charm a thirsty loud-mouth chick at the bar, and she blabbed where the gang spent the majority of their time.

"That asshole Marquees treated women like shit. He would take me to the stash house off Fondren & W Airport Boulevard to work for some extra cash. All the men tried to do was sleep with the women and not pay us for bagging their drugs all day," she rambled.

"What does the house look like, beautiful?" Ja asked. She flashed her yellow teeth at him.

"It's a white house with a black door. You can't miss it. It sits down a side street, right next to a small pond," she answered. Ja got all the information he needed. He got up and walked off.

"Heyyy, where are you going?" She screamed after him.

These men thought they were untouchable, hiding behind their gang's reputation, but Ja knew how to get to them. He had been trained for moments like this, and now it was time to go to war. This part of town was filled with industrial parks, run-down neighborhoods, and junkies. The stash house was easy to find. Ja parked a little ways from the house.

He crouched behind an abandoned car, watching as a couple of armed gang members stood by the entrance. They laughed and passed a cigarette back and forth, unaware that tonight would be their last. Ja had everything he needed: a duffel bag filled with a silenced Glock, homemade Molotov cocktails, and enough gasoline to burn the place to the ground. He was done waiting.

Timing his move, Ja slipped around the corner and crept along the building's wall. In one swift motion, he pulled out his Glock and fired two silent shots. The guards Boogie and Sean dropped, their bodies crumpling against the doorframe. Ja recognized Sean from the church, but it was too late. Ja pushed through the door, moving swiftly and quietly, just as he had during countless raids overseas. Inside, the place was a mess—graffiti-tagged walls, crates of drugs and cash scattered around, and the smell of cheap cologne mixing with gun oil. The sound of voices echoed from deeper inside, but Ja moved without hesitation.

He made his way to the living room where the rest of the gang was lounging around, playing cards and drinking, oblivious to the carnage Ja had already unleashed. Ja kicked the door in, his weapon up and ready. The room exploded into chaos.

The gangsters scrambled for their guns, but Ja was faster. He moved through them like a ghost, each shot precise and fatal. Marquees and Wakumbe, the men Ja recognized from the restaurant, tried to rush him, but Ja side-stepped Wakumbe and put him down with a quick shot to the chest. Ja, skillful in combat, did a fast spin move, and Marquees received a bullet to the head. His body collapsed on a glass coffee table, breaking it to pieces.

Within seconds, the room was silent. Ja reached into his duffel bag and pulled out a canister of gasoline, dousing the walls and floors, letting the smell of fuel fill the air. The Molotov cocktails were next, the fire catching quickly as he smashed them against the ground. Flames danced up the walls, hungrily consuming everything. Ja stepped outside, watching as the stash house became a roaring inferno behind him.

He walked away from the blaze, jumped in his car, and fled the scene. He had done what he came to do, but he knew this wasn't the end. There were two major stakeholders in this game that needed to be dealt with. Ja arrived back at Sharpee's crib. Sharpee, Reese, and Kyra were sitting in the living room looking like someone ran over their first pet.

"Trinity's gone, man! I think Von got her!" Reese hollered.

"What! How the fuck did that happen? You were supposed to be watching her," Ja yelled. Sharpee got up from the couch.

"Reese and I were in the backyard talking, and she stole my car keys. We traced the car back to an open field, but she was gone. We found a cell phone in the car, and a detective told us she had just given that phone to Trinity," Sharpee said. It had been a whole three days, and still no leads on where Trinity could be."

"I have a plan; it might be a reach, but we are out of options," Kyra said.

Back at D'avyonne's crib, she waited for Von to come over. She had on a red negligee. The gown barely covered her naked ass. She lit candles and blasted R&B music throughout the house. She heard a knock at the door. She opened the door, and Von rushed in.

"What's the emergency, girl?" he asked.

"I haven't seen you, baby. You've been busy!" she pouted.

"I got stuff to do," he said, about to leave out the door. D'avyonne grabbed his arm to stop him from leaving. Then she bent over and bounced her ass.

"Well, do me first," she suggested. He bit his tongue, and she led him into the bedroom. He removed his bottoms and laid on the bed. D'avyonne mounted his hard wood and began to ride him. His eyes rolled in the back of his head.

"You like that," she asked while grinding on his dick. Von's eyes remained closed. D'avyonne slowly moved her hand under the pillow and grabbed the syringe filled with a high dosage of propofol she was hiding. She continued to ride him. When she found the perfect spot on his neck, she quickly injected him with the liquid.

"What the fuck?" Von whispered. He backhanded D'avyonne. He tried to get up, but his body was woozy. He felt the room spinning. Within thirty seconds, he was out cold. Kyra and Dr. Taylor came out of the next room.

"We need to tie him up. The dosage only lasts a couple of minutes," Dr. Taylor said. After D'avyonne put his pants on, Kyra and Dr. Taylor tied his hands and feet. They used his fingerprint to unlock his phone. Kyra quickly found Tank's name and dialed the number.

"Sup V?" he answered.

"We have your boss, Von. Send us the address, so we can trade him for Trinity. You got one minute to comply," and she hung up the phone. In less than a minute, Tank texted the address. They called Ja and Reese to come get Von, since he would be too heavy to carry. They were already waiting outside. Von began to wake up. He saw all three ladies standing there and began to squirm.

"You backstabbing ass bitch," he yelled at D'avyonne. She blew him a kiss. Reese and Ja entered the room. Von looked like he had seen a ghost.

"We might need to give him another sedation," Kyra stated.

"Nah, I got your sedation right here," Reese said. He began throwing punches across Von's face. After he took a few good hits and gave him a bloody lip, the men carried Von to the car.

"I hope y'all will be able to hold up your end of the bargain," D'avyonne said.

"I promise we will," answered Kyra. The men headed to the warehouse, hoping Trinity was okay.

Kyra and Dr. Taylor followed behind them in another car. No way were the ladies going home. They had to see this all the way through.

When they arrived outside the warehouse, Ja untied Von's legs. Ja and Reese walked him deep into the creepy-looking warehouse. Ja held a gun to Von's back. Reese gripped a Glock he got out of Ja's duffel bag. Suddenly, a low growl echoed from the shadows. Two vicious dogs emerged, their teeth bared, eyes gleaming with a predatory glint. The animals sprinted toward the men, their snarls filling the air.

"Reese, watch out!" Ja yelled, but it was too late. One of the dogs leaped at Reese with incredible speed. He lost his footing, and his gun went flying off to the side. The dog was on him in a heartbeat, snapping its jaws, claws raking at his chest.

He quickly grabbed the dog by its collar, twisting sharply to throw it off balance. The dog yelped, but Reese didn't let go. He swung the animal around and slammed it against a nearby stack of crates. The impact was enough to disorient the beast.

The other dog stood there barking ferociously, deciding whether to make a move. Reese quickly grabbed his gun and shot at its feet. Both dogs took off, running down a dark hall.

Tank and Kentrell were standing behind Trinity. Tank held a gun to her head, while Kentrell had his weapon drawn on Reese. Trinity's hair, arms, and legs were dirty. It was obvious she hadn't bathed. Her lips were dry, and she looked dehydrated. I bet she hasn't eaten in days. She was standing there, fragile as ever, and crying.

Kyra and Dr. Taylor were in the car discussing if they should wait or go in.

"There are men with guns in there. We will be sitting ducks," she said. All of a sudden, they heard cars rapidly approaching the warehouse. Numerous men with weapons run into the building. They see one of the men open the door for someone to step out of a Rolls-Royce. That's when Kyra's heart dropped. It was the same man she saved after being shot.

He looked one hundred percent better. He sported expensive silk garments and shades. He walked inside the building.

"I got to go inside. Stay here," Kyra said. Dr. Taylor tried to stop Kyra, but she moved fast. She opened the door to the warehouse and walked towards several men who had their guns drawn on her. Kyra held up her hands, terrified of being shot. Alejandro spotted Kyra and immediately yelled for them to lower their weapons. He walked up to her.

"What are you doing here?" he asked. It was quiet in the warehouse.

"Those are my childhood friends. That girl there is my best friend," Kyra said, pointing to Trinity. Alejandro looked at the people he was supposed to kill. Tank had called him for backup.

"Von is an evil person. He's abused my friend for years," she told him. Alejandro liked Kyra more than Von. In fact, he never could stand him.

"You saved my life. Tonight, we're even. Let's go, guys. This isn't our fight," he said.

"I knew your pretty ass was soft. That's why I could have never seen myself answering to you. If only Boogie had stayed to finish the job that day," Von confessed to being responsible for him being shot.

He got Alejandro's attention now. Alejandro walked up to Von.

"So, you were responsible for the shooting?" he asked. Von smirked.

"I'm about to show you how soft I am NOT!" he stated. The door to the warehouse was heard opening once again.

"You got to be kidding," Alejandro said. Everyone heard heels tapping on the concrete. As the women got closer, Kyra recognized Sydney, who was Von's mother.

"Who is this?" Alejandro asked.

"That's his mother," Kyra replied. "It's okay, trust me," she said. Kyra called Sydney when Von and Tank snatched Trinity after she left the police station. She figured maybe Sydney could convince Von to let her go. To her surprise, Sydney expressed her true intentions regarding her son.

Sydney walked up to Von.

"Son, it's time you leave this earth. I feel responsible for all the turmoil you have caused others. I knew you were evil from the moment you were born. In the womb, you damaged my body to where I couldn't have more children, and I was sick all nine months carrying you. I asked you one last time to give your life over to God. You refused. Now, it's time I send you to hell, where you belong," Sydney stated.

Von tried so hard to keep his composure. A couple of tears fell down his face. Von hocked up as much spit as he could and shot it in his mother's face. His saliva and germs landed smack in the middle of her face. She wiped it off with a handkerchief she kept in her purse.

"You're the evil bitch. I'll see you in hell, Mama," Von said.

"I brought you into this world, son, and I'll take you out," she replied. Alejandro looked at Kyra with a stunned expression. He wasn't expecting a mother to want to kill her son. Kyra shrugged. Kentrell raised his gun to shoot Sydney, and Ja quickly put multiple bullets in his chest. Tank still had the gun pointed at Trinity's head. He knew that was his only leverage.

"The book of Genesis talks about how God formed man of dust from the ground and breathed the breath of life into his nostrils. Then, man became the living. Von's body shall return to the ashes. Who has some gasoline?" Sydney asked. Trinity gasped, covering her mouth. Ja handed Reese the keys and told him to get the extra gas can out of the trunk and the matches. Reese quickly went to the car. Von stared at his mama with so much hatred.

"You plotted on my parents. You both deserve to die!" Trinity screamed. Tank pressed the gun harder on Trinity's skull. A bullet came flying in from the top window and into the back of Tank's skull. It instantly knocks him off his feet. Just like that, he was dead.

Ja looked up to search for Sharpee, but she was nowhere to be found. Her aim was just that good. Reese returned with the large can of gasoline. Ja and Reese stood back.

Sydney opened the gasoline can and poured it on his head and all over his clothing. "God is simply using me as a vessel to hand down his wrath," Sydney stated and wholeheartedly believed. She tossed the match on him, and the torch descended his body. The flames roared to life, consuming Von in a fiery cocoon. He screamed not just in pain, but in defiance. The fire crackled loudly as he squirmed on the ground.

"Ahhhhhhhhhhh!" Von screamed as his body burned alive. Sydney left the warehouse. She didn't stay to watch him suffer. After a few minutes, Von stopped moving, and his body was almost a pile of crisps. Nobody had words at that moment. It was bittersweet but weird this man's mother just murdered him. Alejandro reached to grab Kyra's hand. She looked at him for a second, then gave him a big smile. She was happy to hold his hand. They walked out of the warehouse together.

Ja hugged Trinity, although she smelled awful. "I'm glad you're okay. I don't know what I'd do if something happened to you. I feel like you've been a little confused since Reese got home. I'm going to fall back and let you two be happy. If you're happy, I'm happy," Ja informed her. He turned away from her and headed for the car.

Reese hugged Trinity. "I would love to see if we can rekindle what we have. I still love you, Trinity," Reese acknowledged. Trinity grabbed Reese's hands and gave him an endearing look.

"Reese, I love you too. I truly considered us since the moment you came home. I never want to hurt you, but I'm madly in love with Ja. He holds the key to my heart. You will always have a special place in my heart," Trinity acknowledged. She kissed him on the forehead and ran out of the warehouse. Ja was about to get into his car.

"Ja, wait," Trinity shouted. Ja turned around and noticed Trinity was out of breath.

"Ja, I never said I wanted Reese. The truth is he holds a special place in my heart. You hold the key to my heart. I'm in love with you. I choose you, forever and always!" Trinity shouted. Ja was so happy to hear that. He picked her musty tail up and kissed her lips.

"Let's get a hotel for the night. I need to take a long shower," she informed him. Alejandro said his goodbyes to Kyra. Reese decided to let Trinity and Ja have some alone time. He hopped in the car with Kyra and Dr. Taylor.

As Ja and Trinity sped down the highway, they heard a buzzing noise. Ja forgot he grabbed the phone that Detective Jean Whitfield gave Trinity.

"Hello," Trinity answered. Jean, great news! We finally got everything we need to arrest multiple members of the 163, including Von and Tank," she bragged. That's awesome! Please let me know when the arrests are made," Trinity said.

Ja looked confused. "What did she say?" he asked.

"Oh, she said they have everything they need to arrest Von, Tank, and the 163 gang," she stated, rolling her eyes. They both found the humor in that. They laughed hysterically down the highway.

The city of Houston labeled what happened at the warehouse an incident of gang retaliation. When they found Von's remains, they called Sydney to pick them up. She had the remains buried in a plot and even got him a tombstone.

Mr. Hopner, Von's lawyer, called Trinity and Sydney into his office for the reading of the will. He informed Sydney that the penthouse is now hers because Von and Trinity weren't married. Trinity was okay with that. She never wanted to step foot in that penthouse again. He informed Sydney that she would receive all the money on the accounts without Trinity's name attached to it.

She will now be awarded $48 million. He informed Trinity that she would be awarded $217 million, plus their 30 rental properties, since Von had her listed on the businesses as an equal partner. Trinity was now the owner of the Vanderbilt property. Both women left his office satisfied. Two-Tyma was smiling like he had just hit the lottery. He was waiting in the lobby and couldn't wait to kiss her when the meeting was over.

Trinity and Kyra showed up to D'avyonne's house.

"You made a deal with my best friend, and I will honor it. Thank you for helping us," said Trinity. Trinity handed D'avyonne a large stack of cash.

"Go buy your building," Kyra said, smiling. D'avyonne was excited.

"How did you know I would help y'all?" D'avyonne asked.

"I didn't, but I know one thing women want is money and to be their own boss," Kyra said, shrugging. "Well, you were right," D'avyonne said.

Ja and Trinity visited the cabin. They recently bought a large home in Houston and had been busy for weeks getting settled in. Reese and Dr. Taylor stood on the porch, welcoming them. Reese kissed Dr. Taylor passionately on her lips.

"Get a room," Ja joked as he walked up the steps. The four of them enjoyed each other's company for the rest of the evening.

Kyra and Alejandro made things official. Dealing with his overprotective mom, Karena, was difficult until she discovered Kyra was a future surgeon. Now, she loves her to death. Kyra is still skeptical about dating a crime boss but has grown to accept it. Their love story might be one for the books! Literally.

Jean and Desmond both were promoted to detectives. Although Jean was a tad bit late solving the Coleman murders, she went on to do excellent police work. Des and Jean got married. Captain Dan Marley transferred Desmond to another precinct, where he wouldn't be a distraction for Jean. Deontae Wiley was released on parole. Detective Whitfield spoke at his hearing about how he helped her solve two cold case files. She talked about how he put his life on the line to do the right thing. The local gangsters labeled him a snitch, so he packed up his family and moved to Virginia.

JOHN 10:10

"The thief cometh not, but for to steal, and to kill, and to destroy: I come that they might have life and that they might have it more abundantly."

If you or someone you know is a victim of domestic violence, there is help. Please call the National Domestic Violence Hotline:

1-800-799-7233 (SAFE)
1-800-787-3224 (TTY)

Please follow my social media pages to keep up with discussions and new releases:

Facebook Author Page:
https://www.facebook.com/profile.php?id=61557246986676&mibextid=LQQJ4d

Instagram:
https://instagram.com/jenspeaksvictory?igshid=OGQ5ZDc2ODk2ZA==

TikTok:
https://www.tiktok.com/@jenspeaksvictory18?_t=8fBvircwjbH&_r=1

My Amazon website includes unique coloring books and activity books.

https://www.amazon.com/author/jennieturner44